PROPHET

PROPHET

A NOVEL

SIN BLACHÉ
AND
HELEN MACDONALD

Grove Press
New York

FIRST EDITION

Printed in the United States of America

Lyrics from "It Was a Very Good Year" by Ervin Drake
used by permission of Songwriters Guild of America.

This book is set in 11-pt. Janson Text LT Std
by Alpha Design & Composition of Pittsfield, NH.
Designed by Norman E. Tuttle at Alpha Design & Composition.

First Grove Atlantic hardcover edition: August 2023

Library of Congress Cataloging-in-Publication data is available for this title.

ISBN 978-0-8021-6202-1
eISBN 978-0-8021-6203-8

Grove Press
an imprint of Grove Atlantic
154 West 14th Street
New York, NY 10011

Distributed by Publishers Group West

groveatlantic.com

23 24 25 26 10 9 8 7 6 5 4 3 2 1

The ultimate hidden truth of the world is that it is something we make and could just as easily make differently.

—*David Graeber*

PART I

CHAPTER 1

The room she ushers him into smells of stale cigarettes and air freshener. The decor is '80s mil-spec Holiday Inn. Dark-green carpet, striped armchairs, a smoked-glass table, a print of two F-15s trailing vapour set high in a gilded frame. The scream of their engines outside has been softened in here to a dark, low-frequency roar.

Miller pulls off her jacket, drops it over the back of a chair, winces at the half-drunk coffee cup on the table, and looks apologetically at Rao. Her eyes are the colour of airmail paper, the wrinkles at their corners attest to years of sun. Her hair is bleached, tousled on top, very short at the sides and back, and her business suit hangs far too perfectly on her spare frame to be worth anything other than a fortune. There's a Cartier tank solo on her left wrist, gold studs in her ears, and she is trying so hard to be friendly Rao feels his teeth ache.

They sit.

"Can we get you anything?"

"A drink."

"Mr Rao," she chides. "I can offer coffee, tea, or soda."

"Water," he says tightly. "No ice." She's amused by that—and for the right reasons. She can read an insult even when it's placed gently in front of her. Not a lot of Americans possess that talent, in Rao's experience.

"There's a cooler in the corner."

She doesn't expect him to get up. He doesn't.

"I expect you don't know why you're here."

"Why I was escorted from prison by two MoD AFOs and driven to an American airbase in the arse end of England? No. I don't. They didn't want to tell me."

"They didn't know. Do you want to guess?"

Ugh. Rao stares at her day-for-night reflection in the top of the smoked-glass table between them, the curve of her jaw, the interrogative tilt to her head. "Respectfully, fuck off. Tell me what you want, and please attempt to do so without vague requests for me to perform for your amusement, or I'll find my way back to my cosy remand cell and get on with the rest of my life."

"It's like that?"

"Yes, it is."

"Ok," she says mildly. She reaches into the bag at her feet, pulls out a file, flips it open. "Sunil Rao, thirty-six years old, born 1974, Kingston upon Thames, UK. British citizen, OCI cardholder. Parents Himani and Bhupinder. Mother works for Christie's. Father's family business, fine jewellery." She reads on, raises an eyebrow. "*Very* fine. Educated St Elgin's, BA in art history at St John's College, Oxford. Six years at Sotheby's, fraud and attribution, then MI6." She glances up, smiles. "Very patriotic."

She's definitely looking for a rise. Which could mean she's not in possession of enough information to push him in any other way. More likely it means she's purposefully testing his patience. Both possibilities make it less likely they're going to put him on a plane back to Kabul in the next twenty minutes, but that doesn't make her strategy any less exhausting.

"Eight-week joint operation in Central Asia, last fall." Her voice softens. "Your partner at the DIA spoke highly of your abilities."

"Did he. I've quit."

"We're not unaware." She frowns at the file. "Then Afghanistan. Where things went less well, I see. It says here you became unreliable."

"Highly."

"It says here there was an overdose in a hotel room."

"There was. It wasn't a cry for help."

Her response to that is silence, but not the kind he'd wanted to provoke. It's thoughtful. "Could you tell me about the incident in rehab?" she tries, gently, after a while. "It's not in the file."

"Isn't it?" He holds her eye. "I punched an obnoxious cunt in group therapy who was lying through his teeth."

"I heard it was far more than a punch."

Rao spreads his hands flat on the tabletop, breathes in once through his nose, exhales.

"Why am I here?"

"Are you fit enough to work?"

"I doubt it."

She lays the file on the table between them, pushes at a corner to straighten it. Drags a finger down the cover—a slow, considered movement. "We think we need you, Mr Rao." She doesn't sound happy about it. "We've no one with your skill set."

"Yeah," he snorts. "I guessed."

She raises an eyebrow. "Guessed?"

"Yes."

She walks him down a corridor to an empty conference room where a Stars and Stripes hangs limply by a projector screen. Set out along the length of the long central table is a line of cups, mugs, plates, and bowls. Miller runs her eyes over them, looks at him expectantly. He knows what this is now. Rubs the back of his neck at the familiarity of the setup. Recalls the light slanting from the windows, cigarette smoke rising through it, his father's question as he gestured to the trays of jewellery on the desk. *Which, would you say, is the most interesting of these, Sunil?*

"Kim's Game, is it?"

"No, Mr Rao," she says.

A radiator ticks and hisses. Rao buries both hands deep in the pockets of his jeans and waits to be asked to do what he knows he'll be asked to do.

"I'd be grateful if you could examine these objects and tell me if any seem unlike the others."

"Third from the left," he says. "White mug."

"That quickly, by eye? Could you tell me what's different about it?"

"It's wrong."

"Wrong?"

"Simplest way I can put it in the circumstances."

She brings the pad of her thumb to her closed mouth, rests it there for a few seconds, pulls it away.

"Mr Rao, we'd like to show you something. I think you'll find it interesting. If you could follow me, there's a vehicle waiting outside."

The urgency of whatever this is is suddenly so apparent Rao stops in the corridor to read a random noticeboard. *Baseball practice, commissary tours, missing dog, zip-lining trip, garage sale, pizza night, motorcycle competition.* He glances over at her, registers her clenched fists, her silent agitation, and with a burst of pettiness reads it all again.

Their steps echo on wet tarmac. Suffolk is buried in fog: thick, inconstant air that glitters and shifts around the base lights in the dusk. Miller drags a parka from the back of an unmarked Land Cruiser, hands it wordlessly to Rao. Inside, their driver is tense. He tries to start the ignition while the engine's already idling, hits the indicator far too early for the junction. It's not Miller's presence. He's spooked. Rao splays his hands on his thighs, looks down at his fingers, and knows that he is too. There's a lie to all this that isn't the usual bullshit dissimulation, and the taste of it is beginning to press on his mind. He looks out the windows to push it away. Lights in the mist. Passing bulks that are barns and chicken farms, smears of headlights over roadside hedges. After half a mile they turn up a potholed farm track. A few hundred yards later they halt at a high-security fence set in concrete blocks. A guard steps forward with a torch. After a brief negotiation he opens the gate; the rutted track behind it veers back towards the base.

The driver slows, cuts the engine. Miller gets out and opens Rao's door, informing him it's a three-minute walk. He clambers out into dank, still air and follows her, trudging over rows of fleshy leaves that squeak underfoot. Wet clay clumps on his Converse, making each step a little slower, a little more effortful than the last. He has no idea what this is. Wonders what he's being taken to see. A crash site, a corpse, a cache of arms, a burned-out car. No. None of those. Perhaps a pub? Yes. Let Miller be taking him to a pub. A pub with an unexpectedly fine selection of single malts and a blazing log fire. He knows she isn't, but he's imagining that blessed, forbidden idyll when they reach the crest of the rise.

He stops.

"The *fuck*," he breathes.

Below them, stranded in fog, right in the centre of the field, is a small, one-storey building with a panelled facade of shiny sheet steel. A circle of floodlights haloes it in soft, candescent air. The scale of it is peculiarly uncertain. For a fleeting moment it seems to Rao no bigger than a matchbox, as if he could just reach down and pick it up. There's no doubt what he's looking at. It's an American diner. Not only does it look like the most generic roadside diner ever built, but there's also a red neon sign over the entrance that reads AMERICAN DINER. The lights are on inside. But no roads lead to it, there's no parking lot beside it, and no sign of disturbance in the crop growing around it except the narrow, muddy trail that runs from their feet straight to its double doors.

"Not right, is it," says the voice next to him.

"No, it isn't," he says. He rocks on the balls of his feet in the mud, licking his lips at the sight below. "Not the usual at all, this."

"Is it like the mug?"

"Yes. But—" He blinks, finds himself unable to finish the sentence. Looking at the diner is like watching water swirling down a plughole, and he balks at chasing the intuition any further. In his peripheral vision there's something that could be a smile.

"The mug you identified came from inside. But you already know that, I think. Want to take a closer look?"

"Lead on."

"It's seventy to eighty hours old," she announces as they walk downhill. Her voice is easier now. This has become a briefing, the nature of which is to turn a thing into someone else's problem. "To clarify: that's how long it's been in this location. It's weathered and aged in a way that would date it, ordinarily, as a midcentury building. But we don't know how old this structure is."

"It's seventy to eighty hours old."

"You're sure?" she says.

"Call it a hunch. The lights?"

"It's not connected to utilities. And there's a zone around it that's apparently of interest."

"To whom?"

"All of us."

"It's an us, is it?"

"I hope so, Mr Rao."

"And who are we, exactly?"

"I can't lie to you, can I?"

"You can lie as much as you like. I'll just know you're doing it. You want me to go inside?"

"Go ahead."

He walks to the door. The air smells of fried onions and behind that the faintest hint of diesel. He stretches out a hand, brushes the chrome with two fingertips. The metal is cold, bright, beaded with water. When he pushes, the door swings easily. He steps in. Looks down at his muddy sneakers on the black and white tiles, hears Miller behind him.

He tried to describe it, later. Said that it felt like getting into a hot bath. Not the temperature change but the suddenness of the alteration, how deep it hit, the welcome of it. He's never been inside a fake before. He's never experienced a fake like this before. His skin itches with wrongness. But warring with the wrongness is a surge of elation running up his spine, a quickly unfurling warmth in his chest. After a few seconds, he's surprised to find himself close to tears.

There's no one inside. It's deserted.

It feels full of people.

"It's lovely in here, isn't it?" he says.

She's not sure how to respond. Her arms are folded, her expression complicated. "Look around, Mr Rao. Take your time. The griddle is hot. I wouldn't advise touching it."

He sees a turquoise counter faced with checkerboard tiles. An illuminated jukebox in one corner. Red banquettes, steel chairs with padded seats and backs. Framed photographs across the cherry-coloured walls. Elvis, Sinatra, Marilyn, Bill Haley, the Everly Brothers, a *Gilda*'d Rita Hayworth. These, Rao realises, after they snag on his eye more than once, are wrong in a very specific way. The more he looks at them, the less recognisable their subjects become, and isn't *that* interesting. He walks up to the nearest. Blinks. Diner lights reflected in his eyes against a face that isn't quite Sinatra's. It could all be in his head. He knows he's not right. But he doesn't think so; he doesn't think that's what it is. He looks over his shoulder at Miller. Judging by the stance she's taken by the door, he's not going to be given all night in here. He decides, reluctantly, he has to let this particular mystery wait.

The more Rao looks about, the more wrongness is revealed. Behind the bar, the griddles are indeed on full—he holds a palm just above one to check—and gleaming with oil. There's a row of torn paper orders stuck along a narrow steel strip on the wall—*eggs over easy* scrawled on each one—but there's nothing else. No sink, no grill, no plates, no cooking implements. Scores of coffee mugs, flasks, no means of making coffee.

"And no bathroom," she says, watching him. "What do you think?"

"It's like a model. A full-size prop. What's this thing about the zone outside?"

"There are no foundations. It sits on exactly six inches of sand. And exactly six inches of sand extend from it on each side before it meets the soil of this field."

"What kind of sand?"

"We've not had time to analyse. It's only been here for seventy to—"

"Eighty hours." He's looking at the ruby cursive glow of the neon sign over the counter. SERVICE, it says. There are no wires. None at all. "So, you've shown me this, and before you'll tell me anything more about what it is, you'll need me to sign an NTK declaration, yes?"

She nods.

"In blood."

"It's cold tonight, Mr Rao. Let's eat. They can bring us food from the Officers Club, and I'll do my best to be helpful."

Miller picks at a Caesar salad while Rao devours a plate of chicken fajitas. When he's done, she picks up her coffee, sits back in her seat, and looks at him speculatively.

Here we go, Rao thinks.

"So, the term your former employers used about you, Mr Rao, and they were very keen to explain how off the record it was, was 'fucked.'"

"Just Rao will be fine."

She considers her cup for a while, swirls the coffee a little, watches it circle.

"It must have been hard."

"What?"

"What you've been through."

He closes his eyes. "Let's not, shall we? I've had an awful lot of that lately. If you want to play 'let's make friends,' let me ask the questions."

"Go ahead, Rao."

"What's your department?"

"Defense."

"Job?"

"Investigator."

"Ah," he says. "Columbo."

"No dog, no wife, and I loathe cigars."

"Where did you grow up?"

"Wyoming."

"Where did you get your watch?"

"That's none of your business."

He grins. "No, it isn't. Does this thing scare you?"

She blinks, twice. "The diner? Yes."

"Good." She's looking at him very seriously. He wonders what she sees. She's treating him less like a live grenade now, more like a terrible liability, which is more than fair. He wonders if she has a son somewhere. A difficult one. Something in her expression tells him she might. Yes. He pulls at a loose thread at the hole in the cuff of his sweater, rubs it idly between finger and thumb. "You can get your need-to-know form out now. I'll sign it. Do you have a pen, or should I open a vein?"

"I have a pen."

He signs. Doesn't bother reading it. He's signed them before, and none of them mean shit.

"So what's the deal?"

"There's no *deal*, Rao," she says. "This isn't transactional."

"Not literally. Figure of speech. What's going on here?"

She bites her lip, speaks carefully. "There's been a death on base. Surprising and suspicious circumstances. I'm here to act as liaison between UK and US investigations."

"But you're really here for the diner."

"My liaison role's not cover, Rao. But we're not solely concerned with the diner. I've been tasked with assembling a small team to investigate other recent events at this location. They might have some connection with the diner, maybe with the death. You were recommended highly."

"By whom?"

"You'll be working with Lieutenant Colonel Adam Rubenstein."

"Fuck, is he not dead yet?"

A wry smile. "No."

"What's the point of this team, if anyone asks?"

"Investigation. There's a body, and a lot of people need answers."

"And what's its actual role?"

"Investigation. Just a touch more complicated. A series of objects have turned up around this site. Mostly inside the wire. No one knows where they came from. Base operations assumed they were a practical joke. Then the diner appeared."

"What kind of objects?"

"Various. A surprising number of children's toys. The first was a Cabbage Patch Kid doll picked up on the main runway during a routine FOD walk. The last was a ticket stub for a performance of *The Philadelphia Story* at the Arlington Theatre."

"Awful play."

"Deflection isn't a helpful strategy," she says, "but I agree with you. I should note that this particular production was from 1982."

Rao yawns. It's a stress response. She misinterprets it, looks at her watch, and frowns. "It's late. You were denied bail because you were assessed as a flight risk, Rao, so I'm afraid there'll be a guard outside your dorm. But we're not placing you in the confinement facility, and you'll be more comfortable here than in Pentonville. Do you need anything?"

Rao shakes his head. He doesn't need anything. He wants several things right now, but none would be good for him and none will be given to him. He watches her nod at the uniform sitting three tables away, watches him rise, waits to be escorted away.

CHAPTER 2

See, the main problem with the way Sasha's life shook out is that she hadn't really planned for this to happen. Truthfully, speaking from the heart and all that crap, she hadn't really planned for a lot of stuff, but this really took the cake. She could have probably handled the loss of a limb better than her uptight older brother getting some poor woman pregnant. Not that disappearing for five years and losing her brother's number after she got the happy news could really be counted as handling anything well.

What was she supposed to do with that information? Grab his wife's shoulders, shake her carefully, scream at her to get the fuck out before the baby dropped? It was too late for that. If Sasha had wanted to do something for her, she should have done it before they got pregnant. Should have done it before the damn wedding.

They weren't really a family equipped with healthy coping mechanisms. Growing up like they did, they'd learned early that if they had a problem the best thing to do was to keep it to themselves. Bottle and bury it.

Then she'd kind of forgotten about the whole pregnancy thing during those years. She'd gotten into her own shit, bottled and buried too deep to remember that she was supposed to keep her head above-ground. So, five years later, with an impressive array of gambling debts and a few scars nobody needed to know about, Sasha found herself at her brother's doorstep. Funny thing about family, right? No matter what happened, neither of them could ever manage to fully burn that bridge down. There was always enough left over to cross.

He didn't even say hello when he opened the door. Just looked at her, looked at the suitcase leaning against the back of her legs, watched the taxi drive away. "How long do you want to stay?" he asked.

"How long you got?" she answered.

"I'll get the spare room made up," he told her and stood aside. Never offered to take the bag, but she wouldn't've let him anyway. "Lunch is nearly ready, I think. Go meet the family."

That's about when Sasha remembered about the pregnancy and how cruel she'd thought the whole thing was. Locking his wife up in a prison made of something she guesses he'd call love. "Yeah, lunch sounds good," she said.

"This is your aunt Sasha."

Do you offer to shake a five-year-old's hand when you meet them? Probably not, but there was something about the kid's eyes that made Sasha want to. She fought it.

"Hey, kid. Wow, you're like a whole person these days, huh? Last time I saw you, I don't think you were fully cooked yet." She grinned down at the little boy sitting at the table with a perfectly square PB&J in front of him. He didn't respond. Nobody in the kitchen did. Her brother, his wife, the kid all just looking at her like Sasha just spoke Italian at them and danced a jig.

"The last time your aunt was in town was when I was pregnant with you," her brother's wife explained.

The kid nodded. "Oh."

That's all he said. He ate his sandwich in silence while Sasha avoided answering questions about what she'd been up to for the last few years. He sat quietly, watching with big brown eyes while the adults in the room skirted around how long Sasha was going to stay. As far as she could tell, they landed on "indefinitely" with some underlying threat of that being yanked away as soon as there was a whiff of bad behavior.

Bad behavior, with her brother, was sort of a gray area. Smoking inside the house, talking about her artist friends, playing music he considered subversive: all those were Bad Behavior. But if she sat outside on the porch even though all his neighbors could see her smoking, which she kind of assumed would freak him out, that was okay. If she brought him and the wife to an art gallery in the city, managed to score them some comped passes, then that was culture. That wasn't bad behavior at all. And if some of Sasha's favorites happened to come on the radio, well, what was he going to do about it?

It was a lot like living with their dad again. People cope in their own ways. Sasha went crazy and moved to the city way too young. Her brother went crazy and turned into a slightly softer version of their father. Shit happens. She never blamed him for how he turned out, anyway. None of that was their fault. Sometimes, and only sort of, Sasha wondered if her brother knew that he wasn't to blame. There was no way she was ever going to find out, though. Easier to bottle it all up. Way better to bury it.

CHAPTER 3

"**D**id you get breakfast?"

Rao nods as they walk. He didn't. He probably should have. He's certain he'll die if he doesn't find coffee in the next ten minutes.

"I've got a meeting, so I'll leave you to it. In there," Miller says, halting in the corridor and indicating an unmarked door to their left. Rao hesitates. He's learned a few lessons over the years about walking blindly into rooms like these. "Rao, please get something to eat," she adds, smiling wearily, gesturing again at the door.

He pushes at it. Walks into an open-plan office. Fabric cubicle dividers, worn grey carpet, mesh desk chairs. People staring at screens. Some wear suits, others BDUs. Four of the latter are frowning over something on a breakout table nearby. Porn, maybe. *No.* He looks about. Has he been assigned a desk? Has Miller stuck him in here so people can keep an eye on him?

No to both. He's looking for a spare desk with a screen to hide behind when he feels a tiny, sliding dislocation in his sinuses and chest. Something's not right in here. It'll be something he's dragged his eyes across but not properly seen. An item from the diner, he guesses.

It's not. It's Adam.

Lieutenant Colonel Adam Rubenstein, bent over a file at the far side of the room. Just another dark-haired man in a cheap suit. There are at least five of those in here. All just like him, none of them anything like him.

He looks the same, Rao thinks, but seems somehow unfamiliar. Perhaps he shouldn't be surprised. There was a Rao before Afghanistan, but Rao's not sure how much of him still exists, which makes the Adam he's looking at now seem a souvenir from an impossibly distant past. The shoulders of his jacket still sag. His hair is just as short and ostentatiously poorly cut. The collar of his shirt is tight, the knot of his tie too snug against it. Adam has always dressed as if he's trying to stop himself from giving anything away. The scruff on his jaw is a worrying sign. This must be a serious situation if Adam's not found time to shave.

He remembers Adam's last words to him. Late afternoon in Tashkent, just under a year ago. Bright, landlocked light beating through plate glass into the departure hall, dragging like sandpaper on Rao's appalling hangover. Weak black tea in paper cups. More than a little awkwardness. "Take care," Rao had said as he rose to walk to the gate. He'd judged it the safest bet, but as soon as he'd said it, he knew it sounded as if he were doubting Adam could look after himself. Adam had nodded once, then lowered his eyes to the cartons of cigarettes under Rao's arm and raised an eyebrow. "You know those are fake," he'd said. Not a trace of a smile, but Rao'd been cheered. Adam's peace offerings, on the rare occasions they're given, have always had something of the nature of knives.

Rao doesn't say a word as he approaches. But Adam wouldn't be as good as he is if he hadn't noticed Rao long before he reached his desk. He doesn't look up.

"You look like shit," he says flatly.

"Yeah, thanks," Rao answers. "You look nondescript."

That makes Adam raise his eyes from the file. They're dark, schooled into the usual faint hostility he uses to dissuade conversation. Rao thinks back, recalls the very few times Adam's smiled at anything he's said. There's a sense of humour behind those eyes: that's an immutable fact. He's made Rao laugh in the past. His habitual impassivity, his immunity to jokes and jabs—it's a control thing, Rao's always assumed. The man is wound up tighter than those intricate Black Forest clocks, and Rao is reasonably sure that Adam himself did the winding. Intelligence officers like him hold their own keys. That's the point of them.

He gives Rao a once-over. He'll have already taken in everything he needs, but now he's decided to extend Rao the courtesy of being involved with his assessment. For Adam, this is an act of consideration

bordering on generosity. "Glad to see you standing," he says. He probably means it, Rao decides, looking down at the file Adam's holding, the
faint, black-inked fingerprints decorating its edges. Writing implements
rebel in Adam's hands. Rao suspects he affects their ink like he does
most people's blood pressure. "I didn't mean it literally," Adam adds.
"You can take a seat."

Rao sits. "Are we just going to talk about my current state of being
or are you going to tell me about that file you're ruining?"

"This is a copy," Adam mutters, pushing the papers over to Rao.
"Doesn't matter what happens to it so long as it doesn't leave the room."

Here we go again, Rao thinks, feeling the vague headache he's had
for days blossom into deep, bruising pulses behind his eyes. He pushes
his fingernails hard into his palms. It'd be good to ask Adam what he
knows about Rao's state, his place in all this, and so many other things,
but there's no way he can do that without a sickening amount of vulnerability. Later, Rao decides. Maybe. When his head isn't pounding
so badly and his eyes can focus properly. He picks up the file, opens it,
flips through it helplessly. "Adam, I might look like shit, but I feel far
worse. Just tell me what it says."

"Three days ago, a civilian contractor working grounds mainte-
nance found the body of an SNCO in an unscheduled bonfire in the
southeast sector of the base. Senior Master Sergeant Adrian Straat."

"Dead before the fire?"

"No."

"Cause of death?"

"Fire."

"Is that in the file, or are you fucking with me?"

"Both, maybe. That's a separate file. Miller's told you about the
objects. They appeared about the same time as the corpse over a four-
hundred-meter radius. No one admits to placing them or seeing them
being placed. They've been bagged and inventoried. Miller wants you
to take a look at them after this. They're all in the evidence room except
a 1950s jeep that turned up behind a munitions bunker and a 28-gauge
Browning Citori in the weapons store."

"That's a shotgun."

"Yes, it is. Specifically, a Citori White Lightning Over and Under, hand built in Japan circa 1983. I'm leaving out a lot, Rao. There are details here that can wait for when you're more able to take them in."

"You're handling me."

"And I'm doing it well."

"Fuck off. Is there any coffee around here?"

"You want *coffee*."

"Don't start."

Adam gets up, returns to the desk with two mugs, sets them in front of Rao. Tugs at the file, extracts two stapled pages, and hands them over. The top sheet is an outline map of the base. Across it is a scattering of numbered crosses, concentrated in some areas, sparse in others.

"These crosses are where the objects were found?" Rao says, gulping down liquid so vile it's like a slap round the face.

"Yes. The circle is the fire."

"Should I be seeing something in the pattern?"

"Do you?"

"No. Do you?"

"No."

"Have you been to the diner?"

"Not yet."

"Surprised at you, Adam."

"Rao, I got in at three a.m. off a flight from Dulles. I didn't have time."

"Sure, yeah."

"I'm telling the truth."

"*Sure*, yeah."

Rao feels the grin on his face, marvels at it. He turns the page, scans a few lines. It's as if a yard sale exploded over the base and someone had itemised the fallout.

29 *Motorcycle jacket (black leather)*

30 *Plush dinosaur (yellow, worn condition, missing one eye)*

31 *Recliner chair (burgundy, leather)*

32 *Toolbox (varnished pine)*

33 *Bunch of roses (red)*
34 *Connect 4 game (assembled frame with complete set of counters)*
35 *Beanie Baby (bear, black, worn condition)*

"Santa?" he suggests. "Maybe all the personnel have been good boys and girls."

"Santa is not a plausible delivery system," Adam murmurs. "Security cameras showed nothing except several bursts of static between zero six forty-eight and fifty-one. Before them, nothing. After them"—he nods at the map—"this." He hesitates. "I don't want to get *Twilight Zone*, but I can't account for it."

"I've always assumed Rod Serling taught you how to knot your necktie, Adam, but no, let's—" Rao stops. Reconsiders. "Yeah. Well. I've been in that diner, and it was full *Twilight Zone*. A guy died in a mysterious bonfire and weird shit appeared all over the shop. Why shouldn't we go down the freaky rabbit hole? Do you have a time of death?"

"Approximate." Adam pulls another file towards him, opens it. "There are photos of the scene, if you—"

"Not now, thank you."

"Zero six forty."

"So when was the first one of these objects picked up?"

"Six fifty-one."

"The Cabbage Patch doll?"

"From the flightline, yes."

Rao sees the doubt in Adam's eyes. He drains his mug, picks up the second, takes a gulp, and winces. This one's even worse. He's pathetically grateful for it.

"The diner's mental, love. I've been inside it. And when we look at this Santa shit, it's going to be mental too. There's going to be some kind of logic to all this but I'm pretty sure it's *Twilight Zone* logic and we're just going to have to deal with that as it comes. Keep our minds open."

"Don't patronize me, Rao. I don't care if it's elves. I just need to know why and how it's elves."

It's a three-minute walk, Adam informs him, to the evidence room. Hands stuffed deep in his pockets as he steps over puddles on the footpath, shoulders hunched against the worsening rain, Rao decides he's sufficiently caffeine fortified to broach the subject of how Adam's been.

"So, Adam."

"Rao."

"How've you been?"

"How have I been."

"Yes."

"Busy."

"Busy good or busy bad?"

"Busy."

This, Rao recalls, is what it is like to converse with Adam. "*Classified* busy?"

Adam gives him the barest frown. "More desk work than before," he says after a while.

"You have a desk, Adam?"

"Technically, everyone has."

"Technically?"

"It's more of a concept."

"The fuck does that mean?"

"If you live long enough, you'll end up at your desk."

"Ah, this is a case of there being a bullet out there with your name on it, is it? A bullet, a desk, a grave?"

"Always waiting."

"You're one dramatic cunt."

"Yes, Rao."

"A *desk*," Rao breathes. "Did you fuck up?"

"No, I didn't fuck up."

"No escándalo? Got caught in a compromised position in an embassy broom cupboard?" Rao represses a snicker: it emerges as an almost inaudible squeak. The very idea of Adam having a fumble somewhere. Impossible.

"No."

"Don't tell me you got tired of shooting people? Fucking hell, Adam. Did you find god or something?"

"Rao, you asked me how I've been. I've been busy."

"Of course you have. Christ. Catching up with you is like trying to break into Fort Meade. Don't know why the fuck I bothered asking in the first place." Rao grins. A pair of F-15s passes low overhead, both bristling with ordnance. "Well?" he says when the noise allows.

"Well what?"

"Aren't you going to ask me how I've been?"

Adam shakes his head. "You'll tell me."

The evidence room is in a squat, redbrick building at the far end of the base. Two sad-looking laurel bushes flank its entrance door; the black-painted guttering above gurgles with rainwater. A leftover from the war, Rao surmises. The old RAF operations block? *Yes.*

Adam leads him to the basement and marches straight to a door at the far end of a corridor still decorated in wartime cream and green. Flashes his ID to the guard outside, who straightens, snaps a "sir," unlocks the door, and stands aside. Striplights flicker on.

Rao wrinkles his nose. The air in here smells odd. Aromatic hydro-carbons off-gassing from plastic, he supposes. *No.* Whatever it is, it's redolent of jasmine and mud. Rainwater, sandalwood. He shivers. The room is narrow and deep. Steel floor-to-ceiling shelves stacked with transparent plastic bags run along the walls, and at the far end of the room a number of bulkier bagged items rest on the floor. Rao sees leather upholstery pressed unpleasantly against taut plastic, a Yamaha 50cc.

Adam's businesslike. "OSI forensics said there were no fingerprints on any of the items they looked at except the people who picked them up. Miller wants anything else you can give us."

Rao pulls a pair of nitrile gloves from a box on a steel examination table, puts them on. "So far, all I know is they're all incredibly wrong. Chuck me one?"

"Which?"

"Whatever. Doesn't matter."

Rao takes the bag Adam hands him, squints through it. "I think this is a Care Bear," he decides. "It is a Care Bear."

"It's Funshine Bear."

"Adam, how do you know what a Funshine Bear is?"

"Television." Adam's attention is focused on another item he's pulled from the shelves.

"Bollocks. You definitely had a Funshine Bear," Rao says, then stops dead in wonderment. "Shit, Adam, I never thought about this before. You must have had toys when you were small. What were they? Teeny plastic army men? Retractable daggers? AR-15s?"

Rao expects Adam to greet this with the usual classified silence. Unexpectedly, he answers. "Models," he says flatly. "Scale models. From kits. Mostly aircraft."

"I adore scale models," Rao says. "You still have them tucked away somewhere? Can I see them?"

"No. You should look at these," Adam says, extending his arms.

It's a bunch of red roses.

"Appreciate the sentiment, love, but I've always preferred mimosas."

"Rao."

Rao takes the bag. The blooms are deep scarlet and highly scented: as he unzips the closure, their fragrance hits the back of his throat. He slips them out onto the table. They're a little wilted. He peers at the card attached to a length of red ribbon wrapped around their stems. A message in cursive script, blue ink. *To my Millie. Forever, like we said.*

"There's a date. Ah. The flowers are trying to tell me they're from 1973, Adam."

"Are they. Could you just look at them, Rao."

They look like a bunch of roses. Although there's something about the space between the flowers that isn't quite— Rao frowns, pushes his fingers between the blooms, careful, exploratory.

Holy shit.

They're roses on the outside. But inside the bunch is a monstrosity, a clumped mass of curled, soft, velvety-red vegetal tissue smeared with patches of glossy, veined green, as if leaves and flowers had melted together. Staring at it, Rao remembers a textbook photograph of a plant that had been exposed to gamma radiation and wrought itself into a growth of exuberant and incoherent horror. When he pulls his fingers back, the bouquet snaps shut strangely.

It looks like a bunch of roses.

"Are they roses?" Adam asks slowly, as if the question were not only surprising but unpleasant.

"Well. What's a rose? Look, I did a lot of reading a long while back about the metaphysics of identity. That's not the kind of question that comes in true or false. But there are other things I can test. Like, these flowers were cut from a plant."

"Were they?"

"No. They weren't. *Shit.* Give me something else. Something," he says, thinking carefully, "in a box. There was a toolbox, wasn't there? No, Scrabble. Find the Scrabble box."

"There are two," Adam says, peering at the inventory.

"Give us both."

The first is an old-style set. The board is unremarkable: grey green, dotted with squares of pink and pastel blue. Wooden tile rests. Wooden tiles. The other box can't be opened. When Adam pulls a knife and slices through one corner it turns out to be solid all the way through: fibrous, grey matter that the blade works through with difficulty. Afterwards he spends more time than Rao thinks necessary wiping the blade of his knife on the fabric of his pants, an expression of disgust on his face. He brushes at the spot on his thigh with his fingers several times, looks at Rao.

"They're all going to be like this, aren't they?"

"Yeah, love. Probably. Yeah."

CHAPTER 4

"Where?"

    "In England. RAF Polheath. It's a fighter base, an American one, the name is, uh, misleading."

"I know Polheath."

"Hello? Are you still on the line?"

"Loud and clear. I was thinking. This is deeply suboptimal."

"It's not ideal, no. But, you know, the proverb. Every cloud."

"Every cloud?"

"I was thinking of Dennett. You know Dennett? Daniel Dennett."

"Philosopher of mind, yes. What about him?"

"He holds that making mistakes is the key to making progress. I think this complication could turn out to be quite, quite serendipitous."

CHAPTER 5

"Leave the dishes to me," Sasha told her brother, and the whole family cleared out of the kitchen like magic, not even pausing to talk her out of it for appearances. Now she's alone. Which is exactly right, really, since she offered, and she doesn't mind doing the dishes. It's payment, sort of, and that's what Sasha had planned when she offered, knowing it would be her role for the entire time she stayed with her brother. There were worse things she could've been stuck with, and she'll definitely pick up a few more chores as she goes. No rent, after all. Not even he's so much of an asshole that he'd hound her for a monthly check, probably.

It's suddenly obvious that someone has come into the room, like there's a shift in the air somehow, and Sasha makes a safe guess. "Listen. You can trust me with your china, okay? I'm not a butterfingers like some people I know—" And she's this close to dredging up some old childhood fight just for the fun of it as she turns to face her brother, when she stops.

It's not him. It's his son. He's standing at the door, watching her with those big eyes. "Huh. You're real quiet, kiddo," she says. "Like a ghost."

He shakes his head seriously. Sasha lifts an eyebrow.

"No? Not a ghost."

He shakes his head again. She leans against the edge of the sink, ignoring the wet as it seeps into her shirt and onto her back. It's fine. It's lukewarm and weirdly homey. All the grime and discomfort that comes with a family home. Little things she'd forgotten about while couch surfing with her bum friends. "You want to tell me why you're not like a ghost? Because I'm not seeing any other options here."

She doesn't think he's going to answer. He stands there in silence so long that Sasha shrugs and turns around again. Sticks her hands into the soapy water. Searches for the mug she knows is in there along with the plates and utensils. She'll never know why mugs are more fun to wash, and maybe it's just a lie she tells herself to make the cleaning job easier, but she searches all the same.

The kid talks, so quietly, as her hands find the handle.

"Not real," he says. He's beside her now. Moved from the doorway to the counter right by her side. Neck craned, looking almost painfully tiny, just to see her from where he's standing. "Ghosts aren't real."

Maybe this is the result of a serious family talk, she thinks. Maybe the kid was scared one night, and his parents had to curl up with him and explain that ghosts aren't real. Sasha smiles at the small face looking up at her, thinking about that imaginary scene, all its unlikely domesticity. It doesn't fit her brother or his wife, and it doesn't fit in this house. Like it's too small to stretch over them all and too big to fit into the house. She knows that ghost talk would never have happened, but it's cute to think about. Especially with those big eyes looking up at her.

"Okay. So ghosts aren't real. You got me, kid," she admits. He frowns a little at her, confused. "It's not really a lie when it's part of a story. You get that, right? Like sometimes people tell stories about their days and not everything is all the way true, but they're not all the way lies. You ever hear someone say that it's raining cats and dogs?"

He nods.

"And that just means it's raining a lot, huh?"

He nods again.

"So, saying you're like a ghost doesn't mean that you're fake. Not fake like a ghost," she says, carefully avoiding the topic of death. Maybe that's not a talk she's supposed to have on the first day the kid meets her. "But you're quiet, and you move like it's a secret. Like ghosts. Get it?"

He thinks about it. He really thinks about it. Sasha wonders if maybe it's too much. How old is he again? She's gone too fast and too much. But then he hums at her. A tiny copy of her brother, serious and all straight lines, and far too young to have lost all the laughs inside him. Shit. She needs a smoke.

"I get it," he says.

"Cool. You want a glass of water or something?"

"Yes."

She pulls a glass from the suds, cleans it quickly. "We'll get you to talk more than three words in a row one day, kid. I'm gonna promise you that," she mutters.

CHAPTER 6

Miller listens intently to Rao's report. "Noted," she says. "Rubenstein, anything to add?"

"No, ma'am."

She nods. Her manner is brisk, her equanimity unnerving. "I'd like you to talk to Ed Gibbons," she announces. "The civilian contractor first on the scene at the fire."

"Where is he? In a cell somewhere?"

"No, Rao. He's at home in Brandon with his wife and two dogs. He's been off sick for three days with a migraine. But he's well enough to"—she purses her lips—"have a chat."

"You want us to have a nice chat with the gardener?" Rao asks.

"That's what I want you to do."

Adam glances at Rao, who sends him a sharp side-eye. A wordless *Yes, Adam, I know there's a quicker way to do this.*

Rao remembers that night eleven months ago, driving between Khujand and Tashkent. Tense with the upcoming border crossing, rattled by a desert road littered with broken concrete and ridges of impacted sand, they'd got into a fight about an impending rendezvous.

"He's not going to turn up."

"He'll be there."

"He fucking won't. How did you get to be so *trusting*, Adam? Don't they beat that shit out of you at Langley?"

"I never went to Langley. And it's not like we need to meet him. In fact, I'm pretty sure we don't need to be here at all. Because I worked it out, Rao. I know you're not a polygraph. They think that's what you are, but you're not. You just somehow know what's true and what isn't.

I could write a list of likely possibilities on a piece of paper, and you just point to one. We don't have to be here. We could be in Ohio."

The silence had stretched like molten glass into a thread impossibly fine, impossibly brittle, waiting to break.

"We need to be here," Rao said eventually.

"We really don't."

He'd clutched at Adam's arm. "Adam. Listen to me. *I need to be out here*."

Puzzled, Adam stared down at Rao's fingers until he let go. Turned his gaze back to the road ahead. It took him five seconds to work it out. Rao counted each one.

"They'd never let you out."

"That's the size of it, yes. They'd lock me up, throw away the key, feed me paper. I'd really rather they didn't know."

Then a long and perilous silence. After a while Rao unwound his window, fragrant night air flooding the cabin. Stuck his head out, craned his neck to watch bats dipping over the UAZ to snatch moths drawn in by the headlights. "The asset'll make the rendezvous," he'd said, finally, settling back into his seat.

"Yeah. He will."

Another mile.

"There are limits to what I can do," Rao began, certain that saying any of this was a terrible course of action, but it was happening, and it was happening like an apology happens, and Rao has never been a fan of those. "Exceptions. Like emotional states: there's a lot of vagueness with those. Can't track them. What I *can* do is judge the veracity of propositional statements about the world. Written or spoken, even implied. And no, I don't know how it works."

"What does it feel like?"

Rao shakes his head. "Knowing what's true and what isn't? Fuck, Adam, that's like trying to describe what breathing feels like. You know when the air you inhale is cold or hot. You know how to draw breath and let it out. It's automatic, part of you. It's like that, for me. A sensation. It isn't something I can describe, it just is."

"Did you learn to do it?"

"Nah, it's always been there."

"How far back can you go?"

"What d'you mean?"

"In time. Historically."

Rao rubbed his cheek. "With enough specificity, as far back as you like."

Adam considered this for a while. "Abraham and Isaac? Did that happen?"

Oh that is adorable, Rao thought. "That's impossible. Neither of those people are real enough to track, you know?" He'd glanced across. Adam appeared genuinely disappointed, and Rao felt bad about his lie. Abraham existed, and so did Isaac. As for whether God demanded Abraham kill his son—well, he just didn't want to have to get into the complication of explaining why the "that" of Adam's question was a problem. If statements about gods were testable, Rao'd be in an entirely different line of work than *spy*.

"So, you should probably know. There's one other exception."

"Which is?"

"You. I never know when you're lying."

Rao watched Adam's face harden. An entirely reasonable response, considering. "I'm not fucking with you, Adam. It's been that way since the beginning, and I don't know why."

"The *questions*. So that's why you were like that when we met."

"Like what?"

"Like you were on uppers."

Rao scratched at the corner of an eye. "Erm, to be honest, love, I was. But yes."

Adam nodded slowly. "And you don't know why? Really?"

"I've thought up a fuck ton of theories. But I can't tell if any of them are true. It's a thing, Adam. It's a fucking bizarre thing, and I'm telling you about it now for a reason."

"Which is?"

Rao sat back, heart hammering.

"You're going to keep my secret."

"Of course I am."

"I'm very relieved to hear you say that. I can't know, you see? And cards on the table, it's much weirder than that, because it's not just you. It's anything about you. First time they mentioned you in a briefing my skin crawled. When they ran through your operational history it was like white noise." Rao frowned. "No. Not white noise. What I think of, when people talk about you, it's more like a roulette wheel."

"A roulette wheel."

"Yeah, but not the bit when the ball skips in the pockets. The noise of it circling the rim. Before it falls." He snorted. "I freaked out quite a lot when you told me you grew up in Vegas."

"Outside Vegas. And I could have been lying."

Rao rolled his eyes. "I know. But I've seen you play cards, Adam. And I've seen your file."

"No you haven't. So, you work with me because I made your skin crawl when you first heard my name and because I'm a freak?"

"Yes. Also they told me I had to."

Rao hadn't even caught Adam's name, in truth, only the end of the sentence his name had been in. He'd been staring at his own reflection in the deep shine of the tabletop, letting his mind wander. *French polish. Shellac,* he'd been thinking. *Shellac and denatured alcohol. Layers of it, set one on top of the other. Chatoyancy, the proper name for the way the lustre works light like that. Like in chrysoberyl, like in tiger's-eye*—and he'd been musing on the optical phenomena certain gems display when they're cut in particular ways when he'd heard the phrase "commendable record, six years at the DIA," and his head emptied with a sickening flash of heat. Like magic paper, a conflagration collapsing instantly into absolute vacancy. He'd closed his eyes, and they kept saying things about this Lieutenant Colonel Rubenstein, and all of them were nonsenses, and the sensation in his head bloomed and grew and was so unlike anything he'd ever felt before that for a long while Rao had to grip the edge of the table in terror, convinced he was having some kind of neurological event. The feeling shifted and flickered as the seconds stretched, slowly turning itself into something halfway between a sound and an image. A spinning roulette wheel in that uncertain moment before the ball drops to the pockets below. The moment that's nothing but potential, whose meaning is its own inevitable end. But it refused to end, the entire time they talked about Rubenstein. And there was Rao, trying to follow what they were saying, trying to understand what was happening when they spoke of him, trying to comprehend what could be different about this man and grasping, finally, the point of the entire discussion. They wanted Rao to *work* with him? *Fuck.*

In a black cab en route to their first meeting Rao had wondered if he should have made more of an effort with his clothes. He'd been nervous, and nerves make Rao kick, hard. He'd decided on his oldest, shittiest jacket, threadbare, with a cigarette burn on one sleeve. Vaguely odiferous trainers and a pair of conker-coloured corduroy trousers his mother had once pronounced too short in the leg. A bag slung over his shoulder: laptop, pens, notebook, two packets of Marlboro Lights, a dog-eared 1980s spy-themed Mills and Boon novel called *Cloak of Darkness* he'd stolen from a B&B in Brighton and had become something of a lucky talisman.

A little heavy with the Terre d'Hermès that morning, perhaps, but it separates the men from the boys. Maybe the bump of coke before he left the house had been a bad idea—he was expending a degree of effort in the back of the cab trying not to talk with the driver about *everything*, but he wasn't going to worry about it unduly. They'd seen him worse.

The meet and greet had been in the kind of room Six loves to use when it does performative Britishness for Americans. Magnolia walls, Axminster carpet, leather armchairs, a muddy sub-Landseer oil of a stag above the fireplace, elaborate plaster cornices blurred with layers of white gloss paint covering decades of cigarette smoke.

As soon as he walked through the door, Rao stopped in his tracks, his usual disarming smile dying on his face.

Rubenstein.

Huh, one part of Rao thought. *Cute.* But the rest of him recoiled, like he was seeing something against the laws of nature. Rubenstein wore a dark grey suit, black tie, white shirt, stood at military ease. His eyes were dark and expressionless, but Rao understood they'd very rapidly assessed him from the way Rubenstein tilted his head, just a little, before saying hello.

Baritone. Unplaceable American accent, entirely without emphasis. Hearing it was like trying to climb a sheet of glass. Rao had no purchase at all.

"Hi," he said back, looking a little desperately at his handler on Rubenstein's left. Morten Edwards twitched his nose, smiled back. On Rubenstein's right, a white-haired man in the well-pressed blue shirt and red tie that is something of an unofficial uniform for unofficial elements in the American government nodded at him.

Edwards cleared his throat. "Well here we are," he said cheerfully. "Lovely. Shall we run through everything?"

They sat, and for almost two hours Rao listened to red-tie man— who remained unnamed—run through their upcoming op. Eight weeks in Central Asia, primarily in Uzbekistan, assessing the reliability of intelligence sources and assets in place. A lot of talk of FVEY and interagency cooperation. Rao's lips twitched a little whenever he heard that. He knew he was being loaned to the Americans as a favour, part of some tit for tat. Whatever. Red-tie guy took him through some of the less classified highlights of Rubenstein's career—*Yeah, that's what I've read*, Rao thought helplessly, *but I still don't fucking know?*—and emphasised that he would fulfil a personal protection role in addition to being Rao's operational partner.

Over those eighty minutes, Rubenstein spoke for less than three minutes in all. Everything he asked was acutely to the point, and Rao, struggling to make sense of things using methods quite alien to him, eventually decided that he might be the sharpest man in the room. Also, he thought, considering the blankness of Rubenstein's face and the tone of his voice, he's going to be the most boring man alive to spend time with. Eight weeks. Eight weeks of mission-mandated shared hotel rooms. He's going to drive Rao up the wall. He's going to go absolutely fucking mad.

CHAPTER 7

He learns a lot of things without lessons. He learns by watching, without asking questions, without being sat down and told. If he asks questions, that means he's stupid. If he has to be told, that means he's in trouble. He learns by watching where his mom keeps the wine for Friday, and that it's different from the wine she drinks during the week. He learns that no one is supposed to touch the lighter in the cabinet unless his mom is lighting candles. He learns the words of his dad praying. He knows all the words for what they're doing, but he can't remember when he was told them.

He can't remember figuring out that it's better to watch than to ask. It's just how things are.

Now he's watching and nobody notices him, and his parents are talking about his aunt staying in the house. How his dad thinks she's a hassle, but she's family. How his mom thinks that it's great timing that his aunt turned up when she did, since they have an important dinner and now they don't have to get a babysitter.

That night, after his parents leave for dinner, his aunt smiles at him. Says that they have the house to themselves, that they can do anything that he wants. He can't think of anything, but his aunt doesn't get mad. She finds a pack of cards and starts teaching him games. He doesn't talk much, and he doesn't ask her questions, but it's okay. She's telling him the rules to the game, but he's not in trouble for not already knowing them.

She asks him what they do on Fridays. He tells her. Says the right words. Tells her where the wine is. She doesn't ask, but he tells her that he doesn't like how it smells.

"Like if vinegar could be too sweet, huh?" she says, and she's agreeing with him, and they're both smiling, and everything is fine.

She lights the candles but not like his mom does. She waves her hands to him, gesturing for him to come closer. Places both hands on his shoulders. He cranes his neck to look up at her, but her eyes are closed. And when she prays, it's not the words he's used to.

He listens. He watches. Tries to memorize the words she says.

"What is it?" she asks when she's done. Her hands are still on his shoulders. "Did I get it wrong?"

He shakes his head, but he doesn't know if she did or not. He stays quiet. Doesn't ask questions. He has a lot of them, but he doesn't want her to think he's stupid. But she guesses.

"Your mom and dad don't do that one," she says. It sounds like a question. He shakes his head again. "That's okay, kid. That'll be the one I say, if you want."

He isn't sure why his opinion matters, but he doesn't tell his aunt that. He's not supposed to argue. "Yes," he says. He doesn't move after that. He barely breathes. She's still holding on to his shoulders, but she's not holding him in place. He could move away from her if he wanted to.

He doesn't.

He's the only kid in the house, she tells him, so that means that prayer is just for him. "My lips," she says, "to God's ears, if he's paying attention." Says that it's all about God keeping an eye on him. Shining a light on him.

Peace, she says, and she takes one of her hands from his shoulder. Rests it on his head. The one she'll say on Fridays makes sure he gets a little peace. He's not sad, but he wants to cry.

CHAPTER 8

E d's house is a 1950s bungalow at the far end of a rural cul-de-sac. Purple violas bloom in a planter shaped like a pair of cowboy boots next to the yellow front door; there's a motorbike under a tarp, a square of well-kept lawn. The man who opens the door is in his fifties, open-faced and weather-beaten, with thinning fair hair, a checked flannel shirt rolled to his elbows, and faded tattoos of playing cards dancing up one arm. He's wearing a pair of dark-blue 501s, a belt with a silver rodeo buckle.

Rao apologises for calling on him like this out of the blue. Says, as he always does in situations like these, that his name is Ray. Explains that he and Adam are journalists working on a story about spooky happenings in Suffolk. Ed's face is all caution when he hears the word "journalists," but as soon as Rao says they've heard Ed knows something about this *diner* that's turned up in a field, he perks up. "I might," he says.

"Can we have a chat with you about it?"

"Yeah, why not? Lucky you found me at home. I've been a bit under the weather the last few days. D'you want to come in and have a cup of tea? Roz's just put the kettle on."

Rao knows this is the place.

He knows it as soon as Ed walks them through the hall, and he sees the photo of Roy Rogers, the framed Polaroid of a younger Ed leaning against a pink-and-white Oldsmobile and the metal license plate fixed below it bearing the slogan: HOME MEANS NEVADA. In the lounge a movie poster for *Western Jamboree* on the wall above the TV catches at him almost viciously. He stares at Gene Autry's off-register face for so long, Ed asks if he's ever seen the film.

"No," he says. "Maybe I should."

"It's mad," Ed says. "Absolutely mad. It's about a gang of outlaws trying to steal helium from under Autry's ranch."

"Helium?"

"The gas. There's a blimp and everything."

Rao struggles a bit with this. "And songs?" he says, recovering.

"Of course!" Ed says.

Sinatra is playing on the stereo in the corner and motocross on a muted TV. There's a leather sofa with a Navajo-pattern fleece throw, a lurcher sprawled across it, and a wiry, steeped-tea-toned terrier that jumps onto Rao's lap as soon as he sits in the armchair he's offered. It circles a couple of times, lays its head on his knee, and sighs. Outside, Rao can see ferret hutches, more violas, the woody stems of some kind of climber trained on wires along a fence.

Adam refuses a seat and stands by the door. He's not at ease in domestic spaces. Rao's given him shit for it any number of times, has more than once suggested he was raised in a forward command base, not a family home.

Roz appears.

"This is Ray and—"

"Adam," Rao says.

"They're journalists, want to talk to me about *you know what.*"

"What?" she says. She starts collecting mugs from side tables.

"The diner."

She shakes her head, looks sidelong at Rao. "He knows sod all about it. Either of you want a cup of tea? Milk? Sugar?"

Ed is gleeful. He pulls out his Nokia. Clicks through, holds it out to Rao. On the screen, silvered and foggy, is a photograph of the diner, taken at some distance, its leftmost side obscured by the shadow of a thumb.

"Is that it?"

Ed nods and grins. *Ed*, thinks Rao. *Oh, Ed. You're so eager to please.*

"How did you get this?"

"I know the guy who found it," he says, lowering his voice conspira-torially. "Tomasz. He's Polish, that's Tomasz with a zed, but he lives in Thetford. We were on JCBs together back in the day. He was spraying off the field, came over the hill and there it was, and he sent this to me 'cause he knows I'm into Americana. It's amazing, isn't it. Can't stop looking at this photo."

Rao stares at the phone, shakes his head, says with some wonderment, "No one we've talked to knows how it got there."

Ed laughs. "Well it wasn't the farmer. Garnham's already pissed off at the acreage of sugar beet he's lost, and he hasn't got the imagination to come up with something like this. He doesn't even watch TV, can you believe that? John at the Bells says it's an art installation, but why would someone come up from London and do it here? Waste of time. Then the Yanks came and walled it up, so it's got to be something to do with them. Roz thinks that too. Right, Roz?"

"Yeah. We don't know half of what goes on in there. It's not bad living this close, except the noise. You think you'll get used to it, but you never really do."

Ed nods. "You don't. We've been here fifteen years," he adds. He adores her. Rao's prickling with the weight of emotion between them; it's not right. He already knows why.

"They're alright," Roz says. "Some of the Americans are a bit up themselves, but most of them are nice. We had one next door for a bit. He went off to another base in Idaho, somewhere called Mountains Home."

"*Mountain Home*," Adam corrects.

Ed's eyebrows go up. "You're one, are you?"

It's one of Adam's tightest smiles. "Not by choice."

Ed nods thoughtfully.

Fuck's sake, Rao thinks. "This is a good song, Ed," he says. "Who's this?"

"You don't know who this is?"

"Why would I ask if I knew?"

"The best of the Rat Pack!"

"That's subjective."

"Alright, yeah, ok, if you want to be like that about it." Ed grins. "It's Dean Martin."

"No. Really? I don't think I've ever heard this one."

"One of the best."

"Of the Rat Pack?"

"No, his *songs*."

That kicks off an animated conversation about the Rat Pack that segues quickly into all the things Ed knows about Sinatra and the Mob. "So, this Americana," Rao says, "how did you get into it?"

"He's always been into it," Roz explains. "His dad was as well. I think it's infectious. Few years with Ed and I even got into line dancing."

"She's *really good*," Ed says seriously before launching into a disquisition on the gloriousness of America. America back then. The cars, the music, the clothes, the movies. Ed's trip to Graceland. All Ed's favourites. Sloppy joes, '50s jukeboxes, diner coffee. Diners.

Then Rao says softly, "I love diners, Ed, but I've never been in one. What are they like, inside?"

"Well," Ed says. "They're all the same, basically."

"Tell me. Describe one."

Ed's eyes shift left, shift up as he conjures one inside his head. "Well," he says, drawing it out. Right now Rao knows Ed's thinking of him as something like a stage hypnotist, is thrilled at being in the spotlight, and Rao feels the heavy weight of all his unwarranted trust.

And then it happens. He and Adam sit in the room with the hissing gas fire and the muted TV, the terrier and the sleeping lurcher, and they hear Ed describe the interior of the diner in the muddy field. They hear him describe it *exactly*.

They're quiet driving back.

"How?" Strain in Adam's voice.

"I can't even start to think about tackling that question right now." Rao grimaces. "Also, his wife's having an affair. And he sort of knows it."

"Is that relevant?"

"Fuck knows."

They hit a squall line, water battering the windscreen, blurring the road between each sweep of the blades. "Miller's going to pull him in," Rao says. The knowledge sits sour inside him, a chestful of curdled milk.

"It'd be stupid not to," Adam says, glancing across to the passenger seat. "But they won't be rough with him. It's not like that, here."

Bullshit. Rao looks at twisted roadside pines and runs through all the definitions of "rough" that apply in these cases, all the ones he knows, all the ones he's seen, until Adam, registering the silence, starts complaining about how much he hates driving in the rain. They're almost back at the base when Rao swivels in his seat. "You're babysitting me again," he observes. "But this time they think I'm a lost cause. So, what are you going to tell Miller in your one-on-one?"

Adam flicks the indicator, turns in to the gatehouse lane. "That you're better than I thought you'd be."

"We'll bring him in," Miller announces after they brief her on their visit. Rao swallows past the lump in his throat. It's not just the thought of Ed in one of those rooms. It's the betrayal on Ed's face.

Ray, you said you were a journalist.

"Ed?" he says lightly. "Nah. Leave him for us."

"I understand your position, Rao. But he has to come in. I want to talk to him and I can't be seen leaving for this. It's complicated."

"Ok, but first— Look, I think me and Adam should take him to the diner."

"Your rationale?"

"Ed's got an attitude. Stick it to the man. Bit of a poacher vibe. He thinks we're journalists. We can work with that. Get conspiratorial and sneak him into the site, see how he reacts. Have a chat. We'll get more that way than by shouting at him over a desk."

"Shouting isn't my style," she says. "But I'm willing to permit this. Rubenstein, you want me to send someone else with Rao? Anything to finish up in Washington?"

Adam shakes his head. "No, ma'am. I'll see this through, if that's alright."

"Ok, good. Call Gibbons. Be persuasive."

At eight, a clean-shaven Adam turns up at Rao's dorm with takeout from the base McDonald's, tells him they're picking Ed up at 10:00 a.m. For a while they sit in silence picking at fries tipped out upon a torn-flat bag spread out upon the tiny desk. The smell of grease and salt is overpowering. Rao knows it'll probably turn his stomach later when he's looking to sleep, but right now the heavy olfactory blanket feels welcome. Safe. The silence, on the other hand. The sound of paper rustling and quiet chewing. That feels like a small death with each bite. Can't hack it. Can't stand it. It's going to turn him feral soon, and he won't like who he'll become out of sheer annoyance, hot frustration. He has to fill the silence.

"Adam?" he begins, submerging a chicken nugget in BBQ sauce, munching on it.

"Rao."

"Riddle me this—"

"The Greeks," Adam interrupts. Doesn't look up. Picks another chip from the pile.

Rao blinks. "What?"

"Nothing. What were you going to ask?"

"Right. I was wondering, as I tend to do, but have never actually got round to asking, what you get up to when you're not working."

"I'm always working."

It's what Rao expected him to say. Entirely automatic. *Everything's always work, everything's a job, Rao. I'm always working.* Rao's willing to take a chance on it being a deflection; what spurs him to enquire further is partly curiosity, mostly a desperate need to stop hearing himself chew.

"Legally, you must have downtime."

"Officially, of course I have downtime. Operationally, however, no, I don't."

Rao snorts. "Fucking hell. That might be the most depressing thing you've ever said to me."

Adam frowns as he reaches for the stack of napkins. Wiping his fingers, his eyebrows pucker more deeply. "Is it?"

"No, probably not," Rao allows. Adam says a lot of shit that would be heartbreaking to hear from anyone else. But Adam exists in a weird little covert reality. And he isn't anyone else. Half the time he doesn't act like other human beings. Rao sometimes forgets he's in the room until he moves or speaks. Barely human, Rao's informed him, many times. "Whatever. Answer the question. What do you get up to?"

"On my downtime, which does not exist."

"On your downtime, which does not exist." Rao grins. "What do you get up to?"

Adam peels back the lid of a waxed cardboard cup, inspects the liquid inside, passes it over. "I don't have an answer that's going to satisfy you."

"Try me," Rao says, punching a straw into his Sprite.

Adam looks at him evenly. Chews. Rao can't hear him do it, so it's fine. It's all fine. This is just Adam looking for the simplest route to say something. He's not a voluble soul.

"I watch TV, read books. Go for walks."

"Yeah, you're right." Rao's amused by how disappointed he is at this predictably vapid answer. "That's shit."

"Told you."

"You can't be this boring, love. You can't. No one is."

"Maybe I am."

Rao flicks the hard end of a french fry at him. Adam doesn't even look at it, just snatches it out of the air. If anyone but him had pulled a move like that, it would be remarkable. There'd be astonished laughter. Awe. But it's not anyone. In absolute silence, Rao watches Adam place the fragment back on the flattened bag.

"But you're not, though," Rao tries. "Are you? You're one of the scariest men on America's payroll. Am I wrong?"

"You could be. That could be a lie. Who told you that?"

"No one told me that. But a lot of people have intimated it."

"Mm." That's all the fucker says, but he lifts an eyebrow and passes Rao his Filet-O-Fish. He's laughing, Rao realises. The bastard's laughing at him.

"That's funny, is it?"

Adam unwraps a burger from its now-sheer paper, inspects it. "A little," he admits and takes a bite.

Shithead. He's *such* a shithead. Rao snorts again. Can't help it. "Ok. Here's another question."

"Shoot."

"How many weapons do you have on you at any given time?" Rao doesn't expect Adam to answer this at all. But he might. They used to have nights like this in the field: a shitty dinner and beers, Rao firing off questions, Adam answering them, or more usually not, and somehow never, not once, pissing Rao off in the process. Rubenstein's far too much of a government weirdo for Rao to take his silences personally.

"Depends."

"Depends on what?"

"A lot of variables."

"Name one."

"Carry laws of the state or country I'm in," Adam answers flatly. It sounds true, and Rao's sure it isn't.

"Currently?"

"Currently . . ." He sits back in his chair, looks off to one side.

"Fucking hell. Are you counting?"

A flicker of amusement. "Currently, I have my service weapon."

"Ah yes, your beloved M9. Anything else?"

Adam inclines his head again. "Knives."

"How many?"

"Why are you asking this?"

"Just tell me," Rao says. But really, why is he asking this? He wants to know. And he'll never know for sure with Adam. And it's just fun, talking with his old partner again like they're normal—even if they are talking about how many blades one of them is lugging around at any given time.

"Calf, boot, waistband."

"Three? Bloody hell. I didn't know they were there."

"That's good. That's what you want from concealed weapons."

"No, but— Adam, you don't even move like you're armed."

"Yes, Rao. Because if I did, then people would know that I am."

"See, you are a scary fucker."

Adam hums before taking a bite out of his burger. He thinks while he chews. "You're not scared," he observes eventually.

"No, love," Rao says, rubbing his cheek with the flat of one hand. "But in all honesty, these days I'm not exactly sane."

CHAPTER 9

He keeps hearing things he doesn't mean to. Yesterday he was in the yard, the window was open, and his mom was talking inside the house. First, he heard her say it was just a phase. Then she said Judy's daughter was obsessed with a book last year, but she'd gotten bored with it after a couple of months. That crazes were things kids just go through. Then he heard his dad saying it was something he'd better grow out of soon, that his son was carrying that book around like it was a goddamned teddy bear, and he was too old for that shit.

He shouldn't have heard that. His dad cursing makes him feel inside like when you put your hand into water that's way too hot. He'd looked down at the book he was holding. It was true he had been carrying it around, but he didn't know he wasn't supposed to.

The next morning his mom asks him about it. "Where's the book your aunt Sasha gave you?" she says.

He puts his spoon down into his bowl of Cheerios, looks at the floating Os, tells her that it's in his room. "You read it a lot," she says. He nods again. Then she asks him why he likes it. He's not sure how to answer, so he tells her it's educational. To begin with this seems the right thing to say, but after a bit he's not sure it was.

"What's your favorite story in it?" she asks him.

He explains that it isn't stories; it's all one story. Because the book is about a Greek Hero called Hercules and how he has to do a series of labors. Those are all different though. He thinks about what he's just said, then tells her that he guesses you could call them stories.

She is doing that thing now where she is looking at him but somehow it's like she's thinking about something else. Then she asks him another question. "What's your favorite?"

He thinks fast. He's not going to tell her the one he reads over and over again is not one of the labors. It's the ending. When Hercules puts on a shirt that is soaked in the blood of the Hydra, and it burns him, but he won't take it off, even though he knows he's going to die from it. And when he is dying, Hercules wants to get burned on a fire—because that's what happened back then, people didn't get buried—but there was nobody there who would light it. So the gods—the Greeks thought there were lots of gods—take pity on him and because he had been very brave, they burn him all away with lightning and make him into a god, too, and take him up to where they live, a place called Mount Olympus.

He's read that bit so many times he can see the page in front of his eyes sometimes when he's dreaming. He doesn't dream of Hercules; he's never done that. He dreams of the page the words are on.

"The lion," he decides. "There's a lion called the Nemean Lion." He's not sure if he's said that word right. "And it is . . . impervious to weapons, but Hercules strangles it with his bare hands and then he skins it by using one of the lion's claws to cut through the fur and then he wears the lion's skin as armor afterward. To protect him."

She looks at him. She's really looking at him. He said the right thing.

CHAPTER 10

"**D**o you like her, Adam?"

"Miller? She's good people. Checks out. Doesn't get in your way, doesn't want to control you. You, specifically, Rao, is what I'm saying."

"Yeah. About that . . ."

"In my experience, she's trustworthy."

"Fucking hell. Now I can't know that for sure."

"Why would I lie?" Adam pulls up outside Ed's house, leaves the engine idling. Grips the top of the steering wheel tightly, taps at it with his thumbs. Something's agitating him. Rao doubts it's the prospect of the diner.

"What is it?" he enquires evenly.

"We're in a different vehicle."

"It's exactly the same make, colour, and model. You think he took our number plate last time?" Rao snorts. "This is Brandon, we're not in the Red Zone. Toot the horn. Let him know we're here."

"What's funny?"

"Nothing. I just. I don't know how you manage to make a car horn sound like a hacked-off drill sergeant."

When Ed appears, grinning and waving, he's clad head to toe in camo. Adam lets out a short, sharp sigh. "Fucking hell," Rao breathes. "He's gone full Raoul Moat."

They've been driving for a while now and Ed's still bouncing about on the back seat like a nine-year-old on a school trip. *Calm the fuck down,* Rao thinks at him, hard. "Ed, we had no idea you found a body the other day," he says. "Rough. Are you doing ok?"

"Used to work lairage for an abattoir, years back. Seen a lot of dead stuff. Doesn't bother me. How did you find out about that?"

"Adam knows someone who knows a guy at the base. What happened?"

"Is this for the paper?"

"No," Adam assures him.

"Good, I don't think they'd like me, you know, talking about it."

"Completely off the record," Rao says.

"Off the record," Ed says, grinning. "No one's ever said that to me before. Yeah. I'll tell you. I'd come in that morning and I was heading over to the workshop, turned the corner by the munitions bunkers and got a faceful of smoke. Smelled like barbecue, which is grim, looking back on it. Then I saw this bonfire. Flames were about six foot high, and right by the doors of a weapons store isn't an ideal place for a fire so I grabbed an extinguisher off an outside wall and started putting it out and then I saw a boot and a leg sticking out."

"Bloody hell," Rao says.

"Yeah. I pulled him out." He screws up his face. "Then I reported it. They asked me a load of questions, took me into the base hospital, they said it was smoke inhalation, but what a load of fuss over nothing. I told them I'd done worse on Guy Fawkes. I didn't know the guy. Might of seen him about, but they all look the same in uniform." He sighs. "I hope his family are ok."

"They'll be looked after," Adam assures him.

Ed looks speculative. "So you going to ask me if I think it's murder?"

"Is it?"

"Yeah," Ed says. "Has to be. No one's gonna off themselves like that. But I don't know what whoever it was was thinking. Can't think of a worse place to dispose of a body, and that fire would've taken ages to build and get going. What I'd have done is stuck him in a car, taken it out to the forestry, torched it." He drops his voice. "But you know the best way to get rid of a body? Pigs."

"Pigs?"

"Yeah, they'll eat anything."

"He's right, Ray," Adam says, eyes on the road. "They're efficient. And in this area? Lots of farms. I'm sure no one would look too hard at a pig farmer."

"Teeth, bones. Crunch up everything."

"They can't digest teeth," Adam says. "You need to remove them first."

Rao makes an agonised noise. "Adam. Ed. Please."

They park up on the far side of the hill, strike out up a muddy track that runs alongside a plot of adolescent pines. Spiderwebs are everywhere, slung between branches and stalks, the sky turned blank and gold. Rao watches the hems of Adam's suit trousers darken as they drag through grass and herbage still wet from yesterday's rain. He looks absolutely fucking ridiculous in this environment, Rao thinks, amused, before glancing down at his own sodden hems and yellow Converse high-tops and deciding he might be in no position to judge.

He wiggles his toes. They're cold. Wet. He wonders if he'll get chilblains. He's not had chilblains for years. Then he stops dead. Feels ice blooming in his veins, pushing up his spine. The thought of chilblains— it's so ordinary. And nothing else, nothing else is. None of what's happened here, what's still happening, makes any sense at all. A theory has just occurred to him, and it's a pretty fucking convincing one. All of this could easily be the last, florid kick of his own dying brain in creative overdrive. If this is a dying fantasy, nothing'll be real and testable. He's probably still there in his hotel room in Kabul; his exit plan had worked after all. He wonders how much longer it has to go on for.

He's staring dully at his toes when Adam appears by his side.

"Rao? You ok? Need to wait one?"

"Got a bit dizzy all of a sudden," he says slowly. "It'll pass. Where's Ed?"

"Over there. Are we sure about this?"

"A little fucking faith, love," he says. Takes a deep breath. *A little fucking faith, Rao.*

Ed's eyes widen when they reach the top of the hill. His face lights up and crumples into an expression of tight and painful longing. Then he runs. Runs downhill towards the diner as if he were running into the arms of someone he'd thought lost. Twice he stumbles, nearly falls. He disappears through the doors. Sun flashes from them, sharp, as they swing back into place.

Adam halts, stares. "That was unexpected," he observes.

"*Shit.*"

They jog down to the diner and find Ed perched on a stool at the counter, forearms stretched flat across turquoise melamine, fingers spread wide.

"Alright, Ed?" Rao tries.

No reply.

"What is this?" Adam says, like there's a bad taste at the back of his mouth.

"No idea. It isn't one of those 'it's because he's British' things."

Ed's staring straight ahead, eyes unfocused, an expression of such palpable bliss on his face Rao feels uncomfortably like a voyeur. Whatever this is, he thinks, it's deeply private. He's speculating on the nature of Ed's connection to this place when there's a sharp *clunk*. Deep, metallic, coming from somewhere on the far side of the room. He jumps in alarm, sees Adam reflexively uncoil into a combat stance, then moves his eyes slowly along the slide of Adam's pistol to the source of the noise.

It's the jukebox. It's on. On and *moving*. Mutely, he watches the record selector travelling slowly behind glass, watches it halt with a second solid *clunk* and pull a record from the rack. A flicker of something mechanical, a damp *bump*, a hiss, then a high oboe melody and a floating harp arpeggio. The music's loud. Feels as if it's playing inside Rao's skull. He shakes his head, trying to dislodge it.

And Adam? Adam's still got a bead on the jukebox. Adam's got a bead on Frank Sinatra's voice.

When I was seventeen
It was a very good year

"Are you hearing this too?" he whispers.

Adam holsters his Beretta, face grim. "Yeah," he says. "I hate this song." He looks at Rao expectantly.

"What?"

"This is your department."

"Sinatra?"

"Catatonia."

Rao supposes it probably is.

"Ed?" he tries again.

Nothing. He should be doing something. Adam gives him a vaguely impatient look, then slips two fingers under one of the wrists on the counter. Frowns after a while. Leans in and drops a hand over both Ed's eyes, waits a few seconds, pulls it away. "No reaction to light," he concludes.

Rao winces when Adam brings the base of a ketchup bottle down sharply on Ed's left thumbnail. Numbly, Rao watches the nailbed turn from shocked white to deepest rose.

Still nothing.

"Ok, let's get him out," Rao says.

And it came undone
When I was twenty-one

They pull Ed from his seat and carry him supine, Rao gripping his ankles through thick woollen socks, Adam locking elbows under his armpits, walking him backwards through the swing doors into the open air. Fifteen feet from the diner, he wakes. Wriggles convulsively, shouts. Kicks Rao in the shins, breaks free, falls, scrambles to his feet, and runs inside. They find him back at the counter, hands covered in mud, as unresponsive as before.

It poured sweet and clear
It was a very good year

"Don't slip this time," Adam says.

"Fuck *off*. You take his legs."

Ed wakes again as they carry him over the deep, muddy troughs he made in the field the first time he broke free. This time his waking is more violent. He wails wordlessly, eyes wide and wet with panic, back arching, fingers clutching at the air, stretching his arms back towards the diner. Rao swears under his breath, a litany of soft curses in time with the music in his head that's louder than ever, lodging itself even deeper, a slowly driven nail. He's sweating now with the effort of keeping Ed's writhing, not inconsiderable weight off the ground and the contagious terror of the noises Ed's making. Rao's back aches now, his knees too. It's a struggle to keep moving. He stumbles, catches himself, keeps going.

Forty yards from the diner.

Fifty.

Sixty.

Silence.

Abruptly, Ed's quiet. He's stopped resisting their hold, arms fallen slack, muddy fingers curled. *Thank fuck*, Rao thinks, relieved. But when he glances down, Ed's face is ashen, eyes rolled sickeningly up and back, and Adam's already lowering his feet to the ground. They lay him down on mud and sugar beet. Rao loosens his collar, Adam his belt. They listen to Ed's gasping breaths, hear them turn to desperate hauls. Hear them rattle and stutter, then stop.

Rao can hear himself calling Ed's name. Fruitlessly, pointlessly, stupidly. Rao is watching Adam administer CPR, thinking dully, *But that's not what Adam's for.* And all the time Sinatra, growing fainter now and turning far too slow, as if the voice is slipping, pulling him under, and Rao knows the truth of what this is, knows exactly when it happens, sooner even than Adam does.

After a while Adam sits back on his heels. His expression is glacially cold. He checks his watch. Pulls out his phone, calls it in. The music is distant, now, like it's back in the diner, and Rao sits on the ground hugging his knees. Breathing is an effort. The air stinks of sewage and crushed beet leaves. He doesn't want to look at the diner. He doesn't want to look at Ed. He doesn't want to look at Adam, and he's sure as shit not going to look at himself. He raises his eyes to the heavens. A flock of birds is passing overhead, making noises far too much like Ed's

last, ragged breaths. He watches their slow and shifting constellations and screws his eyes tight, knowing the darkness won't help, won't make any of this go away.

Halfway along the corridor to Miller's office, Adam slows and stops. "You're not needed in the debrief."

"Miller's orders?"

"Mine. I told her you wouldn't be there."

"Thank you, Adam. I'd entirely forgotten the delights of you deciding what's best for me," Rao replies, because sarcasm is easier than gratitude. But as Adam nods and turns to leave, he's gripped with panic. "Wait, what am I supposed to do while you explain to Miller this is all my fault?"

"I'm not going to do that." Adam tips his head to a couple of soft chairs and a low table. "Sit."

"Oh, wonderful. Back issues of the *Stars and Stripes*. Go on. I'll be here."

He sits. Picks up a newspaper, opens it, stares moodily at a photograph of smiling assholes standing by a gunmetal-grey drone. A new DOD contract with Lunastus-Dainsleif, the Pentagon's corporate fuck-buddies in Sunnyvale, California. Money to be made, people to kill. Same old same old.

Bile rises. He tosses the paper back onto the pile. Snaps his fingers compulsively to fill the silence. Stares at the skirting boards and door-frames, watches feet walk past, counts them, counts the chips in the paint by the side of the chair, the snagged threads in the orange fabric of the chair he's sitting on and the one next to him too. Ed's death is right there waiting for him if he puts a foot wrong in his mind. It's on a perpetual reel. Ed's face in the diner, the smears of mud on his hands after their first attempt to get him out. The sounds he made as they carried him. The colour of the inside of his mouth as he gasped for air. That stupid, stupid fucking camouflage jacket. Rao knows his defences are crumbling fast. He thinks of a number. Four. He says *four* in his mind. Repeats it. Imagines the word, the shape of the letters. It's like holding up a crucifix to a vampire. It keeps it at bay, but only barely.

Sweat's prickling in his armpits, in the small of his back. He wants to throw up but his head doesn't hurt, and that's freaking him out too because he doesn't know why. His head has no business being clear.

Ed's death wasn't his fault, Rao knows. But it was, all the same.

It's like that time with *the cold*. He'd been small when that happened. They'd been out in the West End on a frozen winter afternoon. There were lights, Christmas lights, he thinks now that's probably what he'd been taken to see. His mother was pointing them out, and yes, they were pretty, but his hands hurt from the cold and his feet hurt worse, he'd wanted to cry, and he'd looked at all the people passing by in big coats, all kinds of people, some of them looking up at the lights, most of them not, and a thought had lit on him out of nowhere. *One day I'm going to die.* And then he'd whispered it, because he needed to test if it was true. And the truth of it, spoken, had grabbed him like a cat grabs a sparrow in its jaws, and then everything inside his head ballooned outwards and upwards until it seemed to fill all of London, and everything inside the rest of him crushed itself down and constricted to a point so fine and cold it trembled on the edge of not existing at all. It's there, still. He can still feel it, or whatever it did to the places around it, the burn of the hole it made.

Rao knows the story isn't a special one. There's a moment in everyone's childhood when the great and terrible secret makes itself known. But Rao's particular relationship with truth, he thinks, might have made it different for him, because after all that he'd fainted, right there on the pavement, and he'd woken in the London house with the family doctor and his parents by his bedside and the light from his Transformers lamp making his hands gripping the covers look like they were made of metal, and he'd been looking at his hands when they'd asked him about what happened, and he'd thought again about how after he dies and his soul's reborn in another body he won't remember himself. He won't be *him*. And he'd looked at his mother then and known he couldn't lie. He said, because it was simple, *I just got cold inside.* And that was true enough.

Adam's face is blanker than ever when he reappears in the corridor. As he draws nearer, Rao sees it's more than the aftermath of a difficult debrief. Adam's exhausted. The pallor, the darkness below his eyes, his blink rate, the faint tremor in his hands: seeing them, Rao feels an unexpected burst of compassion. A weird compulsion to tell Adam to fuck off home and let someone else deal with this shit. Whatever this shit is, wherever home is for Adam. DC, probably. Or some condo outside Vegas, maybe. Home gym in the garage. Knives in every drawer.

"She's taking the guard off your door."

"Why?"

"She's putting me in with you."

Of course she is. Adam'll be there to stop him going out and getting fucked up. No. Not that. Adam's on fucking *suicide watch*. Rao lets the complicated, heavy mess of gratitude and outrage wash over him and ducks out the other side.

"Roommate?"

"Suitemate."

"Sleepover. Lovely. Will you want me to do your hair?"

"Sure," Adam says. "I want French braids."

"Yeah, and I want a handful of oxy and a blow job, Adam. Life is cruel."

CHAPTER 11

He's so tired. The only sounds he can hear are his own breaths, the beating of his heart, the sharp echo of his wrist snapping in his ears. Time doesn't always work the same, he thinks dully. When he fell from the tree, it felt like forever before he'd hit the ground. It feels like seconds since he sat on the porch steps but also it feels like days. It took him twelve minutes to get a grip, stop crying, and start walking home after it happened. He checked the time on his watch. The watch in his jeans pocket. The watch with a cracked face. He had to take it off his wrist. That took forever too.

He knows his arm is broken. He knows it's all his fault.

The crack when he hit the concrete was scary, and the pain was worse, but the only thing on his mind walking home was what his parents would say. How he should have been more careful. How he shouldn't be crying. How he's torn his shirt. Cracked his watch. How this is just what they need. How he's ruined their nice evening. He was feeling cold all over by the time he made it to the porch. He was sitting before he knew what else was happening.

Time isn't always the same, he thinks. He doesn't know how long he's been sitting here, waiting for the shakes to go away, waiting to warm up, waiting to get brave enough to knock on the door and tell his parents what happened. When he thinks about his aunt, about how she never seemed to get mad at him, it feels like someone else's thought. He blinks it away, but even that feels like he's pulling the strings of himself to make it happen. He's not there with her, and it wouldn't help even if he were.

He doesn't mean to sleep. He doesn't know if he does. All he knows is that when he comes back down to himself it's because his mother is saying his name and his dad is pressing a bag of frozen peas into his hands, right where he has his wrist cradled against his body. He starts crying, starts apologizing. His dad tells him to shut up, to keep it to himself, so he stops saying the words. But he can't stop the tears. The pain is bad, but the crying is worse. He hates it.

He hates the tears more than anything.

CHAPTER 12

"Ah, the usual five-star accommodation," Rao grumbles. "So, which room of this delightful suite do you like best, Adam? The one with the bald eagle print or the one with the old aeroplane?"

"It's a P-51 Mustang."

"Of course it is. I'll rephrase. Which room do you want, Adam?"

"I think this room is yours," Adam says, staring down at a bed. "These are."

Rao pads over. Two plastic bags from the base PX have been dumped on the covers, SUNIL ROY printed across each in black Magic Marker. He sighs, tips their contents out, rifles through the clothes. "What the fuck is this?" he demands, holding one up to Adam.

"It's a Union Jack T-shirt, Rao."

"Ugh."

He showers, pulls on a checked flannel shirt and a navy sweater, a pair of beige chinos. Stares dubiously at his reflection in the narrow mirror bolted to the wall. Swivels to take in all angles.

"I look like I'm having a midlife crisis. Just not the one I'm actually having," he mutters. Then he perches on the side of the bed, looking down at the wine-coloured, horribly patterned carpet. There are stains on it, tidelines running out from the wall. He hopes they're water. Mostly they are.

Adam is staring into space from an armchair. They sit in silence for a while.

"Alcohol's off-limits?" Adam asks.

"It is, yes."

"Want me to turn the TV on?"

Rao shakes his head. "No, I don't. Adam, have you ever been to India?"

"Yeah."

"Jaipur?"

"No."

"It's a good place, you should visit. So. Listen. There's this thing happens there. In the evenings, the sky's full of kites. Everyone goes up onto the roof to fly them. It's competitive. You show off your moves and you're trying to cut other kites down with yours. And to help them do that, a lot of the kite lines are coated in glass dust."

Rao thinks of the dancing mosaic the kites make of the sky as it tips to dusk, notices himself breathing. It's always strange when you remember that's what you're doing, what you're doing *all the time*. "I was flying one once, I was eleven, they're not big, these kites, this one had the glass *manjha*. And a bird flew into it. Cheel, a kite, that is, same word but a bird of prey. They're everywhere in the city, really slow wingbeats, look like little eagles. Graceful. This one was gliding fast on its way somewhere and it hit my line. It sheared through one of its wings. It crumpled up midair, fell out of the sky." The words are just spilling out. Rao doesn't hate them yet. "I ran down to look for it."

"Did you find it?"

"Yeah. It was huddled up against a wall, covered in blood. I picked it up and it sank its talons into me. Dug them right in. Tore at me. Don't blame it for doing that. I mean, it's what I would have done. I've still got the scar." Rao turns his arm, points at the faint, pale line across the back of his right wrist.

"You rescued it?"

Rao shakes his head. "It died."

Adam nods thoughtfully. "So, in this story you're the bird."

"No, Adam. Of course I'm not the fucking bird. I was the kid with the kite."

Ed's death—it wasn't his fault the same way everything in Afghanistan wasn't his fault. He can taste Kabul in his mouth right now, vinegar and rust and radiator water. He feels suddenly vicious. "How much do you know?" he demands.

"About what?"

"Kabul."

"Some."

"You'll have found the intel like a ferret scenting blood. *Some* isn't enough."

"Ok. They had you ground-truthing interrogations. British citizens only, to begin with. Then you got loaned out. CIA pushed you too far and it all went to shit."

"It did. Have you seen these places?"

Adam shakes his head. "I'm glad," Rao says. He's surprised to hear himself say it, but Adam doesn't seem surprised to hear it. He looks unhappy. Wipes his mouth with the back of one hand. Gets up, walks to the kitchenette, returns with a pack of Marlboros and a mug. Sets the mug on the bedside table for an ashtray, passes the pack to Rao, who extracts a cigarette and lights it. Doesn't quite get round to smoking it. "I'm not going to talk about what they were doing in there," he says slowly. "It was obscene. Still is. It's happening right now. There's a cabal of sadists in possession of the conviction that they're saving the world running that shithole and its redacted fucking city."

A long drag on the cigarette, a longer exhale, both of them watching smoke threading its way through the close air of the room.

"Should we be smoking in here?" Rao asks.

"Probably not," Adam says. "But if you trigger the alarms, I'll take the rap."

"Colonel Rubenstein. Always looking out for me," Rao says a little sourly. "You know what happens to you if you're tortured, day in, day out for months? You start to give the people hurting you gifts. You tell them things you think they want to hear. A plan, a map, a bomb, some HVT. There'd be a cousin in Islamabad who knew someone who knows where bin Laden is, some fissile material coming in from Iran, something *sexy*. The interrogators'd look at me to truth it, and I'd shake my head. They hated me for that. And the people coming up with the stories? They hated me even more."

"You were everyone's problem."

"I was."

Another long silence. In it, Rao realises he's going to tell it all. "They put me in a hotel in Kabul for the duration. One night, there was a guy in the bar. There were a lot of guys, Adam. This one was American. Ex-marine. I was—at this point it didn't really matter who. I remember him being taller than me."

"And that's relevant?"

"No, but not all of us are short arses, love. Taller doesn't happen often. Didn't, back when it happened." Rao's viciousness has receded; he feels a little violent flutter of skittishness. It comes out as a breathy giggle. "Can you even handle this? Listening to my hot man-on-man action stories?"

"I don't understand the question."

"Most straights can't handle it."

Adam frowns. "Oh. No, I'm—it's fine."

"So. This marine. He had a very beautiful smile. I can't remember much about us getting off," Rao lies, "but afterwards he pulled out a bag and some foil and we smoked. I'd never done brown before. He was surprised about that. Really surprised. Anyway. That happened, and I lay back on the bed feeling good for the first time in forever."

Adam's watching him carefully, now. Cautiously. He'll be memorising all this for his next debriefing and Rao doesn't care. "He was there again the next night. And two nights later, when he said he was shipping out. But by then I'd managed to sort myself out, easy, because one thing Afghanistan is very good at, Adam, is heroin. Famous for it, you know?"

"Does it—did it—work like your fights do?"

Rao smiles. "Ah, that's a clever question, love. No, it doesn't. Get hurt enough and the world disappears. No truth, no untruth. You can't tell what colour the room is when the light's off, right? Opiates are different. They don't stop me reading the world. They just put the world *over there*. Which turned into a couple of months of me sitting in the corner of the room listening to pain like I was looking into a glass case at a museum. Didn't fucking care."

"But something happened."

"Adam, questions like that are going to make me think you keep a therapist in a cupboard back home."

Adam's laugh at that is sudden, pained, apparently genuine. "No. I don't do those."

"This does not surprise me. Yes. Well. Something happened."

Rao pulls the cigarette from his mouth, taps it on the side of the mug, holds it horizontally in front of him. Blows carefully on the coal. It glows fiercely. He watches little petals of spent ash grow around the incandescent core. Lets his breath die; smoke curls into his eyes. He widens them and blinks it in for as long as he can bear, screws them tight and grimaces. Wipes water from his cheeks, takes another drag.

"They broke people in there, Adam. Took me too long to work out torture's got fuck all to do with innocence or guilt. I watched them carry a body out once. *Oh, that one got wet somehow overnight, was he naked in that cell, oh well, cold night, shit happens. Must have been the guards, they're locals, we don't get involved. Whatever, one less to worry about.* They brought this new guy in, and he was so fresh, Adam. They picked him up in Birmingham. Not Birmingham, Alabama. England. He hadn't a clue. Went to the wrong mosque. He was an apprentice heating engineer. I told them, *This guy knows fuck all.* Less than. I kept telling them. They decided I was lying. They decided I'd got unreliable. They didn't take me out of the room, though. Everything this guy said was true, and I told them, and they didn't stop. They were rough with him with me right there. Slapped him first, then threw him against the wall a dozen times, and I think most of that was punishing me. And they put him back in his chair and he looked at me and he hadn't looked at me before, and he said, *Brother, I'm not getting out of here alive.*"

"Which was true," Adam says slowly.

"Turned out to be, yeah. And that was the *something*. I wanted out. Made myself an exit strategy. Thought it was a good one, at the time. Didn't work. As you can see. And here we are again, happy as can be. With you on suicide watch."

"That's what they asked me to do."

"I'm not going to."

"I know that, Rao."

"And just how the fuck do you *know* that?"

"Don't be an asshole to me for being in your corner. I *know* because I figure it's going to take a hell of a lot more than today."

Rao thinks about that for a while. "Not much more."

"Get some sleep."

He tries. At three in the morning he's frowning at the ceiling wondering if Adam's following his orders to the letter. Ten minutes of idle speculation evolves into an insistent need to know, so he throws back his blankets, swings his legs to the floor, and sneaks across the room to the connecting door. There's enough light through the curtains to confirm that Adam is indeed asleep, which is always a wonderment, because sleeping Adam looks like an eleven-year-old *this* close to asking for hot milk. Not quite: the analogy doesn't fit the long scar along his right collarbone that according to Adam may or may not have been something he'd picked up in Iran. He's on his stomach, face pressed to the sheets, one hand curled over the edge of the bed, pillows stacked neatly on the floor beside the frame. Seeing him, Rao's hit by a wave of exhaustion so total he reaches for the wall to steady himself. Some part of him, he supposes, understands that if Adam's sleeping, he's safe. He staggers back, falls atop his covers, is almost instantly out. When he opens his eyes again Adam's standing over him, looking blank and impatient at once.

"Get up. I'm taking you to breakfast," he says.

"Ugh, no. I can't cope with the whole DFAC thing right now."

"Good, because we're going to IHOP. How's your mental health?"

Rao rolls his eyes. "Fucking outstanding, Adam."

They perch on padded vinyl by an expanse of rain-streaked glass. Looking up from the laminated menu, Rao sees a badge on a red shirt that reads MADDY. She's tiny, with blonde hair scraped from her forehead and an expression of such obvious boredom Rao knows she's English before she opens her mouth.

"Short stack buttermilk," Adam says. "Rao?"

"Give me a sec—"

Adam gives him five. "He'll have the Split Decision Breakfast."

"It's *not* called that," Rao protests.

Maddy looks at him pityingly. "Yes, it is."

When Adam pours an obscene amount of syrup over his pancakes, Rao stares, fascinated. "Are you a bee, Adam?"

"What? Oh. No. This stuff doesn't get graded. It's not maple syrup. Just corn syrup with colour and flavouring. It's pretty bad, but some people prefer it. Reminds them of their childhoods, I guess."

"Like Angel Delight," Rao suggests.

"Sure."

"You have no idea what I'm talking about."

"No."

"Good. I shouldn't have mentioned it. State secret." Rao's rambling on autopilot watching Adam dissect his stack. The cuts he makes are neat and precise, but the quantities of syrup involved make the process of eating the result teeter on the edge of uncontrollability.

"You should eat."

Rao looks down at the food in front of him, makes a face. "I'm not hungry."

"Doesn't matter. We have a ten a.m. with Miller."

"That information is not improving my appetite."

"Eat your breakfast, Rao."

Miller doesn't ask Rao how he's feeling, which raises her greatly in his estimation. So do her earrings du jour: pink gold brilliant-cut Cartier Diamants Légers.

"Lot to get through, but I'll keep this short," she says, pulling a sheet from a file. "Straat's autopsy gives cause of death as thermal injuries from the fire. Apart from a stomach ulcer, he was in pretty good shape. There was no antemortem bruising. Which makes me think, in light of preliminary findings from Mr Gibbons—"

"He ran into the fire," Rao says and discovers it's true.

"You think? Mr Gibbons died from what's called takotsubo cardiomyopathy. I called the pathologist just now to get a clearer summary. It seems he experienced a sudden, massive surge of stress hormones that first stunned the heart then ruptured the left ventricle wall. She told me it's very rare and happens mostly in postmenopausal women. She also told me it's called broken heart syndrome."

"Ah," Rao says.

"You have a theory?" she asks.

"No, just thinking what you'll be thinking. These objects have some kind of intense attraction for some people. For Ed, it was the diner. The bonfire for Straat. Don't know what they have in common."

"They were both fifty-two-year-old white men. But that doesn't seem much of an explanation. There are a lot of those around."

"Mind-altering drugs?" Adam offers. Rao snorts. Miller shakes her head. "Toxicology came back clean. Or at least nothing they could detect."

She sits back, contemplates Adam and Rao for a while, then looks down at the watch on her wrist. Licks a thumb, rubs at its crystal face. "Everyone," she says softly, "needs this to be suicide. Unfortunately there's no evidence that Straat wanted to kill himself. So it's likely we're heading for an open verdict, which is suboptimal. There are a few financial irregularities, an ex-wife, child support. Things could pan out. Depends on the coroner. But you should both hear this. Straat's last leave is very much of interest. He spent the first twelve days of it on base. Golf. Two trips to London. Then he hopped on a transport from Mildenhall to Nellis and dropped off the map."

Adam sits up, listens intently. *No*, Rao thinks. He was doing that before. He's just somehow giving the impression he's doing it *more*.

"Phone?" Adam asks.

"Bricked. I assume a burner was in play. When he reappeared, he went around telling everyone who'd listen that he'd spent a week with friends on a camping and fishing trip in the Jarbidge Wilderness area, and he talked a lot about trout when he got back here. A lot. In a very spiritual way."

"Eventually, all things merge into one," Rao observes portentously. "And a river runs through it."

"That's not a bad Redford," she says.

"Thank you."

Adam frowns. "There wasn't a fishing trip."

She shakes her head, looks disappointed. "It was terrible cover. Fishing trips generally are. But we have a possible lead. It concerns the contents of his laptop."

Rao sits up. "You want us to watch his porn? I'll do it."

"You don't want to watch his porn, Rao. He was a commanding officer," Adam says quickly.

"Oh. Missionary only, huh?"

"Aggressively heterosexual," Miller confirms in passing. "But that's not what I meant, Rao. Straat had been in contact with a lecturer at the University of Cambridge. A Dr Katherine Caldwell. I've asked forensic IT for copies of their correspondence. Should have been here by now, but you can pick them up from"—she checks her notes—"room 26, building 832. There's not much there. I'm told it's mostly concerned with scheduling a series of telephone calls. So, I've talked to Caldwell, told her we're investigating Straat's death, exploring all avenues, and set up a meeting this afternoon. Three p.m. Go speak to her."

CHAPTER 13

He knew he would be taken to the playground after the cast came off his wrist. *It'll be good for him*, he'd heard his dad tell his mom. *Soldiers need to retrain after injury.* His mom replied that he wasn't a soldier, but it wasn't an argument. She wasn't fighting. They never fought.

Two days after his cast came off, his dad took him to a quiet playground and put him on the monkey bars. He hadn't been good at this before the break, and now he was even worse.

"What's taking you so long?" his dad asked, standing on the far side of the bars.

He hung there, pain shooting up his arm. He knew better than to show it. "It hurts."

His dad looked at him.

"It hurts, sir," he corrected.

His dad shook his head and took out a soft packet from his shirt pocket. Tapped out a cigarette. Lit it with a match as he spoke. "Pain's one of those things," he said, like everyone knew what *one of those things* was. "It's all in your mind. If it's in your mind, then you can think past it."

The whole memory is blue, like he can only see it through a thin film of grease. Like he's looking at it from far away or underwater. It feels hazy even though he can hear every single one of his father's words to him clear as a bell in his head. He'll always hear them.

He only managed to get to the third bar before it felt like progress was an impossibility. He hung there in silence, watching his dad finish his cigarette. Willing him to look over. To notice. He didn't want to say anything. He didn't want to speak first, but he had to. His dad wasn't just not noticing him. He was looking away. He didn't want to see.

"I need help," he said quietly. The pain was getting too much, and he was going to drop soon. Not that it was all that high from the monkey bars to the dust and scorched grass underneath him, but the thought of falling again so soon made his stomach feel cold.

His dad didn't look at him. He tried again.

"I need help, please." No response. He tried again, with urgency. "Sir."

His dad finally looked up. Shook his head so minutely that— Did he imagine it? It's hard to remember. He remembers the look on his father's face, even through the haze. His expression stays with him like the words.

His dad wasn't just disappointed. It was worse than that. He looked sad about being asked for help. His dad, in that moment, looked just about as helpless in disappointment as he felt on the bars.

"Help yourself," his dad said. Flicked the cigarette away. "I'll wait in the car."

It was after his dad had left him alone that his arms finally gave out. He dropped, but it wasn't as bad as when he had fallen from the tree. He didn't hurt himself. His wrist hurt again, inside, but he hadn't hurt himself.

CHAPTER 14

The rain has stopped and the sky has no colour at all. Rao sniffs the air as they walk. He can't smell kerosene in it anymore. It feels like a personal failing.

"We should do a truth run," Adam says.

"*We?*"

"You. Why haven't you?"

Rao shrugs.

"Answer the question, Rao."

"Are you pissed off with me?" Rao asks.

"I'm not pissed." Adam still sounds tired, though Rao knows he slept. "Miller's on my back. Someone's on her back, and someone else is on theirs."

"Ah, so this would be a personal favour, would it?" Rao doesn't wait for an answer. "I need a fag. You can go on if you want. I'll find the place." He halts by the corner of the accommodation block and lights up. Adam stands at ease and watches a golf buggy labouring across the green of the base course a few hundred yards away. An F-15 screams low overhead on its final approach. Rao glares at it, leans back against the wall, waits for the noise to subside.

"Look, you know they think I need a real live person to work from," he sighs. Adam isn't looking at him. His head is tilted up, watching a second Eagle coming in. "I can't just go in and give Miller the answers."

"But you can find them."

Rao nods. "Some, maybe." He drags on the cigarette he doesn't want. "Brute force it. But we'd have to keep whatever I find to ourselves, and the way I am right now, I don't know if I'll be able to do that. So I've been inclined just to follow the mood, you know? Work to rule."

Eyes still fixed on the now-empty sky, Adam's expression turns sour. "But if you'd done it before we took Ed to the—"

"Don't you *fucking dare*," Rao splutters. "You want the reason why I've not done a run? Here it is, Adam. The truth. I'm not inclined to do one because I'm not looking forward to what I'll find out. This shit isn't right. It really isn't right, and it's doing my head in."

Anger is a weakness, he remembers too late. A vulnerability. Which is why, he realises with a flush of fury, Adam must have said what he did, and *it fucking worked*. "It feels like I'm standing outside an extremely haunted house," he spits out. "And pardon me if I'm not particularly thrilled about the prospect of walking up the path and knocking on the door."

"You won't be walking in alone," Adam says.

"It's a *metaphor*, not an actual building," Rao hisses. "Not that you know much about houses, homes, or the kinds of people who might live in them, Lieutenant Colonel 'vat-grown in a government facility' Rubenstein."

"It was air force housing in Vegas."

Rao's eyes widen. "What?"

"Housing for personnel on base for a term or two. Temporary accommodation. We always stayed. My dad wasn't constantly there, obviously."

"Obviously?"

"He hated anything that wasn't work," he says tonelessly.

It sounds more like a tape recording than human speech, but—this is personal information. From Adam. Rao's astonished. He wants to know more, but he's not going to ask. No fucking way. He hates, absolutely *hates* how much he wants to. "Military workaholic, was he?" he snickers instead. "Now I see where you get it from. Like father, like son."

"Rao, could you . . ." Adam rubs both eyes, one after the other, with the heel of one hand. "Could you *not*, right now?"

Rao tosses his cigarette to the ground, grinds it beneath his heel until it's flat and frayed on the tarmac. *Fear is the mind-killer*, he thinks. He's always hated that quote. He's always hated that fucking book.

"Whatever," he mutters after a while. "I'll do you a run. When we get back from this thing."

Persuading a Cambridge college porter to open the gates to a Cambridge college car park is at least 80 percent harder than getting into GCHQ without a pass, Rao decides: it takes two minutes of crackly negotiation over the intercom and a call to Dr Caldwell before the porter admits defeat and lets them through. They follow the narrow road past a rugby pitch, park up under a bruised-looking chestnut tree. "All you need to know about Cambridge," Rao mutters, pulling his jacket tighter around himself as they walk to the Porters' Lodge, "is that it's awful. My world, Adam, for my sins, so leave this to me."

Caldwell's rooms are at the far side of a three-sided court of yellowed wisteria and honeyed stone. The outer door is open. Rao knocks, and the inner door swings wide.

"Dr Caldwell?"

"Kitty, please. Come in."

Rao stares. He'd expected a patrician, middle-aged Englishwoman in tweed, someone with whom he could forge an instant and mutual dislike. But Kitty is not that person. She's Black, has a New York accent, a soft plaid shirt, and a burnt-orange jacket, and is so instantly likable Rao's surprised to find himself vaguely cross they're not already friends. Her rooms are warm and spacious, with arched Gothic windows, oak bookcases, and—Rao's eyes widen—a flood of *things* spilling over and across shelves and tables and sills. Stacks of board games, an ant farm kit, a lava lamp, figurines and statuettes from *Star Wars, Spy vs. Spy, Mars Attacks!*, the Sinclair dinosaur, a full-size plastic Canada goose. There's a jackalope mounted on a trophy shield hanging by a Caesars Palace mirror, a pile of *National Geographic* magazines on the floor by Rao's feet, and in the far corner is a mannequin dressed as fucking late-stage Elvis.

"I was sorry to hear about what happened to Adrian," Kitty says. "I was told he was in the air force?"

"He was a master sergeant," Adam says.

"Huh. Ranked," Kitty replies, looking Adam up and down. "He always called himself Mr Straat."

"You never met?"

"Not in person. I don't think I'm going to be much help to you," she says. "And I don't have long. Thirty minutes before my next supervision. But until then, I'm all yours. Please, sit. Coffee? Tea?"

"No thank you, ma'am." Adam shakes his head. Kitty's mouth twitches momentarily before she resumes her expression of respectful solemnity.

"So." She gestures again at the brocade-covered armchair. Rao sits. "What can I tell you about him? He contacted me just over a month ago. An email, a couple of follow-ups, then a series of phone calls. I don't normally work with independent researchers, but he was an exception."

"Why?"

She looks shamefaced. "He *paid*. I'd have farmed him off to a graduate student, but he paid *well*, and I want a new kitchen."

Oh Kitty, Rao thinks. *That's not why you wanted the money.*

"What did you talk about?" Adam asks, while Rao silently determines that Kitty's screwed herself with credit card debt.

"He'd read one of my books and wanted to discuss the subject."

"Which was?"

"Nostalgia."

"Ah," Rao says. "Could you elaborate?"

Kitty shrugs, turning one hand palm up, letting her eyes close for the briefest of moments. "You could read the book."

"An executive summary would be very helpful, Dr Caldwell," Adam says.

"I was joking. I can lend you a copy, though." She looks up at the clock on the wall, her face shifting into an expression so familiar to Rao that he prickles with angry guilt at having somehow failed to write another essay. *Oh god*, he thinks, suppressing a horrified laugh. She's going to give us a tutorial.

"Do you know the history of the concept?"

"Of nostalgia? No, ma'am," Adam says.

"It was a military disease. Back in the eighteenth century, Swiss mercenaries in France and Italy started falling ill. They lost all interest in life, pined for the mountains, had hallucinations, saw ghosts."

"Ghosts," Adam repeats, so quietly it's hardly a word at all.

"A medical student called Johannes Hofer coined a term for it: 'nostalgia.' It was a kind of homesickness. From the Greek *nostos*, meaning a return to home, and *algos*, meaning—"

"Pain," Rao says.

"Yes," she says. "Or longing. Classicist?"

"Art history."

"Where?"

"St John's."

She nods, looks intrigued. "You know Tom McAlister?"

Kitty, Rao thinks. *You are sharp as a fucking knife.* "Can't recall," he says, with a moue.

She grins at him, continues. "They hit on a couple of cures. Pain and terror, that worked. Or opium." Rao glances at Adam. His face is as impassive as ever but he'll be thinking it, the fucker.

"Much later it evolved into a more Romantic concept, got tied up with nationalism." She pauses. "The problem with imagining a home you want to return to is, of course, that you tend to exclude people from it you don't want there with you." She lets that thought breathe in the open air before continuing. "Anyway. One model of nostalgia sees it as a psychological response to trauma and discontinuity. A defence mechanism. Big social changes can conjure it. Wars, revolutions, 9/11. People feel dislocated, so they conjure an imaginary past they long to return to. This fantasy place of safety. So nostalgia is emotional and psychological, but it's also political. Highly manipulable, either politically or in the marketplace. And that's what my book's about. Specifically, on how material history and nostalgia and politics coincide." She waves her hands around the room. "All this stuff, you know?"

Rao nods, frowning. "So if nostalgia is a defence mechanism, something like a Mr. Potato Head can feel to someone like a safe refuge from harm?"

"It's complicated, and we could talk about transitional objects, but yes. There's some pretty convincing work by Starobinski and Roth on how nostalgia got privatized and internalized in the twentieth century, on how the longing for home got shrunk into the longing for one's own childhood. So childhood toys or things associated with your childhood memories tend to feature pretty high up on the list, yeah."

"Kitty, can I show you something?" Rao says, pulling a file from his bag and holding it out. "We'll get back to Straat, but I'd really value your thoughts on this collection of things."

She takes it, flicks through the photographs of the objects picked up at the base. Rao sees her linger on a toy rifle, a red velvet comforter, a plush rabbit, a rocking chair.

"Yeah," she says. "Beautifully curated. Makes me think of the Valley of Lost Things. There's a chapter called that in my book. It's a literary device, a place characters visit in stories and find all the things people have lost. These, though"—her voice turns speculative—"seem to me not so much lost things as things *made* of loss. Where are these from?"

Adam cuts in before Rao can answer. "Dr Caldwell," he says, speaking as delicately as if he were walking through a minefield, "can you tell us how an object can be made of loss?"

"I can try. Have you ever read Philip K. Dick?"

Adam nods. Rao's not proud of his surprise.

"*The Man in the High Castle*?"

Adam manages to smile without smiling. "Of course."

"Remember the scene where the memorabilia dealer is talking about historicity?"

"I remember it," Adam says. "Roosevelt's lighter."

She looks delighted. Then blinks rapidly. "Sorry," she says to Rao—and isn't. "It's a wonderful scene. The novel is set in an alternate universe where the Nazis won the war. A memorabilia dealer shows someone two lighters. One was in Roosevelt's pocket when he was assassinated, so it's worth a fortune. The other one wasn't, so it's not worth anything. The dealer points out that you can't tell them apart. There's no mystical aura; you can't detect which is which. It's impossible. *The* line comes later in this scene, when the dealer talks about a gun that's been in a famous battle. He says it's just the same as if it hadn't, unless you know it has been through the battle." She taps her head. "It's in the mind, not the gun."

"Not entirely," Rao says.

Adam's expression shifts to solid, Rao-directed remonstration.

"Well, that's a position," Caldwell says.

"It is," Rao agrees, scratching his beard. "Ignore it. I get carried away, sometimes. Devil's advocate, terrible habit. And I hate to interrupt," he lies, "but time's marching on. I'll be happy to give Adam the rest of his Semiotics 101 later. Can we get back to Straat? What did he want to know, specifically?"

"To begin with, he kept asking me about the neurological basis of the nostalgic experience," Kitty answers. "I told him I was the wrong person for that. We talked some more, and then he wanted to know about how loss and nostalgia relate to homesickness. There was a lot of general discussion, we had two hour-long calls, but it seemed to narrow down, for him, to the question of whether people who are geographically far from home experience nostalgia in a different way."

"Do they?"

She shrugs gracefully once more, an upturned palm. "Depends. First-generation immigrants often refuse nostalgia completely. Second-generation sometimes get lost in it. Imagined homes, imagined places can have a power far greater than real ones."

"Like an imaginary American diner?"

She looks at Rao closely. "That's a very specific example."

"It is."

Adam speaks up. "Do you know why he was asking you these questions?"

"No. He just said he was interested in the subject."

"Did anything he said suggest a motive to you?"

"Nothing I can remember. I'll let you know if I do. Is there a way to contact you if I think of anything else?"

Adam gives her his phone number. She gets up, walks to a bookcase, pulls out a book. "Here. Keep it as long as you need. This conversation hasn't been what I expected, and I've got a feeling I'll be seeing you again."

———

Adam's deep in thought as they walk back to the vehicle. "What was all that about Tom McAlister?" he asks, eyes on the worn flagstones beneath his feet.

"Yeah, I couldn't believe that. She's fucking on the ball, Kitty is."

"Who is he?"

"Oh. History professor. Talent spotter. Not me, obviously, he wouldn't have touched me with a barge pole. They sent someone else for that when I was at Sotheby's. Apparently one of my cousins-in-law got expansive after three bottles of Lynch-Bages at one of those dreadful dinner parties in Chipping Norton and told everyone at the table I had this miraculous ability to detect fakes and frauds. Word got out, and after a while Morten Edwards appeared. Blond with a deep Welsh accent and a spectacular suit. Came in asking me to authenticate a Sebastiano. You know him, for fuck's sake. He was in that meeting, the first one."

"I didn't know he was Welsh."

CHAPTER 15

Before

You can get a lot about a person from how they present themselves. Sunil Rao was the type of mess he'd seen a bunch of times before in cryptanalysts. Guys like that get cut a lot of slack because of what they can do. They push back. Make a point of it. The file he'd been given suggested Sunil Rao wouldn't be easy to handle. The meeting confirmed it. Rao talked incessantly, told unrelated anecdotes and jokes. The jokes were pretty funny, considering, but wildly inappropriate in context. Adam quickly put most of this down to him having taken some kind of stimulant. His pupils were dilated and he found it hard to sit still, kept brushing the arm of his chair with his palms, drumming the desk with his fingers. Half an hour in he took out some gum and chewed it for so long and so energetically Adam's own jaw started to feel uncomfortable.

After the meeting, Rao came up and told him, conspiratorially, that he didn't have to believe all the stuff in his file.

"I have to take it on trust," Adam replied.

Rao laughed. "Trust, yeah. Very, very important concept, Adam."

"It is, Mr. Rao."

"So it's very important, you know, you don't lie to me."

Adam blinked. "I don't intend to."

"Good. Good. How old are you?"

"Thirty-five."

Rao shook his head in wonderment. "Fucking hell. Have you been to London before?"

"Yes."

"Are you in London now?"

Adam frowned. "I am."

"Am I?"

He hadn't answered that, just stared at Rao, and Rao had laughed, high and hysterical. Which was when Adam reassessed his previous assessment. Slotted this operation into the category *potentially very difficult*.

It was, and it wasn't.

Several weeks in the field proved Rao was as chaotic and uncontrolled as Adam had predicted. He waved his arms a lot, scratched his head compulsively. Always laughed at his own jokes. It always looked like he was wearing someone else's clothes. He was uncomfortable with silence. Had to fill it with words, hummed tunes, snapping fingers. And there was a degree of oppositional behavior. It wasn't directed at Adam, but sometimes that made it worse.

Operationally, however, he was superb. First, he was a natural at soft interrogation. It was fun to watch how quickly people trusted him who shouldn't. Adam knew the mechanics, but there was more to it than tone, word choice, body language. There was something intangible involved, a form of *Fingerspitzengefühl* that couldn't be learned if you didn't already have it. Adam never had. Second, Rao's Russian was flawless, and from the pace of the conversations he heard, his Uzbek nowhere near as bad as Rao insisted. Third, no matter how much vodka he'd drunk, Rao's reports were admirably clear and concise. One evening, Rao had told him the trick, smugly tapping one temple. "I'm cursed," he'd said. "With perfect recall and a photographic memory. It's *awful*."

Most of all, Adam had been impressed by Rao's specialism.

They'd informed him Rao worked like a polygraph, but his numbers were better, said he was near infallible. Which sounded bullshit. Predictable bullshit: Adam had long been entertained by how much of a hard-on certain sectors had for supernatural intel. It'd be so much cheaper, if they could ever get it to work. They never could. Like those phonies holding their temples in Fort Meade back in the sixties, trying to put Soviet missile silos on bits of unexposed film.

But the evidence stacked up, day by day, and eventually Adam couldn't deny it. Rao could tell when assets were lying, when DOD personnel and embassy staff were lying. Waiters, taxi drivers, receptionists, anyone. But maybe he needed to concentrate to do it, because he wasn't infallible, and it wasn't all the time. Adam had lied to Rao a bunch of times and he hadn't seemed to notice.

On a Bukhara backstreet, listening to Rao complaining bitterly about how some cruel fluke of fate had deprived him of the excellent driving skills that everyone else in his family possessed, Adam tested him again. Informed him, deadpan, that their vehicle had gone.

"Gone? As in stolen? Shit. Shit. This isn't good. What are we going to do? We have to be on the road in—" Rao stopped, then glared. "You're fucking with me."

"I am."

Adam was very familiar with the kind of person who could dish it out and not take it. He hadn't thought Rao was among their number, but he must have been wrong, because Rao was suddenly furious.

"You're just another tool in the kit, is it?" he spat out.

"What?"

"I just can't tell how you're doing it, that's all. I need to know."

"Years of training in marksmanship, close quarters, and hand to hand?"

"No, not the creepy stalker hit man stuff."

"I'm not—"

"How are you doing it?"

"Rao, I'm afraid I'm going to have to ask you to talk in full, complete sentences. Please attach as much information to these sentences as you can."

"Get fucked," Rao said. "Seriously."

CHAPTER 16

"What culinary delights are the American air force offering us this evening, Adam?"

"Specialty oatmeal night."

"What? Is that a— Oh fuck off." Rao squints at the DFAC menu on the wall. "What the shit is turkey spaghetti?"

"What it says," Adam says, pulling a tray and walking down the line.

"BBQ Beef Cubes?!" Rao calls after him. He opts for fish and chips, dumped on his plate by a server with a fixed smile and doubtful eyes. Rao smiles back. *Good evening to you too*, he thinks. He likes his terrorist beard. He's not shaving it off. He looks over to Adam. He's sorted himself a plate of mac and cheese. If he didn't know Adam, he'd assume it was comfort food. They sit. Rao forks up some chips.

"This place is like the diner," he observes. Adam looks up, alarmed. "Not like that," Rao says, gesturing at the faux-Tudor beams, the tabard-wearing mannequin, the heraldic shields on the walls. "It's Olde England. Like those American movies from the 1950s, you know. *Robin Hood. The Flame and the Arrow.* Old America's version of Old England. The thing being that it feels fake, but actually . . ."

Adam's still not eating, is waiting for him to finish, and Rao's already tired of what he's saying. He's relieved when Adam starts chowing down again, having evidently decided that none of what Rao's saying is operationally relevant. It's his usual metric, one that means that most of what Rao says most of the time can be safely disregarded.

"Hm," Rao grunts. "What's on the docket for the rest of the day?"

"No more meetings."

"Thank fuck."

Twenty seconds later Miller appears in the room, catches sight of them, walks over. Rao mouths "meeting" at Adam, gets a flicker of irritation that's sufficient to count as a win.

Miller politely asks the airmen sitting with them to fuck off, then sits. "How did it go?" she enquires.

"Caldwell doesn't know anything," Adam says. "Their discussions were on the subject of nostalgia and homesickness. She says she'll contact us if she recalls anything that might relate to the reason behind Straat's interest. And she's loaned us a book she wrote on nostalgia. Rao's going to read it."

"Good. Rao, let me know if it's useful. I'm sorry to disturb you both while you're eating, but this is new." Miller slides a photograph across the table. "It was found in the fire. It was missed in the initial search." She glances at Adam. He blinks, nods minutely.

Rao puts his cutlery down, wipes his hands on his trousers, pulls the photograph towards him. It shows a small, scorched, broken glass vial by a millimetre scale, the label curled and burned.

"What was in it?" he asks, handing it to Adam.

"We don't know. It's gone to the lab."

"Anything on the label?" Rao asks.

"A few letters. An *e* and an *o*. Possibly a *p*. We'll run the ink, too, but there's no reason to think it's anything other than a standard label."

"Except it being found at the site of a master sergeant's self-immolation."

"That doesn't mean the label ink is going to be unusual," Adam says.

Rao gives him a weary look. "No, it doesn't."

After dinner they make a detour to the base food court Starbucks, where Rao loads a venti Pumpkin Spice Latte with shedloads of nutmeg and cinnamon. Back in the room, he sets the cup on the table. Places the photograph next to it. Picks up a legal pad and a pen, hands them to Adam, sits.

"Right, let's do this, Adamski. Truth run time. Can you keep tabs?"
Adam nods, pulls up a chair.

Rao takes a breath. "Straat was murdered." He shakes his head. "Straat's death was accidental," he says. "Ok, that's true. Straat brought the vial to the base. *True*. The substance in the vial was involved in the appearance of these objects on the base," he says. "*True*. Humans were involved in the appearance of these objects on the base. *True*."

"Not aliens?"

"Shut up, Adam. The substance in the vial created these objects. *Unclear*. How about . . . people created these objects. *Unclear*." He tries again, selecting his words with more care. "Exposing people to the substance in the vial caused the objects to appear. *True*."

He sits for a moment. "The fuck is this stuff?"

Adam's dark eyes are on his, expecting the truth of what this is, if Rao can reach it. For the benefit of the American government. Does Adam see Rao as anything more than a sentient ticker tape spooling out intel? Times like these, he's not sure.

"I don't know," Adam says.

"That was a rhetorical question," Rao snaps. "But thank you for your contribution." He shakes his head, goes on. "The substance was in the smoke from the bonfire. *True*. The objects that appeared around the base were a consequence of people inhaling the substance in the smoke. *True*."

He's quiet for a while.

"How did—"

Rao waves a hand in dismissal. "I'm thinking."

"A single person was involved in the creation of each object. *True*. These objects contain the substance. *False*."

He breathes in, breathes out. "Ok. The objects are . . . memories. Ugh. Not quite. *Maybe*. The objects have psychological significance to the individuals who created them. *True*. The significance of the objects is related to safety. *True*. The significance of the objects is related to a sense of refuge. *True*."

"Can I ask something, Rao?"

"What?"

"Caldwell said that nostalgia was a kind of knee-jerk response to psychic trauma."

"She didn't say knee-jerk, Adam, or psychic trauma, but good point. How about this: the substance causes psychic trauma to people exposed to it. *True.* That's a definite yes. The effect of the psychic trauma is to make people nostalgic." He tilts his head, listens. That one is a very near truth that isn't quite the right shape, exerts a pressure like the feeling in his sinuses when a plane ascends, and he's still not sure why his brain thinks that listening will take him any closer when this occurs. It never does. He thinks the word "nostalgia" isn't the right one. But it's close enough. He's going to put that one down as true.

Vagueness and indeterminacy are sensations that Rao can worry at until they scratch at him unpleasantly, even when he knows that a statement he generates can't be reduced to truth or falsehood. On a run like this, he constantly falls into the trap of convincing himself that truths can always be found if he could just find the right way to ask for them. The longer a run goes on, the more he feels that his questions aren't precise enough, that the words he's choosing are the wrong ones. Sometimes he'll slip into Russian or Hindi or Dundhari, Spanish or French. Not because words in those languages connect more accurately with reality but because the sentences are angled differently, are new ways to engage with it.

Truth runs are always exhausting. He knows that someone brighter than him—someone with a clearer mind—could do them better. They always remind him of his inadequacies. They make him tired and frustrated. They make him hate himself. Right now he knows he's too much of a mess to go much further. Has a good idea where he'll end up if he does, and then he'll be no good to anyone.

He stretches, runs both hands savagely through his hair. "This is hard. It's a conceptual minefield and right now I'm too freaked out to think clearly. Let's get back to it in a bit. I'll take a look at the vial instead." He takes three long gulps of tepid coffee, leans to squint at the burned label in the photograph, mutters under his breath. "Two words," he says. "This could take a while. You can go and lie down or have a wank or whatever. Chuck me that paper and pen?" Adam hands them to him, then sits back, starts doing the expressionless sniper thing, behaving like he's not really there. It's one of Adam's specialities, making himself unremarkable to the point of invisibility even when someone's looking right at him. It should be infuriating, but it's surprisingly easy to ignore. Rao supposes that's the point.

It doesn't take long. Six minutes later he takes a fresh sheet, scrawls on it, pushes it across the table to Adam.

EOS PROPHET

"Shit," Adam breathes. Rao, fascinated, watches his face drain of all colour.

"The fuck, Adam. You look like you've just read your own death sentence. What is it?"

Adam's throat works a couple of times. "Us," he says eventually.

"What d'you mean, 'us'?"

"Sounds like a project nickname."

"A nickname?"

"That's the correct term."

"Correct for who?"

"Defense."

"So it's a military project. Can't you look it up, find out what it is?"

Adam meets his eyes.

"Ok, so it's a black project."

"Likely an SAP, yes."

"In English, love?"

"Special Access Program. There are," he goes on, speaking quietly and more hesitantly than Rao's ever heard him before, "various different categories of classified initiatives."

"Well, shall we find out what kind this is?"

Adam doesn't respond for a long while. Then he nods. "Worst case, this could be an unacknowledged Special Access Program."

Rao tests the supposition, nods.

"Yeah, that's what it is."

"Fuck."

Another long silence.

"Does Miller know?"

Rao whispers under his breath, shakes his head. "She hasn't a clue. Well. Isn't this exciting. Make yourself some coffee. I'll keep going."

"No, you won't. You'll stop right now."

"The fuck?"

"An unacknowledged SAP is a world of shit. The ramifications aren't pretty. I need time to think."

"Knowing more about what it is isn't going to stop you thinking, Adam."

"It might, Rao."

It's late. Rao is asleep, and Rao is dreaming. It's the usual dream, and it starts in the usual place, just outside the door of his great-uncle's business room back in the big house in Jaipur. The dream is a memory. In it, he's small and uncomfortably full of dinner. It's getting towards bedtime and this summons is unexpected. He's not been allowed into this room before, though he's sneaked in a few times just to thrill in the agony that someone might catch him. It's a dark room, the windows always half shuttered, and it smells of pomade and jasmine and, on one of his secret visits, strongly of perfume. It must have been a visitor's perfume because these rooms are where people come to buy things. Not the kind of people who go to the showroom but people who are very famous or very rich. That's what his father had said. And it was true. He'd even seen a man come out of the room once that he'd seen twice before, not in real life, but on the big screen at the Raj Mandir.

He knocks on the door and a voice behind it tells him to come in. The bottom of the door brushes a little against the rug as it swings. He approaches the desk where his great-uncle sits. He is as stern as usual, his collar buttoned tight. And his father is there too, sitting this side of the desk, which is a relief, but the atmosphere is forbidding, like it always is when his great-uncle is there. His father is smoking a cigarette, and Rao stands there watching the smoke climb through shafts of setting sunlight that have come through the bottom of the blinds. He can hear pigeons cooing just outside the window, traffic. He's worried. Has he done something? He must have done something to be called in here. He can't think of any particular thing he's done of late that would mean a big punishment, and he doesn't forget things. Sometimes he doesn't know that what he is doing is bad, that's true. But still he can't think of what it could be.

Then his father smiles at him, so he knows he is not in trouble. But the smile is odd, like his father's worried. Rao feels a new tug of anxiety. Maybe he's not doing this right. He links his hands behind his back and stands even taller.

His father nods at his great-uncle, and then turns and spreads three padded trays across the mahogany desk. They're display trays, like the ones in the showroom in the city. They're full of assorted jewellery, which is strange, because usually, he knows, they are all one thing. All rings, or all bracelets, or one kind of other thing.

Then his father turns back to Rao, his face very serious. His voice is low. Almost a whisper.

"Which, would you say, is the most interesting of these, Sunil?" he says.

Rao's not sure what he means. He thinks he should be, but he isn't. He whispers back. "You mean beautiful, papaji?"

"They are all beautiful in their different ways. I mean, which is the most interesting because it is different?"

Sunil nods. Points. It's easy. There it is, on the second tray, a sapphire pendant whose gleaming stone isn't a sapphire at all.

"This one?"

He nods. And he sees, then, his father and great-uncle trade a significant look. He didn't know what it meant back then, but in these dreams he does, because that was the moment they discovered that Rao could ascertain fakes by sight alone, and things after it were not the same as they had been. Which is why, Rao presumes, he has this dream a lot. Sometimes he knows he's having it, is aware and lucid inside it. When that happens, he always tries to point to a different jewel, but the dream never lets him. It's a horrible feeling, his inability to change the narrative. The dream runs always like the dream always runs.

But this time it doesn't. This time the dream veers off its usual course. Instead of nodding gravely, his uncle laughs. Hearing it, seeing him do it, is a shock. So much so, Rao wakes, all his senses tingling. The whole dream felt far more real than usual. He feels like he's just been dragged back here from thirty years ago. Then he hears a low murmuring from the room next door. Adam. Adam's talking. He must be on a call. And then, blinking in the dark, Rao hears it again. It's not his uncle. It's Adam. Adam is *laughing*.

CHAPTER 17

"**W**hat's this?"

His dad kicks the box across the floor to him as he walks into his room. He winces because the impact could knock the optics out of alignment, maybe break the lenses. That's his first thought: the telescope, the impact of his dad's foot. Then he catches up with the scene.

There are worse ways to find out his dad searches his room.

"It's a telescope," he answers.

The telescope was his. It was his before he bought it. It was his the second he saw it in the faded print of the mail-order catalog. It was his the entire time he was saving for it. He mowed lawns. He did extra chores for his mom. He stood dutifully nearby while his dad worked on the RV, ready to pass whatever tool he needed. He spent so long outside doing things, working, finding chores and little jobs that his mom told him he was getting a tan just like normal kids.

His parents never asked why he wanted to work so hard for the money. They were distracted, he supposed, by the work ethic. That was the most important thing to them. He was showing dedication to something, putting in the time, and he wasn't complaining about the tasks they laid out for him. All that showed something. Character, probably.

He'd ordered the telescope when his dad was out of town. It wasn't planned, but it was better that way. He didn't want to answer any questions, like *Why a telescope?*

Why *not* a telescope?

When it arrived, the box was a lot larger than he thought it would be. His mom stood on the porch with him, both of them staring at it.

"Did you tell your father that you were spending your money on something big?"

Of course he hadn't. He should have. His aunt liked to say it was better to beg forgiveness than to ask permission, but she never sought either from his dad. The former was infinitely worse to beg for than the latter.

"It'll fit under your bed," his mom said. Looked at him evenly as she lit a cigarette with a match. "But I don't know when you'll get to use it."

"I'll figure it out," he told her. Sounded like he believed himself.

"Good."

He figured it out. He got to use the telescope twice while his dad was away. His eyes watered the first time he used it, which messed with his ability to focus. He was crying, but somehow that wasn't bad. There was so much more above him than he'd expected. It wasn't even the stars, more the darkness between them. Looking up there, seeing what there was, it made the band around his chest go away. Felt like being lost, but somewhere he wanted to be.

"That's a telescope," he answers.

"Don't give me back talk."

Back talk is answering questions when he isn't supposed to, or knowing things too early, before his dad has a chance to teach them to him, or not wanting to do something his dad wants to do, or wanting to do something his dad doesn't. Back talk is saying anything that isn't right. He's usually smarter than this, usually knows to shut up when he's asked a question, especially when his dad is this mad. Why is he so mad?

"Who gave you this?"

He waits. Doesn't answer right away. Isn't going to be stupid again. Opens his mouth only after his dad gives him a nod, a go-ahead. "I bought it myself."

"With what money?"

"I worked for the money, sir."

They look at each other. He watches his father remember. He'd pressed notes into his son's hand. Hadn't thought about it at the time.

"Why are you hiding it?" his dad asks.

Good question. Because his mom told him to. Because he was scared about asking for permission and terrified to beg for forgiveness. Because he'd wanted to avoid this anger that came from nowhere and made no sense.

He doesn't have an answer to give his dad. That's enough.

"I hope it wasn't expensive," his dad says, picking up the box like it weighs nothing. "No one hides anything from me in my own house. Do you understand?"

"Yes, sir."

They look at each other again. A beat of silence. An unasked question.

"The searches are random," his dad tells him on the way out of the room with his telescope under his arm. "No secrets from me in my home. I'll always know."

A threat, a simple fact. Flat and absolute. He'll always know.

CHAPTER 18

Back at IHOP for breakfast, Adam's pouring coffee in a peculiarly talkative mood. "Do you know why IHOPs keep a pot of coffee on every table?"

"I see you're making conversation, Adam."

"So you don't."

"Come on then, out with it."

Adam tears open a pot of vanilla creamer, dumps it into a mug, inspects the result, adds another. "Back in the fifties, there was a guy making films for the Federal Civil Defense Administration about surviving atomic attacks. Logistics, delivering essential emergency provisions. Coffee was one of the necessities. He got thinking and it ended up with him opening this place." He pushes the mug across to Rao.

"Huh," Rao says, picking up a sachet of sugar. "That can't possibly be true." *It is.* "Are you working right now, Adam?"

Adam regards him blankly. "I'm talking to you, so yes."

Rao taps the sachet and tilts his head to watch the sugar fall. "No, besides all this. Are you on a job? Go on, tell me. I can help."

"If I were, then you might help. That's true. But I'm not."

"So what was all that last night?" Rao says, stirring.

"Elaborate," Adam says.

"All that laughing at two a.m. I heard you, Adam, so you can stop lying to me."

"Laughter proves that I'm working because . . . ?"

"Because you don't have any friends."

Adam shakes his head. "I have friends, Rao."

"With a sense of humour?"

"Some of them. This one does."

"So what does this funny friend do?"

"Combat controller."

"What's that?" Rao knows what a combat controller is, but there's no satisfaction in admitting it. There is considerable satisfaction, however, in the precise and irritated diction of Adam's reply. "AFSO CCs are the MVPs in pretty much any theatre. Their training's the most rigorous in existence. The instructors spend fifteen weeks pretty much trying to kill the recruits. They use CS gas for negative reinforcement. The washout rate's over eighty percent. Survive that and you're the best. Period."

"Better than the SAS?"

Adam stirs his coffee. "Yes, Rao."

Rao narrows his eyes, recalling all the times he's heard the USAF dismissed as the lamest branch of the American military. Decides not to raise this particular point with Adam. It never goes down well. "So who is this guy?" he asks.

Adam rolls his eyes. "She's not a guy."

"Well fucking *sorry* for not working out that this friend is a woman. You can't tell me that's a piece that fits in the grand puzzle of Lieutenant Colonel Fucking Rubenstein."

"Explain your logic."

"Don't women hate you?"

Adam twitches his lips. "No, women don't hate me. Everyone dislikes me. There's a subtle difference."

"So what's this guy who's not a guy's story?"

Adam drinks his coffee, considers. "We go back a long way. She's just back stateside."

"From where?"

"Afghanistan."

"And what was she doing over there?"

"Rao. I wouldn't tell you even if I had the specifics."

Rao waves vaguely. "Not specifically. *Generally*."

"CCs are attached to special ops," Adam explains. "Delta, SAS, all sorts. They do everything special ops do and simultaneously provide terminal guidance and control for fire support."

"So your not-guy calls in air strikes."

"She directs air traffic for that purpose and others." The fondness in his face shifts to something nearer awe. "The role's complex as hell, Rao. Like playing chess, only—"

"Yeah, yeah." Rao cuts Adam short. "So she's an air traffic controller."

"She's qualified, yes."

"What's her name?"

"Hunter."

"Just Hunter?"

"Hunter Wood."

"Like Dr. Quinn, Medicine Woman."

"Rao."

"Hunter Wood, ATC."

"You don't want to call her that."

"If I ever meet her, I will certainly be calling her that."

Adam's eyebrows rise. "Your funeral. She's a master sergeant. She called because a guy who went through training with her has gone AWOL."

"That's what Special Forces do, Adam. They disappear. Like we need more problems right now. Your friend's mate vanishing has nothing to do with what we're working on." He feels his jaw drop, slack. "What's his name?"

Adam narrows his eyes. "Why do you need to—"

"Humour me."

"Flores. Danny Flores."

"The disappearance of Danny Flores is related to the substance in the vial. *Shit*. Adam."

Outside Miller's office, Adam gives Rao a warning look that resembles a straight razor made into a facial expression. Rao sighs, lifts his eyes to the ceiling.

"I've been briefed on the matter of deniability, love. Extensively, by you. I won't mention the thing."

"Because it's crucial that you don't."

"You've made that exceedingly clear. Stop nagging."

Miller's arms are crossed. Her perfectly annealed surface manner is intact, but her hair is a little wild and there's a chaotic intensity to her stare that makes Rao suspect she's about three seconds from imploding.

"How are you?" Rao says, with genuine concern.

"I'm good."

"No, but really," he insists.

"It's nice of you to ask," she says, surprised. "I'm quite tired, Rao. But things are getting done. You have an update?"

"No. A theory. And it's going to sound insane."

She looks at Adam. He looks back. What passes between them is opaque. She turns her eyes to Rao. Periwinkle blue, the faintest shadow above their upper lashes. *Such a striking colour*, Rao thinks. Evening sky. They're wonderful. He watches them narrow.

"Try me," she says.

"Right. Ok. Yes. So, I think the substance in that vial got into people and made them create the objects."

"Create them?"

"Yeah, I know. The physics makes no sense at all. But it fits. Look, let's say Straat was carrying the vial, brought it back from his covert holiday, and it breaks by mistake. He gets contaminated and creates the bonfire. Right in front of him. Runs straight into it."

"But—"

"Like I said, it makes no sense. Bear with me. The substance in the vial boils off, gets carried in the smoke. Ed gets a huge hit, makes the diner. A way away, for some reason. Then the smoke drifted downwind—"

To his surprise, Miller nods, finishes his sentence. "Base personnel breathed it in, and they"—she flexes her fingers in front of her—"*made* everything else we found. The dolls, that theatre ticket, the board games."

"Exactly."

"Which is why the objects seem wrong to you."

Rao makes a face. "It's the best word to describe what they are. 'Fake' isn't right. They just don't have histories." He scratches his beard, rubs his knuckles over his mouth, decides to go for it. "I think they're made out of feelings. Not memories, though memory is part of what they are. They're constructions. A blend of things. Like the diner, right? Ed made that out of things he felt should be in a diner, how he felt a diner should look and feel and smell. It isn't a memory of any particular diner he's visited or seen. But it has absolute phenomenological fidelity to what diners are in Ed's mind. So there's no way of making coffee in that place because that wasn't relevant to him. The coffee was, though. He didn't think of toilets when he made his diner, so they're not there."

Adam nods. "Same with the Scrabble box and the roses."

"Exactly." Rao lets out a long breath and wishes he'd not used the word "phenomenological." "And I'd keep people away from that storeroom."

Miller stares at the desk for a while. "Well, boys," she says, finally, with a weak smile. "This isn't the working hypothesis I'd hoped for." Again, she wipes at the face of her watch with a thumb. It's one of the most delightful tells Rao has ever seen. "You know there's a department that deals with stuff like this?"

Rao's eyes widen. "There's a real *X-Files*?"

"Mulder wouldn't last a week. The Extranatural Incident Office employs actual professionals, Rao. But yes. Turning it over to them might be inevitable. But . . ."

"They're assholes?"

"Legendarily so. I wonder if we could—"

"We have a lead," Adam cuts in.

"What is it?"

"Sensitive source. At present, I'm not in a position to—"

"Rubenstein," she says warningly.

"Allow it," Rao says. "If we can wrap this up for you, you can present it as a fait accompli to Mulder and Scully."

"To the EIO. Are you trading on my professional ambitions, Rao?"

"He's not, ma'am," Adam says.

"I totally am, Adam."

"So what *can* you tell me?" Miller asks.

"We need to be in Colorado ASAP. There's a transport to Peterson tomorrow. Can you authorize?"

She looks at them both for a long second. "I'll need to speak to the UK authorities to take the flag off Rao's passport. I'll action that now."

"You have my passport?"

"We have your passport. How long will you need over there?"

"Fuck knows," Rao says. "But Adam'll give you as many sitreps as you need."

Miller closes her eyes briefly. "Don't make me regret this, Rubenstein."

"No, ma'am," Adam answers.

"Rao, go and pack. I need a word with your partner."

Rao hangs around outside. When Adam emerges a few minutes later, Rao's surprised to see him looking almost cheerful. "Adam, she *said it*," he hisses.

"Said what?"

"'Don't make me regret this.' I thought that was only in movies."

"It's not only in movies."

"So? What did she say?"

That's definitely amusement in Adam's eyes.

"A few things. She was very clear on one matter. She says I have to keep you safe."

"Well, listen to her, Adam."

"I'm thinking about it, Rao."

Rao stomps his feet beside his loaned kit bag and swears in several languages, breath clouding the air. The morning smells metallic, like snow or blood, and despite his numb fingers and toes, he feels a shiver of grudging delight. Last night's freezing fog transformed the base into Fairyland. Fence wires, asphalt, spiders' webs, the leaves of the car park shrubs—all are furred with delicate, geometric threads of frost. He rubs his fingers across the top of the bollard by his side, watches the crystals melt away in front of his eyes.

When their car draws up, he and Adam stow their bags and are driven to Mildenhall in silence. Twenty minutes later, he's trying to place the atmosphere inside the passenger terminal as he thaws. Decides it's a late-night Walmart, maybe a haunted parking garage. The floor is so highly polished he jumps when he glances down at check-in and makes eye contact with his own reflection. Leaving Adam at the desk, he wanders off to find a seat, stopping to stare at a flowerbed tucked under a staircase: fleshy houseplants bordered by the fakest fake rocks he's ever seen, amateur dramatic props in a village hall production of *Dracula*. He finds a bank of five chairs already occupied by an older couple, sits.

"Hi," he says. She has an ash-blonde bob, a cream gilet, pearl-templed rimless varifocals. He's bulky with a thick neck, a brown cow-hide jacket, an Omega Seamaster, a copy of *Newsweek* folded in one hand. All-American. Apple pie. "You off on vacation?" he asks.

"Kind of," she answers hesitantly. "We're visiting our son." Their son is called Gary, she explains, a first-class cadet at the Air Force Academy majoring in space operations. They're an air force family, he says, and Gary makes them very proud. Rao knows a thing or two about family traditions, says a few words about carrying on legacies. She beams at him.

"Rao," he says, extending a hand.

"Heather," she says, shaking it. "This is my husband, Bill."

A photo is pulled from a wallet, passed across.

"Looks like he's born to it," Rao says.

Bill nods. "He loves it there. Duck to water. So what takes you to CONUS?"

"Work," Rao says with a significant wink.

"Ah," he says, pleased. "Good for you."

Adam reappears, looking askance at them all. "Also," Rao announces, "I'm going to meet my friend here's girlfriend for the first time, which will be nice."

Adam hands him a bulky puffer jacket. "Showtime," he says, ignoring Heather and Bill. "You'll need this. C-17s get cold at thirty thousand feet."

CHAPTER 19

Before

Adam cursed under his breath as he drove back to their Tashkent hotel. The last thing he needed was a stop from Uzbek police at two in the morning with a bloodied and bruised man in the back of the vehicle. Keeping to backstreets, he recalled what had happened at the end of that first London meeting, just after Rao had left the room.

"So," Morten Edwards had said to him, not quite making eye contact, "that's Rao. There's something you should know about him, and I thought it might be politic to wait until he was out of the room before discussing it."

"The drinking?"

"Well, there is that, yes." An awkward smile. "But that doesn't affect his particular skills, so we don't worry too much about that side of things. It's more that Rao's a little"—Edwards hesitated—"I suppose you might call him punch-happy. Fighting's fighting, as I'm sure you know, but we really don't want any trouble on the books. So if you could keep an eye on him, don't let it get too out of hand, we'd really appreciate it."

Adam nodded. Sunil Rao was a savant with an attitude problem. He had to keep him clean without losing him. Sounded about right.

"Understood," he answered.

Rao got into a fight three days after they arrived in Uzbekistan. Adam didn't catch what Rao said to the guy who punched him, but he'd obviously earned it, already bloody-mouthed, swaying, drunk in his chair. Adam considered stepping in immediately, but he'd wanted a fuller understanding of what this was. Why start a fight at all?

Rao stayed upright. Impressive. Sometimes he was on his feet, some-times fallen back onto his seat, but he took every blow like he didn't feel it. He ended up laughing at the big guy he'd chosen to fuck with, out of breath and frustrated by Rao's passivity.

Adam didn't get it. He didn't even really have to break up the so-called fight; mostly he just pushed past the guy beating bruises into Rao and called it. "Whatever he said to you, he's sorry," Adam informed him. Rao laughed at that, high and wet, continued laughing as Adam dragged him away from the bar.

Adam didn't see the next fight. Rao had sneaked out late one eve-ning. Impressive again. Not many people would have been able to get away from under Adam's nose like that. He got a call from a dive twenty minutes from their hotel. The bar was a bitch to find. He parked two blocks away, followed the smell of shashlik smoke and rowdy Russian voices. Found Rao laughing, bleeding freely, sitting in the dirt outside. "There he is!" Rao shouted, pointing at him as he approached. He took a breath and looked at his partner. He could have done a better job than this. He'd been told Rao liked to look for trouble, and he'd known what that meant. But over the years, Adam had learned not to care about all this. If someone was going to get their ass kicked, and if Adam wasn't doing the actual kicking, it really shouldn't involve him at all. It was very rare he'd been told outright to stop it from happening, however. He definitely could have done better.

He sat on the curb next to Rao. "Bored, huh?"

Rao dabbed at his split lip, examined the blood on his fingers. "Let me ask you something, Adam," he said, tonguing at the wound as he spoke, sounding close to laughter with every word. Adam suspected he was high as well as drunk, but in this light—two strings of dim light bulbs between the front of the bar and a tree—Adam couldn't see his pupils clearly enough to tell. "You don't really talk to people."

"That's not a question," Adam replied.

Rao laughed, a little hysterically. "That's *true*, isn't it?"

"It's true you didn't ask me a question," Adam observed. "And it's true that I don't talk to many people. We're working, as you know, and considering my role, contacts are limited."

"That's the most you've said since we've met," Rao pointed out.

Adam had never known how to respond when people told him things like that. *Is it everything you hoped for?* Too sarcastic. *That's factually accurate.* Too cold. "Mm," he said.

Rao considered Adam through the eye he could still open. "You don't say fuck all to anyone, and that's how you block them out," he continued. Adam was struck by how clear and cutting Rao's speech was. No trace of slurring at all. This could be a learned skill or just a natural one, he mused, if it could be called a skill at all. "We all have our things, yeah? Yours is being a dickhead."

"That's my thing, huh?" Adam sighed, pulling Rao's arm around his shoulder.

"Yeah. Your armour," Rao insisted, doing his best to stand as Adam pulled him up. "Yours. This is mine."

Adam didn't follow this reasoning. He considered the merits of continuing with this conversation. If he understood Rao's justification for finding his way into fights, he might be able to predict his moods. Good enough.

"Getting pummeled every other night isn't the best armor, Rao."

"Depends, doesn't it? Whether the armor's to protect or whether it's there to block," Rao answered, chuckling low and thick like he had a bubble in his throat, but at least the hysteria was gone. Adam made a mental note to check for bruising around Rao's neck when they were back at the hotel.

"You're precise with your words when you want to be," Adam observed. He'd known for a while that Rao preferred statements to questions. It didn't matter if he was doing his focused shit on them or not. He liked statements. Facts. Liked having them in the air. Adam supposed that it was something they had in common.

Rao raised a hand. "Precision, love, always throws people off. You've noticed that, surely? I reckon you notice a lot of things." He tried to waggle his fingers. It was probably meant to be a playful gesture, but the attempt failed. He grimaced and aborted the action. *Funny*, Adam thought and didn't laugh. The whole night was sort of funny in its own way, in the Rao way, which was something he was still getting used to. It was when nothing made sense, when the words were precise and evasive at the same time. Frustrating more than anything else. But pretty funny too.

"I'm sure I don't know what you mean," he replied evenly.

Rao considered Adam sideways. "Fucking hell," he murmured, shaking his head enough to quickly shut his working eye. *Concussion check*, Adam added to his list. The list grew longer as they walked to the truck. Rao's habitually uneven pace had become a limp. His hands would need examining too. More than likely bruised rather than broken, but he needed to be sure.

The streets were quiet. Lines of whitewashed tree trunks in the dark. A white Moskvich 2140 slowed as it approached; Adam put himself between Rao and the car. Private taxi, he decided, as the driver reconsidered his speculative stop and accelerated away.

As Adam watched its taillights recede along the street, Rao seemed to realize he didn't have all his attention and started on some godawful, deeply inappropriate drinking song. Sung it right into Adam's ear, trying to get a rise. Rao had no idea how easy it was for Adam to shut everything out while making a list. How easy it was for him to turn his focus elsewhere. Check out.

"You're no fun," Rao grumbled as Adam dumped him in the back seat.

"Is that true?"

"Fuck off. Of course it fucking is," Rao said, wincing. "Fuck."

PART II

CHAPTER 20

It's cavernous inside the cargo bay: grey paint, stencilled signs, pipes, alcoves packed with steel hardware. Strapped-down boxes, pallets and crates, passenger seats along both sides of the fuselage. It's bright outside, but as soon as the bay door closes it feels like the end of a long night inside the plane, everything foggy and tired and old, the light strange, as if it were tipped on one end.

Rao buckles himself in, asks Adam which inflight movies are showing today.

"I don't know, Rao," Adam says patiently. "Ask the flight attendants when they come around with champagne."

Rao smirks. He knows he's easily bored. It's one of his worst qualities. Well, no, it's far from his worst. But flying has never bored him. He adores the dissociation it brings, the mild hypoxia, the way it picks you up and hides you from the world. And it meant family, for years. Home to home on his school holidays. London Heathrow to Delhi, onwards to Jaipur, up on the top deck of the 747 where the upholstery was the colour of apricots and candlelight, and small Sunil rejoicing in all of it, tracing the murals on the walls with his fingers, poring over the route maps, transfixed by the cabin crew. The Air India Girls. When he was a child, they'd been *everything*. He'd told his mother he wanted to be one once. She'd nodded gravely and told him she absolutely understood why. There was laughter in her eyes, but Rao had heard the truth behind her words and basked in the joy of being known.

His last plane journey had been on an aircraft like this one, but Rao doesn't remember much of it. He'd been barely conscious. It returns to him in disconnected images, like damp newsprint photos, grimy halftones adhering to his skin. And the one before? An ancient TriStar from Brize Norton. Dirty side-eyes from scores of Royal Marines and bouts of nausea from what the pilot had called heavy chop. But the worst recollection of that journey was how excited he'd been throughout, grasping the knowledge that he was going out there to help as tightly as he had his mother's hand back when he was a child, slowly, determinedly, climbing the steep steps to the cabin.

Heather and Bill have taken seats opposite them on the far side of the bay. Rao nods at them, opens Kitty's book as the engines spool up. He always feels guilty reading books like these. Having perfect recall and an ability to discern truth in things made his university career a case of outrageous academic fraud. "You're a smart guy, Rao," Adam had said once, and Rao had grimaced. "I'm educated, Adam. People regularly mistake the two."

Two hours into the flight he's munching on chocolate-covered pretzels and deep in a chapter called "The Valley of Lost Things." Lots of writers have conjured such places, he discovers. Have filled them with things long forgotten and things still longed for. He reads that L. Frank Baum made it a valley filled with pocketbooks, shoes, toys, and clothes, just over the desert from the Land of Oz, and that P. L. Travers put lost things on the moon: Mary Poppins escorted children through the clouds to reach it. And four hundred years before Mary Poppins, the moon was also the home of lost things in Ariosto's *Orlando Furioso*. Things lost in error, lost through time or chance. Ruined castles, lost towns, lost reputations, lost loves, lost fame, people's wits stoppered tightly in jars. *Sanity sealed into vials*, Rao thinks, frowning, and reads on.

These are places, Kitty tells him, that you can only visit if you're accompanied by a guide. *Like the underworld*, Rao thinks, pleased by his analogy. He recalls the *Inferno* and Doré's etchings for it, and these bring Piranesi's *Carceri d'invenzione* to mind. He closes his eyes and wanders about inside Piranesi's impossible spaces of chains and walls and wheels and stone. There are lost things in these prisons, too, he muses, and with a jolt exactly like expecting a step underfoot that isn't there, he realises with horror that what he's done is put himself right back in Kabul. He opens his eyes, grips the book tightly. Tries to read on but can't resolve the words. His concentration's gone. Everything has, except a visceral, desperate need to use. *Fuck.* Could anyone on the plane help him out? He looks at Bill and Heather doubtfully. But the pilots? Surely. Those assholes get handed drugs by the kilo. Rao is thinking about getting out of his seat to go see when he feels a nudge against his shoulder. His whole body tenses for a punch. *How does Adam know?* he thinks, outraged. But the nudge doesn't stop. It becomes a weight. And it's not an admonition, he realises. Adam's head is on his shoulder.

Adam has fallen asleep.

He's astonished. Then gleeful. He's going to give Adam *so* much shit about this. The prospect makes him grin. He's still grinning when a burst of turbulence hits the plane. The seats shudder, there's a low swoop in his stomach, the head resting on his shoulder shifts slightly, and so does Rao, and suddenly he's feeling the prickle of Adam's shit crewcut right against his cheek and the corner of his mouth. And he's overtaken all at once by a wave of dreadful longing. It fills him so completely he shuts his eyes and drifts in it for a while, lost in the sensation, the scent of cheap shower gel. He shouldn't be feeling this. But he is. It's not arousal—well, it is a little bit, for fuck's sake, of course it is, this turbulence isn't helping—but *Adam*? Fuck.

Maybe he should cut himself some slack. It's been a wretchedly long time. Plus, Adam looks out for him. In fact, these days, Rao muses, he's probably the only person who does. He deliberates on this pathetic fact for a while and decides that he'd look out for Adam, too, if that were ever required, which it won't be, of course, and none of this would mean shit to Adam anyway because Adam doesn't need anything. Rubenstein is the most self-contained, emotionless bastard in existence. Rao feels a peculiar burst of self-pity at the thought. Pulls his head back and does his best to ignore the continuing weight on his shoulder. *You know what,* he thinks, looking down morosely at the book spread over his lap, *I really need to get laid.*

When Adam shifts back to his seat, apparently unaware of his transgression, Rao masters himself sufficiently to read. He reads. Adam sleeps.

Then Rao sleeps. When he wakes, Adam's still asleep. Two hours before landing, he blinks back into consciousness. Rubs his neck, stretches, checks his watch, looks surprised. "I missed the flight," he says.

"You left me alone with my thoughts, you bastard."

"Won't happen again, Rao."

CHAPTER 21

Before

The morning after the bar fight, Adam watched Rao angle his head in front of the mirror, touch the swelling around one eye, tentatively massage his jaw. "You've been lucky with the police," he observed.

"Uzbek police can always be bribed."

"Lucky," Adam repeated, sharp and weary. "There's redundancy in our schedule. But not much. And it's not just what this is going to look like when we meet the people that count. Those bruises are a liability on the road."

Rao fussed about in his wash bag. Brought out a small bottle and a sponge. Wet the sponge, squeezed it into the sink. Shook the bottle. "Keep your hair on, Adamski," he said, uncapping it. "Stop worrying. We'll be fine."

"We."

"I will. You will too." He upended the bottle onto the pad of one finger, dotted the finger across the bruise on one cheekbone, then dabbed at the place with the sponge. "Concealer hides a multitude of sins."

Adam didn't respond. Sins weren't a topic he wished to raise with Rao. He walked closer, looked at the bottle, then up at Rao's face in the mirror.

"You carry this around with you."

"Just in case."

Adam began to calculate exactly how much more fucked up that was than Rao getting himself fucked up in the first place, but he stopped, because this was fascinating to watch. Like an actor preparing for a role. He'd never thought about makeup. His mother used to use it.

Sometimes thicker than other times. This was different. And not different, because Rao was putting it on with the same short, assessing glances at his face his mother had used that time he watched her from the bedroom door when he was small and snuck away feeling he'd seen something he wasn't supposed to.

He forced himself to keep looking, watched the paint slowly cover Rao's bruises, hiding his damage, making it disappear.

"Is makeup a lie?" he said without thinking.

Rao paused, sponge an inch from his face.

"Now Adam, why would you ask a thing like that?"

Adam felt an obscure sense of shame then, and it must have shown on his face because Rao kept talking, smoothing over the cracks with ease. "Depends on the makeup, depends on the person. This? Yeah. I'd say this was a lie the same way you telling people you're an international freight coordinator is. It's cover."

But it wasn't. It wasn't a lie. Adam stood there somehow knowing it wasn't but lacking the words to articulate how or why. He looked away, troubled.

"You've never messed about with makeup, have you?" Rao said.

"No."

Rao frowned at something that wasn't quite right under one eye. Patted at it with his little finger. "Not even for a school play?"

"I'm not good at drama."

"Could have fooled me, love. Anyway, you'd look killer with a subtle wing on those eyes. Want to give it a go? You can always wipe it off."

"No."

"Go on."

"No, Rao."

"I'll get you someday."

Adam didn't reply. What was bothering him, watching Rao in the mirror, wasn't Rao's freedom to indulge in his own brand of masochism. Wasn't even his fucked-up makeup routine. It was that Rao said things. Just *said them*. At first Adam had assumed this was a calculated act. He had a fine-grained knowledge of distraction techniques, knew how effective a strategy verbal chaff could be. But recently he'd figured

out that usually Rao had no idea what he was going to say until after he'd
heard himself say it. In fact, Rao regularly didn't seem to hear the words
he'd been saying at all, because he was too busy doing something else,
thinking about something else. What would it be like to live like that?
Adam wondered, watching Rao cap the concealer, stow it back in his
bag, fuss with his hair. What would it be like to be so unconcerned by
the words that leave your mouth. To not wonder if they were the right
ones or if they should have been spoken at all. To just *say them*, like Rao?

Lifting the heel of his hand to one eye, he rubbed at it so hard lights
blossomed against the black. "Five minutes," he called, picking up the
keys from the table and walking to the door.

"Someday," Rao shouted after him. "You'll love it."

CHAPTER 22

Another bloody hotel. This one has a lobby of varnished pine, rustic stone, cheap leather armchairs, and framed photographs of elks bellowing in snow. Rao hates it and is pathetically grateful for it. He needs to sleep. The silence that follows a flight is something he's habitually filled with alcohol, and he's hoping unconsciousness will claim him before the craving gets too insistent to ignore.

Adam gets them a second-floor room. Two single beds with dark-brown comforters, regulation Air Force Inn pub carpet. Rao unlaces and kicks off his sneakers, falls back onto a bed, laces his hands behind his head, and stares at the ceiling fan. After a while he turns his neck to watch Adam. He's already unplugged the TV at the wall and set the small radio he'd brought on the windowsill. Now he's pulling folded clothes from his bag and stowing them carefully in the wardrobe. Rao'll never cease to be bewildered by Adam's inability to leave his things in a suitcase like a normal human being. It's not like they'll be staying here long. There'll be another hotel. There always is.

"You should keep hydrated," Adam instructs, angling another white shirt onto a hanger. "We're over a mile high. You'll feel the altitude for a couple of days."

"Thank you, Doctor Rubenstein." He clears his throat. "Adam?"

"Mm?"

"Heather and Bill, our nice friends on the flight. They came into the lobby after us."

"Yeah, I saw."

"They told me they were here to visit their son. They aren't. And I don't know who the fuck they are, but they're not called Heather and Bill. They're tailing us."

"Yeah. That's why I rejected the first two rooms they gave us."

"Is that what you were doing? I just assumed you were being a dick. Are we in danger?"

"We could be, if we wanted," Adam murmurs. "Or we could get some sleep."

Jetlagged and itchy under his sheets, Rao sleeps fitfully, dipping in and out of dreams in which something obscure and massy is writhing inside him, dark and patently desperate. He wakes just before seven with a coughing fit. The dawn light is a surprise. The fact that Adam's bed is perfectly made up is not, nor that Adam is fully dressed. He's standing to one side of the window, gazing down through the net curtain, and his posture is highly professional. Something's up.

"What's going on?"

"Come and look at this," he answers with evident irritation.

Rao hauls himself from the mattress, walks over, and peers around the edge of the chequered drapes. There's a Dodge van pulled up on the verge of the narrow access road behind their room. Dark blue, a bit beaten up.

"Ah. A van. Good morning to you too."

"Watch."

"What am I watching?"

"Predictability. They're going to put the hood up like they've got engine trouble."

That's exactly what they do. Three clean-shaven guys in casual sportswear clamber out of the van, two of whom make a big show of shaking their heads at whatever the one who's stuck his head under the hood is saying.

"Ah. Heather and Bill have friends."

"Yeah. The van'll be there for the duration. I'll put the radio against the glass and close the drapes." He sighs. "They're shit, Rao. I'm insulted."

"Come on, Adam, don't take it so personally."

"How the fuck else am I supposed to take it?"

"It's nice to know we're wanted, love."

"Yeah," Adam says flatly. "Just like old times. I almost feel nostalgic."

Rao whistles along with "Bad Moon Rising" on the radio laid against the window and futzes with the coffee machine. Adam's at the desk setting up an encrypted remote meeting with Miller on his laptop. "Sorry about the diner logo," he announces, handing a mug to Adam.

"Thanks. Huh. Ok, we're through."

Rao pulls up a chair, stares dubiously at the screen. The feed is tinted like a video transfer of an '80s sitcom. Intermittently it stutters and freezes. It's the hotel Wi-Fi, but Rao amuses himself with the theory that Miller's clipped, executive manner is simply too much for the technology to handle. Her right hand is laid flat on the papers in front of her, her left clasped around a vacuum-walled coffee mug. Perfect manicure on brushed steel. "Rubenstein?"

"We're being tailed. Skeleton team."

She nods. "Useful."

"Yes, ma'am."

"News here is that vial's gone missing. Disappeared before it got to the lab. I'm assuming someone's taken it. We'll work through everyone in the chain."

"Understood," Adam says.

Rao blinks. A sliding *thump* from the laptop speakers and Miller jumps in her seat. "Just files falling off the desk," she explains. She pushes her chair back a fraction, leaning down to retrieve them.

Rao feels a trickle of foreboding.

"Miller—" he starts.

She reappears with a snub-nosed revolver in one hand. The puzzlement on her face shifts to astonished recognition. "Oh! I had one just like—"

"Miller! Shit. *Shit.* Adam, call the base medics. Call them *now.*"

Adam's pulled his phone and is already dialling. Miller is cradling the gun like a doll now, pressing it tight to her chest with both hands, her face rapt, beatific, wet with tears. Rao can hear Adam requesting an emergency paramedic team to her office in a voice so impossibly calm he wants to scream. He waits until he can't wait any longer, grabs the phone out of his hands.

"Right, this is important," he says through his teeth. "Tell the paramedics. She'll be in a trance. And she'll be holding a gun. Yes. A gun. I don't know what— No. It's a revolver, why the *fuck* do you need to know? Don't take it off her. Don't even think about— If you take it away from her, she'll probably die. What?" He can barely hear the question down the line over the roar of blood in his ears. "Rao," he snaps. "R-A-O. Sunil. Yes. No. I'm not . . . Will you *fucking listen to me . . .*"

He exhales heavily. Turns to Adam. "They keep telling me to calm down—"

Adam takes back the phone. "Who am I speaking to? Ashley, hello. This is Rubenstein again. We've seen cases like this before. Under no circumstances should the medical team remove the revolver from her grip. Or attempt to. She can't and won't use it and taking it from her will lead to severe complications up to and including her sudden death. Clear?"

He listens for a while, furrows his brow.

"Yes. We're working on that, but it's complex. Results won't be immediate. What I need right now is a verbal confirmation from you that these orders will be followed."

Rao hears a "yes, sir" down the line.

"Keep me updated. And, Ashley, this is super-secret squirrel. I'll liaise with the DIA about forward options. Just keep her alive."

Another pause.

"Thanks." He cuts the call.

Rao can't drag his eyes from the screen. Miller's bent forward over the desk now, her face completely obscured. He stares at the pale curls on her crown, the wrinkled seam along the shoulder of her jacket, the clock on the wall behind. At milky coffee from her upended mug seeping slowly through paper, wetting the side of her sleeve. His heart hurts, his hands itch. "*Fuck*," he spits out.

He and Adam sit there in silence until the paramedics enter the room, administer to Miller, produce a stretcher—carefully avoiding the weapon in her grasp—and ferry her away. When the room is empty,

Adam cuts the video call, pushing at the screen and snapping the laptop shut.

It's then Rao glances up. Sees Adam's face. It's alight with rage. When Adam catches his eye, the briefest flash of something like panic races across his features before he adjusts them, fixing them back into their usual impassivity. Rao sees the effort this takes, the perfection of the result. There he is, as he always is. Or was. Adam Rubenstein: nothingness made manifest.

CHAPTER 23

They were having a great day. His aunt picked him up from his house in the morning, telling his parents that they were going into the city for the day for "lunch and stuff." She fed him, as promised, then she took him to one of the last locally owned ice-cream parlors in the city. He ate a bowl of pistachio with slivers of nuts on top and listened to his aunt talk about work and the people she worked with. *Artists*, she said, rolling her eyes. *Painters*. He doesn't know what his aunt does, but he knows it has something to do with art galleries. She isn't an artist but sometimes it seems like they must be the only people she talks to, because they are the only people she talks about. He doesn't think he's ever met one.

After ice cream, she takes him to her little apartment. It's not permanent, she tells him as she unlocks the door. She won't be in this place forever. But it's close to the family, and it's close to her favorite nephew. When he points out that he's her only nephew, she grins and agrees that he has an unfair advantage.

It's a great day. He ruins it.

He's talking about cars. He doesn't know that much about them, but not knowing much about things doesn't matter when he's alone with his aunt in her apartment. Here with her he doesn't need to know everything about a topic to speak about it. He can just like a car sometimes and say so.

"What car are you going to have when you can get one?" she asks. They're both acting now, he knows. It's all pretend, make-believe, that when he gets to have a car he'll have any choice to make about it.

"I want to fix mine up," he answers. He hadn't thought about it at all before she asked, but the words come out of his mouth, and it feels like he's telling the truth. "I want to get some old piece of junk and fix it up."

"You want a project."

"I've seen some cars that people say are beyond hope," he argues. "It's not true. It's just hard work, and they don't want to do hard work."

His aunt throws her head back and laughs. "You sound like your dad," she says. It's not an insult. He laughs back. Not because it's funny but because it's true. He sounds like his dad, but both of them know he's nothing like the man. His aunt gets up to get another drink from the fridge, walking around him to do so.

He turns to her, still talking. "Hey, do you think—"

There's a crash, and he forgets what he was going to ask because his brain turns white at the noise. It only takes a blink for him to realize what he's done: he wasn't paying attention, he'd been too loose, too careless, and his elbow had bumped one of the mugs on his aunt's table and knocked it to the floor. He hadn't even been aware enough of what he was doing to have managed to catch it in time. It's smashed into irreparable pieces, right across the kitchen tiles.

"Shit," his aunt says under her breath.

His heart kicks against his chest. Hurts him with the force of it. "I'm sorry," he says quickly, getting up only to kneel and begin gathering up the bigger pieces as fast as he can without cutting himself. It'll be worse if he starts bleeding on everything as well as making a mess of the kitchen.

"Sit down, kid," his aunt says, but he doesn't do what she says. He keeps cleaning. There's a broom in the corner, he tells himself. The bigger pieces pile into a ceramic pyramid in front of him as he tells himself repeatedly that there is a broom in the corner. He can clean this all so quickly. Like it never happened. The quicker he goes, the more it feels like he might be about to outrun his aunt getting mad about it. He's never seen her mad. The thought of it makes the world turn grayer somehow. She's not always smiling, and she's not always laughing, and he wouldn't classify her as a Happy Person like people always seem to be outside their family or on TV or in magazines. But that doesn't mean that she's angry. She's definitely not angry.

He's seen what angry looks like. His aunt's not that kind of person. And there's no way he's willing to risk making her into one.

She's saying something else to him, but he's ignoring her. Can't hear her. He says that he's sorry, again, and finishes cleaning up his mess. At least there wasn't a drink in the mug. He sits back down at the table and closes his eyes. At least there wasn't a drink in the mug.

"Okay," his aunt says slowly. She's got a fresh glass of orange juice in her hand. Very calmly, she sets it down on the table. "Are you alright, kiddo?"

"I didn't mean to do that," he tells her. "I wasn't thinking. I wasn't paying attention. It was stupid, but that's no excuse, and I'm sorry."

Her eyebrows go up, but she nods. For a second she looks like his dad: serious and pensive and unreadable. Then, without saying anything, she picks up the matching mug on the table. Meets his eyes. Lets a second pass between them. Then, with a grin that banishes all semblance of his father from her face, she lets the mug drop to the tiles.

It smashes worse than the one that he broke.

There's no breath left in his body.

"I hated those things anyway," she says, sipping her orange juice. "Thanks for doing me a favor. I never would have gotten rid of them otherwise."

There are broken mug pieces and dust everywhere. It's going to be dangerous to walk in here without a dedicated and deep clean. His mouth feels dry, but the white in his brain is gone, and he doesn't feel like he's out of place in the world.

"Do you have any more of those mugs?"

"Now you're talking."

CHAPTER 24

Before

"Uhh," Rao said, and froze.

He'd always taken personal pride in being open to the unexpected, in taking all life's switchbacks in his stride, but coming back from the Chorsu Bazaar to find his colleague pressing a gun to the kneecap of a terrified man tied to a chair in the middle of their Tashkent apartment? There are limits. There really fucking are.

The man was middle-aged and looked Russian. Patterned sweater, knockoff Levi's. Sweat shining on his face, he was looking down into Adam's eyes. And Adam, crouching, was looking up into his.

I'm interrupting a private moment, Rao thought, shocked into stupidity, tucking the bag of warm pastries he'd brought from the market a little closer to his chest. Adam turned his head to look at him then and—his expression. *Christ.* Whatever desperately deflecting bit of schoolboy humour Rao'd been assembling died in his throat, right there.

"What's going on?" he managed.

"Close the door."

A few seconds of silence while Rao tussled with the ambiguity.

"Which side," he asked carefully, "of the door do you want me on?"

Then the man with the gun against his knee started to talk. A long outpouring in Russian. Pleas for help, attestations that the man with the gun was crazy, a total psycho—*quite possibly you're right*, Rao thought, *now I've seen this*—interspersed with lavish protestations of ignorance and innocence and—

Ah.

Rao made no move to shut the door.

"You've zip-tied him to the chair."

"Yeah."

"So he's not going to fuck off if we have a quiet word, is he?"

The undeniable fact appeared to require deliberation. And Adam wasn't deliberating with his usual impassivity; something about the set of his jaw made it look as if he were taking on the pros and cons in close quarters combat.

"No," he said finally, rising to his feet. As he drew near, Rao clutched the pastries even tighter to his chest. Some visceral sense of self-preservation was screaming at him to get the fuck out of the way, and it took him a deal of courage to master it.

"You weren't supposed to be here," Adam points out in the corridor, low and deeply accusatory.

"I am. Who's this guy?"

"He's tailed us for two days. I concluded they're either amateurs, short of personnel, or I'd made a mistake."

"You've not made a mistake, have you."

The briefest of smiles. "No."

"Ok," Rao says. "You don't know who's running him."

Adam shakes his head.

"And you want to."

"Obviously."

"So before you start really hurting this guy, might I suggest I sit in?"

Adam's not dumb.

"Sit behind him. Blink twice if he's lying."

Rao jerks his head at the Beretta in Adam's hand. "I'll do that. Can you put that away?"

Adam opens his mouth to protest, stops himself. Nods slowly. "It's a problem."

"No," Rao lies. "I just think you've already made your point."

Rao wasn't assisting with this interrogation for solely humanitarian reasons. Felt like it, to begin with, but no. Occupying the moral high ground. Showing off, a little. Having a chance to do some real spy shit. And as the minutes passed it was gratifying to see how freaked out the man got when he saw Adam knew when he was lying. Maybe a little too gratifying. Gratification, if he was being honest, well on its way to being very fucked up.

After fifteen minutes and a lull in the proceedings, Rao became impatient enough to do some covert truth-testing on the sly: he left his seat, started whispering suggested questions in Adam's ear. Questions he'd tried to make sound like guesses. But he got carried away. Pushed his luck way over the line when he told Adam maybe he should ask about the guy's sick sister. A lurch of apprehension in his stomach when Adam frowned. Another after the guy had heard the question and stared at Adam in disbelief.

But the sister had been the key. As soon as she was mentioned, the man started talking, stumbling over his words like he was running too fast down a very steep hill. He sat there sweating, explaining that he wasn't good at surveillance, it wasn't his job, he was just a driver—a good driver, he drove the important guys—but their usual team was working in Termez because some VIPs were up there now. That he'd been told to follow them because there was a tip-off from someone, he didn't know who. He apologised for that. He apologised for a lot of things, for not knowing things, but he'd heard a lot of conversations, and he knew the names, he explained the Turkish connection, told them exactly where the goods came through from Afghanistan and then, his voice rising even higher, how worried they were getting these days, because the government was wiping out a lot of the smaller importers because heroin was lucrative, and the government wanted the trade. Nationalising it, that's what they were doing, under the table. Because, he went on, the government's very happy to have the Americans here, to help on their war on terror, and they're also happy to buy from the guys in Afghanistan, the ones that are killing the Americans, because that's what Americans don't understand about here, is that things don't work the way they do in the movies.

Rao sat there listening to it all. But all he kept thinking when the guy was finished, all he continued to think after Adam cut him free and set him loose, was: *Which movies?*

CHAPTER 25

When Hunter marches into the lobby through the doors of the Air Force Inn, the first thing Rao notices are her eyebrows. They're absolutely perfect. He's instantly envious. The eyes beneath them are the kind that veer between dry amusement and outright challenge. A khaki T-shirt, fatigues. Box braids, bitten fingernails, a bunch of woven and leather bracelets, a *lot* of tattoos. *She's not what I expected,* Rao decides, before realising he'd no clear expectations at all. She's hot. Shit. She's *very* hot, and she makes him incredibly nervous. This is a combination dear to Rao's heart; in any other circumstances he'd be all over it like a rash.

Seeing Adam, Hunter raises her chin a fraction and does the Adam thing, the frown that's a covert smile. She jerks her head at Rao. "Is this the guy? Your lie detector?"

Adam grins. There's nothing covert about it. "Yeah. And he's not."

"Not yours or not a lie detector?"

"I'm right here," Rao says.

"So you want to hear about this?" Hunter says. "I've got a room. But we can walk and talk if you want—"

"Secure?" Adam checks.

"Secure."

"Then inside's good. Rao wants to pick up a Starbucks first."

"Of course he does." She's looking at Rao like she's his bloody mother. How is she doing that. "Ok," she says. "Hi."

"Hi," he says.

"Pleased to meet you." She turns to Adam again. "He's exactly what I expected, Rubenstein. Let's get him a Frappuccino or whatever the fuck else it is he needs."

She leads them to a block of offices designated as a Distinguished
Visitor Area and opens a door onto a room that's little larger than two
king-size beds: cloth walls, no windows, a dark wooden table surrounded
by high-backed chairs upholstered in cream-coloured leather. She sits.
Adam drops into the seat next to hers. Rao pulls up a chair at the farthest
end of the table and regards them both over the Americano he didn't
really want. Adam sends him an enquiring glance and gently taps one
earlobe. Rao shakes his head. No one's listening in.

"So," says Hunter. "Flores."

Danny Flores, Rao learns, was invalided out last year after taking a
round to an ankle while doing something unspecified in an unspecified
location in Afghanistan. Hunter maintains that Flores "knows his shit
cold," whatever that means, and that he's reliable. "Reliable like Rubenstein," she says, looking right at Rao. He picks up his cup, works out he's
only done so because he wants to hide behind it, puts it back on the table.

"Where was he living?" he ventures.

"Boulder. I just came from there," she says. "But he dropped off the
map fifteen days ago."

Huh, Rao thinks. He's gone AWOL for longer than that without
anyone getting even vaguely worried. His scepticism must show, because
Hunter tells him about Flores's dogs. How he'd booked them into a
boarding kennel for three nights but never returned to pick them up.
This, in her opinion, means Flores is likely dead.

"Hunter—" Adam begins.

She cuts in quickly, vehemently. "Can't see it. That's not his kind
of broken. And his mom's still alive. She's got dementia. She's in a care
facility a few blocks from his house. It's why he moved back out West.
I've heard him talk about her. No way he'll kill himself if she's still alive,
even if she doesn't know him from a stone."

"He's alive," Rao says quietly.

She stares. "You can't know that."

Adam's looking at him, wary and surprised. *Yes, you bastard*, he
thinks. *I'm willing to trust her because you do.* Which is nuts. He nods.

"Actually, he can," Adam says. "Rao can tell when things are true.
Not just whether people are lying. It's a talent."

She rolls her eyes. "He's a goddamn psychic investigator? Jesus, what is this? Have you joined the EIO?"

"They wish."

"Don't fuck with me, Rubenstein."

Ten minutes later she picks her bottle of peach tea from the table, slaps the cap with the flat of her hand, twists it off, and drinks. Her eyes regard Rao very seriously as she does. She's tested him, provided him with a series of statements to verify. Some were personal; some were shading to classified. In this particular area she's not found him wanting.

"This is insane. So, he—" She stops herself, addresses Rao directly. "You know what's true and what isn't. Anytime, anyplace. Except when it's about *him*."

"Yes," Rao says. He's learning the less he says to Hunter the better. Using words in her presence is like putting out targets in a live-fire exercise.

"Insane," she says, again to no one in particular.

"It's not insane," Adam says. "It's just Rao."

She gives Adam a side-eye for the ages, drains the last of her tea, pushes the bottle across the tabletop, and leans back in her seat.

"Ok. So you said you had shit to tell me. Quid pro quo. I'm listening."

"It's connected with Flores, and we don't know how," Adam explains. "Yet. But we're pushing into full unacknowledged territory. Hunter, this is strict ears only. And it's going to sound crazy. You have to trust me that it's true."

She tenses at that. "I trust you," she says quietly. "You know this. Don't need to ask for it."

"Ok," Adam says. And he tells her. He tells her about the diner and the fire. He tells her about Straat and the roses, the proliferating objects, the static cutting in on the surveillance footage. He tells her what happened to Ed. What happened to Miller. She winces. He tells her about the vial and the vial going missing—she winces at that too—and Rao's conclusions about what the substance does. How Rao had found out that Flores's disappearance was connected. She listens with fierce attention, asks a bunch of perceptive questions, and she buys all of it.

"Huh," she says. Stares at the wall for a while, rubbing at the corner of her mouth. "Miller. Shit. I'm sorry, Rubenstein. Someone dosed her, yeah?"

Ugh, Rao thinks. That hadn't occurred to him. He's losing his touch. Lost it. He tests possibilities, exhales. "No, her contamination was accidental."

"Fuck." Hunter breathes. She gazes at Rao. "This is messy. Don't end up dead, Rubenstein."

Adam twists his mouth. "Not able to promise you that."

When Adam heads off to the bathroom, Rao sends Hunter his sweetest smile. Feels like the bravest thing he's done for a while. She meets it with a level stare. "What's the deal with you and Rubenstein?" she asks.

"You are aware we work together."

"Don't be a smartass. You know what I mean. How do you take him? You ride or die?"

Rao nods slowly. "Ah, we're talking professional bonding. Battle buddies."

"Sure," she says, like she's joking. But Rao knows she's not. She *knows*, now. She deserves the courtesy of a proper answer. What comes out of his mouth surprises him.

"I, uh, was going to die. Seems like ages ago now, but it wasn't long at all. And while it was happening, I thought about Adam." He frowns. "Actually, he was the last thing I thought about, which is weird. I've thought about that. Why, I mean. It's because he's unknowable to me. Which means he's just like death. Like what comes after, if it comes after. And . . ." He assumes a smile, aware he should lighten the tone. "I guess Adam's a bit inevitable too. You know what he's like."

Hunter mutters a low "Jesus" and shakes her head. Rao's gratified he's knocked her off-balance, but he's feeling off-balance, too, now, and the silence between them is strained.

Adam halts three paces into the room, regards them with suspicion. "Rao. Hunter," he says.

"Rubenstein," Hunter replies.

"How very formal," Rao observes. "I was just telling Hunter here that you'll probably be the last thing I see before I die, one way or another."

"That's not going to happen, Rao."

"Well." Rao grins. "Sorry to inform you, love, but it's kind of inevitable."

They arrange to meet for dinner at a nearby smokehouse grill.

"It's called *what*?"

"Racks 'n' Butts," Hunter repeats.

"Ok," Rao says eventually. He watches them both disappear around the corner of the building, stares dully at the space they'd walked through. Time, he decides, for a swift personal sitrep. He'd liked Miller and has likely just killed her. He'd kind of liked Ed and definitely killed him. Hunter's doing his head in. He's jetlagged, achy, getting seriously scared of this EOS PROPHET business, and is fighting a slew of silent, increasingly insistent cravings.

It's not optimal. He sets off on an aimless walk, staring for most of it at the few inches of asphalt or grass around his feet. Then he sulks his way to a local Denny's and eats his way through a Chicken Philly Melt, a double portion of fries, and a chocolate lava cake a la mode, which have the double benefit of upping his self-hatred and dulling the worst of the cravings to a level he thinks he'll be able to live with for a while.

He drags himself back to the Air Force Inn and throws himself full-length on his bed. He'd have a wank, but the surveillance van outside their window is a little off-putting; exhibitionism really isn't his thing. He doesn't want to think about why they've come here. So he stares at the ceiling and wonders what Adam and Hunter are doing. Decides, considering Adam's perpetual disinterest in having any kind of fun, that they're probably not having the dangerous sex he can't seem to stop imagining. He tells himself they're probably sitting in a room some-where comparing their respective knife and firearm collections, which, he realises gloomily, isn't any less libidinously confronting. *Fuck's sake, Sunil*, he tells himself. *Get over yourself.* He gets up, showers aggressively, opens his kit bag. Stares moodily at the terrible suit and shirt and tie that the Department of Defense saw fit to gift him with. Stretches out on his bed again, shuts his eyes.

What he wants and needs is sleep. But he can't get near it. He's remembering that last night in Tashkent, eleven months ago to the day. By virtue of who and what he is, he recalls every second with agonising fidelity. He doesn't want to, but he has no choice. The memory has found him and fallen on him entire.

They're in an old-style Soviet hotel, a vast brutalist hulk of stained geometric concrete that reminds Rao vaguely of a monumental Triscuit. Inside, dark, glossy wood and peeling corridors, light-deprived houseplants dying slowly by the lift doors. The city outside smells of lignite, salt, and woodsmoke, but inside the lobby all is bleach and turpentine, and Rao had felt a surge of grandiosity as they approached reception and agitated for a whole suite. Adam, to his surprise, had agreed. It turns out to be shabby and magnificent. Acres of brocade wallpaper, tired ornate chairs, chandeliers holding half-blown arrays of tiny bulbs.

Rao's never seen Adam drink like this. He's never seen Adam behave like this. He's rolled his shirtsleeves up, loosened his tie. He's eating ravenously, black bread and cheese and pickles and beetroot-stained Russian salad on a side table drawn up to the couch. He's found a pack of cards in a drawer, is playing with them between mouthfuls of food and shots of vodka. Rao draws near, fascinated. Adam looks up, still chewing.

"Adam, this is what I was talking about."

He swallows. "What?"

Rao waves a hand vaguely.

Adam grins. "That's a vodka answer. Try using words."

"Cards."

"Yes."

"What are you doing?"

"Just fucking around."

"Yes but . . ." Rao watches him. It's mesmerising.

"There are hundreds of different kinds of cuts," Adam says after a while. "Thousands. They all do the same thing. It's just the same as splitting the deck. Another kind of shuffle, always working towards random order. The whole idea of cards is that there's random order. It's the lie everyone agrees to."

"Everyone," Rao concurs, but he's not really listening. The cards, Adam's deft fingers, the peculiar combination of fluidity and decisiveness in the way both move: he's getting a little lost in it.

"Everyone. So you have a thousand legitimate cuts, a thousand legitimate shuffles. For every legit one, there's a false one. So *this* is a false cut. But it looks like . . . *this*, which is a legitimate cut."

Rao nods. "Where did you learn this stuff, Adam?"

"Around."

"Just around?"

"Just around."

"Is that classified?"

"Everything about me's classified, Rao," Adam says, deadpan.

"Including me?"

Adam gives him a quick, glancing look. His eyes meet Rao's for a fraction of a second, get pulled away like they've been scalded. *What's that*, Rao wonders. He sits down on the other end of the couch, eyes on the ever-moving cards. Finally he works out what the look had meant.

"Yeah. Fair. I know you know."

"Know what?"

"I'm not a real agent. Thanks for not giving me perpetual shit about it, actually. I appreciate that."

Adam stills the cards in his hands.

"What are you talking about?"

"You know what I'm talking about. You practically said it. Definitely implied it. I'm not a real agent. It's bullshit. I'm only here because I can do tricks. What I am is a bit of kit to deploy. You know"—he waves a hand—"Geiger counter, navy-trained whale, Sunil Rao."

Adam shakes his head decisively. "No," he says. "That's not what you are."

"Adam, do me a favour. You should know by now I'm the world's most fraudulent asshole. I'm not a proper intelligence officer. Never did the induction. I wasn't a real art historian. I conned them all at

Sotheby's. I've never been anything real." This is vodka and he should shut up. He should stop talking right now. "And it goes all the way down. I've never felt properly Indian and I'm certainly not English. Not quite a man, but not a woman either. I'm just . . ." He sighs. "Ignore me. Ignore this. I'm drunk." But one more awful sentence crawls out of his mouth. "It's not that I don't fit in, it's not that bullshit. It's that I'm not . . . anything real. I mean, I'm just *not*."

Adam shrugs as easily as if Rao'd asked him about the weather outside. "You're not *not*. I'm an expert on *not*, Rao. You're *all*."

"Right. Care to enlighten me further, or is this full Adam koan shit?"

Adam looks at him like he's in dire need of remedial education. "You're like this pack of cards. You can pull any combination. It's all there. You carry all of them at once, but you don't have to show anyone shit unless you want to. You get to choose. You're lucky."

Rao is a little blindsided. That was a hell of a speech from Adam.

It was a hell of a speech, per se. He thinks about that "lucky" and what it might mean that Adam said it. But his head isn't clear enough. He shakes it instead, says, almost angrily, "What the fuck do you know?"

Adam laughs at that. Properly laughs. Another thing Rao's never seen before. There are *dimples*. "True," he says, reaching across for the bottle. "That's true."

A few hours later, Rao walks carefully into the bathroom and succeeds in taking a piss without getting any on the tiles. *Absolute triumph*, he thinks, awarding himself a small imaginary medal and a round of imaginary applause. Zipping himself up, he spots his wash bag on the shelf beneath the mirror and remembers. Snickers out loud. Walks back into the lounge. Marches up to the couch that Adam is sprawled across in a way that in literally any other individual Rao would consider bewitchingly dissolute.

"It's time," Rao says.

Adam cracks an eye. "What?"

Rao brandishes his eye pencil. "I told you I'd get you someday. Today is that someday. It's today."

"It's not day. It's three in the morning."

"Don't deflect, Rubenstein. Take this like a man."

Adam sits up. He assumes an expression of intense resignation, then picks up his glass from the table, drains it, slams it back down. "Ok. Alright," he says. "Ok, do it. *Do it.*"

Rao's taken aback. "It's not like I'm going to throw a punch, for fuck's sake. Stop psyching yourself up, you complete and utter lunatic."

Adam, Rao suspects, has just worked out that this joke is not entirely at his own expense, because a flicker of something like wonderment crosses his features before they turn distinctly apprehensive.

"Don't worry, it's hypoallergenic," Rao assures him, waving the pencil, and this is sufficient to start Adam laughing. So much so that Rao's fighting a losing battle to grip his face to keep it still enough to apply the pencil. "Fucking keep still," Rao mutters. "Stop it, this is *serious.*" They're both cracking up now, and Rao's squinting in the low light of the room, focusing on where he's going to apply these bloody wings. Adam blinks. *He has stupidly long eyelashes*, Rao thinks. Stupidly. And his eyes are. Yeah. And that's when Rao jettisons his hypothesis that whatever sexuality Adam possesses has been entirely sublimated into government-sponsored violence. Forgets the eyeliner in his hand. Forgets himself. Because it's obvious now that they both know what this is. Rao looks down at Adam's fractionally opened mouth and thinks, *Fuck. Yeah. Why not.* He shifts his grip on Adam's jaw minutely and meaningfully, leans in, and is so buoyed on the longing he knows Adam is feeling, too, he expects Adam to meet him first.

Adam does not.

Adam flinches.

He looks away. He pulls back. Rao gets the full, awful trinity. He even raises a hand to Rao's chest. Doesn't touch him, just keeps it there between them. Rao looks down at it. It's trembling violently. Looks back up. Adam's eyes are a mess of refusal and panic.

"Fuck," he begins. He'd been so *sure.*

"It's fine," Adam says.

"Adam—"

"It's *fine.*"

CHAPTER 26

Wasn't nightmares that woke him. He's too old for those, and he never remembered having them anyway, even when he was told that's what they were. And it's not that he's away from home. There are kids in his class who still have problems with that, which is pretty fucked up, considering. He woke up because it's hot. The air in the RV is stifling because the generator's been off all night. He breathes in the dark, knows he has to get outside. He has to do it without waking his parents, but that is not going to be a problem because they're sleeping in the bedroom at the far end of the vehicle, and he is very, very good at being quiet. He gets dressed lying on the mattress, picks up his boots, and pads to the door. Eases the mechanism of the door catch open, slips outside, softly closes the door behind him, and releases the handle back into place so slowly there are moments in the process that feel like falling through space, like they'll go on forever. Outside, he puts on his boots, laces them tight, starts walking toward the shore.

It was a long drive to get here. His dad had been in the kind of mood that was red flags from the start. Kept talking about how great this place was, how much they'd love it, how it was a real American Riviera. He didn't need to listen too hard to what his dad was saying, because there wasn't any instruction in it and besides, his mom was listening, and she was starting to make the very blank face she makes when she's bracing herself against bad things. He knows what that face means because he makes it, too, sometimes. He didn't know until he caught sight of himself in a window once, and there it was.

She'd pretended to sleep most of the way. She always does. She's never really asleep. He'd sat between them in the front, and after a couple of hours he had felt her hand grip his. Secretly he was glad, because his dad's mood had been getting tighter by the mile, and he'd tried to look more interested in everything, and that had worked for a while but then there was a song on the radio that he hadn't heard before and hearing it was a bit like the feeling of falling asleep, like being hypnotized. It sounded English, and he thinks it was called *golden brown* but that could have been the chorus, and his father noticed him listening to it, and looked at him sideways and said, *You like this song? You know it's about foreign women?* Which made him suspect he shouldn't like it at all, and he knew that silence would be the wrong response but so would talking, so he nodded and said *mmm* and that's when his mom had taken his hand. Not for too long, and he didn't look down to where her fingers gripped his, but out at the shoulder of the interstate instead, where the palms were fat and dusty and sneakers tied in pairs were thrown over wires.

When they arrived, it wasn't what he'd expected. It wasn't what his dad had expected. The place was a ruin. People had been leaving for years, the only other guy at the RV park said. He was here to make a documentary, and he had told them about the history, everything about what had happened. He thought it was funny that they had come here for a weekend away, and his dad's face when the guy laughed was something he's trying to forget. But he remembers very clearly wanting to take the guy down and hurt him very badly, knowing there was no way he was going to try it. Nothing happened. Nothing was going to happen. This weekend was like a lot of weekends. It was going to be a thing to get through, is all.

It's a long walk. The sky's already lighter. He can make out birds wheeling and flapping overhead, hear them squawking. The air smells bad. Like rotten eggs. Sulfurous. He knows he'll get used to it. Takes deep breaths to make that happen quicker. When he gets close to the lake, each step sinks into something that's not sand and not dirt. Something in between. Sludgy and crunchy, like sugary cookie dough. The stuff doesn't get any deeper as he nears the waterline, but when he looks back over his shoulder and sees a dim trail of his own footprints pointing to where he stands there's a little kick of adrenaline in his stomach. He turns his back on the evidence of his movements. Keeps walking. Soon he's treading on what feels like scattered, grainy drifts of white gravel. But it's not stones. He crouches and picks up half a handful of the stuff. It's dry and light, and he stares in puzzlement at the heap on his palm before he figures out that he's looking at fish bones.

He looks at his watch. He's been out here a while. He knows he should be back at the RV.

He's not. He's here.

He brushes what looks like salt off the wood of a section of wrecked jetty and sits on it, facing the lake. After a while he pulls a packet of his dad's illicit smokes and a box of UCO matches from his pants pocket. He lights a Lucky Strike looking out at the water.

The sun's rising behind the hills on the farther shore. The sky is blue, then pale blue, then lemon, then gold. There are seagulls flying everywhere, and he sees, as the light increases, that the shapes on the palisades far out in the shallows might be pelicans.

He sits there and looks at the water glowing under the low California sun and thinks about this lake. How it was a mistake. How some engineers messed up a river diversion, and until they managed to stop the flow, all this water had poured into this place. And now there's nowhere for it to go. How it's full of salt and poison getting more and more concentrated under the sun. First all the fish will die, and then the birds, and the shoreline will shrink as the lake dries up, and one day everything in front of him will be desert again, dust. He looks at the water. Its surface is completely still, like a pool of mercury colored blue and gold from the sky above, and as he looks at it something happens. It's another stab of adrenaline in his stomach, but this one is joined by a weird creep up his spine.

He looks at it and realizes he loves it.

He loves it. It's showing him that everything will end. Everything he knows, all of it will disappear one day. It's the weirdest thing to think, because it makes him feel calm. It might be the most calming thought he has ever had, and he knows he hasn't seen much of the world, not yet, but he also knows this: this is the best, the most perfect place in it.

CHAPTER 27

Adam looks up at the night sky after Rao makes them stop so that he can take a piss around the side of a closed store. Hunter sighs and rests against the wall with him, leaning forward to swing a look at where Rao is. "He's a tactical liability," she mutters. Adam smiles a little. He knows what she means.

"You get used to him."

Hunter snorts. Offers him a cigarette. Shakes her head when he declines. "I don't think I want to. Seems like a hell of a lot of wasted effort."

"Wasted effort."

"Sure. I don't have the same patience as you do for these babysitting gigs, Rubenstein. I don't get off on this like you do."

"It's not like that." *That's not entirely true*, he hears himself think in Rao's voice. Watching Rao return from bar restrooms wiping his lips, hustling pool badly for attention, having to roll with the verbal punches whenever Rao is in a bad mood: none of that feels good. He doesn't crave it the way Hunter thinks he does. He knows it's not simple. Is fully aware that his role in this partnership doesn't allow for his fulfillment. But that doesn't bother him. It never has. He's not an idiot. He knows his odds in life. Knows that dedication doesn't have to be a two-way street for it to mean something.

"He's asleep," Hunter observes, leaning forward again. The smoke rises from her hand into Adam's face. He doesn't hate it. He should quit. He's quitting. He's not smoking right now. But the smoke is a nice bonus. "He fell asleep pissing against the wall."

Adam closes his eyes briefly. "He does that."

"How the fuck."

"He puts his forehead against the wall and closes his eyes. Either he falls over or he wakes up. Several points to inner ear function in that case. But it doesn't take longer than thirty seconds," he explains. Hunter stares at him, incredulous.

"How come you're always there to clean up this mess?" she asks. She must know the answer, but she wants to know if Adam does too. If he will say it out loud.

"I have nothing to say about that," he tells her. It doesn't work.

"How long are you going to do this? Have you thought about that? Because there's going to be one night when you aren't around to stop him from drowning in his own vomit."

Adam frowns. People get Rao wrong. "That won't happen."

"Rubenstein." Hunter sounds genuinely disappointed in him. Adam flips her the bird. She grins, but only briefly. "I'm serious. You're not usually the one to get suckered by optimism."

"This isn't optimism. This is being in possession of all the facts. You aren't aware of the intricate details related to the subject," Adam says simply, flatly, honestly. "You have surface intel, which only gives you an idea of a fraction of the field."

"Don't give me jargon just because you're cornered."

"Don't decide that I'm cornered just because you don't like the answer you're getting."

She looks at Rao against the wall. "By your count, he'll wake up soon."

"Or fall over," Adam reminds her.

"I know you see things to the end," Hunter sighs. "I know that 'do or die' is the Rubenstein credo. But I've never seen you like this about anything but work."

It's not an unfair observation, but she's a little off the mark. She thinks that he's dedicated to the cause, whatever that might be, once he has an objective. An airman down to the marrow. Adam knows that's not exactly an untrue observation, but being a good airman, being reliable, aiming to always stay standing until the last, that isn't dedication. That's inevitability.

He was always going to enlist. That was going to happen from the day he was born.

"I thought Rao was work," Adam deflects. "Babysitting."

"That's not what this is, Rubenstein."

Rao's head falls back by an inch and he startles awake with a snore. "Fuck," he mutters.

The conversation ends there. Adam's not sure if he's relieved. Hunter's known him best since they went through basic together, and she still doesn't really get it. She might not ever get it. Adam doesn't even know where he could start.

Rao likes to say that he's a tool in a box, like a James Bond gadget on the belt of international intelligence agencies, and he's accused Adam of being the same more than once. But he's never been right about that. Adam's only a gun to point at a problem. Even holstered, he's meant to be dangerous, and that's how he's always been used, from intelligence to target elimination to babysitting. He's a weapon—and a simple one.

Nobody's ever used a gun to finesse a complex situation.

"I don't know what to tell you, Hunter," he says. Makes his way over to Rao before he falls backward. "Rao just knows where to point me."

"Doesn't strike me as a man with a plan. Now you're saying he gives you direction?"

"That's not what I said."

"That's what I heard."

"Barely my problem," Adam responds and gets flipped off again. There's no malice on Hunter's face, just exhaustion. It's been a long night for all of them and, with some luck, maybe she's done trying to talk sense into him, whatever that means to her.

He gets an arm around Rao's waist and braces, pulling him from the wall. "Come on, Rao. Put your dick away."

"What? Oh. Right you are, Adam."

*

Rao wakes and immediately wishes he hadn't.

He wakes because Adam's turned on his antisurveillance radio, and right now KMFC: The Bullshit—or whatever the local station is called— is serving up Rick Astley. Rao feels so atrociously unwell he wants to die. No. No, he wants Rick Astley to die first, and he wants to watch.

Then he wants to die.

"You're alive," Adam says.

"Jury's out," he mutters. He tries to turn to bury his face in the pillow—it's appallingly bright in here—but the attempt is far too challenging, and he comes perilously close to throwing up. "For the love of god, close the curtains," he whispers. "Or shoot me."

Rao can't see Adam through the sickening patterns on the back of his eyelids, but he hears the ratcheting drag of a single curtain being drawn, then the sounds of a series of objects landing on the bedside table like heavy artillery at point-blank range. He groans.

"Tylenol, water, coffee. We have breakfast in forty minutes. Hunter's shipping out."

"Fuck. Forty minutes."

"I factored in the hangover."

"Can't you just leave me here to die?"

"I'm not doing that, Rao."

Through the near-opaque walls of his hangover, Rao slowly comes to understand there is a bit of an *atmosphere* at breakfast. He keeps his head as still as he can, chews slowly on dry toast, and listens to Hunter and Adam talking. In his fragile condition, Adam is the more bearable. His voice is lower, and he doesn't keep shooting him glares. Hunter doesn't like him, does she? Which isn't fair, considering.

Rao thinks about it a little more, decides it might be fair, considering.

"So," he says to her. "Last night."

She fixes him with a look that's remarkably like the pins entomologists use to stick insects onto plywood.

"Do you remember what happened?" she says.

Adam frowns. "Hunter . . ."

"No, I don't," Rao lies. "And I'm blissful in my ignorance, thank you."

She turns to Adam. "I'm going to tell him."

"Why?"

"Why wouldn't I, Rubenstein?"

"Fuck's sake," Rao breathes. "Listen. Could I finish my coffee first?"

"Finish it while I'm talking. I don't care."

"Patently obvious, yes."

She sits back, folds her arms. "I think we lost you during the pool game. You don't remember that? That's when you started to get messy, anyway. Told us that you were going to hustle some poor assholes. Ended up draping yourself on the first dude that would let you. Loudly asked him if he wanted to follow you to the restroom."

"You called it the loo at the time," Adam interjects, the fucking turncoat.

"Devil's in the details, Adam. *Cheers.*"

"You instantly ignore this dude as soon as you emerge massaging your jaw and licking your lips, by the way," Hunter continues. "Obnoxious."

"Sounds like he got the best result from the night, quite frankly."

"Then you spent an hour talking about, quote unquote, *amazing* things you've done while high. There was some shit about being on acid and discovering money?"

"Inventing the concept of currency from first principles," Rao supplies. There's something wrong with his voice as he speaks. No. It's Adam. Adam just said exactly the same sentence he just said at exactly the same time he said it.

Hunter's world-weariness increases by several tonnes.

"Jesus," she says.

"Got to that one, did I? You could've stopped me," Rao points out, reasonably.

She tilts her head at Adam. "That fucker wouldn't let me."

"It's better to let it play out," Adam says very seriously.

"I didn't go on about how I'm a god, did I?" Rao can't forget things, but sometimes he mislays memories on purpose.

"Do you want me to lie to you?"

"Fuck me," Rao groans.

"*That* came up a few times too. I'll tell you now what I told you then—"

"Adam," he whispers.

"Sorry, Rao."

"You're not my type," Hunter finishes.

"What *is* your type? You'll find me very accommodating when there's decent incentive."

"Shut up. You told us about how you were a god among men, alright. For some reason *this* is what made you go to pieces. What the fuck was that about?"

"I mentioned my mum?" Rao sighs, turning to Adam.

"You asked me not to tell her that you called yourself a god."

"I've asked that of you before, haven't I?"

"Haven't told her yet."

"Deeply appreciated, love."

Hunter's gaze has now turned baleful, getting on for full Medusa. She's not finished.

"We had to shepherd your ass out of the bar and back to the inn."

"*In?*" Rao frowns.

"Hotel."

"Ah."

"And that took fucking forever. You fell asleep pissing, at one stage. It's not funny, you shitheads."

"Hunter," Adam says, with the barest ghost of a grin, "I think we're done here."

"I'll tell you when we're done," she snaps.

"Yes, ma'am."

"Fuck you, Rubenstein."

They glare at each other. For a teetering moment, Rao thinks they're going to kick off. But then Adam snorts with open amusement and Hunter dissolves into giggles. "Were you fucking with me?" Rao demands irritably.

"I absolutely was not," Hunter says. "You were a pain in the ass. If you'd—"

"Hunter, you remember Tampa?" Adam cuts in.

What happened in Tampa?

Hunter rolls her eyes. "It was once."

"Last night was once."

"It felt longer than one night. Fuck." She shakes her head, turns to him. "Rao?"

She used my name, he thinks, alarmed. "Hunter?"

"When you've gotten over yourself, you're gonna put yourself on Flores's case, right? Find out where he is with your magic powers. I'm on leave for a while now visiting my folks, so keep me in the loop."

"Where are they?"

"Alaska."

"No they aren't."

"No, they aren't. Your battle buddy's got Flores's photo. Call me. No. Don't call me. He can call me."

At the door of the breakfast place she gives Adam a highly military hug that lasts, Rao thinks, a good four seconds longer than military hugs ought. She slaps his back to break it. "As you were, fuckhead," she says. Adam grins. *Dimples.*

Then she turns to Rao. She's hard to read, Hunter, but judging by how his skin prickles as she stares at him, under all that hostility and humour is someone truly terrifying. He's not going to get a hug. Possibly a punch in the mouth. But after looking him up and down, mouth downturned, she finally extends a hand. He shakes it firmly and is about to say something suitably lighthearted when the words turn to ash in his throat. He's met her eyes. Seen deep, deep resignation in them. *Ah*, he thinks, slowly. *She doesn't think I'm going to survive this.*

CHAPTER 28

Before

A dam had stopped the vehicle to let a small flock of turkeys cross the road, skinny, long-legged things shepherded by a small girl in a dress that brushed the dust. Rao was oblivious, slumped low in the passenger seat with both feet on the dash, continuing the complaint he'd started twenty minutes earlier. "Just because you don't eat, Adamski, doesn't mean other people don't get to. Come on, you must be hungry?"

Adam assured Rao again that he was not. But all this was moot. He'd diverted their route to the nearest town as soon as Rao started needling about lunch. He parked the UAZ in a leafy, shaded street. Explained that he needed to stretch his legs, so he'd come into the market too.

"Feel free," Rao muttered. "But I can buy food without getting murdered, you know. I do it all the time."

"Only takes once," Adam observed.

"Is that so? You're like the worst maiden aunt in existence. I keep expecting you to tell me to wear clean underwear, just in case."

"In case of what?"

"Doesn't matter. World War Three. Are you coming or not? It's a very exciting experience, watching me buy lunch. You won't want to miss it."

Sun-aged melons, bunches of greens, apples in piles, bowls of nuts, dried grapes, ash-coated apricot pits. Birds that hopped about his feet, chirruping through Persian pop, woodsmoke, pale-yellow sun. Adam kept his distance, but after establishing there was no sign of a local tail, he walked closer to Rao, overheard him telling the woman behind the

bread stall that she was so beautiful he'd forgotten what he was here
to buy. She threw her head back and laughed at him, and he grinned.
She told him he'd better be wanting bread, because that's all she had,
this being a bread stall, but it'd cost him more if he threw out compli-
ments like that to a woman in her sixties—one married at that—and
he arched his eyebrows at her in mock horror. Another line, this one in
Uzbek, not Russian, conspiratorial and low. She laughed again, called
him an idiot.

Rao's so dumb, Adam thought. Stupid. Look at him. The angle of
Rao's jaw, the curl of his shoulders, the threads of silver at his temples,
how he used his hands to help him speak, the shape of his mouth as
he did. All familiar. But somehow not. Adam wondered, absurdly, if
he'd ever seen Rao before. Then stood there, totally nonplussed. For a
moment, he'd forgotten why they were here. Not just in this market.
All of it. The tactical knives, the 9 mil at his back. The most reassuring things he owns. The express weight and presence of what he's for.
But now the knives and pistol felt entirely insubstantial, like they were
made of water. Hands would slip right through. He felt his heart contract, looking at Rao in the smoke, in the lemon-yellow morning light,
staring at Rao's mouth as he spoke. And realized the fact, all at once.

Oh, he thought, astonished. *I'm in love with him.*

"You're being bloody quiet, even for you," Rao observed, back on
the road. "You're not sulking because of the maiden aunt thing? Get
over it, Adam. I've said much worse."

"I'm not sulking, Rao. I'm driving."

I'm compromised.

"Uh-huh."

Adam glanced down at the bags stuffed into the footwell around
Rao's legs, at the two plate-sized rounds of lepeshka on his lap. Stamped,
patterned decorations like needle marks, tiny black seeds scattered over
glossy crusts.

"Break off some of that bread for me?"

"You *were* hungry. I knew it."

"You don't know shit, Rao."

"Shut up, you tosser," Rao said amiably, tearing him a section, handing it over. "I got cheese, roast chicken, samsas, gumma, pickles, fruit. Just let me know what you want when you want it."

"I'm all set," Adam said, biting into the piece, pulling a strip away, chewing it. He wasn't hungry.

The bread was good. He hated it. Kept his eyes ahead as he swallowed, staring as far down the road as the haze permitted, to where the Silk Route disappeared in a chaos of light and dust.

CHAPTER 29

Back in their hotel room, Rao whistles as he unfolds the map.
"I've not done this for ages. Have you got it?"

"What?"

"The photo Hunter gave you. We've been through this before, love. There are other Danny Floreses; the name isn't a rigid designator. Seeing a picture makes it easier."

Rao takes the photo, looks at it. Moves it a little farther from his face, hoping Adam doesn't start his usual "you need glasses" routine. It's a matte 4 x 6 print of a pine-panelled room, and it's a room in Afghanistan, because the man front and centre is wearing a pakol and a grey wool waistcoat over a white shirt. No. It's Pakistan. He's got a tawny, spec-ops fashionista beard, and he's giving the camera a half smile that doesn't reach anywhere near his eyes.

Flores. Ok. Rao lays the photo down, mutters at the map spread across the table before picking it up and folding it once along its vertical axis. "He's not in the Rockies. Shame. Always wanted to visit." He ladders his index finger up the sheet, dropping it on panel by creased panel, asking each one if Flores's current position is within its bounds. "Ah," he says eventually. "He's in Denver. Denver-*ish*," he peers. "Aurora?"

"Aurora."

"Yeah. Ah! That'll be why it's EOS."

"What?"

"Aurora's the Roman goddess of sunrise, Adam. Eos is the Greek goddess of sunrise."

"I know that, Rao. It won't be why. Project nicknames are generated automatically."

Rao ignores that after whispering it to himself, pushing past the usual weird resistance he feels when he's retesting one of Adam's statements and finding it's true. Rao scoots his fingers about, zeroing in on a location.

"Have you ever been lost?" Adam asks suddenly.

"Emotionally?"

"Rao."

"If I know where I have to get to or I've someone or something to find, no. How long will it take us to get to Aurora?"

"Who's driving?"

"Fuck off." Rao is an excruciatingly slow driver.

"Just over an hour. Hour and a quarter. But we should move base. I'll get us a motel."

"Yeah, good plan. Let's go full Bates. Find one with those vibrating beds."

"Magic Fingers."

"Yes, Adam. That's what I have, or so I've been told. Many, many times. Right. Fire up your laptop, we're taking this to Google Earth."

"So, Flores is in this block of buildings across the road from Buckley Air Force Base," Rao concludes a little while later, gazing at the screen, at the aerial view of long shadows falling from rooftops across a parking lot before losing coherence in a mass of summer foliage.

"That's Space Command," Adam says.

"You think he was retraining as an astronaut?"

"Unlikely."

"It was a joke, Adam. Let's find out who owns this place." He googles the address and blinks. "Fucking hell. Lunastus-Dainsleif BioScience."

"Huh," Adam says. He doesn't sound surprised.

Lunastus-Dainsleif, Rao thinks. Raytheon for the new millennium, the RAND Corporation in hipster suits. Big data and defense contracts, fingers in all the pies.

"So what's the plan?" he asks.

"We walk in."

"That's a terrible plan."

"We don't have time to recruit assets and we're in no position to SWAT team it."

"Adam," Rao says patiently. "They won't let us in."

"You can brute force sufficient intel to get us in."

"Right. Then they shoot us. Or dose us and make us make Furbys."

Adam's silence isn't reassuring. "What would you make?" Rao asks. "If you got, *you know.*"

"What?"

"Dosed with this stuff."

"I've got no idea."

Rao narrows his eyes. "A knife."

Adam rolls his. "I'm not nostalgic about knives, Rao. They're kit."

"Bullshit. I've seen your knives. They're a bit flashy for kit."

"They're not flashy."

"They bloody are. Ok, not a knife. One of your airplane models."

"Stay on target, Rao."

"Al-most there."

Adam closes his eyes for a moment. "Give me my laptop. I'll book a car and a hotel."

Rao throws himself upon his bed, flings the back of one hand theatrically over his eyes, and lets out a self-pitying groan. For the last forty minutes he's been generating statements out loud and ascertaining the truth value of each one. He's found out that Flores is alive but incapacitated by the substance, along with fourteen others in that building, all but three of whom are ex–Special Forces. Volunteers.

After that, Adam handed him a pen and paper and asked him to run through the alphabet to find the name of the guy at the top of the hierarchy on-site, who happens to be someone named Montgomery. Adam intends to tell whoever this Montgomery turns out to be that they've come to conduct a spot check on project progress. Drop the words "EOS PROPHET."

Rao's not happy with this plan. "With a bit of time and a lot of paper, we can just find out the names and roles of everyone involved in the project," he'd pointed out quite reasonably, because it's fucking obvious that's what they should do. "You know, now you've decided I'm allowed to."

"Names don't get Flores out," Adam had said tightly. "We need to go in."

Rao had struggled with this statement. Adam's mission prep has always been infinitesimally granular, and it's disturbing how ready he is to go in on such limited intel. *Must be because of Miller*, he thought, remembering the rage on Adam's face. Or did he call Miller's boss and get explicit orders while Rao was having a smoke outside? Maybe. More likely.

He yawns. He's ok. Tired but ok. Agitated the way he always is after a run but ok. His hangover has been lessened by time, water, and Tylenol, but its diminishment has exposed all his self-recriminations, and those are far trickier to handle. All day he's been telling himself that last night's relapse was a one-off, but Rao's a past master at lying to himself. He's going to do better. He had been. He has to.

Adam walks back in from the bathroom. Rao hadn't noticed he'd gone, and startles slightly. "How're you doing?" Adam asks.

"Headache's gone, but my brain's leaping about like an ant on a hotplate." He waggles his brows. "Might go back to that bar and start a fight."

Adam snorts. "That won't be happening."

"You punch me in the face, then."

"Rao. Please."

"Adam, *please*."

"I'd suggest we raid the minibar, but I think you already did that."

"Leave off. I get it. I went off on one. I'm not going to apologise."

"Wasn't asking you to," Adam says, pulling the chair from the desk to sit. He leans back and folds his arms; there's the faintest suspicion of a smile. Rao closes his eyes to shut it out.

"I was really awful though, yeah?"

"No. Hunter just doesn't know you. I had a pretty good night, considering."

"Considering what?"

"Nothing, never mind."

Rao's not going to let *that* lie. He props himself up on an elbow, fixes Adam with an enquiring eye.

"Fine," Adam acquiesces. "If you weren't giving me shit last night, then Hunter was. I'm not used to pincer manoeuvre ass kicking."

Rao grins. "I'd never be able to kick your arse, and I think it's alright if we both admit that."

"Mm. There's kicking someone's ass and then there's giving a friend an ass kicking."

"Ah," Rao says sagely. "It's all becoming clear now, Adamski. So what was Hunter's problem? You don't look at her during?"

"We're not a thing, Rao."

"But you have, though. Haven't you?"

Adam's mouth twitches. "Wow. No. Extremely no. She's a friend, and that's it. I'm not her type, and she's very much not my type."

"Out of your league?"

"Hunter's out of everyone's league."

"Alright, alright. So what was the problem, then?"

"I don't think you want to know."

"Fuck off, Adam. Stop being a wanker."

Adam shrugs minutely. "She thinks that you're taking advantage of my patience."

Rao laughs at that. "Fuck right the fuck off. Are you serious?"

Adam's covert smile hovers on the edge of being in the clear. "You asked," he says.

"Your *patience*?"

"Not her exact words, but yes."

"Does she *know* you?"

"Yeah, she does. Apart from you, better than anyone."

Rao's not sure he heard that right. He doesn't want the moment to pass unmarked. "I'm touched," he says eventually.

Adam frowns. "Don't."

"No, I'm being serious. You know I always sound like this, love. Can't help the sarcastic lilt to my tone. Social camouflage at school. I was surrounded by silver spoons, you know."

"Right. I know."

Liar, thinks Rao, amused. He can hear Crosby, Stills and Nash on the radio. Housekeeping in the corridor. The dopplering drone of transport planes outside. Adam's quiet, studying the floor.

"Would you believe me if I said that I feel similarly?" Rao offers.

"You don't have to do that."

"I don't *have* to do fuck all, Adam. Yet here I am, telling you the truth when I don't have to. Sober, too."

"Lucky me?"

"Fucking right. I trust you, you berk. Always have," he says. *No*, he thinks. *That's false.* "Well, not from the start, obviously, but it was a close thing. I had to, really. Trust you. If I didn't, I'd have gone mad with uncertainty and second-guessing. So that paid off, professionally speaking, pretty quickly. But, you know. Turns out I started trusting you as a friend as well."

"Rao—"

"I know, I know. Maybe I'm still hungover. All this sharing."

"You're not hungover. You'd be complaining more."

"That's true."

Adam looks up, eyes dark and serious. "I trust you, too, Rao."

"I should hope so."

"But I think you should be more careful about where you place your trust."

"Don't be a twat. I know you think I don't notice things, but I do."

"Do you."

"Yeah. I know it's always you that keeps us right when we're working. I'll wander off the second anyone gives me a chance, and I'll kick at any bastard who tries to stop me. But you manage it. Don't know anyone else who can do that. I see that, you know. I'm not an idiot."

"I know you aren't."

"You've probably kept me alive way more times than I know about, yeah? Just a hunch."

"There are some things you don't know about—"

Rao raises a hand. "Don't tell me, love. I really don't want to know about all the people who could have killed me if you hadn't been there.

I just hope you know that if I were of any use at all in that arena, I'd have returned the favour by now."

"That's not a concern."

"So what's this revelation?"

"It's not just your protection I've been tasked with when we're partnered, Rao."

"I know you're not just a bouncer with a gun because I was there, if you recall. You're a Defense Intelligence Agency officer. We met with your assets."

"Yes. But I've filled other roles." Rao waggles his brows. Adam rolls his eyes minutely. "*Roles,* Rao. Not *holes.*"

"Was that a joke?"

"You know I'm not capable of jokes."

"Right. I say that a lot, don't I?"

"I haven't noticed."

"Stop lying, Adam."

Adam is staring at the floor again. He's thinking. "What?" Rao asks eventually. "What is it?"

"Are we still sharing?"

"I'm rather hurt you feel you need to ask. You know me better than that."

"I guess I do. I just wanted to say . . ." Adam starts, then hesitates.

"Spit it out, love."

"I do my best not to lie to you."

"Nice to know. You have an unfair advantage, after all."

"Lies would mess things up."

"Without a doubt."

"Lies by omission are worse than making things up, though. Aren't they?"

Rao feels a soft flutter of foreboding. "What are you getting at?"

It takes Adam a while to speak. "I was contacted," he says, "by some people, a few times, for advice on how to get you to focus on a job."

"And when was this?"

"You were in Afghanistan."

The air is cold, suddenly. "Is that so," Rao says. Precise diction. Each word honed to a point.

"Yes."

"Go on."

"I let them know that you're happier when you indulge and that it was in their best interest to let it happen. That your limits with that kind of thing are higher than average."

"*Indulge.* Right. I see. Better drug tolerance than your average bear, is that what you told them?"

"Not word for word."

The coldness is now so searing Rao half expects his breath to fog the air when he opens his mouth and speaks. "No. You don't get to joke. I get to joke. You get to shut the fuck up."

Adam raises his eyes briefly to Rao's, drops them to his feet.

"Well? Go on. Tell me what you're not saying."

"They misused that information."

The ice inside Rao spreads and ramifies. Reluctantly, he recalls the details. Sees them for exactly what they were. What it was. How much of a setup it had been. And now the coldness inside him isn't cold anymore. It's molten metal, it's magma, incandescent, and Adam's still talking. "You said something about meeting a guy at a bar—"

"Yes, thank you. I'm capable of following the bread crumbs of shit you're trailing around. Fucking hell. This tall fucker, too. Did you tell them to use him too? Do you keep a file on my sexual preferences, Adam?"

"No. I don't."

"CIA, I suppose. Nice little chat. You'd be happy enough to open up to them. Everything's a job, right?"

"They already had the reports I wrote on you after our time in Central Asia."

"Reports. Fucking *wizard*, Adam! What else? Been calling my mum each time I piss on the toilet seat?"

"I—"

"Don't fucking answer that," Rao hisses. It's astonishing how difficult he's finding it to breathe. It hurts. Feels like he's inhaling scalding steam. It's astounding that he's not already beating six shades of shit out of Adam. He knows from his face he'd let it happen. And it'd be happening right now if it weren't so very hard to move.

"It's not just your advising the cunts it'd be a good idea to get me hooked on heroin, is it," he says slowly. "Your reports were why they wanted me in the first place."

Adam doesn't respond. Rao sits. Rao waits.

"Well?" he says finally.

"Well what? That's all of it."

"You're shitting me."

"That's all, I swear."

"No, you prick. You're not even thinking about apologising, are you?"

Nothing. Silence.

"You wrecked my life, Adam. And you can't even fucking apologise."

Rao watches Adam inhale and exhale slowly before he speaks. "What's done is done."

"There. That. The *arrogance* that oozes from you, deciding what matters from someone else's past just because you never pay in sanity or blood like the rest of us. And no one can see it, because you're so boring and god-awful to be around. But now—would you like to know what I have now?"

"You're going to tell me."

"Yes. That's true. I am going to tell you. I have my wits about me now. My eyes are open. I know what you are. You're broken on the inside and that's why I can't tell with you. There's nothing even remotely human in there. It's just all the missing parts from every other soldier on the roster jumbled into the cage you call a body. Under your shitty, *shitty* suits." He takes a deep breath, trembling with rage. "Say something," he says. "No. No. On second thought, don't say anything. Don't talk to me. Don't fucking look at me. Fucking *trust*. That's it. That's me taught."

They sit in silence.

"Rao," Adam says eventually. "You should go home."

"Home."

Adam nods:

"What the fuck would you know about home? Yeah, an evasive look, what a surprise. Home's a meaningless concept to a military shit like you. Also," he spits out, "home for me isn't a nice house in the country, if you recall? What's waiting for me back in Blighty is prison. Sorry. *Jail*."

"I'll talk to some people. Write up a report on—"

"Fuck you and your reports, Adam."

"Rao, please go home."

"Care to tell me how? I've got no wallet. I've been spending *your* cash. My passport's locked in *your* bag. What do you want me to do? Suck off a trucker for a ride to an airport, walk up to check-in, and beg?"

"I can get you to Andrews, then—"

"I'm not some faceless goon like some people. I can't just plug in at any charging station at any fucking military outpost, you cunt."

Rao killed Ed. He's probably killed Miller. All those poor bastards in Kabul. Guilt, sour, stacked high, wet paper in his chest. "I'm coming with you tomorrow," he continues, voice like it's held in a vice. "No matter how much you'd rather I didn't."

He is. Mainly because he's gripped by an inchoate desire to find whoever's responsible for this and beat the shit out of them. That would be satisfying. While it lasts. Considering the scale of this project, what it's already done, he has no illusions about how an encounter like that would end. Maybe Adam'll watch him die. Yeah. That works.

"Rao—"

"Conversation's over."

CHAPTER 30

His parents are gone for the day. They've been leaving him alone in the house since he turned ten. Now that he's nearing his fourteenth birthday it's barely worth mentioning he's home alone to a neighbor or anything. Nobody will poke their head in. It's fine. Only, that day, his aunt comes to visit.

"Got the house to yourself, kid?" she grins as she walks in. Her voice is scratchy from the cigarette she's just stubbed out on the porch. He smiles back at her but doesn't answer. He doesn't have to. She never minds if he is a little quiet or slow to warm up to a conversation. "Are we having a party or what?"

"They're back at midnight," he explains. He isn't going to have a party, but that wasn't the question she was asking.

"So you have some time to breathe, huh?" She nods.

Aunt Sasha gets it. He never has to say the words to her. She understands. She knows how sometimes being in his parents' house feels like being held underwater, and no matter how hard he wants to kick and buck against it, he is always going to go under. He tells her how his dad has needed to get out of the house. How he's said he's been having trouble looking at his son lately. How he needs to go out and be normal with his wife. Talk out some things.

Then he tells his aunt about the camp. About how some friends of his dad's had sent their sons there. Their sons were older than him, already enlisted now. Tells her how, when they came back, their dads kept talking about how disciplined they were.

He isn't sure why, but that's when he tells her about Mark.

He knows it'll be fine to tell his aunt about Mark. She's safe. He knows she'll always be safe. Whenever he's messed up, she's never cared.

And this? This was a big one. Several clicks past messing up. Mark, and being caught with Mark, wasn't messing up. It was a fuckup.

She listens to him like she always does. Asks him if Mark was his first kiss or just the first boy. First everything, he tells her. She smiles like she's proud of him. It doesn't matter how much he messes up. She always smiles at him like that in the end.

"What's the name of that camp?" she asks.

He doesn't know. He's never listened to the details because there's no point in fighting his dad about it, he tells her. She knows how he is.

She nods and speaks slowly. Carefully. "How about, instead of that camp, you come live with me for the summer?" They look at each other in silence. She shrugs. "Or forever. Get away from your dad. Get away from that camp."

He thinks about it. It's not a real option. He'll never be allowed. Doesn't get a chance to say that to his aunt before she starts talking again.

"We gotta get you out of here, kid," she says quietly. They're the only people in the house, but she speaks quietly like there might be someone listening. "All I need is a few days and I can get us tickets to somewhere else, anywhere else, and your mom and dad won't find us."

"He'll kill me," he tells her. It isn't a no.

"He's going to kill you if you stay. One way or another, kid, he's going to kill who you are. You know what that camp is, right?"

CHAPTER 31

The building is a smoked-glass corporate pile set behind trees just off the air base perimeter road. Rao steps out of the car, brushes the lapels of his stupid suit jacket, pulls at the knot of his tie. The parking lot is half empty. Movement catches his eye. A vulture, flying past the mirrored facade of the topmost floors, reflection following it tilting and flickering frame to frame to frame. He stares at the bird's double until it winks out of existence, then shifts his eyes to the living vulture as it flexes its wings and soars higher.

"Rao."

"What."

"You ready for this?"

Rao hunches his shoulders, starts walking towards the doors.

Reception is a built guy in a black shirt whose sternocleidomastoid muscles are so outsized that when he opens his mouth Rao half expects him to ask him how much he can press.

"Good morning," he says. "How can I help you, gentlemen?"

"We're here for Montgomery," Adam replies.

"Misters Rubenstein and Rao?"

Credit to the asshole, but Adam doesn't blink. He nods. When reception guy looks down at his desk, he shoots Rao a tense look. It's a question. Rao doesn't dignify it with a response. Maybe they'll both get bullets in their heads once they're through those shining walnut doors. He doesn't fucking care.

Reception guy pushes a confidential visitor book across the desk and Rao watches Adam print in capitals across the black panel that says: WRITE YOUR NAME HERE. When Adam offers him the pen, he doesn't take it. Waits until it's laid back down on the page before grabbing it and filling out the form. When the passes are slid across the desk, Adam picks them up.

"Take a seat," built guy says. "I'll call him now."

They sit.

Adam's going to say something. Rao waits for it with infinite weariness. When it comes, it's even more absurd than he'd predicted. Even more maddening.

"Does this feel right to you?"

"Now that's important, is it? Suddenly my feelings on the matter are important."

"I'm serious. They know our names. We just walked in."

"No shit."

"This is weird, Rao. You should—"

"If you finish that sentence I will honest to fuck break your nose. Leave it. Shut up."

They sit in silence for another six minutes until a harassed-looking white man in his late fifties with close-cropped receding hair and wire-rimmed glasses walks through the doors into the foyer. His smile is speculative and hopeful: the kind Rao's always read as hoping for a punch in the face.

"Hi. Welcome," he says, opening his hands. "Look, I was given your names, but I wasn't told much about this visit, so I don't have a working brief—"

"Well, we've only just been brought on board," Rao says and shudders. The unexpected truth of that statement sets up a runaway physiological panic. He collects himself with difficulty. "We're here for a site tour, a rundown of the project history, and a progress report, if you have time."

"Sure. There's time." Montgomery smiles. "Dr Rhodes is managing day-to-day. She's our clinical research associate." He looks at his watch. "Let's go to the boardroom, I'll get you up to speed, and then we can head down to the clinical floor."

It's the worst boardroom Rao has ever seen. Futuristic art deco lit in Cherenkov blue and cotton candy pink, it's like a team at Industrial

Light and Magic had got fucked up on K and designed a grotto for a cruise ship.

"Wonderful, isn't it?" Montgomery enthuses.

"It's impressive," Rao agrees.

The vast glass tabletop rests on cubes of crushed automobiles. It's awful. The coffee brought to it by an urgent young man with pomaded hair is, however, sensational. Rao pops a Godiva chocolate in his mouth, then another. Glances at Adam. He's being worse than fucking useless. Rao might as well have brought a Care Bear and propped it on the table opposite him. Would have been more fun to look at.

Montgomery's eyes dart from Adam to Rao and back again. He looks down at the space in front of him as if expecting an agenda to magically appear. "Right," he says. "Yes. I don't know how much you—"

"Assume we know nothing. Start at the beginning."

"Ok. Yes. Twenty-two months ago a materials lab at Duke University synthesized a novel high-temperature superconductor. Shortly afterward, there was an incident. An outbreak of psychological instability. Started when one postdoc became convinced he'd lost something important under the refrigerator in the break room and kept pulling it out to look underneath it."

"Did he find it?"

"There wasn't anything there. He wouldn't leave the fridge alone. EMTs got called and they had to sedate him to get him home. The PI didn't come in the following morning because she'd spent the previous night throwing all the furniture in her bedroom out of the windows into the yard. Said she needed to re-create her childhood bedroom. They had to sedate her too. One of the lab technicians vanished. Wyoming state troopers picked him up nine days later on a ranch near Sheridan, dehydrated and delirious, raving about how he was a cowboy. They're all still unable to work."

"How unable?" Rao asks.

Montgomery swallows. His professional expression shifts to something more haunted. "The tech still thinks he's a cowboy, and the PI's marriage collapsed. Psychologically, she's regressed to a seven-year-old. They're both doing ok, though, considering."

"Are they," Rao says. "What about the postdoc?"

"He's not doing so well. Stopped speaking. Doesn't eat. Has to be tube fed. And he's still trying to look for what he thinks he's lost. He's—"

"DOD flagged the lab," Adam interjects.

"Well, yes." Montgomery looks at Adam. "Turned out there was a thin film of an unknown substance on the sample in the vice. Defense considered it a potential battlefield incapacitant. You with them? Thought so. I can tell. And you"—he turns to Rao—"I mean, you're a creative. Lunastus, right?"

Rao smiles thinly, reaches for another chocolate. "Very recent hire."

"And Defense reached out to us." Montgomery gives Rao a shy, conspiratorial grin. "You know how Lunastus-Dainsleif was a CIA start-up. A natural home for a project like this. We put materials scientists and neuroscientists on the case, looking at the structure of the substance and its affective mechanisms. We got some results. Then . . ."

"Then?"

Montgomery frowns. "It started growing."

"Growing?"

"Yeah. It increased in volume. Also in complexity. It's still doing that, actually. But how and what it used—uses—to polymerise, we've not yet been able to determine. And the effect it has on those exposed to it, that's changed too. Early iterations, exposed subjects got obsessed with things they'd lost or thought they'd lost. Later, they stopped getting upset about things they'd lost—"

"And started making them," Adam says.

Montgomery nods.

"How?" Rao says.

Another frown. "What kind of how? There are—"

"The physics of it. Conservation of energy, for one thing. Where does the matter come from?"

"Yes. Well. Our physicists are pretty freaked out. No one's got any idea."

He's not lying.

"And now?" Rao says.

Montgomery's looking a little uncertain. "You're here for the mani-festation program?"

"We are. How's it going?"

"Mixed results," Montgomery says. "Look, it's an elegant idea. We want it to work as much as you do. We've recruited the right volun-teers and put them in a hostile VR environment. But so far, none have generated defensive weaponry. We expose them to a virtual firefight and they . . ."

"Make Care Bears and get incapacitated," Rao offers.

"Not all of them," Montgomery says.

"I think you should show us," Adam says.

The elevator doors are glossy Kubrick white and open into a roomy elevator with scuffed yellow walls. On the lower floor, Montgomery leads them down a corridor and through two sets of airlock doors into a clinical lab. A petite woman in a white lab coat turns to them as they enter.

Hello, Rao thinks. She looks almost exactly like the house rigger at a fetish club in Berlin he used to kick about in back in the day: the same simultaneously welcoming-and-unwelcoming demeanour, the same straight-cut auburn bangs, narrow chin, and wide grey eyes. She has the kind of face that gives nothing away and a mouth—wearing what he's pretty sure is Rouge Dior 999—that hovers disconcertingly close to a smile.

"Dr Veronica Rhodes, clinical research associate," she says. Cut glass RP. She extends a slender hand.

"Hi. I'm Rao."

She glances enquiringly at Montgomery.

"They're here for the manifestation program," he says.

Her mouth twists a little as she takes them in. Adam doesn't appear to interest her at all. Her eyes slide off him, return to Rao. Excellent judge of character, he decides. She looks at him curiously. When he finally takes her hand, she smiles warmly. It's like the sun's come out. Winter sun, for sure, but still Rao can feel it on his skin.

"A pleasure to meet you," she says. "What might your particular expertise be?"

Rao winks, lets her hand drop. "I'll tell you mine if you tell me yours."

Adam clears his throat. "He's an expert at spotting fakes and forgeries."

Rao's mood instantly plummets back to the pit it was in. Fucking Adam and his long history of cockblocks. *Fucking who asked you?* he thinks venomously.

Veronica's eyes haven't left his face. "How interesting," she says. The smile's still there, but a little fixed. The merest furrow has appeared on her otherwise perfect forehead. Rao's fascination ratchets up a few notches. She's a fake. He's just not sure what flavour yet. "And where does one learn to do that?"

"Long story. Spent a few years in fraud and attributions at Sotheby's."

She nods, turns to Adam. "What about you, Mr . . ."

"He can't talk about it," Rao says firmly.

"Can't or won't?"

"He's constitutionally unable."

"Defense," Montgomery explains.

"Ah. In which case I'll refrain from further questions. I'm about to head down to the ward," she says, gesturing to the door and smiling her pale sunlight smile. "Shall we start there?"

Rao's heart drops, skips, and swings into a too-rapid rhythm as they enter a large clinical space. Sallow light, lemon-scented air with an undertow of shit and bleach. Serried sounds of heart rate monitors, light refracted through pouches of saline. Submerged memories surface sharply: his stomach churns and sweat prickles under his arms. He takes a series of deep breaths, counts the beds. Thirty. Fifteen occupied.

Two nurses in white rush up. Veronica hastens forward and draws them a little away. Rao can't hear what she's saying—it's hurried, sotto voce—but from the looks on their faces as they leave the room, she's just told them to fuck off. She turns back to Rao and Adam, bringing one finger up to tuck one curled end of her fringe behind her ear, though not a single hair is out of place. The gesture is an obvious act, and Rao finds himself charmed by it. "We've had some issues with sores," she says. "Placing even a partial physical barrier between skin and object generates poor outcomes. But I'm happy to say that with our current regimen they're all doing very well."

In his peripheral vision, Adam is scanning the rows of unconscious bodies. He moves towards a bed, considering its occupant for a while before turning towards Rao. Rao, who's ignoring Adam so thoroughly that he knows exactly where in the room the fucker is and exactly what he's doing. He tries to listen to Veronica, but he can't parse what she's saying because Adam is looking at him and Rao knows that look. It's one of Adam's *significant* ones. He tries even harder to listen, hears the phrase "memory-reward coactivation," then gives in and joins Adam and his fucking significant looks.

"*What is it?*" he hisses, making his way over. Adam's looking down at the bed. It's Flores. Clean-shaven, a tube through one nostril, a bruise on his forehead, but Flores all the same. He's gripping something small in both hands, tucked tight under his jaw, and his expression is a rictus of such manifest bliss Rao feels a tug of unexpected envy.

"So, tell us about this one," Rao asks Veronica.

"It's a cassette tape. Specifically, a cassette single. 'On Our Own' by Bobby Brown, taken from the *Ghostbusters* soundtrack. It's one of the easier objects in terms of patient management."

"Not the object. The subject."

"Oh, yes. One of our first. Invalided ex–special ops, like most of our volunteers. This one"—she frowns—"Flores. We had high hopes for him."

High hopes. Rao's skin crawls. Flores is trapped in a moment of absolute emotional truth: looking at him makes Rao tight chested, like his lungs are packed with sugar. Dread ticks under his skin. He still wants to punch something, and even though that urge isn't going any-where while Adam Fucking Rubenstein is in the same room, he knows he has to focus. For Miller. For this faded Flores. For Ed. He drags his eyes away from the corner of the cassette pressing into Flores's reddened jaw, looks down at the bed to his left.

This patient's face is pressed against a wooden box. An old-style radio. Oatmeal grille cloth, a rose-and-gold dial. It's the source, Rao realises, of the soft, sibilant noises he's been hearing under the hum of climate control. Whispered squeals and hisses, snatches of barely audible voices, as if someone were searching for a station. He listens. The hissing whispers, the static highs and lows all loop back to their starting point every four breaths. He can't tell if the radio is syncing with the breathing, the breathing with the radio, or if there's any meaningful causal distinction to be made between breathing and radio at all.

"This one's notable," Veronica says. "It's a 1952 Raytheon tube radio. We've ascertained it wasn't a feature of the subject's childhood environment, so it doesn't possess the usual autobiographical affect. Our working theory is that this EPGO, that's Eos Prophet Generated Object, is the manifestation of a more generalized cultural nostalgia." Rao nods. The radio is a tiny version of Ed's diner. "And secondly, it's the first that's emitted sounds."

Adam looks up from Flores's chart. "You've had others?"

Rao's very close to snapping, *Of course they fucking haven't.* He doesn't. He recognises that covert, enquiring glance he's getting, and he's not going to fall in line. Adam's working. Adam's on mission for the military, like he always is. Always was.

Fuck him and fuck them.

He stares dully at the rows of beds, the racks of monitoring machinery. Thinks of what this is. How it works. How it's always fucking worked. Thinks, *complicity.* Thinks, *Kabul.* Thinks, *naïveté.* Thinks of Adam's betrayal. Feels a fresh, rolling wave of outrage.

He needs to ask. Turns to Montgomery, and despite the bile in his throat, keeps his voice low, soft. Manages, even, to sound impressed. "How on earth did you get this past an ethics committee?"

Montgomery makes a small, private smile, shakes his head. He looks like John Denver, Rao decides. An amoral, balding, asshole John Denver.

"There isn't an ethics committee. Very technically, the manifestation program isn't classified as medical research, so the Declaration of Helsinki doesn't apply. Any adverse effects on test subjects fall under the category of nonoperational casualties."

Rao wonders who taught him that fluid little speech. He didn't quite follow it. Adam, apparently, did. "It's a military training program," he says slowly.

"Indeed," Veronica clarifies. "No limits on training if the ends justify the requirement."

"Deaths?" Adam asks.

"Two," Veronica says. "Before we developed our current postinfusion protocols. A pity, but these things happen."

Adam opens his mouth to respond, but Rao cuts in, addressing him directly. "Well, you know how it goes with these things, Adam," he says, voice like silk. "What's done is done, after all."

He watches that land. Detonate. Adam's face is expressionless, but there's agony in his eyes. *Good.* Rao needs to see more of that. Adam should suffer. Because, as people have always been so fond of telling him, there should be consequences to one's actions.

Adam struggles back into the conversation. "You're working on fixing this?" He looks to Rao again. Unbelievable. He's still working. Still trying to generate statements for Rao to read. Still fucking using him.

"Fixing?" she says.

"Waking the subjects. Getting them out of their comas."

"They're trance states."

"Getting them out of their trance states," Adam corrects.

Everything she's said so far has been true. Everything except the line about her patients doing well. That was a barefaced lie. And, considering the supine bodies surrounding them, an impressively ballsy one.

"Oh, yes. A priority," she says. "We're making progress."

And that's two more.

Adam is giving him another look. This one's even more hopeful.

"Adam, fuck off," he says flatly. He couldn't give a shit about the questioning looks. Couldn't give a shit about anything. Fuck this horror show. He sees how it works.

What Adam is leads to all of this.

And what all of this is leads to Adam.

Adam, who's standing there looking at the floor.

He's not evil, Rao thinks. He's a blank cassette, a wet clay tablet. Lieutenant Colonel Tabula Rasa. Something they could write on. Train. Make. Use. Or maybe that's not true. Maybe he is an evil bastard. Absolute psychopath. No feelings, no blood, never gave a fuck. Yeah. *Because he gave me up for what?* For *work.* Because it's his job. Because CIA asked him and Adam's the Rao expert. Better at handling Rao than Rao is. All those times Adam's done things for him. Water and Tylenol on the nightstand. All the times he's bought him cigarettes. Checked his vision with a penlight after Rao'd let off steam. The time he laid out that asshole who threw a slur in Rao's direction. Even that. All of it was work. Adam, babysitting. Rao's astounded by the extent of his naïveté. Even after Kabul. Feels like he's grown up, wrenched into the world. Curtain twitched away. Plato's fucking cave. Now he's behind the—

"Mr Rao?"

It's Veronica. She's been trying to attract his attention for a while.

"I was saying, perhaps you'd be interested in viewing the test footage?" she asks.

Rao shrugs. "Sounds good, yeah."

CHAPTER 32

His dad taught him how to pack. Told him the key was practice. Repetition. Like stripping and reassembling a weapon. Do it enough times and you won't waste any mental effort on it. It's more efficient in the long run. Plus, if you pack and unpack and repack a bag a bunch of times, then you get to know where all the items are inside, which makes them easier to find when you need them. First you need a staging zone, where you can lay out the contents and organize them. Then you pack in reverse order, so the things you need last are the things that go in first. You have to break the pack into thirds. Bottom third is medium weight, middle third is heavy, top third is light. And the heaviest things always go closest to your back.

He knows this is a good go bag, but he also knows that if he messes up and doesn't pack something important, he'll never get another chance to pack it.

Nothing inessential, his dad always said, when you pack a bag. He looks down at the things arranged neatly on his bedroom carpet. Some of them aren't essential. The Swiss Army knife is. The buck knife really isn't. But he's packing it anyway. He thought about taking books to read but decided they weren't necessary. His aunt has a lot of books already. But he's bringing the book she gave him when he was a kid. He hasn't read it for years, but he doesn't want to leave it behind.

Two shirts, three tees, two pairs of socks, three pairs of underwear, two pairs of pants.

Sneakers. He'll wear his boots.

Jacket.

Wash bag.

His passport. Social Security card. He went into his dad's den while his parents were out and picked the lock of the filing cabinet, which was easy—he's done it before—and pulled out the file with the family passports and cards. He flipped his dad's open. *Joseph*. His name is Joe. Nobody calls him Joseph except his aunt. But nobody calls his aunt Alexandra except his dad, so he guesses that's fair. He opened his own and looked at the photo. Blinked at it. It's an old photo and he looks different now, but he's not good at recognizing himself in photographs anyway. Even in mirrors he never quite gets who it is looking back. This photo, though. He looks like a dumbass in it. Doesn't matter.

He finishes with his backpack. Slips the passport with his SS card tucked inside it into the secret pocket at the back. Then he undoes the top and looks in. Pajamas rolled up and fitted neatly on top. He closes it. The tightness is happening, the band around his chest, and he knows that if he took everything out of the bag and packed it again that would help. But he doesn't. He's already done that twice. He sits on the carpet and holds his knees instead. He wants to do the thing, but maybe he won't have to this time. Sometimes it goes away on its own without getting really bad.

Not always.

There's got to be something wrong with him. Something wrong with his heart, probably, because he can feel it beating in his throat, times like this, and that tight feeling is what people talk about when they talk about heart attacks. He hasn't told anyone about it. Never will. Especially his dad. If there's something wrong with him, they won't let him enlist. And he doesn't like to think about that, but he's thinking about that now, and it's making his heart worse, it's beating stupid fast now, thumping in his ears, and it's a bad one, he knows it is, because he's getting that shivery, trickling feeling, and he's sweating, and when he lifts a hand from one knee it's shaking.

He's going to do the thing because he has to.

He gets up and goes to the bathroom, blinking because the world is dark. He doesn't turn on the light. He shuts the door, locks it. Steps into the bathtub, sits in it, curls up over his knees, closes his eyes, takes deep breaths, and waits.

CHAPTER 33

Veronica leads them to a dark, luxuriantly carpeted room that smells of expensive hotel. Montgomery hovers by the door. She takes a seat before a wall of monitors, pulls a keyboard towards her, and brings up time-stamped footage on two of the screens. When she presses Play, both run synchronously.

The first shows a moving landscape. It could pass for real. It isn't. All digital. A hillside, crags. Bare trees, stretches of dry grass pushed by breeze. Midday glare, gullies in deep black shadow. Rocks. No truth to the flocks of birds in the sky except the algorithm that's making them wheel and turn.

The other footage is a man in a white-walled room. He's wearing a white singlet, sweatpants, and laced-up boots. Flores.

Veronica moves into view beside him on-screen. She wrinkles her nose fondly at him, her mouth moves—there's no sound—and he laughs, shoulders easing as she speaks. She's flirting, Rao sees, and she's good at it. He watches her hand Flores a virtual reality headset. The manner in which Flores puts it on, his ease as he walks about to test his orientation: the routine is familiar to him, and as he turns and walks, the landscape on the other screen shifts to match his movements.

He nods. She takes his hand, guides him back to the centre of the room. Picks a syringe, a vial, and a small packet from a surgical dish on the shelf beneath the observation window, walks back, tears open the packet, and wipes his upper arm. Then she draws Prophet from the vial, slips the needle into the muscle just below his shoulder. When she withdraws it, she speaks again.

He nods. She leaves the room.

"You'll need sound for the cue," Veronica says, pressing a key. Wind, sifting grass, and birdsong fill the room. She fast-forwards the video; when it resumes normal speed, three minutes have passed.

Then something like the crack of a whip, loud and unmistakable. Rao hears Adam inhale, sees the subject's head turn, then realises it's the sound of a round passing far too close. Flores drops to the ground—perhaps less fluidly than he would have done back in the day, that right ankle is definitely off—but he's prone, on his elbows, and there's another crack, rippling into an intermittent fusillade.

"As I said, we had hopes for this one. You can see he puts a hand to where he expects his rifle to be."

Rao blinks. He doesn't want to. Doesn't want to miss any of this. But he blinks despite himself, watching Flores reach for the rifle that isn't there. In its place, the cassingle. Flores raises it to nestle it under his chin, his face bright with joy.

Veronica cuts the video. Brings up another. "That was subject three. This is six."

The same setup but a different man. Shorter than Flores, wirier. Same outfit. He's treated to the same flirting as Flores, though this time it doesn't seem to land. The same goggles are handed to him; they show the same arid, virtual scene. Veronica administers her dose. Time passes. Same crack of ordnance, same response. But no object. Nothing appears. A little while later, the virtual scenery cuts to slowly flashing red text: PLEASE REMOVE HEADSET. And the guy pulls off the goggles, gets up, and grins.

"What's the difference?" Adam says.

"Prophet appears to provoke flash memories of objects with deep psychological salience to our test subjects," Montgomery explains. Rao doesn't jump, but it's a close thing. He'd entirely forgotten about Montgomery, though that's probably a regular occurrence for the man. "Some people don't have those." He glances at Veronica.

"Have what?" Rao asks.

"Emotional memories," she says. "The combination of flattened emotional affect and less-than-vivid autobiographical memories is found in approximately one percent of the general population, but individuals of this type are overrepresented in our test demographic."

Rao suspects she's trying to lose him in the jargon, but he's hanging on with glee. "Veronica," he breathes with mock horror. "Are you telling me that Special Forces hire *psychos*?"

She gives him a dangerous smile. "That's not a term recognised in the *DSM-IV*."

"Well," Rao says. "Whatever you call it, this is good news for you, Adam."

"I'm not a psychopath, Rao."

"Is he?" Veronica asks.

"Yeah," Rao says. "Full Tin Man. No heart. That bastard'll be immune."

He waits for Adam to kick back after that. Expects something properly vicious. To prove him right, prove him wrong, do fucking anything at all. He gets nothing. Just a mute mask and downcast eyes. It's *enraging*.

Montgomery coughs a cartoon *ahem*. "Mr Rao, individuals with limited empathy are essential to this project. The substance aerosolizes readily. Infusions can only be carried out by people who are immune."

Veronica's beaming at Rao. Ah. *So* that's *her flavour of fake*, he thinks. Of course. All that flirting. He sees it for what it is. Doesn't care. She's good.

"I don't think I've ever met a psycho that isn't a bloke before," he lies.

"I'm sure you have," she says sweetly. "We're just much better at keeping it under our hats."

Next stop on the tour, Montgomery informs them, is the test suite. En route, Rao keeps his eyes trained on the art on the corridor walls. It's dreadful: corporate always is. But he'd rather stare at shitty sub-Rothkos than look at Adam, who's matching his pace, walking inches from his side. His skin itches with that unwelcome proximity, right hand bunching into a fist. He imagines the swing, the force he'll put behind it, the satisfaction when it connects.

"Rao—" Adam begins, voice low.

"Whatever it is you feel you have to say," Rao spits, "keep it to yourself. I can do this on my own. I don't need you. You're entirely fucking pointless."

They file in, silent, through a pair of airlock doors into a room so fiercely ventilated a breeze tugs fitfully at Rao's hair. The steel wardrobe near the entrance hums softly: a refrigerator or freezer, Rao assumes. *Refrigerator.* Three chairs, two workstations, three screens. It's spotlessly clean. Rao rubs at one wrist, feeling grimy. Out of place. Pathogenic.

"Observation room. The test room is through there," Montgomery explains, gesturing at the wide window next to a door on the far wall. Rao walks up to the glass, peers into the space beyond. Complicated ceiling ductwork, plasticised floor, wall-mounted cameras, everything white, wipe-down, a whole Michael Crichton vibe. It's dimly lit, far smaller than it looked on-screen. *They're going to be fucked*, he muses, *when some poor bastard re-creates their childhood house in there.* Would the created house push all this out of the way into rubble, or would it manifest itself right through it? He imagines being trapped in that impossible architecture. Rooms cut into dead-space angles by facility walls, bisected by sheets of glass.

No. Everything in the ward upstairs was small. Nothing bigger than that bulky radio. He remembers the diner, clouds over beet fields, sun on wet clay. Maybe it's—

"So where do you keep the substance?" Adam's bastard voice, breaking his concentration.

"In the refrigerator," Veronica says. "Shall we take a look?"

"Are we—"

"It's perfectly safe."

She opens the door. Rao walks over to see. Bathed in white light and laid on wire racks are a score or so of syringes in separate, glass-like containers.

"That's it?"

"Yes, Mr Rao. That's Prophet."

Rao takes another step towards the fridge, hesitates.

There's impatience in her voice. "It's safe, as I said. We no longer use vials. The syringes are predrawn at the point of manufacture and shipped here in vacuum containment vessels."

"Prophet," Rao says, feeling the word curl on his tongue.

"That's what we're calling it."

Close up, the substance in the syringes gleams.

"It's a metal?" he says.

"No. It's a very unusual substance. Our physicists have begun calling it a supersolid. The infusion is a colloidal suspension. Point six percent by volume. It looks like that because it has very particular optical properties. Even at this concentration, it scatters light with phenomenal efficiency."

Rao blinks. The syringes are right there, right in front of his face. At the same time he has an unpleasantly compelling intuition that they're also *somewhere else*. Worse, the intuition feels true. The dissonance grates horribly. Glass paper in his sinuses, a low swoop of motion sickness. He's relieved when Veronica shuts the refrigerator door. But the dim reflection of his face in brushed steel feels precisely the same: somehow both here and somewhere else. Revulsion, suddenly, and Rao moves quickly to the far side of the room, dimly aware that he'd prefer to put a wall between himself and the stuff in the fridge. Turning his back on everyone, he looks again into the observation room. But he can't focus on what's inside, only the surface of the window, and when his eyes find his own reflection, they get stuck on it.

Somewhere else.

The last time he'd stared like this at his own face was in his hotel bathroom in Kabul. He remembers spending a long while before that pacing about his room, then slowing. Slowing to look at everything in it, the filled ashtrays, the clothes on the floor, the glass in the window, smoke in the sky outside, the spaces between all these things somehow more real than the things themselves, before he'd walked into the bathroom and stood in front of the mirror, drawn to commit his own face to memory, knowing that in a little while there'd be no memories left to have. Such a relief. So quiet, those long moments before he went back into the room to make it happen. So quiet. It's not that he'd expected his life to flash past his eyes. But the quietness of it all was still a surprise, his own eyes in the mirror looking back at him from somewhere else.

Another face joins his reflection. Pale, clean-shaven. Takes him a few seconds to work out it's not a ghostly hallucination. It's Adam, standing far too close, looking into the test room as if he's trying to comprehend exactly what Rao can see in it.

My death, Rao thinks. *Which was on you. All on you.*

He closes his eyes, hears Adam asking about the current status of the testing program.

"It's slowed lately," Montgomery admits. "As you can imagine, the pool of suitable volunteers isn't large."

Rao speaks then. Keeps his eyes shut and speaks. Every syllable is hot and vicious. "Being a cunt doesn't interfere with the test, does it? Because if it doesn't, I volunteer Adam. He's a *huge* fan of secret military drug programs."

Montgomery hesitates. "I'm not sure if you can volunteer your partner on his behalf."

"Don't worry. Literally no one will miss him."

Adam says something too low to hear.

"No," Rao says evenly, opening his eyes. He turns to Adam, stares him down. "If you've something to say, do me the courtesy of saying it out loud."

Barely a whisper. "I hate you, Rao."

What a fucking child.

Rao rolls his eyes at Veronica. "That's a lie, of course. He's bloody obsessed with me."

Adam looks at him blankly. Doesn't say a word. Turns his back and walks towards the door.

Good. Fuck off back to the car.

"Right," Rao says. "Veronica. Where were we? Questions and answers time."

"Questions and answers," Veronica repeats, her grey eyes holding Rao's. Then her gaze slips past him. Her eyes widen. A quiet sound then, an indrawn breath, a light bulb dropped. She reaches forward and pushes him. He stares down at her hands on his chest. She pushes him again, harder. Rocking back on one foot, he opens his mouth to protest when he catches sight of the floor by the door. Glitter of broken glass. A jacket.

Adam's jacket. Adam's jacket is on the floor. And above it, Adam.

Adam, head bowed low over his forearm.

Adam with his sleeve pushed up, needle sunk into his skin, and everything is moving sickeningly slow, but he's depressing the plunger appallingly fast.

He's saying something. He's saying, "I'll find an answer."

He's not looking at me, Rao thinks stupidly.

Even before Adam tugs the needle free, Veronica's hands are on him, propelling him backwards towards the test room. He yields to her insistence. No protest, not a sound. He still isn't looking at Rao, and this, more than anything, is what drives him. Before Veronica gets Adam through the door, Rao's already slipped through.

"Not you," she says tightly. "Get out." He slips around her, slams the door. "Foolish," she hisses, shaking her head rapidly as if ridding herself of him.

Adam's right arm has fallen to his side, the syringe still gripped in his hand. The fingers holding it are white. Blood on his fingers, a track running down his right wrist. He's looking at Rao now, eyes wide. Rao has seen eyes like them before in a mirror in a hotel room in Kabul at sunset, and for one impossible second, he's certain he's looking at himself.

The full weight of what Adam's done falls on him. *No. Oh no.* Mutely, he watches Veronica prise the syringe from Adam's fingers. She turns her wrist to glance at her watch, strides quickly to the far side of the room.

"How long?" Rao manages to croak.

"Radial artery? Seconds."

Adam's already looking rough. His eyes have lost Rao's. His skin is clammy, pale. He's breathing with effort. Rao steps forward, takes his face between his hands. Rasp of hair against his fingers, skull beneath skin.

"Adam, please," he hears himself say. "Get through this. Just be ok. Anything you want. I'll do anything."

Adam's mouth moves, once. Barely a whisper.

"Don't—"

CHAPTER 34

Rao thinks it's fear, at first. It's a scent, close, thick, wet, deep as blood, but it's not metallic and doesn't cut that way. Not blood. Heady as arousal, but not that either.

No. He knows what it is. Exactly what it is, but it shouldn't be here. He's smelled it in Rajasthan, in Uzbekistan, in every desert he's walked in after rain, fragrance rising from the ground after water hits dry soil. He's holding Adam's face in his hands in a room that smells of petrichor. And woodsmoke, now, threading through it, strengthening until smoke is all there is, hazy and sweet. Abruptly, an atmospheric shift: the room pales, lit like morning sun. Then noises, a quick succession. One ping, like an oven timer, makes him jump out of his skin. A scrape of something like a cry, a distant *burr* that might be jet noise, the drumming of heavy rain, charred toast, then that lemon-yellow light again and more woodsmoke and then the smell of a just-fired pistol and then Rao can taste vodka in his own mouth. Turpentine, gun oil, something sharp like grapefruit juice, a snatch of what he thinks is a song by the Seekers playing on a transistor radio. It's too fast. The sensations are being pulled over him like striplights in a freeway tunnel at top speed and over all of them, or under, is the growing tick of a metronome. Burned toast, again. Thickly acrid, almost makes him choke. Rao battens himself against the rising barrage of sensory information, turns his head to follow Adam's gaze and sees it fixed on the wall across the room. On it is a languid patch of brightness that's moving like sun on water, and the sounds are slowing now, the shifts of light, too, a dying zoetrope, the perpetually rattling roulette wheel finally coming to a halt, and the blank wall is no longer bright and glittering, it's no longer blank at all, because it's honey-varnished pine panelling, golden with evening sunlight, and hanging on it, right at eye level, is a clock, hands set at

5:45 p.m.

He was supposed to leave the house at six. It's a fifteen-minute walk to the traffic lights at the intersection, the rendezvous his aunt had picked. She said she'd be there, waiting. Motor running. Ready. He just had to leave the house without arousing suspicion. That was supposed to be the easy part. But it hasn't been so easy. Until recently his parents hadn't cared where he was. They'd give him a time to be home and tell him to stay out of trouble. They never asked questions. That changed a few weeks ago. The reason was obvious.

He was supposed to just walk out. Dodge questions. Check his packed bag. Open the door. Walk away. His mom was supposed to be upstairs. His dad was supposed to be working. They were supposed to be busy. Easily ignored, easily avoided.

This was supposed to be the easy part.

He wasn't supposed to be sitting at the kitchen table watching his dad standing at the countertop fuming over the broken toaster. He wasn't supposed to be watching the clock on the wall, waiting for a chance to leave. He wasn't supposed to be here. At 5:45 p.m., he was supposed to be double-checking his packed bag, opening the door. Walking away.

His aunt was going to be at the lights.

"Do you think you could fix this thing?" his dad asks suddenly, jiggling the toaster. There's bread in it. He can smell it burning. Smoke is rising from the slots.

He's surprised. Why would his dad ask him if he knows how to fix a toaster?

"I don't know anything about that right now, but I could probably figure it out," he answers, speaking as honestly as he can without sounding like he's back talking. It's always a fine line to walk. "If you gave me time."

Right now he's supposed to be double-checking everything.

Right now he's supposed to be getting ready to leave.

"You're a smart kid," his dad mutters.

The toast doesn't pop. It slides up after a soft *ding*. Burned, black crusts. Smell charring the air. Sharp. It's 5:50 p.m.

He isn't sure if his dad has ever said he was smart before. It shouldn't matter that he has. He knows he's smart. He just doesn't think his dad has ever said it out loud. Trust the man to drop that at 5:50 p.m. He doesn't reply because he doesn't think this is a conversation. But then his dad starts speaking again, so apparently it is.

"You're going to think all kinds of things about life soon, you know," his dad says, looking down at the toaster. He picks a single black slice out of it. Turns it in his hand. Doesn't do anything to it. Doesn't bother to get a knife to run down its surface. Doesn't bother scraping the carbon off. "You're going to come up with explanations about life, about growing up. About me. About your mom. While you're out of this house, you're going to be told all kinds of things. And you'll come up with more. You're smart."

He's talking about that camp again. He talks about it a lot.

"It's complicated, Adam," his dad goes on, sitting down at the table. He sets the burnt toast down on the table. No plate. Just rests it between them on the tablecloth. Neither of them looks at the other. They look at the toast. "It'll get more complicated as time goes on. That's life. That's what they don't tell you, but I'm telling you now. It gets more and more complicated. The only way to make it through life intact is to figure out your own way to think about it."

"And I don't think about it the right way," Adam says.

It isn't a question. He gets what his dad is saying. He usually does.

The sun is setting. Golden light is falling over the kitchen in pools that warm the parts of his leg it touches. His eyes catch on the tip of his dad's air force tattoo, just visible below the edge of his tan shirtsleeve. It would have been black once. Now the ink is kind of blue. He's never been sure what it is. He's never seen all of it. It's probably a bird.

He doesn't know.

He looks up. There's sunlit dust in the air. Little points of light, moving slowly, like stars.

The clock says 6:00 p.m.

He was supposed to be gone by now. He's not supposed to be here.

"You don't think about it the right way yet. That's all."

The clock ticks over to 6:01 p.m.

*

Adam mustn't, must *not*, *cannot* touch the thing on the wall. Rao isn't going to let it happen. He flings his arms tight around him, braces his feet against the floor. Takes a deep breath, grips harder, waits for the struggle. He knows this is pointless. He's seen Adam fight, knows he could kill him without breaking a sweat, expects to be thrown to the ground in less than a second. But there's no retaliation. No movement at all. Beneath his shirt, Adam's muscles are locked tight. It's like clinging to a statue. Blank. Inert. The only heartbeat Rao can feel is his own, wild and high in his throat. The seconds slip and drag and thicken until Rao feels a flutter of wild, uncertain hope. Unlike Ed, unlike Miller and those poor bastards in the next room, he realises, Adam isn't being drawn to the thing he's made.

He loosens his hold a fraction. Nothing. He loosens it a little more. Adam's legs give way. Taking his weight, Rao helps him down to the floor, where he sits, frozen in place. Rao gets to his knees in front of him to block his view. Takes both of Adam's hands in his own. Talks to him. Low and urgent, edged with hysteria. The words are nonsense. They're barely words at all. But it doesn't matter. He's pretty sure Adam can't hear him. He's certain Adam can't see him.

His fingers twitch, spasm weirdly, a painless cramp. Adam's skin is *hot* suddenly. No. *Cold.* Freezing. Something else. *Something—*

He turns Adam's left hand. Sees something like sweat beading on his palm. Something. Like drops of mercury. Metallic. Silvery. Palladium grey. They're hard to focus on, as if they don't want to be looked at, but he can't tear his eyes away. They're like the vulture. Like the diner. Like that small, cold night. And as he stares at them, the room, the building, the whole world flows smoothly, inexorably inwards, contracting into Adam's outstretched hand, taking Rao with it.

Helplessly, he drops a finger, soft, onto Adam's palm and stares, entranced, as the beads move towards it, tiny droplets coalescing into thin rivulets that run along the lines of Adam's skin into his own. He watches it soak into him like ink into a wick. Like capillary action, as if he's pulling it in. Feels it, senses it slipping into his blood. He shivers. A weird, weird hit. Yes. *Yes.*

He grabs both of Adam's hands. Laces their fingers. Presses their palms together. Screws his eyes tight like Dorothy—*there's no place like home*—and wills every single atom of the stuff into himself.

Fuck, he thinks. *Fuck.* This is new. *Holy shit.* It's like he's being bent backwards to the floor. He's not moving. Sprays of phosphenes bubble up in front of his eyes to obscure his vision and he blinks them away. He's falling through all the things that ever existed or will exist and now they are carefully pleating themselves inside him into something so fine and perfect he's not sure he'll ever need to breathe again. It—

There's a tug on his hands. Through his eyes he sees the man whose hands he's holding double up. Fold over himself. Hears coughing, a desperate hauling in of air. For an instant the room is his cell at Pentonville, his hotel room at Kabul, his flat in Clapham, his college set, his childhood bedroom, that suite in Tashkent, all at once, and he blinks their ghosts away and looks at the man who's now sitting back on his heels before him, swaying a little, trembling violently. He's so—

He's so—

Rao can't think of the word. It's important, it's crucial. He searches for it in vain, searching the man's face. It's perfectly expressionless. His eyes are closed. He's crying. Not sobbing, no noise at all, just water coursing down his cheeks.

Rao remembers a little more. Turns his head to the wall behind him. The clock's still there, light still gilding the pine boards behind it, shining on the curve of its metal case.

"Oh," he hears a woman say breathlessly. "This is *very* interesting."

"Adam?" Rao says, though it takes him a few tries to remember the name.

Adam's mouth opens and moves and shuts again. He furrows his brow, opens his eyes, tries again. "Rao," he whispers. "Can we leave?"

Unsteadily, Rao gets to his feet. As he does, the room snaps abruptly into a negative of itself and slips precipitously to one side, but he manages to tilt it back into something approximating normality as he hauls gently on Adam's hands to pull him up from the floor. It takes a while.

Rao slings one of Adam's arms over his shoulders, grips his wrist tight, and turns them both to the door. There's a woman in front of it. *Veronica*, he remembers. Her face shines as she speaks.

"You need to stay for observation. This is a highly anomalous result."

Rao shakes his head, works hard to assemble a sentence.

"We're leaving. Adam, love, can you walk?"

Another room. Rao remembers it. A mirror. Adam's jacket. He leans to pick it up as they pass. Broken glass crunches underfoot. Harmonics, high-pitched, like voices. A man rushes up. Rao can't remember him at all. He's agitated, fists clenched, eyes wide. "Are you ok? Is he ok? Was this a test?"

Rao ignores him, concentrates on getting Adam into the corridor.

It takes forever to get to the car. He leans Adam against the passenger-side door, drags the keys from his inside jacket pocket. Gets him in the seat, buckles him in. He's cold, shivering, shirt soaked with sweat.

Rao pulls the GPS out of the glove compartment, plugs it into the cigarette lighter. "Where's the motel, love?" he asks. He's scared he can't remember its name, can't remember where it is.

Adam looks at him blankly.

"Our hotel. We left our bags there. Can you remember what it's called?"

A long silence, then Adam manages some words. They're almost inaudible, but one, Rao thinks, might have been "King." Yes. He stabs at the GPS screen with a finger, flinching at each keystroke tone. The King's Inn. He drops the GPS in his lap, starts the engine. Judders out of the lot, merges with the traffic. At the first intersection, he looks over to the passenger seat. Adam's face is red with reflected stoplight. Bad grey underneath. Rao jumps when his face shifts green, is hit by another wave of disorientation. More amplitude to this one. Deeper, wilder. The car behind them sounds an impatient horn. *Lucky*, he thinks, as he gets the car moving again, that he's had comprehensive experience of driving while off his face. Lucky. *You're lucky.*

"Fuck's sake, mate," he breathes. "Psychos are fine with this stuff. Why couldn't you have been?"

Adam speaks so quietly Rao can barely hear. "I'll be fine."

CHAPTER 35

Chills, a cold sweat, the smell of his childhood kitchen, his father's burnt toast acrid in his nostrils, charred caramel of spent rounds, thick sludge of dread and self-loathing fresh and new in his stomach, everything balling up inside. He can't care. He won't care. He cares too much.

They're driving to the motel. Rao's talking. Rao's driving. Adam doesn't care. Dangerous to care. Rao's driving, he's talking, and he looks shaken. *Mate*, he's saying. Adam knows that there's a meaning behind every one of Rao's pet names, Rao's endearments. They're an arsenal. Needlelike, and every single one a weapon or a piece of armor. He's only ever heard Rao call people mate when he's worried about them. Armor, then. Much easier to bear than Rao's everyday velvet-wrapped bullet of "love."

Rao asks him a question. He feels the click of his own mouth opening, how much air he uses up to answer. He says he'll be fine. A violent wave of shakes hits him and he wonders if he's going to die. He considers asking Rao if he's dying—but what's the point? Rao won't know. The only thing they both know for sure is that he's a black hole. A cigarette burn in the fabric of Rao's tapestry of truth. Adam is the promise of a migraine without a trigger. No point in asking. He'll never get an answer.

The car halts. "I'll be back. Just stay here," Rao's saying. After some time, the vehicle's moving again, Rao biting his lip and pulling at the wheel. Where they park has windows in front. A door. Rao helps him out of the car and walks with him. It's not hard to walk. Adam can do it unsupported. He doesn't tell Rao that.

He learned the merits of keeping his mouth shut when he was young, but the way his aunt Sasha talked about him made Adam suspect that he was always kind of quiet. "You grow up around all that noise, kid, and you lose your voice," she'd said, once. Only once. He remembers the smell of her cigarette smoke in the air as she said it. How the sunset through the curtains hit her, made everything seem brightly colored and unlit all the same. He remembers her saying it and how it made him feel like he was a chipped cup in a set.

"Look, I know you're not talkative, love, but this is next-level," Rao complains from the kitchenette. Adam watches from the end of the nearest bed. Two queens, one large TV, good floorspace, a desk. Upmarket. Stakeout rooms. Recoup motel. "Usually I'll get at least a grunt from you to let me know whether you're ignoring or humoring me."

He has no idea.

"The problem is, if you don't say anything, I'll just keep talking," he continues. "Have to fill the silence." A pause. A frown. "Fuck me, Adam. That's true. I have to fill the silence? Compelled? Fuck. Wasn't ready for that little nugget of impromptu self-reflection."

Normally Rao's monologue would be entertaining. It's different in the recoup motel. Here, it's not funny. Here, Rao being Rao is prying Adam's chest open. Cracks into marrow. He can breathe but feels like he can't. His arms ache with an effort he doesn't understand.

"Please," Adam rasps and slowly lifts a hand to his face. Doesn't cover his eyes. Can't bring himself to. He has to stop caring. He can't.

Rao looks up from the fridge, eyes wide. "Didn't think that would actually work," he admits. He leaves the kitchenette, pulls one of the chairs from the desk, and drags it across the carpet to Adam's bed. Sits. His eyes dart around Adam's features, taking him in. Adam's ribcage feels weak. Might collapse at any second. He can't ask Rao if he's dying. He'll never know. "What do you need?" Rao asks.

Adam works his throat. Knows what he wants. Knows what he can ask for. "I need you to shut up," he says quietly. His voice. It sounds like he's been strangled. The bruised swelling that follows. The rasp and dryness of a healing throat. The constant ache of minor internal bleeding, tiny shards of glass inside his words. It'll pass. In a day. Maybe two. "Rao, please shut up."

Rao laughs. He laughs and the laugh blocks out the ticking of a clock somewhere in the room. Adam hadn't even noticed the sound until it was gone. Feels like he can't breathe again. Needs Rao to laugh again.

"Fuck off," Rao says, grinning, gripping his knee like they're friends. Maybe they are again. Some people, they just need to shed some blood together. But Rao telling him to fuck off sounds like he's saying something else. Adam doesn't know what those other words are. They just aren't the words coming out of his mouth. "So you're alright?" Rao adds.

"I'm fine," Adam lies. Looks around the room to find the clock he'd failed to notice. Locates it on the wall opposite the bed he's sitting on, to the left of Rao's head. He focuses on its face. Doesn't know if that's a good idea or a bad idea. Can't care. Probably should.

"Don't lie to me, Adam. It's a dirty trick."

Adam snorts humorlessly. It hurts. Like he has a cold. Sinus pain, throat pain: cousins, not siblings. "I guess I really look like shit, huh," he croaks.

Rao considers Adam carefully. Speaks gingerly. Might be the first time Adam's seen him so gentle in all their time working together. "Let's just say that you look fucking terrible and leave it at that."

Adam blinks at him.

"What? I'm not going to get into it. You know where I've been and what I've seen. Imagine all the comparisons I could make with my vast experience of just how ragged a human being can look and apply them. And don't get ratty with me because I'm choosing to be kind."

"Kind," Adam repeats. Hard to say. Makes his throat cut into itself. Rao talked about kite strings made to cut others before. Glass dust. Adam feels a sudden kinship with something he's never seen.

"Extraordinarily kind. And trust me when I tell you that right now you need to get something to drink and make an attempt at solid food."

Adam sighs. He could fight. The clock ticks beside Rao's head. He could fight it all. But he can't pin down if he should fight, if he wants to

fight, or if any of this will matter in the long run. "So you're primary
on this?"

"This isn't a job, Adam."

"Everything's a job, Rao."

"You're delicate right now, love, so I'll leave that morsel of innuendo
on the table to enjoy later." Rao pats Adam's knee and gets up, walks
back over to the kitchenette. Adam tears his gaze from the clock on the
wall to watch him. Rao's standing by the fridge, making a face. "There's
a Safeway a block away. I could get groceries. But I'm not a cook."

"No shit."

"We'll get takeout."

By the time he was thirteen, he could cook pretty well. His mom taught
him. Told him there's no point in being in the world if you can't look
after yourself. Told him he wouldn't be "one of those boys," a designation Adam wouldn't understand until he was living in barracks with
scores of "those boys." His mom could cook, but she was also a practical
woman. Most of their family meals came from cans or jars. They all
knew that a homemade sauce was better, but who could find the hours
in the day for that kind of dedication? She used to put different herbs in
the sauces. Made it personal. It was fine. Adam still thinks nobody can
cook up a box of mac like his mom. They didn't do takeout. "It's lazy,"
his dad told him. Lazy was the worst thing a person could be. "And you
don't know who's making your food. They could put anything in it."
Adam thought that realistically that could happen anywhere. Anyone
could do that. Anyone. He never said that to his mom. He figured she
knew already.

He watches Rao eat his fourth slice of pizza. Rao seems unfazed. That's
good. Rao's the one with experience in situations like this one, so Adam
has to assume that if Rao seems calm, then his own crushing feelings of
doom are just his own. Maybe therapy would've helped him to figure out
where to put these feelings. He has no idea what to do with them now.
Never imagined he'd have them. Therapy's not a dirty word to Adam,
not a sign of weakness. He's known a lot of people in the service who

needed it, got it, came out the other side better for it. He's known a lot of people who needed it just as badly but did nothing about it. Once you know that type, you can see them everywhere: the ones who think getting help is a weakness.

He's never gotten help. He's dealt with everything himself. Coped. Driven on. The higher-ups would check in sometimes. Ask him if he needed to talk to someone. He never took them up on their offers. Didn't want to visit that kind of hurt on anyone else's head, especially when they meant well enough to offer him help. And because, realistically, where would he start?

Turns out, Prophet knew exactly where he would start.

"You've been giving me and this pepperoni the evils for a solid minute now," Rao observes. "Not hungry anymore?"

Adam isn't hungry at all. "I spaced out," he says. "Wasn't really looking at you."

"Fucking hell, Adam, you always know how to make a man feel wanted."

Rao sounds playful. Upbeat. What you're going through is normal, he'd assured Adam earlier. Wanting to die, wanting to scream, feeling like you're moving when you're not, feeling like you'll never breathe right again. It's all normal.

Adam doesn't feel normal. Adam's never felt normal.

He watches Rao deposit his half-eaten slice on top of a napkin. Pizza oil leaks and blooms into the paper. He blinks back a memory of blood welling through sand-dusted DCU.

"Did you space out on anything specific?" Rao says carefully.

Therapy, Adam doesn't say out loud, and how it might have helped him now. Not then. He still doesn't think he'd have been anything but disturbing to the people with the notepads at the time, but right now, after what's happened, he thinks he might like to possess the tools to hold a conversation at the very least. "I should get some sleep," he says instead.

It's not an answer, but it gets a nod. "Which bed do you want? I don't care which you pick," Adam assures him. "I just want to sleep."

"Then sleep. I'll put the telly on low."

"You need the TV on?"

"You know I do."

Adam nods. Radio, TV, the voices of strangers. Doesn't matter what language, doesn't matter where, Rao needs white noise to relax and sleep. Adam's never minded. It's standard countersurveillance. He's found scores of talk radio stations for Rao during jobs. Has always liked the way Rao's features ease after a few minutes of background chatter. How there's always this one split second before he gazes out the window or picks up a book when he seems honestly at peace.

CHAPTER 36

Unscheduled calls break unspoken rules, but Steven needs to know. When he appears on-screen, Veronica's relieved to see he's at his Maine residence. The house resembles a nineteenth-century cabin, but as with so many of his things, this is merely an impression it's designed to give: there's a T1 line into the property and sufficient security to repel whole armies. Steven will be in Maine to search for heritage apple varieties in the woods, which is good because it means he'll be—as far as Steven ever is—receptive to conversation. He shifts in his seat, fiddles with the wick on the oil lamp; the light dims in the wood-panelled room. He doesn't like to be visible, even here.

"Do we, uh, have a breakthrough?" he says in his familiar whisper.

"We had two visitors today, Steven. I didn't know they were coming. It seems Lane let them in: he'd passed Montgomery their names."

A pause, a sigh. He pushes at an unsharpened carpentry pencil on the desk, shifts it an inch sideways. A longer pause.

"I'll talk to him," he says eventually. He looks unhappy to be discussing this. It means nothing. He's never, in the years Veronica's known him, ever looked comfortable discussing anything other than apples.

"I'd be grateful, Steven. Were you aware of them?"

He wrinkles his nose. Another long silence. "I talked with Zachary two days ago. He, uh, notified me. Rubenstein and Rao. Said they might turn up at the Aurora facility. They were Miller's hires."

Veronica frowns. "I didn't like that."

"Like what?"

"How Lane used her."

He looks mystified. "Morally?"

"No, Steven. Unwitting agents aren't my favourite flavour. But in retrospect—" She rubs a thumb along the fingernails of one curled hand, shrugs minutely. "What's the state of play in England?"

"The coroner returned a favourable verdict. The, um, the objects have been removed from the base into level four storage and Miller's off-site and secure."

"And we're clear her exposure was accidental?"

"As far as we, uh, yeah. It was. We also have the vial in our possession. So that project's complete."

She nods, exasperated. That EOS PROPHET side project never got off the ground. It was a little gift for Steven from Lane, and like most of Lane's little gifts, an embarrassing one. It's highly irritating to her that Straat's death had such fascinating consequences.

"What do we have on Rubenstein and Rao?"

"One's at the Defense Intelligence Agency. Rubenstein. The other one is, uh, damaged goods. Ex-MI6. Miller got him out of prison. He's supposed to have some kind of extranormal ability to detect lies. CIA overtaxed him and he tried to kill himself. He's Indian, I think? I suppose he must be. The name."

"Rubenstein said he could detect fakes and frauds."

A snuffle of laughter. Steven doesn't laugh like any other person Veronica has heard. A high-pitched grunt, no facial levity attached. "Maybe those, too, yes, maybe, maybe. Lane was keen to bring him in. He thought he'd be useful, ultimately, but the odds seemed too long to me. He's apparently, uh, you know, quite unstable."

Veronica enjoys the ambiguity, says nothing.

"What's Rao's relation to the DIA operative?"

"Rubenstein's . . . a bodyguard? We couldn't get much on him. Lane said he wasn't interesting."

She sits back in her seat and smiles. "He is."

CHAPTER 37

Adam's propped up against his headboard staring at the motel wall opposite, at the unlikely blue-on-blue wallpaper printed with geese and flowers. He's blinking slowly, taking deep breaths he doesn't seem to ever exhale. Rao's been watching him for a long time. Knows he's barely registering on Adam's consciousness, is little more than a shadow on his periphery. Adam certainly looks like he's in a dissociative state, brain slipped into protective mode to unshackle him from himself and the world. Yeah. Well. Rao is familiar with dissociation. Knows the safety of that disconnect. He's looked down at himself and felt his body doesn't belong to him more times than he can count. But he's certain that's not what's happening here. There's something about Adam's stare, the way his right hand grips the coverlet. The way fear scents the room like rain the air.

No, Adam's not dissociating. This is the opposite. He's thinking and feeling too much. Inside his skull, there's a crescendo of white noise running in a terrible, screaming, silent loop. Rao knows this. He doesn't know how, but he does.

He has to get Adam out of it.

"Adam."

Another blink. Adam doesn't look over. "Yes, Rao."

"Can we talk?" Rao regrets his choice of words instantly. *Far too intense, Sunil. You're usually so much better than this.*

Still, it makes Adam look over. His eyes look black. "Is it a big talk or a little talk?"

"No, just a little talk."

"Ok. What do you want to talk about?"

"Anything at all. Tell me something about yourself no one else knows."

"You already know so much about me that no one else knows," Adam sighs, rearranging himself against the headboard. That's true. Rao knows it is, but it doesn't feel like it. It just feels like Adam.

"Yeah, well. I'm a greedy bastard, then. Tell me something new."

"I can't think of anything."

"You didn't try."

"Rao, this isn't as fun a game as you think it is."

"I'm not having any bloody fun! You're not telling me anything."

Adam closes his eyes, but he's smiling. It's barely there, barely a smile, but it's not a frown. That counts. "Ask me a question and I'll answer it."

"Alright. Give me a second," Rao instructs, suddenly desperate not to waste this chance. As if it were the only one. Yes, he has questions. Questions about the clock on the wall, what it meant. About Adam's family. Why he chose this career. What the real deal is with Hunter. Why Prophet didn't work the way they thought it would. He *really* wants to know why Adam chose to tell him about his involvement with those fucks from the CIA. But he wants to keep Adam from the white noise in his head. None of what he wants to ask will keep him clear of that.

Something easy. Softball.

"What was your first kiss like?" he asks with a bit of a grin. Easy. Softball. But real, and something he knows Adam would never talk about otherwise. "Let me guess first. Was she your high school sweetheart? Yeah, I can see that, with you. Apple pie shit. Probably kissed her cheek while an American flag waved behind the two of you."

Adam's eyebrows tick down in a frown. "Incorrect. Guess again."

"Piss off," Rao laughs.

Adam opens his eyes.

"Just tell me," Rao says.

There's a pause. A breath. Long enough for Rao to realise how much he's enjoying himself. Begin to worry that Adam's right, and this game might just be for him.

"For a start, I think I was still in middle school," Adam tells him, speaking slowly. Nice and careful. *Adam's like that*, Rao thinks with sudden fondness. Always takes his time when he's saying something more than a statement or rebuke. "There was a ball field near where my house was. My dad found us at the fence by the diamond."

"What was she like?"

Adam snorts humourlessly. "*Mark* was taller than me. I don't really remember a lot about him. I know he had green eyes. I remember keeping my eyes open. I saw my dad coming before Mark did. Man, you know—" He laughs, genuinely: a sudden shift in energy. "My dad made him piss himself. We were so scared."

"Wait."

"Yes, Rao."

"This isn't like, you know, a girl called Alex, is it?"

"No."

"Adam. I rather think that after everything, you should be honest with me. We're rebuilding trust here."

Adam takes a deep breath and sighs it out. Sits back against the headboard. Rao'd missed when he'd sat forward. Missed that entirely. The laughter is gone. Might as well have never existed. "I'm not lying to you."

This demands some thought. Adam in his early teens with a boy a little taller than him. Eyes open during the kiss, because of course Adam would kiss like that. Low sun, dust in the air, asphalt and dry grass. Rao can picture it so clearly it's like it's a memory of his own. Feels the ghost of a hand gripping his shirtfront. He shakes his head. None of this feels like a lie. It doesn't feel like anything. Feels like Adam.

"But you're straight," he continues to argue.

"I never said that."

The makeup. The eyeliner. They were so close, and Rao had been *so sure*. "That time, we didn't kiss, but it was fucking close—"

"Are you suggesting," Adam interrupts, exasperated, "that I must be straight because I didn't kiss you?"

"Yes."

"Rao."

"Well! Alright, maybe not that exactly." Only, *that*. Exactly that. "Are you bisexual?"

Adam rolls his neck to level a raised eyebrow at him.

"It's alright if you are, obviously," Rao says quickly. "I'd say that's what I am, if I ever stopped to think about it. I reckon I'm alright with anything, actually, if we're—"

Adam interrupts him again. "What's your obsession with me having sex with women?"

"What?"

"Why do you fixate on that?"

"I don't fixate on anything about your sexuality, Adam."

"That's bullshit."

I've never seen him like this, Rao thinks in some wonderment before correcting himself. He's seen him like this before, and he'd hated it. Adam is like this with Hunter; he laughs and he swears. Doesn't just roll with the verbal punches, doles them out too. Wait. No. That's wrong again, isn't it? Because he'd seen Adam like this before he knew Hunter existed. Adam with his sleeves rolled up unscrewing the cap of a bottle of Tashkentvino vodka, Adam sprawled on a couch, messing with cards.

"If you're not deciding that I'm making out against the flag or sleeping around with every female soldier at the base or just banging my friends, then you're declaring me sexless." Adam doesn't sound mad. He sounds tired. "It's one of your favourite topics."

"Do I go on about that?" Rao asks, his words feeling oddly pointless. Like all of this, somehow, was inevitable.

"You once told me that if I had any animal magnetism in my system, I might be considered handsome," Adam says, then laughs like he had when he'd talked about his dad finding him by the fence. It surprises Rao all over again. "And I think it was probably the nicest thing you've ever said to me."

"Bloody hell, Adam. I'm sorry."

Adam's face twists. "You don't have to do that. You were right. You're always right."

"You know how desperately I'd like to agree with you on that one, love." Rao lifts his chin, scratches his neck, sees Adam's wince deepen.

"But I did just find out that my extremely heterosexual best friend has, in fact, no interest in women whatsoever."

"I'm not your best friend, Rao."

"That seems to be a choice I get to make, Adam."

Adam frowns. "Make a better choice."

Rao clicks his fingers as he thinks. Weighs up his options. Decides he doesn't care about safety or stability. They were probably well beyond that already. "What if this were a big talk?"

"It's not a little one."

"No," Rao agrees. "Which means that I'm well within my rights to bring up the whole . . . well, you know."

"Ruining your life," Adam prompts, flatly.

"Ruining my life, yes."

Rao watches Adam gather himself up, far more slowly than usual, in order to present his mask of cold indifference. There sits Adam as he's always been before: a forgotten cigarette burn in the tapestry of the universe. Nothing tangible for Rao to hold onto, nothing ever true or false. A spinning wheel.

The only proof he has that Adam might still be hearing that white noise in his head, might still be a mess, is how his fingers tremble as he wraps them around his left wrist.

It's not just the straight thing, Rao realises with a start sudden as laughter. He's misunderstood everything about Adam the whole time.

"Ok. Let's talk about it," he says evenly. *Such a professional.*

*

Desk work after time in the field makes Adam's skin crawl. Low ceilings, fluorescent light, gray DC skies outside. He's good at it. But it always feels like a shackle. And it's thoughts like these that had been getting Adam through the day, snorting under his breath and thinking how Rao would call him a drama queen. *An incredibly boring drama queen, but we work with what we're given.* Because Rao was on his mind. It would have been easy to get pathetic about that, blame it on all the time he had to let his mind wander while he wasn't in the field, but the truth was that recently he'd been asked to provide a more detailed file report of their operations in Central Asia. He had dug up all his memories, stripped them clean of sentiment and camaraderie, packaged them up for another set of eyes, and passed them on.

So it made sense that he was thinking of Rao. Expected, after reliving all the moments that don't make it into reports. The jokes and quiet evenings. Stories shared. Market stalls. Dust and cologne and cigarette smoke. The way Rao always complained about the scratchy blankets, lumpy pillows, moldy couches with too-hard armrests.

He wasn't surprised when he got the call.

"A follow-up on your report." A male voice, a crackly line. Adam wondered exactly where this one was posted.

"You should have all the details you need," Adam sighed, acting like he had something better to do. What did he have lined up? Meetings. A 5:00 p.m. sit-in with a service chief, a four-star general, a politician with a thousand-dollar-a-day coke habit, and a diplomat fucking his au pair.

"We need to know about Sunil Rao."

Adam sat up. "What do you need?"

"We're working with him at the moment and we're finding his behavior . . ." A pause during which Adam smiled grimly at nothing. "Challenging."

"He's being an asshole."

"Yeah, he really is."

Adam nodded. "Fights?"

"Nearly every night. Grounding doesn't stick. He slipped out of cuffs. He drinks, gets his ass kicked, causes havoc," the agent continued. He was off script already, but that's the whole point of knowing the right words to say. "I'd get rid of him but . . ."

He didn't need to finish the sentence. Adam got it, and so did the strung out agent. Rao's something else, even when being a pain in the ass.

"You're giving him what he wants," Adam said. "Something to kick against. You cuffed him?"

"Desperation."

"Obviously."

"I need solutions, Colonel Rubenstein, not a dressing down."

It was hard not to laugh. "I don't have any special instructions for you."

"You're the only person who's managed to work with him without punching him."

Adam grinned. "I've punched him."

"It didn't make it into the report."

"No, it didn't," Adam allowed, wondering how many people had included all the times Rao had goaded them into retaliation in their reports. He'd say he was immune, the way Rao told him he was, but that wasn't true. He wasn't immune like that. "I suppose I've already given you the best advice I can give you."

"Don't cuff him."

"Don't treat him like a prisoner," Adam corrected. "He's an asset. Treat him like he is. Whatever the situation—"

"Classified."

"Of course. But whatever the situation is, you need him. The fights are his way of letting off steam," he explained. It wasn't hard to talk about Rao. Never has been. What's always hard is getting people to understand. "Give him another outlet. Let him drink. Let him smoke. Let him go further than that if you need to. Encourage it. His tolerance is higher than you think, and he'll always bounce back, so long as it's done in moderation."

"You're encouraging recreational drug use."

Adam paused. Was he? Yes. But it's Rao. "If there are substances floating around, he'll find them anyway. It's in your best interest to be aware and in control of the situation if you want to work with him without the headaches, agent."

"Littlewood."

"Excuse me?"

"Agent Littlewood."

Poor bastard. No wonder he's having trouble with Rao. "I hope this has been useful to you, Agent Littlewood."

"Extremely."

The call clicked to an end and Adam sat for a moment, rapping his fingers on the desk, remembering the time he punched Rao, too early in their friendship to know he was doing exactly what Rao wanted him to do. Before he realized Rao was an asset.

The asset.

He got up from his desk, convinced for the first time in a long time that he'd actually done some good.

CHAPTER 38

Rao sits in silence after Adam recounts the phone call. Then, pursing his lips, he asks him if he wants to order in more pizza.

"I'm not hungry."

"Nor am I," Rao agrees. "They were shit anyway."

"You ate five slices."

Rao smiles bleakly at that.

"Why didn't you just tell me that they were cunts?" he asks seriously. "The way you said it before sounded like you just told them to hold me down and stick me with a needle to control me."

"That's basically what I did," Adam says. "If I had more intel on the situation, I would have been more careful." He's shaking his head. He doesn't believe what he's saying.

"This really doesn't suit you."

"What?"

"Guilt," Rao sniffs. He hates it. "I've never seen it on you before and it's not your colour, love."

Adam shoots him one of his not-frown smiles. "Like it's a hat I'm trying on."

"Yeah. Take it the fuck off."

"It's not that easy, Rao."

"It should be."

Adam stares at him blankly.

"I'm the injured party, and I'm expressly forgiving you," Rao says. "Which should knock that shitty guilt hat clean off."

Adam hums tunelessly. "And if you're wearing a shitty guilt hat of your own?"

Fuck. Trust Adam to be a total pain in the arse even in recovery from impossible experimental substances. "Leave my hat alone," he says.

Adam nods, slow and silent. He's thinking. They're having a big talk now, after all. All their guts on the table. All of Adam's guts on the table, anyway. Rao blinks, suddenly comprehending the power imbalance. Aware of it and hating it.

"You don't have anything to feel guilty about," Adam says eventually.

"That's bollocks. The shrinks kept telling me that when I got back. They didn't understand that everything in those rooms in Kabul was a weapon, Adam. Everything. And I was in the room," he insists. "I'm guilty as fuck."

"Yeah, all that is true." Adam speaks slowly. Eyes back down to his own hands.

Rao follows Adam's gaze. Remembers those hands holding a gun to the kneecap of a man in Tashkent a lifetime ago. The man who'd ended up telling them both, his voice tight with fear, that things in Afghanistan aren't like they are in the movies.

But they are, Rao thinks. They *really* are. Just the movie happens to be *Goodfellas*, not *Saving Private Ryan*.

Adam raises his eyes. "But . . . I don't think you have anything to feel guilty about as far as I'm concerned."

"It isn't that easy." Rao shivers, though he feels warmer. Doesn't hate it right this second. Hell of a ride. "This is my fault."

"What is?"

"This. You. Right now, you and now."

"You didn't make me do anything."

"Yeah, but—"

"Shut up, Rao. You didn't make me do anything."

A propositional statement that can't be read. But Rao knows it's a lie. Because he was pushing Adam in the facility, pushing as hard as he could. He wanted—

He doesn't know what he wanted. He knows exactly what he wanted. But what he got was something else, and he got it at Adam's expense. Rao looks down at his own hand. Turns it, regards the creases on his palm. Remembers the beads of Prophet climbing out of Adam's skin and slipping into his own. The unnatural heaviness behind his eyes that doesn't feel right, feels so right. Shivers. Lights behind his vision when he blinks. What he got was something else, and there's no going back. But it's Adam. Adam who's in recovery. Adam, who's looking at Rao closely now, leaning forward to get his attention, as if he didn't already have it, as though Rao weren't the most alert and aware he's ever been in his life. Everything's firing at once. He's feeling like he did when he was a kid, when he wanted to be able to do everything in one day and getting tired was a waste of time. Feels like he did when he tried coke the first time. Just that first time. Like he'd figured out how to do everything at once. It was a fleeting intuition and confusing after an hour, but insistent. He feels insistent. All of him feels insistent.

"What is it, Adam?"

"You look like you have more questions."

Rao suppresses a laugh. "Well, given the brand-new information laid at my feet about your formative years, not to mention a whole retelling of your narrative, I do indeed have quite a few more questions."

Adam blinks at him. Sits back. Seems disappointed.

"You want to ask me about my love life?"

"Now that I have something to give a fuck about, yes."

"You didn't give a fuck when you thought I was straight?"

"Neither of us want me to answer that, Adam."

One of Adam's eyes is twitching spasmodically. He's haggard as fuck. Exhausted. Rao should let him sleep. But he can't let this go. Not yet.

Adam laughs, low and tired. "I really hate you, Rao," he says.

"You said that before."

He'd whispered it before. Rao'd pulled it out of him before. Humiliated it out of him.

"Yeah, I did." Adam's eyes are closed again. Back against the headboard.

Two steps forward, Sunil. "Did you mean it?"

Adam opens his eyes to meet Rao's. That heavy feeling comes back, resting just behind Rao's ocular nerve like a migraine without pain. Pressure.

He shakes his head. "No," he mouths, voiceless.

He's spilled single malt on the table. It's right there, a splash of it the size of his little fingernail. If he leaves it there it'll eat through the varnish and scar the wood. If he leaves it longer it'll evaporate, rise into the air, alcohol molecules bumping around under the low ceiling, suspended in cigarette smoke. Rao leans down to examine the spill more closely, is reaching for it with a finger when it disappears. Which is not, he realises after a confused second or two, his doing. The bar's gone dark. Another power cut. Cheers and jeers from the surrounding tables. He waits to see if this time the hotel generator will cut in.

It does. He exhales. Lights another cigarette. His hand is shaking. That's the whisky. But if it weren't the whisky, it'd be not enough whisky. If he were sober right now, he'd have to listen to the room. International agency pricks bragging about how many war zones they've been in. Journalists swapping photographers and vehicles. Brittle expats being weird about everything. Everyone everyone else's best friend. Everyone loathing each other. Everyone mendacious. A rotating cast of lies and liars. Faces he knows, faces that come and go and return and go again. Faces staring into phones, arranging cars. Faces that most often greet him, as he walks in, with suspicion, with irritation, or the fixed smile that means fuck off. The usual. *When did this get to be usual?* he thinks. *When wasn't it like this?* He lifts his hand to his forehead to rub at the frown that's a pressure between his eyes. It doesn't go away. Drags his fingers lower to massage his cheekbone. It hurts, a bit. His skin's doing that thing where it feels like it's not his. Then he remembers that tomorrow will happen, and that's a sickening turn, like skidding on ice, the wheel going light in his hands.

Ash falls everywhere when he stubs out his cigarette. He stares at it on his fingers. How long has he been here? Good question. He looks up to the line of clocks showing different time zones on the wall above the bar and is surprised because none of them are there. Someone'll have nicked them, yeah. Because things go missing around here all the time. Clocks, minds, wallets, wills to live. He turns his wrist to find his watch. Stares at it for a while. The bastard face refuses to resolve, so he recites numbers. Discovers, to his surprise, that it's not even midnight, though it feels like four in the morning.

Then blankness falls on him, heavy and damp and far too stifling, and it goes on a while, until eventually a question hauls and heaves its way out of it.

What do you want, Sunil?

Well.

He wants to pass out.

There's a problem with that. Experience has taught him that the hotel staff aren't big fans of unconscious patrons on the floor. They don't like fights, either. He's not their favourite guest. So. Where was—yes. Somewhere upstairs is his room, and he supposes he's going to have to get himself there first. The mechanics of doing so are vague.

Adam, he thinks. Or says out loud. One or the other, anyway. Because he has a sudden sense of Adam's physical presence. It's odd, he decides after a while, how Adam never smells bad. Maybe it's the way the American government stamps them out. Maybe they put something in the mix like Twinkie preservatives. Because sometimes Adam smells hot and clean, like laundry, and sometimes more like vermouth and knives. Sharpest when he's angry, sometimes when he's tired. Iris root too. Hint of motor oil, but maybe it's not motor oil. Maybe it's C4.

He's thinking of Adam again.

That'll be because he's fucked, yeah? Times like these, sometimes he's blacked out and opened his eyes in the morning in a real bed with bottles of water within arm's reach, and that's all Adam. Rubenstein makes things easier. But it's not that. *Fuck*, Rao realises slowly. *I think I miss him.* Is that mad? He can hear Adam's tired sigh. *Yes, Rao*, he says. *That's completely fucking insane.*

Very carefully, Rao turns in his seat, looks about. No. Adam's not here. That's very strange. He should be. Wasn't he here, just now?

The air in the room is darker now. Maybe the generator's dying. No, it's just cigarette smoke. Darker than usual, almost black. He glances over to the blank space on the wall where the clocks should be. The wall's not right. It's not painted vermillion. It's wood panelling rouged with a patch of sun. And when he looks back down at the room it's empty and he's completely alone. There's never been anyone here. And the truth of what this is falls on him. It's death, he knows it is, opening inside him like a mouth, and he opens his own to scream—

He wakes into it. Sweating, constricted, tangled in sheets, one arm trapped behind his back. But the relief of it being a dream is torn away in an instant when he realises the scream he can hear isn't coming from his mouth. It's coming from somewhere else. *Still a dream*, he thinks, desperately, and his throat closes up because he knows it's not true. Can't move. Can't breathe. Couldn't scream now if he wanted to. Because it's Adam. This is Adam's scream. Adam is screaming.

*

"Adam?"

What wakes him isn't the tearing in his throat, the sound of his own shouts dying in his chest. It's Rao shaking him. Rao saying his name. Adam blinks up at his face.

The room's too hot. He's shivering. So is Rao.

"Are you alright, love?" Stupid question. Adam screws his eyes shut. He must take too long to answer because he hears a tap running. Then Rao's feet on the carpet. "Obviously you're not alright. But I mean—are you alright?" he clarifies, badly.

Adam cracks an eye to look at him. He's holding out a glass of water. He looks shaken. Worried. Rao almost never lets it show like this. Panicked and wide-eyed as he puts the glass on the bedside table.

"I'm fine," Adam lies.

Rao sits beside him on the bed. "Is that one of those 'I'm fines' where you're not fine at all?"

Once, not being able to read truth in Adam's words would have freaked Rao out. Lately, he's getting better at figuring him out on his own. Adam gives up on his lie.

"Yes."

"Is there anything I can do?"

So much. He could do so much to help. He could leave, but Adam doesn't think that would actually help. Wanting him to is instinct, some deep wound in Adam's gut crying out for quiet and safety. Rao's never embodied safety, not to anyone, including himself. But if he left, Adam would feel worse. And if he stays, then Adam will feel . . .

Doesn't matter.

"I don't know," he answers. Noncommittal. Another lie.

"Scoot over, then."

Adam acquiesces, giving Rao enough space to get properly into the bed. He stretches out, makes himself comfortable. Turns to face Adam. Streetlights outside. Everything is blue and orange. Rao can't have any idea what his face looks like in the half darkness. Rao's staying, and that seems better than him leaving, but Adam's skin aches like a bruise.

"What was the nightmare?"

"Aren't you supposed to ask if you can ask first?"

"What kind of rule is that?"

Adam sniffs. "One that allows me to run interference."

"Very funny. You don't have to tell me—"

"No, I'm just being a dick," Adam sighs. Trying to distract Rao. Crying out for quiet and safety. Maybe just one of those. "Would you believe me if I told you that I don't remember?"

"Wouldn't have any choice in the matter, love. I'd have to believe you."

"Not the first time you've said that."

"Not the first time it's been true."

Rao's voice sounds deeper when he's being serious. It's different from his regular lilting sarcasm, a distant relative of the biting tone his insults are laced with. Nightmare sweat is cooling in the small of Adam's back and it's making it very difficult for him to figure out if he likes Rao's serious voice or not. He might hate it. He feels strongly about it. He knows he does because he keeps replaying what Rao just said, turning it over and over in his mind.

Maybe he just wants to get away from Rao's voice on repeat in his head. Maybe he doesn't remember the details of the nightmare, but he knows what it was about.

He thinks for a while. Maybe he just wants Rao to know. Yeah. Of all people, Rao. If anyone, Rao.

"I think you would've liked my aunt Sasha. Or she would've liked you," he begins slowly. It's strange to say her name out loud. Feels like it's been years. Maybe it has. "She died when I was a teenager but I always kind of thought—"

Silence. He stops, surprised. He has, hasn't he? Always thought, somehow knew that Rao and Sasha would have gotten along like a house on fire.

"Thought what?" Rao prompts, nudging Adam's shoulder with his own. He leans against him, doesn't move away. It's a tactic. Rao deploys charm to get what he wants, never intimidation. But it's a tactic Adam appreciates right now. He'll take it.

"I was supposed to go live with her," he says. Rao's question is still there in the air between them but it doesn't matter. Has anything ever mattered? "We had this big plan to get me out of my dad's house. All I had to do was leave the house before six."

Adam keeps his eyes open. The clock that Prophet pulled out of him floats in his vision whenever he blinks. He keeps his eyes open in the half-orange-blue light.

"She was waiting for me at a junction near my house, and I was supposed to meet her. We were supposed to get out of the state before my dad even noticed that I was gone. I never found out where we were going to go. She was going to drive, or she got plane tickets, or something. I didn't have to think about it. She had it all planned out."

His eyes sting, dry. He has to blink. Hates it.

"What happened?" Rao asks, quietly. There it is again: the serious drop, that illusion of depth in his voice.

"You can guess."

"I can. But I don't think that's the point, is it?"

"No," Adam sighs. "She waited for me for too long. Didn't see an oncoming truck. Truck driver wasn't expecting her to be parked where she was. The coroner called it for just a little after six."

Rao doesn't say anything for a long time. Maybe it's not that long. Time doesn't always work the same way. Maybe it's just a single second stretched out forever in front of them. Pulled out into the silent wishes that Rao could have met Sasha, the questions Adam can feel bubbling under Rao's skin and into the other thing that can't ever be spoken. "That's what I saw. What I made was me failing to leave and go live with my aunt. Not a model plane. Like it probably should have been. Not one of my knives, like you predicted."

Rao swallows. Blinks in the half light. Adam woke him and he must be exhausted, but he's just going to have to suck it up a little longer. He's always wanted Adam to talk more.

"Well," Rao says quietly, unexpectedly gentle. "You know I'm a kinky bastard. I've always liked knives. Always liked how they work, you know? People are very much themselves when they're wielding a knife. People are very much themselves when they're underneath a blade."

Adam frowns. He's not following Rao's reasoning. "You're talking about lies again," he concludes.

"I'm talking about truth," Rao counters, shaking his head. "You made a moment like a knife."

"Oh." He knows what Rao's trying to say about him. "It must have confirmed some theories."

Rao exhales. It's almost a grunt. He's tired and he's frustrated. It's making him relax farther against Adam, press heavier against his side. "What *are* you on about?"

"Psychopathy."

"Ah. That was— You aren't, though."

"I'm not *not*."

Rao laughs softly. "No, love. That's me."

"What?"

*

It's hot in here. Stifling. Adam's shivering again. Affectless tears gleam on his cheekbones in this cinematic half light and the shadows under his eyes are so dark it looks like makeup. He's blinking back at Rao as he waits for an answer. His face isn't expressionless. It's disoriented, confused. Rao hates that it is. His own eyes ache. His sinuses hurt. Hurt like jet lag. Hurt like truth-run exhaustion. Hurt like compassion. He just wants Adam to be ok. So he doesn't bother answering Adam's question. Doesn't consider the manifest idiocy of what he's going to do. He just does it. Slips an arm behind Adam and gathers him up. Drags him down gently until Adam's head rests on his chest, and to his astonishment, Adam lets him do it. Absolute quiescence, unresisting passivity, and Rao is holding Lieutenant Colonel Adam Rubenstein in his arms and his own heart is beating hard. It's probably adrenaline. Probably.

It's just that—it isn't, is it. It's not adrenaline at all. Adam's shockingly heavy with muscle. There are hard biceps under Rao's palm, the faint tug of the scruff on Adam's jaw catching on Rao's stupid Union Jack tee. It's far past disconcerting. Shit. *Shit.* He should have thought this through. It's been a long time since he's felt the weight of a body on his own, this much sweat-soaked solid skin. He takes a deep breath and fights off a surge of desperate, overwhelming need, want so intense he can taste it. Tells himself a little hysterically that this is *Adam having a breakdown at 3:00 a.m.*, not *motel hookup round two*, takes another deep breath, lets it out shakily, shifts sideways a little uncomfortably, and after a few minutes of something like barely contained terror, gets over it.

Just about. A rolling wave of weariness hits him then, so sudden and entire he only barely registers the way Adam's pressing himself closer, has thrown an arm right across his chest to grip him tighter. Only barely registers all this, because Adam is falling asleep, is already asleep, and if Adam's asleep then Rao's good to sleep too.

CHAPTER 39

"You don't have any idea, do you?" he blurts out as soon as Adam wakes. Rao's been sitting in the chair by his bed for some time, impatiently drumming his fingers. He has things to say. Things Adam has to hear.

"Rao?"

"Look, what happened in there was incredible. It came out of loss, obviously, I mean, that's what Prophet does. But you didn't conjure safety. You conjured something else."

"Failure," Adam offers flatly after a while.

"No. Well, yes. Bear with me."

He should shut up. Adam's a wreck and only just awake. But he can't. Because Rao's had a hell of a night. It's not just the revelation that Adam can cuddle. The death of his aunt and what that meant, the sudden apprehension of Adam having been an actual child, his sexuality, his whole— Rao frowns. Adam's got a heart. He's got a *fucking heart*. What's he supposed to do with that information? He's going to have to put it to one side. That's what he's going to have to do, because Rao's hell of a night started after he fell asleep. The dreams were—they weren't dreams. He doesn't know what they were. But he knows what caused them. The Prophet inside him might not have chosen to make doodhia wood dolls or beloved childhood bedrooms out of thin air, but it is very, very far from inert.

What's inside him is busy. It's doing things he can't describe or conceptualise because words weren't invented for things like it. The closest he gets is during the intoxicating shivers up his spine that hit him repeatedly last night, waking him each time. Each one carried with it a ghostly intuition, like a signal harmonic, and all were different. The first was like a chasm of stacked plates of glass, another seemed as if all the music that ever existed had bent back in on itself and become a single tone. In another, Prophet was working on him like a paper thread book he'd played with once at Sotheby's, a faded Zhen Xian Bao. Each page was covered in squares that unfolded into tiny boxes. If you closed them all, you could lift two adjoining squares at once, turning those into different, bigger boxes. Or you could shut them all if you wanted and make the whole of each page a box. And then? Shut those boxes, lay the whole book flat, turn it on its side, and pick up the corners to turn the whole book into one single hollow box. It's like that. Like that, but backwards. As if every inch there is, is folded inside itself uncountable times, and the boxes inside the inches go on forever.

He shivers again. He needs to talk about what he saw in the test room. Needs Adam to know. Needs him to know like he needs to breathe. He knows the truth of what he saw. He doesn't know it in his accustomed way, which is disconcerting. He knows that explaining it to Adam might be impossible. Words. All the trust people have in them, the worlds between them. The ludicrousness of them. But he's going to have to do his best.

"You conjured a choice. You brought a choice into existence, Adam. That's so much better than the things other people make."

Adam sits up. Rubs at one shoulder. "It wasn't a choice. It was a failure. Over and done."

"No. It's not. That's not how this works. Choices aren't traps, like the things regular people make. They're hinges. The world swings from them, you know?"

"Swung, maybe."

Rao can't do it. He can't explain. The frustration is so immense he wants to punch something. Takes a deep breath. "What you did in there, it's important."

"If you say so."

He tries again. "You're feeling like shit because what happened didn't lock you in a fake loop, like other people, it opened you up instead. It opened you up to—"

Adam raises a hand. "I'll take your word for it."

Adam needs him to stop. Which is fine. It's not like he can go much further. "I'm having trouble with words this morning," he admits, and the smile he tries then feels watery, like it's stuck on with paste. He knows he's being an arse. Having word trouble isn't in the same order of difficulty as Adam's full-on breakdown. But he really is struggling. It's not as bad as it had been in the immediate aftermath, when he'd forgotten so many words he'd wondered if Prophet had attacked the language centres of his brain. If it had done, it was temporary, because the words are all back, all there for him to use. It just feels as if none of them are working properly. None of them are talking about what's *there*.

Now he's watching Adam swing his feet to the floor. Push back the blankets. He's getting up. Rao watches the balls of his feet on the carpet, the crook of each toe, the bones of his ankles, the musculature of his calves and knees and thighs, aware of the actions of sinew and blood and lymph and all the vascular patterns that are somehow visible to him though they can't be seen. He knows the temperature beneath Adam's skin, feels the air in the room parting to let him pass through. For a moment he's astonished that Adam's alive. How impossible it is.

But as he watches Adam tuck a filter in the coffee machine, spoon coffee into the paper, fill the reservoir from the tap, something happens inside him. It's deep and final. It's something like a nod, an *ah*, an exhale, like the sensation of taking a seat. It's here, and it's him, but it's somewhere else, and it isn't him at all, and a memory is twisted into it. An ancient banyan in Ranthambore, a grove of trees that was all one tree, streams of evening light through crowded columns of roots. Roots that weren't roots at all, because they'd grown downwards from the branches above, dug themselves into the ground and thickened into trunks. Rao sits in the hotel room and pulls the memory right through himself.

When it's done, there's an intense feeling of relief. He can still hear the sound of one of those forest birds calling a slow metronome through motionless air. But whatever that was, it's over. Every hiss and glug from the percolator bubbles in his chest like laughter. It's going to be ok. It is ok. The chair is just a chair now. The room is just a room. He's come down from whatever Prophet did to him. It's all ok. And Adam's ok too. He's making coffee. He's not speaking, but when the fuck was that anything other than normal for Lieutenant Colonel Rubenstein?

Everything's smooth now, seamless. The coffee smells amazing. He stands, pulls back the curtains, and looks out of the window. His eyes catch on a tattered Jack in the Box bag flapping from the branches of a parking lot maple. The way the wind fills it and drops it over and over again: it's bewitching. Sirens in the distance. The just-risen sun painting the cloudy Aurora sky with swathes of gold and rose. It's fucking lovely.

"Rao."

Somehow Adam's dressed. Barefoot, tieless, but dressed. He's holding out a mug of coffee. Rao takes it. He should have made the coffee. He should have done that. He's not sure why he didn't. He's a fucking terrible friend. "Cheers, love," he says. "It's a beautiful day out there."

Adam looks vaguely amused. "Glad to hear it," he says and sits back on his unmade bed, taking uncharacteristically delicate gulps from his mug.

"How are you holding up?" he asks.

"Don't. I'm fine. I'm—a lot better. Thanks, Rao."

"Yeah, no problem."

"No, I mean . . . last night. Thanks for sitting up with me. And thanks for after. I don't know if I would have slept for very long if you'd left."

He's so *earnest*. "You ever had a cat, Adam?"

"What."

"A cat. You've seen them, right? Fur, tail, arsehole, retractable claws. You've never had one?"

"No."

"Me neither, but people I know do, and I'm hopeless at moving them when they fall asleep on me."

"I'm not a cat, Rao."

"Definitely not. But I still wasn't going to move after you fell asleep. Listen, I'm famished. Shall we go out for breakfast? You up to it?"

Adam thinks for a full two seconds, then nods.

Rao gets up, rests his coffee on the windowsill, retrieves his chinos from the floor, steps in and zips them up, slips on his sneakers, picks up his mug, takes another mouthful of coffee. "Going out for a smoke, won't be a sec."

Mug in one hand, he pulls a soft pack from his pocket, extracts a cigarette with his lips, stuffs the packet back in his pocket, takes the chain off the door, rests a hand on the handle, and what happens next—it's like the fucking Pamplona bull run. The door bursts open, bouncing off Rao and spilling hot coffee down his groin and thighs—he yelps—and then two men are standing in the room. It's the built guy from reception that first day and an even bigger guy with a buzz cut and a jaw like a cartoon anvil. Full G.I. Joe vibe. A proper heavy's heavy. Their eyes register Adam, still sitting on the bed with his coffee, face as blank as Rao's ever seen it. Now the two guys are looking at Rao for all the world like they're bounty hunters and he's a jail breaker. Rao feels a punch of laughter through the shock because he is. He fucking is, isn't he. He takes the cigarette from his mouth. "Can I help you, gentlemen?" he enquires.

"We're here to escort you to Dr Rhodes," says reception guy.

"Not Montgomery?"

"Rhodes wants to talk with you," anvil guy explains.

"I got that," Rao said. "But this isn't very polite, lads. I'm only half-dressed and we've not had breakfast. Why don't you fuck off back to Veronica and we'll think about dropping by later."

"She wants to see you now."

"You know what?" Rao says. "No."

"You're coming with us," anvil guy says. Rao can hear the edge he's put in his voice.

"No we're fucking not," Rao replies, hearing the glee in his. He's light as air, floating, adrenaline ballooning up his spine. So much so, he giggles when anvil guy steps forward, takes hold of his upper arm, and tugs him towards the door. And then. Then—

Rao's seen Adam fight. Or *thought* he had. There'd been a guy kicking about in Tashkent that Adam had trained with back in the day—*no, not at Langley*, he'd breathed wearily when Rao had enquired—and during a few days' downtime, this guy and Adam had arranged to spar in a basement backroom of the US embassy that was fitted out with mats and pads and punchbags. Which amused Rao greatly. Backrooms in British embassies tended more to faux gentleman's club libraries featuring week-old copies of the *Daily Telegraph* and moth-eaten Afghan rugs. He'd come along to watch because he had fuck all else to do, thought he'd heckle from the sidelines like a cunt just to piss Adam off, but that didn't happen. It didn't happen because Adam fighting was a revelation. His usual blankness was stripped away to reveal a being of aggressive fluidity and unholy grace. Rao watched the whole session in stunned silence, barely able to breathe, and when it was over, as Adam rolled his neck, sniffed, and walked back towards him, the expression on his face made Rao snicker. He'd looked so intensely *bored*. So yes, Rao thought he'd seen Adam fight. But right now, in a Colorado hotel room, he understands that wasn't what he'd seen at all.

It's not elegant. It's brutal, and it happens incomprehensibly fast. Adam throws scalding coffee into anvil guy's face. Brings an elbow—Rao thinks it's an elbow—down hard on the back of his neck. Once he's on the ground, a knee with all Adam's weight behind it is dropped squarely on his groin. The guy's making terrible noises now, fighting to breathe, and *shit* the receptionist guy has just put one hand on Adam's shoulder to pull him off, and that was dumb, that was *so* dumb, because Adam uncoils, punches receptionist guy in the throat, pushes him against the nearest wall, smashes his head twice against it, and then suddenly there's stillness.

Relative stillness. Because the guy on the floor is writhing and Rao's heart is beating a ridiculous tattoo against his chest. Right. Right. He's still holding his coffee. He looks down at the mug. His knuckles are locked around the handle so tight he might never be able to let it go. Right. Ok. He shuts his eyes. This is a situation. The situation is— What is the situation? He takes a deep breath, opens his eyes, and looks.

Ok, he might shut his eyes again. The receptionist's on tiptoe, struggling to breathe, head tipped back against the wall. And with good reason, because Adam's pulled a knife from god knows where and has lodged its point an inch to the left of his chin. The tip must be grating against his jawbone. Blood is running down the blade. Rao can't see Adam's face, but the other guy's eyes are wide, nostrils flared like a terrified horse.

Shit. Shit. Rao was only being a dick because it pleased him to be a dick, because he's always a dick. *It's what he does.* Of course they should go to the facility. Of course they should see that psycho Veronica Rhodes. All the answers they need are there.

Fuck.

The man on the floor interrupts his thoughts with a series of hoarse noises shaped a little like words. Rao looks down. His nose is broken. When did that happen? Sees him spit blood and try again.

"Call him off," he croaks.

"What?"

"Call him off, call him off."

It might be the most ridiculous thing he's ever heard. Rao splutters. "You think I'm the one in charge? Adam, love," he says. "Tell him?"

No answer. Rao takes a couple of steps to bring Adam's face into view. Freezes. *Christ.* All those times Rao's told Adam he's barely human. All those stupid jokes. But here it is. There it is. That's not a human face.

"Adam?" he says cautiously.

Adam twists the blade a little. Inhales. Exhales. Blinks a few times. Shifts his grip on the knife. His expression doesn't change, but maybe, Rao thinks, he's thawing, atom by atom, into something fractionally less remote.

"He's not in charge," Adam says, like he's just learned how to speak. "See?"

Adam's knife hand is wet with blood. It's soaked his shirt cuff, is spreading in terrible patches through the cotton of his sleeve. Rao can see drips forming at his elbow. One falls to the floor. *Shit.* He has to *try.* "Maybe stand down a little, Adam?" he suggests.

Adam frowns, turns his head towards Rao. The look in his eyes is almost too much to bear. It's like he's pleading for something, and Rao has no idea what. He nods.

"If he lets you live," Rao says to the guy against the wall, "you're going to back the fuck off, yeah?"

A strangled noise of assent. Adam steps back. Both of them watch the guy slide to the floor, both hands pressed against his jaw. He's coughing uncontrollably.

"Adam, you ok?"

"I'm fine."

"Did you hurt him anywhere else?"

That gets him a blank look. Rao bites his lip. "So look, I know . . . this sounds mad. But I think we should do it."

"What?"

"Go to the facility. I know it's not optimal. But we need to hear what Veronica has to say for herself." He grins. It's a terrible effort. Glances at the mug he's still holding. "Also the coffee there is great, and they might give us breakfast." He yanks his head at the man on the floor and continues. "And doctors, yeah? I don't think we should leave these poor sods here and I don't know about you, but I'm not too keen on calling an ambulance."

All the eyes in the room are on Adam now. All register his nod of assent.

Rao puts his coffee cup down on the table, massages his fingers. "Lads," he says almost sadly. "This could have been a bit easier if you hadn't come in all guns blazing. You could have just asked nicely. We'd have been happy to go see Veronica, but you had to be dicks about it."

CHAPTER 40

The smile Veronica gives him when Montgomery ushers them into her lab is no longer winter sun. It's hungry. Expectant. Her face is a little flushed, her fringe awry. Different lipstick today. Darker. Eyes a little wide. *She's fucking mad, isn't she*, Rao thinks, unfazed.

She purses her lips. "What happened in the test room?" she demands.

Rao steps forward, scratches at his beard, runs his hands through his hair, grimaces at the whole backwoods Elvis thing he's got going on.

"You wouldn't happen to know a good barber in town, would you, Veronica?"

She stares. "No."

"You have the resources to find out, surely. Care to send some more heavies to bundle one in the back of a van and bring them here?"

She catches on. "Your pickup? It seemed a wise precaution, now I know who you both are."

"Do you? Well done. Congratulations. Veronica, the men you sent were assholes. You could have tried calling on the motel phone and asking nicely."

"I was busy."

"Yeah, well. So was I."

Silence. Her face is that of a person who's never learned to smile. *There she is*, Rao thinks. *The real Veronica Rhodes.* "I'm told your colleague overreacted."

"No shit."

"Should we be concerned about his propensity for violence, going forward?"

Yes, you bloody should. "The fuck are you asking me for? Adam's right here." She raises a hand to her fringe, smooths it. Rao steps forward. "A word in private?" he murmurs. "I'll be fine," he adds, answering Adam's dubious look in the same breath.

Veronica complies. He knew she would.

"Right," he says when they're both in the corridor. "Let's talk. What's in this for me?"

"We need to understand exactly what happened in the test suite, Mr Rao. It could lead us to a cure."

"Could, yeah. Maybe. But that's not what I asked. I'm a cynical bastard these days, Veronica. Good of humanity isn't really my thing anymore."

"We can talk compensation—"

"We can certainly talk compensation. We very much should, in fact. But before that we need to talk about Adam."

"What about him?"

"You want me on board, don't fuck with him, don't test him, don't lay a finger on him. Don't bring him into this."

She's frowning now. "But he—"

"Terms. Take them, leave them, Veronica."

The frown deepens. "You're not in the strongest of negotiating positions, Mr Rao."

He giggles. Doesn't mean to, but *really*. "Of course I am. I know what happened in there, and you're going to need me onside to get more of it. It wasn't . . ." He searches for the right word. Finds it, after a while. Picks it up, wet paper from asphalt. "Passive. It wasn't a passive thing."

That piques her interest. "What do you mean, passive?"

He raises his eyebrows and waits.

"Ok," she says finally. "If you work with us, Mr Rao, we'll leave him alone."

She's lying, of course. Rao doesn't mind. It's enough for now, and he's pretty sure that however blank Adam can be, he's going to know if they lobotomise the fucker. Maybe.

Montgomery and Adam are gone when they reenter the lab, and Rao turns to Veronica, ready to kick off. She raises a placatory, perfectly manicured hand. "He's being taken to have a blood test, Mr Rao. That's all. It's nothing to worry about. We'd like you to have one too.

You both appear to be well, but we don't want to take any chances with your health, do we?"

If he weren't so weirdly antsy about Adam's whereabouts, Rao'd enjoy these ludicrous falsehoods, empty reassurances in primary school teacher tones. "Where is he?"

"Mr Rubenstein is in a treatment room off the main corridor. I'll be taking his bloods personally. Dr Montgomery is in the room next to it. He'll take yours."

*

Adam watches as Dr. Rhodes finds his vein and begins to extract blood with practiced efficiency. Doctors always have trouble finding Adam's veins, but not this one. She speaks first. Bright and pleasant. False. "Your reaction to Prophet suggests you aren't a psychopath, Mr. Rubenstein." She smiles, looking up from his arm. "But you're far from normal."

"No shit," he says under his breath.

"You aren't surprised?"

"To find out that I'm not a psychopath?"

"Mr. Rubenstein." Dr. Rhodes makes a complicated vial swap look as simple and routine as replacing toilet paper. Adam wishes he liked her like Rao seems to. "I've just told you you're not normal. Doesn't that bother you? Interest you?"

"Colonel."

"I'm sorry?"

"Lieutenant Colonel Rubenstein." He's too tired after the last few days to let her weak power plays slide. Too tired after the motel and Prophet and late nights and too much truth with Rao.

"As you like."

"Thank you. Where's Rao?"

"He's also having his bloods taken."

Another vial change.

"Mm," he hums, noncommittal. "What other tests are you intending on running?"

"What makes you presume we have other tests in mind?"

"Dr. Rhodes, you're drawing a lot of blood from me right now."

"It does seem a remarkable amount, doesn't it?"

They're locking horns. It's not about rank. Not about authority. Rhodes isn't trying to intimidate. They're both after the same thing. Apart from Rao's whereabouts, all Adam cares about is finding the avenues in front of him that will grant him as much information as possible. Tit for tat is an easy road to walk, but it's tricky to make it to the end with more intel than the other person. Still, it's the route Adam chooses.

"Fine. I'll play along for now."

"Appreciated."

He sighs, gives her what she wants. "What do you mean, not normal?"

"Ah, that *is* the question." Dr. Rhodes smiles again. This one is genuine, and it does nothing to change Adam's opinion of her. "Do you know what you made after your exposure to Prophet?"

"No, I don't. What was it?"

She shakes her head. "You misunderstand the question, Colonel. What did you make? What was it that you manifested? You didn't respond to it like our other test subjects."

Adam decides to leave the "test subject" designation on the table for now. It'll keep her sweet—or as sweet as she's liable to get.

"That was . . . a moment from my life."

"A happy memory?" She's removed the needle, is taping a wad of cotton over the puncture wound. He presses it with an index finger, eyes drawn to the bruise over the artery above his wrist. He's overtired, skin still jumping after the encounter at the motel. On edge, not knowing exactly where Rao is or what they're doing to him. Blood loss, at this stage, at this level, will only keep him going. Rhodes has stopped short of making him useless, but there is no way in hell Adam is going to let her know that.

"No, Dr. Rhodes," he answers. "It wasn't a happy memory."

"That makes you the first subject who appears to have manifested an object relating to an unpleasant past experience."

"Glad to be of service."

"And you weren't drawn to your . . . moment."

"No."

"Do you think you could replicate it? If you were exposed again?"

"No."

"No, you don't think you could replicate it?"

"No, I don't think that's going to happen."

"You're withholding consent."

"At present."

"Very well. I have more questions—"

"I don't think I have any answers you want."

"But I'll refrain from asking them for now."

She tilts her head. She's expecting more. She's not going to get it.

"Thank you for being such a good sport, Lieutenant Colonel Rubenstein," she says eventually.

"A sport."

"Indeed."

*

Rao massages his inner elbow with a thumb, stares at the tubes of his own blood on the desk. *Dark*, he thinks stupidly. *So dark. Blood's so dark.*

"So, we'll be analysing this," Montgomery says, picking up a pen to fill out labels for the vials.

"No shit," Rao snaps. He's surprised by the flinch that provokes. "Sorry. Sorry, Monty. It's been a bit of a morning. Why've you drained my arm, exactly?"

"We have to determine if you were contaminated in the test room."

Very much so, Rao thinks. *You have no idea.*

Montgomery pauses then, pen wavering. Rao lets the silence stretch. It's a promising one.

"You know, Mr Rao, we had a debrief after"—he clears his throat—"after. We viewed the footage several times. What happened in there wasn't clear."

"Veronica wasn't a happy bunny, eh?"

That gets Rao a nervous, conspiratorial glance. *Bingo*, he thinks. That's the fulcrum. Monty's shit scared of her.

"She . . . exhibited some frustration, yes."

"Fucking hell, Monty," he says seriously. "Don't envy you that experience. Veronica's quite terrifying, isn't she?"

"It's Kent."

"What?"

"Kent Montgomery."

"Ah. Right. Kent. So, Kent. You had a theory about what happened, yeah?"

"I did. I pointed out that her own psychological profile could have negatively impacted her experimental design. She didn't take into account the possibility that emotional bonds, relational attachments could inhibit the action of Prophet. She agreed with me." He smiles. Then the smile slips. "She brought in some volunteers. They weren't military. A couple." His face falls farther. He lowers his voice to a near whisper. "Between you and me, I don't think there was fully informed consent. She put them in the test suite together, dosed the man. He made an orange blanket."

"He's in the ward?"

Montgomery nods. "With his blanket."

"Where's the girlfriend?"

"She's there too."

"Bedside vigil?"

"She's sedated."

"How sedated?"

Montgomery shakes his head sadly. "I don't think Dr Rhodes will stop with these two. I asked her to give you some time to recover, and she was amenable to that. But I'm glad you're here now. I hope you can help."

"Help what?"

"We'll take whatever we can get at this stage," Monty says slowly. "But don't tell her I said that."

CHAPTER 41

Rao watches the door of the room Montgomery ushered him into. Windowless. Cramped. Feels like a holding cell. Maybe that's just how the room makes Rao feel. Maybe he's being horribly unfair to the room. A vending machine clicks and hums itself out of a nap beside him. Moodily, he remembers that he was supposed to be eating some godawful fast-food breakfast. Something too fatty and greasy and absolutely too perfect not to complain at length to Adam about. Because Adam had looked better this morning, and Rao's plan had been to carp about something banal until the man had regained his usual blankness. After all that time in the motel faced with an honestly, immovably, horribly empty Adam, Rao is sorely missing what he'd always assumed was his innate lack of emotion. He watches the door and thinks threats into the air. If they don't bring Adam back out soon, then he'll . . . He'll what, exactly? *Figure it out, Sunil,* he thinks, acid thoughts turning against him in the humming silence. They were supposed to be getting shitty McDonald's pancakes. Egg McMuffins. This day was supposed to be different. This all feels wrong. He's waiting, and he's staring at the door, and he's thinking very hard about not eating every last candy bar in that fucking machine.

*

Rhodes escorts Adam to a small room where Rao is perched on a table swinging his legs and looking bored. She tells them she'll return shortly. He half expects to hear the door lock behind her when she leaves. It doesn't. There's no need. There are eight doors between them and the parking lot, and likely all are controlled remotely from a room they'll never see. If Rao decides to make a break for it, he'll have to come up with a better plan than *run*.

After the door clicks shut, Rao stops kicking the air, starts snapping his fingers. "What did you talk to Veronica about?"

Adam hesitates.

"No one's listening," Rao assures him.

"Dr. Rhodes wanted to talk about what happened last time we were here," he says, pulling a chair up to the table. He sits, looks up at Rao, watches him frown out his thoughts.

"You didn't give her anything?"

"Not much. I told her that what happened, what got made—"

"What you manifested—"

"Was a moment."

"A moment. Yeah. Well. I guess that's true enough." There's something about how Rao says that, something a little *off*. Adam opens his mouth, but Rao doesn't give him the chance to ask his question before he's answering it. "No, I still can't tell with you, you paranoid cunt."

That's not it. That's never been a concern. In fact, sometimes Adam is happy Rao can't tell with him. "Happy" is the only word he has for the feeling. Happy that Rao can't just do a run on him and leave him unraveled like he does everyone else. Rao has no qualms about doing runs on people—and truth be told, neither does Adam. They've never talked about it, but it's clear to him that Rao's knack of zeroing in on a person's vulnerabilities, coupled with his extraordinary talent, his knowledge of the truth, makes Rao one of the most important intelligence assets in the world. Espionage rests on trust, on passing, on leverage, and on betrayal, and Rao's existence breaks the whole system. Nobody seems to get that. Drives Adam crazy. It should be obvious as soon as they find out about Rao.

"Does Rhodes know about you?"

Rao doesn't miss a beat, doesn't stop to test it. Which means he already has. "Yeah. She's had access to some official file or report. Very recently. It's probably one of yours."

Adam blinks a few times. "Probably," he agrees, voice tight. Rao sniffs, holds back from another blow. He's feeling merciful today. "I don't trust her, Rao."

"Of course you don't," Rao laughs. "Veronica's out of her mind. But she's alright."

"You just said that she's out of her mind."

"Quite a few people could say the same about me, love. And after this morning, I suspect a few people are saying the same about you."

Adam sits back in his chair. Thinks about Dr. Rhodes, her fake smiles and plyboard-thin lies. "You like her," he asks. Doesn't sound like a question, but it is.

"I really do."

Adam knows how much Rao enjoys liars. Once, drunkenly, he told Adam he considered himself a connoisseur of mendacity. He explained that he doesn't always know when people are lying. All he can tell is whether a statement says true things about the world. But with the right questions, he can usually find out. And that, he said with relish, is the art of the thing. The only times that liars get to him are when he decides their lies are stupid or messy or lacking in craft.

Adam can see that Rhodes appreciates "the craft." And she—well. Rao has a healthy appreciation for beauty, and Dr. Rhodes is objectively beautiful. Classically so. Silver screen beauty that out of Glorious Technicolor, in faded and muted reality, makes her look a little cruel. Brunette. Gray eyes. Carefully chosen shades of lipstick. She and Rao flirt when they talk, and Adam wonders if either understands the terms of their interactions. Likely both simply enjoy playing the game.

"Is it because she's English?" he deflects.

"You're fucking with me."

"I'm fucking with you."

"Glad to see you're in such a good mood after our highly eventful morning, Adam," Rao observes, a grin spreading on his face.

Adam looks down, picks at the dried brown on his left cuff. Blood is hard to get out of a light cotton blend. "Mm," he says.

"Adam?"

"Yes, Rao."

"Where did that knife come from?"

"Waistband."

"Looked like you pulled it out of thin air."

"I think that's what it looked like to the guy who grabbed you too," Adam says. The words tumble out of his mouth. Truth pulled out of him because he's tired, or is suffering transient anemia after his blood was drawn, or because now he owes Rao every truth he's carefully squirreled away.

Rao looks at him. Adam looks right back. He doesn't think Rao's scared or spooked, though the expression on his face looks like both at once. *He's got to know now*, Adam thinks. If he didn't before, he definitely got a clue after last night, after their talks in the dark, after how quickly he fell asleep when Rao did what he did. And if that hadn't been enough, he knows now. He *has* to.

They hold each other's gaze. Neither of them startles or looks away, but it's too much for Adam to handle. He takes a breath and picks himself up, goes to the vending machine. He's got a few loose dollars in his pockets, and he effectively ruined any chance they had at having a decent breakfast. "What do you want?"

Rao thinks about his answer very seriously. "Butterfinger."

Adam throws the chocolate bar to him, and Rao unwraps it, eats it ruminatively. "Veronica and Monty," he says, taking another bite, "don't know about our tail. They didn't put it on us."

"Who did?"

"Internal. Yeah. It's Prophet. This project has hands that don't know what other hands in the project are doing with themselves."

"Succinct," Adam comments mildly.

Rao ignores that, pops the last of the Butterfinger in his mouth, chews, and swallows. "Also, Veronica isn't related to Elise."

"Elise?"

Rao smirks. "Someone I knew in Berlin. Spitting image. It's uncanny."

"This isn't relevant, Rao."

"I hoped it might be."

Adam exhales. "Miller?"

"She's alive. Still in a trance. Veronica knows what happened in Polheath but wasn't involved. Monty doesn't know about it. Monty hasn't a fucking clue about much, if you ask me."

"Is Miller—" Adam begins but shuts his mouth as the door opens and Veronica walks in.

"Colonel," she says, looking at Rao, "I'd like to have a word with your colleague. Might you excuse us?"

Rao screws up the Butterfinger wrapper, drops it on the table. "Is there somewhere for Adam to get breakfast?"

"There's a canteen. It's on the third floor. I'm sure Montgomery will be delighted to take him there. I'll call him now."

"Rao, I'm—"

"Go on Adam. I owe you."

CHAPTER 42

As soon as Adam and Montgomery leave, Veronica leans across the table, picks up Rao's discarded candy wrapper, and walks it to the far side of the room. Dropping it into a trash can, she looks back at him, smiling brightly. *Mistake*, Rao thinks. He doesn't respond well to being treated like an errant child. But then he notes the professional interest in her eyes. She pulled that move specifically to provoke him. *Yeah*, he thinks. *She's good.*

She walks out of sight behind him to the far side of the table. A scraping noise as she draws up a chair. He considers staying put. Decides, on reflection, to hop off his perch and take a seat facing her.

"Cards on the table, Mr Rao," she says. "Montgomery is concerned with the possibility that you and Colonel Rubenstein are infiltrators."

"Infiltrators."

"Moles. Working for outside agents. He's worried about it."

"I expect Monty worries about a lot of things," Rao sighs. "Who am I supposed to be reporting to?"

"Montgomery suspects corporate espionage."

"And you?"

She purses her lips. "I'd say the most likely recipient would be the British security services."

"I'm not reporting to those wankers."

"And I should take that on trust?"

"I would," Rao says. This is tiresome. He sits back in his chair. "Look. We just came here following a lead. We were trying to find Flores. He's the friend of a friend. But I'm feeling inclined to stick around."

"Are you. I'm a little perplexed about why."

He snorts. "Because Prophet fascinates the ever-living shit out of me, Veronica. I can't stop thinking about it."

"So you're . . . sticking around in the spirit of intellectual enquiry?"

"One way of putting it."

"Better than prison?"

"Another way."

She considers him. "You've rather a difficult personality, Mr Rao."

"I'm being sweet as pie to you, Veronica."

"Your psych evaluations suggest oppositional defiant disorder."

That's bullshit, Rao thinks. Doctors invented ODD so they could diagnose it in patients who hate them. Besides, he's not in the habit of blaming other people for his problems. When things go wrong, it's always Rao's fault. He's just an asshole who's a maestro at fucking things up when he's just trying to *help*.

"You have those evals, do you?" he says.

"I do. I also have a police report relating to an incident at the Laburnum recovery centre."

Rao briefly closes his eyes. "Fucking reports," he sighs. It's not that he didn't expect Lunastus to have fingers in all the pies, but it's still disagreeable to discover how quickly they've got hold of this shit.

"They tell me," she says, "that you're a man capable of unprovoked violent assault."

"It wasn't unprovoked."

"Why don't you tell me all about it?"

"You sound like one of them," he says sourly.

The Laburnum. The group sharing session. The peach-hued walls, the velvet couch, and the marble fireplace. The chairs around the rug in the middle of the room. The black rug. Circular. Like a hole in the floor. Rao staring at his trainers, failing to get anywhere near serenity because his opiate eiderdown has been taken away and memories of Kabul have kept him from sleep for days. They're cutting, continual, snipped into sections like strips of celluloid film, looping backwards and forwards in nonsensical, nauseating patterns. It's not the lack of heroin that's slowly killing him here; it's the memories. It's the lack of sleep. It's the floral room fragrance that's making his throat close. The faux-orchid-scented air.

He focuses on the man opposite. Colonel Foster. It's his time to share. Tattersall open-necked shirt, a patrician mouth. A pair of red corduroy trousers. Brogues. Salt-and-pepper hair with a fringe swept sideways like he's still wearing a beret. He's here with a DUI. He's resting his hands on his knees, looking everyone in the eye, one after the other, telling them about how he started drinking heavily after the first death at the training barracks he commanded.

Well that's bollocks, Rao determines. *Didn't start then.* He's interested now. Listens harder. Foster is strangely at ease in this therapeutic space. It's because he grew up in a God-fearing Roman Catholic family. He's used to confession. How to do it. How to make it sound: everything he says rings with deep conviction. A little tremble in his voice here and there. A catch, sometimes. He's telling everyone how terrible it was as a commanding officer to have such things happen under his watch. The beating squads, the torturing of new recruits. He has tears in his eyes now, and his hands are shaking. His voice is a whisper when he tells the group that he had had no idea what was going on. How the bullying had been kept from him. How he should have known. How those suicides from the bullying were unacceptable, and he'll never forgive himself—

No, Rao thinks firmly. Not all those deaths were suicides. *No.* Foster had full knowledge. Foster is lying through his fucking teeth. And Foster is suddenly all of them. All the bastards who strung up naked men in Kabul and left them soaked through bitter nights, who assaulted them, humiliated them, pissed on them, threw them against walls, broke their souls to shards and ashes, and Rao isn't sitting anymore, he's up and retaliating, he's punched Foster in the face, tipping his chair back onto the carpeted floor, and he's kicked him in the face twice, the second time harder through the fingers that Foster brought up to protect himself, and he's doing it because he *must*. It's not just to stop this cunt talking, it's to obliterate every lie that ever was in the world, to obliterate the knowledge that such things happen in it, and he feels the searing pain in his toes as the kicks connect and usually that would clear his head but this just makes him go harder, there are people reaching for him and he pushes them off and he's on top of Foster now, punching him again and again and there's blood on that tattersall shirt and blood on his knuckles, and a siren is going off and Rao isn't sure if it's in his head or in the room, and then they drag him off and there's a needle and Rao laughs when he feels it and he just keeps saying thank you, because he's never before met unconsciousness with so much simple, desperate gratitude.

Remembering it, his knuckles sting anew. He won't lose it. He *won't*. Rubbing his eyes, he takes a deep breath, lets it out as slowly as he can. "It wasn't unprovoked," he repeats. "He was a lying piece of shit."

"You nearly killed him," she says almost cheerfully. It's calming, Rao thinks, how little she cares. Like she's balancing out how much he does in some cosmic ledger. Now she purses her lips, leans closer. "You should know I've been considering granting you both access to the project."

"As test subjects?"

"Subcontractors. Coworkers."

"Because you'd rather have us inside the tent pissing out than outside pissing in?"

"No. Not for that reason," she responds, unflinching. "Mr Rao, you were flagged as a potential asset to our project before you walked through our doors. I'm told you can detect fakes. Can you identify an Eos Prophet Generated Object, an EPGO, on sight?"

"Yes, as I'm sure you already know. Go on. Cards on the table, Dr Rhodes."

"My sources also say you're a human polygraph, a unique talent that could also be of use to us here." She opens her hands. "So, Mr Rao. Tell me. Using your special powers. Am I being straight with you?"

Yes. She is. And isn't. "Yes, Veronica. You are. Though there's rather a lot of lying by omission, isn't there? Most of your interest in us is medical."

"Could you be persuaded to join us?"

"I'll have to talk to Adam."

She nods. "If you did, will you behave?"

He sniggers. "Really, Veronica? *Austin Powers?*"

"Rao, could we please talk seriously?"

"Alright, alright. I'll talk to Adam. Be nice to us both, and I'll do my best."

"Is that an undertaking?"

"It's as much of one as you're going to get."

The following morning, staring at the TOP SECRET designation printed on the pages spread over the boardroom table, Rao is experiencing a small, silent crisis. He'd expected Adam to painstakingly read the small print, factoring in every possible consequence of them joining the project. Instead, he'd simply picked up a pen and signed everything Montgomery put in front of him. Rao'd never thought Adam capable of recklessness. But the clock had happened. That guy he'd pinned to the wall with a knife. And now this.

This is what Adam wanted, though. Wants. Rao'd quizzed him about it yesterday evening outside the motel, dogs barking fitfully, streetlights flickering on. While he'd sat on the low car park wall and smoked, Adam had informed him they were fine to sign up to the project.

"Fine in what sense?" Rao'd asked carefully.

"Miller's boss wants us embedded in the program."

Rao'd sighed. "They should bring in those assholes she told us about. The paranormal ones."

"I mentioned them. Got told there was no guarantee the EIO weren't involved already and could be antagonistic to our investigation. We have to stay under the radar as long as possible."

"You don't sound enthusiastic about any of this, love."

"They're orders, Rao."

So here Adam is. Here he is. Here they both are. Reckless as fuck. Still, the coffee continues to be great. He pours himself another cup. "We don't get chocolates now we've signed up as guinea pigs?"

Montgomery glances at Veronica. "We can call for chocolates," he says. "And you aren't guinea pigs. You're subcontractors. The forms are quite clear."

"They are. They say I shouldn't have access to this project at all," Rao continues cheerfully, counting on his fingers. "I've taken drugs, I've drunk to excess, I've been arrested, and I'm not a US citizen."

"Technically, neither of you should have access to this project," Veronica counters. "But I wanted you, so I made it happen. Let's move on. I believe Montgomery wants to run through some of our results, and then we can discuss ways forward that suit our needs."

"Whose needs?" Adam says.

"Ours. I'm assuming you want to discover what Prophet is, and why it does what it does. It's what we want too."

"Ways forward?" Rao asks.

"Investigative procedures."

"Vivisection's off the table."

"I've never vivisected anyone," Montgomery says hastily.

"Rather glad to hear you say that."

"Ok, so, let's give you a little more background on my background," Montgomery begins, voice shifting official. "Before this I worked with Dr Rhodes on another Lunastus biomedical project, based in . . . uh, based elsewhere. Before that I was at DARPA, where I was a program manager."

True, Rao thinks, *but so fucking boring.* "Kent, can we skip the CV? Just tell us about Prophet."

"Ok, ok, sure. What do you want to know?"

"What happens to it after it's got inside someone and fucked them up?"

"Near torpor," Veronica says. "Reduced heart rate, periodic breathing, metabolic rate suppression. The state is akin to hibernation. Physiologically fascinating."

"Does it break down over time?"

"Good question, Rao," Montgomery says. "No, it doesn't. After exposure, levels in the bloodstream remain constant. We can't detect any trace of Prophet or any potential metabolites in sweat, urine, faeces, or exhaled air. Once administered, it crosses the blood-brain barrier, concentrating in regions of the brain associated with memory retrieval and emotional regulation."

"You're employing scans? MRIs?" Adam asks.

"Yes," he says. "But we can only scan subjects with smaller EPGOs. Nonmetallic ones."

Veronica cuts in. "Functional MRIs don't directly show the presence of Prophet; they evidence the neurological activity it provokes. For finer structural analysis, we've recourse to histological samples." She smiles at Adam. "In layman's terms, we've been looking at samples of tissue to understand where Prophet collects in the brain."

"Whose tissue?" Adam says.

"Our previous principal investigator has made an important personal contribution to our understanding of the substance. Postmortem. We're very grateful to him."

"Fucking hell," Rao breathes.

She waves her hand. "It won't happen again. Not now we've robust postinfusion protocols."

"And you have Kent."

Montgomery gives Adam and Rao a miniature, self-conscious wave. Clears his throat after a few seconds of silence. "Moving on to test results. Rao, I'm afraid I have to inform you that you have Prophet in your blood."

Rao sits forward. Asks the question that's been burning away at him. The question that's remained bafflingly unanswered by every run he's made at it. "Why haven't I made something and got stuck to it, then?"

Montgomery shifts in his seat. "Well . . ." he begins.

"I'm not a psycho, Kent."

A watery smile. "Individuals with psychopathy show a characteristic pattern of neurological activity after being exposed to Prophet. We can put you through an fMRI and—"

"What about Adam?" Rao interrupts.

"Well. Mr—Lieutenant Colonel Rubenstein is a mystery. His self-administered dose was a full one. But there's no trace of Prophet in his blood."

"Samples got mixed up?" Adam asks.

"No," Veronica says. "Everything was labelled at source. But considering these results, more blood work will be required."

Rao groans. "You're a bunch of vampires."

"I'm a doctor," Montgomery protests.

"So was Renfield," Rao shoots back. Adam looks down at the table-top and smiles. Rao's not seen that smile for a while. He wants to see it again. "He's not going to start eating flies, is he?" he whispers.

"Good protein source."

"Fucking hell, Adam. Ok, Kent, fire up your MRI. I think you should give me a scan."

CHAPTER 43

Rao's voice comes over the intercom. "This is weird."

"How are you doing, Mr. Rao?" Rhodes checks. Adam watches her tap a key to change the image on-screen. Still Rao's brain. The scan isn't fully complete, but he understands what he's looking at. Rao's skull. His eyes. There his brain sits and sparks. "Looks fine here."

"No, I think I'm alright," Rao confirms. He's nervous in the machine, his voice wavering like he's on the edge of laughter. "I just wanted to say that this is fucking weird."

"Please don't move," she instructs. Rao responds with a huff over the mic and the line goes quiet.

Adam decides he hates the scanner. Which surprises him. Generally speaking, he doesn't mind heavy machinery. He understands engines. Aircraft. Cars. Doesn't understand people who feel intimidated by technology, by things built to do a specific job and do it perfectly. He grew up on base surrounded by the roar of jets, the noise of sirens and horns. But the machine Rao is in isn't making the kind of sounds he's used to. They're alien hums and tones that remind him of alarms. In the back of his mind, the Big Voice over base loudspeakers. *Scramble. Scramble.*

"I would like to take you to see the clock, Colonel Rubenstein," Dr. Rhodes murmurs, her eyes on the screen. "Your manifested object."

"I know what clock you're talking about, Dr. Rhodes," he says. "To what end?"

Rhodes smiles a private smile. "To see what happens."

There are a million reasons why he shouldn't tempt fate by going down there. One of them is the expression on Rhodes's face. Adam looks at Rao in the tube, hears the alien clunks. Thinks about how Rao simply wanted to talk through how *weird* it is in there.

"Alright," he says.

Dr Rhodes turns her head to look at him properly. She'd been expecting resistance. "Do you think you can handle it?"

"I suppose we'll find out."

"Told you there'd be aftereffects," Rao complains as the slab rolls out of the tube like a tongue rolling out of a mouth. "I feel fucking dreadful after that."

"The scan is entirely safe," Rhodes says. But once Rao is sitting up, she takes his wrist all the same. Old school. Eyes on her watch as she counts the beats. "You're fine."

"Dreadful," he repeats venomously. "I want to lie down."

"You're welcome to do so, Mr. Rao. There's a bed in the room next door. Take as long as you need. Colonel Rubenstein and I are going to take a stroll down to the testing labs to revisit his EPGO."

"The clock?"

"Correct."

Rao shakes his head, winces. Speaks with his eyes closed. "Adam."

"Rao."

"That's bonkers."

Adam's inclined to agree, but Rhodes speaks before he can reply. "Even when the object was manifested, Colonel Rubenstein showed no signs of wanting to connect to it. I'm confident revisiting it will be a risk-free experience."

Rao opens his eyes and looks at her. Adam knows that look. Rao's pissed that he can't tell if her statement's true because it's about him. Rhodes, he realizes, has no knowledge of that particular block.

"I'm coming with you both," Rao says eventually.

"I thought you wanted to lie down," Adam says.

"Yeah, but that was before I found out you were intending to be a dickhead today."

Adam hums. "Not the whole day."

Rao smiles, despite himself. "Piss off, Adam."

Rhodes leads them to the test room. It's illuminated by ceiling strips of harsh fluorescents, but the clock is lit up like the sun is hitting it just right in Nevada sunset yellow. Time frozen in place.

They stand in silence looking at it. Adam doesn't feel anything. He wonders why. The nothing he feels now is complicated. The loss of his aunt, the absolute failure of that day, the sheer drop of grief—all of it sits in the exact same place inside him as before. Might be sharper. The wound opened fresh again. Maybe. He can remember everything that happened back then more clearly now. There must be something about Prophet that seeks out the part inside you that yearns for safety and pieces it all together. Pulls it out like a lure forged by muscles you didn't know you possessed. The EPGOs are that, in the end. Some kind of lure. A light to entice, an escape. An escape that's a trap.

But he's looking at the clock in the test room, flush to a section of wall decorated like his mom's kitchen, and he doesn't feel a damn thing.

He turns to face Rao and Rhodes.

"You have no urge to get closer to it?" Rhodes asks. Adam shakes his head. "Are you feeling any revulsion at the sight?"

"I'm indifferent," he tells her.

"Remarkable," she murmurs, stepping closer to check his pupils. He hates her standing so close, but in only a second's breath she's moving beyond him to examine the clock for what he can only imagine is the fiftieth time. He watches her lift a pencil tip to the ticking, trembling second hand that will never move any farther. "Could you touch it?" she asks.

He walks to the wall. When he raises his right arm, his hand is pale with fluorescent light, though the clock and the paneled wall around it glow with evening sun. He isn't casting any shadow.

He reaches. Hears Rao take a breath.

The glass is warm, like evenings were. He feels nothing. Lets his hand drop.

"You're alright?" Rao says.

"I'm fine."

"Outstanding." Rao presses a thumb against the bridge of his nose. "I'm going to lie down. You'll find me."

"I will."

Rao grunts, leaves the room. Doesn't look back. Adam watches the door close behind him.

"I wonder if another dose might clarify matters," Veronica muses aloud.

Adam considers it. All of them were expecting *something* to happen when he came down here. His feeling nothing at all is a result of sorts, but it's not exactly thrilling. Funny, considering that the clock is an artifact of the most thrilling thing about him. He's not normal. The clock. Feeling nothing. Being a snowstorm in Rao's cacophony of truth: all point to him being abnormal. *Anomalous*, Dr. Rhodes would say.

"Let's find out," he says. "The scientific approach would be to repeat the experiment, correct?"

Rhodes's lips twitch. "Perhaps more of a military approach, but I'm not inclined to disagree. Intravenous, like last time. Shall we?"

Adam's already rolling up his shirtsleeve, thankful that Rao isn't around to try to talk him out of this. But this isn't like last time. Adam wants to see the other side.

Rhodes isn't prone to wasting time. It's one of the few things Adam likes about her. He waits for her to return with the single dose of Prophet with his back turned to the clock and the Nevada sunset. She doesn't speak again, remains silent as she wipes his skin and injects the dose. Not even the customary *you'll feel a pinch*. He recognizes that this doesn't come from mutual respect, only her desperation to find out something new about a substance she barely understands, but he appreciates it.

Once it's in his veins, she withdraws the needle. Stands back. They wait. Adam looks down at the injection site, expecting to see where the needle went in. It bit like hell. It should have left a mark. And there *is* a mark, but it's not red. And it's not a pinprick. It's black. It looks like a mole. He thinks he's imagining things when the mole starts to grow. He holds himself still, barely breathing. It's not a mole. And it's not black. It's dark gray, then silver. It's Prophet, and it's pooling out of him like he's an overfull glass of water. With every tick of the not-clock behind him, the bead doubles in size until a puddle of Prophet is sitting in the bend of his elbow. He looks up at Rhodes.

"That's . . . unusual," she says, eyes wide. She sounds like she's just seen something beautiful. Singular. The tone people use when they talk about the first time they see some natural wonder. Machu Picchu. Niagara Falls. Adam Rubenstein with a silver puddle on his arm.

"What am I looking at? What's happening?"

"It doesn't want you," she breathes.

Hard not to take that personally. "What does that mean?"

"I'm not sure," she says. Her voice is full of awe. Adam hates it. "Don't move," she adds.

She rushes out of the room and returns with a petri dish and another syringe of Prophet. Silver, like it's solid in there. Adam knows it isn't.

"Tip your arm, please. Carefully," Rhodes says. They both focus very hard on the task of letting the Prophet drip from his skin to the dish. It doesn't flow like a liquid should. Doesn't get caught in the tiny hairs of his arm. Isn't directed along the imperceptible lines of his skin. It drips onto Rhodes's dish like it's flowing over smooth metal. Adam thinks about all the times Rao's called him a robot.

"What is your plan, Dr. Rhodes?" he asks, nodding at her second dose of Prophet.

"I'd like to try again," she says. Doesn't try to hide her enthusiasm.

Adam thinks about that. Thinks about Rao with his headache, lying in another room. Thinks about how ready he had been, when they first arrived, to get Rao his answers or die trying. How much he'd been hoping for the latter. That had been stupid but only because he'd acted without a cushion in place.

Rhodes looks hungry. Adam thinks that she doesn't know what hunger is.

"Let's talk testing," he says.

Rhodes raises an eyebrow. "By all means."

"How far do you want to go?"

"Obviously we must stay within safety parameters," she says. Adam doesn't buy it. It's a line. He doesn't care about her script.

"And if we didn't?"

Her gray eyes darken. "May I ask why you have a sudden interest?"

"I'm wondering how much I should be asking for in return for compliance."

She smiles. "What is it that you want?"

Adam smiles back. "We were talking about you, Dr. Rhodes."

"Proximally, I want to know why Prophet affects you like it does. Ultimately, there is no limit to what I want to know. I want to know everything. And now, as is customary in a negotiation, I'd like to hear your demands in return."

"How deep does Lunastus-Dainsleif go?"

"You're talking about influence?" she asks. He nods. "Deeper than, I think, you currently comprehend."

"That sounds like dick swinging, Dr. Rhodes."

"It does, doesn't it?" She's smug. "It isn't."

Adam hums. "If that's true, then you already know about Rao's record."

"Correct."

"I want that cleared."

"Is that all?"

He shakes his head. He's got a lot more. "You'll employ him. As staff, not as a contractor. I don't care if he actually does a job or not, Rhodes," he tells her. "I don't give a shit. You'll have him on payroll and he will be entirely legit. I want him untouchable."

"To what end?"

"Stability."

"For only one of you?"

"You said there's no limit to what you want to know. Doesn't that imply there's no limit to the tests you want to run? Beyond safety parameters."

"You're willing to commit yourself to this course of action for—"

"Yes," he interrupts, suddenly aware of how little time they might have before Rao comes looking for them. "If I get confirmation, without a doubt, that all of this will be provided. I want certainty that it will go ahead."

"Of course."

Adam inclines his head. "Then we have the beginnings of a deal."

"Seems that we do," Rhodes concurs. "Would you be willing to take another dose?"

"I'll do it again," he nods.

"Now?"

"No. After I get everything we just talked about in writing."

"In order for this to work, you may need to be recategorized as a new hire," she says. "Working for the research department."

"I don't care how you make it work," he says honestly.

"I appreciate your directness, Colonel."

"Fine. Dr. Rhodes?"

"More requests?"

"Rao doesn't need to be in the loop from the beginning."

"You don't want him to know?"

"He will know, eventually," he tells Rhodes. No reason to lie. He doesn't tell her the truth, that he wants to control when and how Rao finds out. He has to be the one to tell Rao every part of the arrangement. Not Rhodes. Not Montgomery. Not any of their Lunastus lackeys. Only him. "He just doesn't need to be contacted directly with any of these details until everything is finalized."

"Ah. I believe I understand."

"I don't think you do, Dr. Rhodes, but I do think you'll do as I ask."

"Very confident."

There's no reason why that statement strikes Adam's last nerve. Could be the simple fact that he doesn't like her. Every smug comment out of her mouth feels like sandpaper against his skin. Then again, he feels closer than ever to snapping since that first dose and the clock, after everything said and unsaid in the motel.

Whatever. Adam gives her the truth again. He doesn't care if she doesn't like it.

"I'm a test subject with my wits about me and free access to a weapon. I could blow my brains out and ruin your chances to get what you want. Every hostage situation begins and ends with confidence."

She doesn't answer for a beat. Two beats. Eventually, she opens her mouth. "I sincerely hope that we get along, Colonel Rubenstein."

"You'll cope, Dr. Rhodes."

CHAPTER 44

Rao complains so incessantly about his headache and nausea that Rhodes sends them back to the motel for the rest of the day. "Fucking dreadful," Rao repeats in the car. Adam smiles tightly at the road but doesn't respond. It's difficult not to. There's a twist in his stomach that surprises him, and every time he looks at Rao, even glancingly, the twist gets sharper. Feels like when he saw Rao in Polheath for the first time in forever, feels like when he found out about the heroin, about Kabul. Feels like he just connected the dots between what he said about Rao that one time and what happened to him. Guilt.

At the door to their room, Adam's not so much struggling with the keys as hesitant with them. Doesn't want to go into a closed space with Rao. Feels like a trap. Hard to tell who's being trapped.

"Rao."

"Adam," Rao sounds exhausted. He's leaning against the wall beside the door, eyes closed, head turned toward Adam's voice. "What does that tone mean?"

"What tone?"

"The way you just said my name means there's a problem," Rao sighs, eyes screwed tighter now. "Are we talking about an external problem or an internal one?"

Adam hums. "Could you define 'external' versus 'internal' for me in this context?"

Rao opens his eyes, annoyed. "'External' as in there are snipers trained on us."

It's funny, but Adam doesn't laugh. "There are no snipers, Rao."

"Brilliant news," Rao says flatly. "In that case, could the internal problem wait a bit? This headache is the kind of monster that demands drugs before it'll leave me the fuck alone, and since I'm moderately sure there are none in my immediate vicinity?" He pauses, looking vaguely hopeful. Adam shakes his head. "Right. Then I'm going to go lie down. Can it wait?"

Adam thinks about that. It can wait, but he doesn't want it to. He rips off the Band-Aid. "Rhodes and I decided to dose me again." Rao pushes off the wall. Looks at Adam closely. "When are you planning to do this?"

"Already done."

"Fuck's sake, Adam." Rao grits his teeth.

"Let's talk about it inside."

"Fucking let's."

In the room, Rao sits down heavily on his bed. "What happened?" he demands.

"Nothing."

"What do you mean, nothing?"

"It means nothing happened," Adam repeats. "I didn't manifest anything. Rhodes administered a single dose." He shrugs off his jacket and rolls up his sleeve. Shows Rao the crook of his elbow. The injection site stings, and there's a dull ache there, like a bruise under his skin, but he's just showing Rao his arm. There's nothing there. "I guess it happened again."

"What are you talking about?"

"My blood work showed no Prophet. I'm not normal, Rao. It doesn't work on me like other people. It did what it did to me last time, then it must have just come out of me. Like today."

Rao blinks at him. "*Fuck off.*"

"What?"

"Are you *serious*?"

"I don't understand the question."

"Then fuck right off. It didn't just come out of you, last time," Rao says. He sounds incredulous. Insulted. Adam frowns, confused. "I took it out of you. I— Fuck, Adam, I *drew it out of you*. It was me."

"That doesn't make sense," Adam says. He feels stupid. Distant. He tries to remember the day. He thought he remembered everything. The injection, the manifestation. But the more he thinks about it, the more he realizes there are breaks in his memory. There was the clock. The clock, everything about it and everything it meant. All the grief he'd felt back then, all the grief he'd buried since, all of it out in the room for everyone to see. He could barely breathe through it. Couldn't think through it. And then—then he could. He knew that Rao was there. He'd asked to leave. They'd left. There were stoplights somewhere. In the vehicle. In the car. That's what Adam remembers.

"What about any of this makes sense?" Rao counters. Adam silently agrees. "What did Veronica say?"

Adam crosses the room, sits on the other bed. "She said . . ." He pauses. Hates that he does. Stupid. "Rhodes said that it didn't want me."

Rao crows with sudden laughter. "Story of your life," he splutters.

It's weird how quickly Adam forgot how to handle Rao saying things like this. The insults that aren't quite insults. It's the purest form of Rao familiarity: find the weak joint and pull until the structure groans into near collapse. Adam isn't ready for it, this punch to the gut.

Internal problem.

It obviously shows on his face. Rao winces.

"Sorry, Adam."

"It's fine," he says. It nearly is.

Adam's grateful when Rao goes to take a shower. He sits on his bed and stares at the chaos surrounding Rao's. Clothes on the carpet and discarded mugs and candy wrappers on the nightstand. He's gotten pretty good at ignoring Rao's clutter, but right now he can't. He picks up the mugs, brings them to the kitchenette, and washes them. Puts the trash where it should be. Picks the clothes off the floor, folds them, lays them on the bed, and he's squaring the books on the nightstand when Rao reappears wearing a waffle robe and hotel slippers. Every time Adam's cleaned like this before, Rao's given him shit for it. But now he looks amiably at Adam. "Cheers," he says. "I'm a messy bastard. Okay if I order in some pizza?"

Pizza's turning into their Big Talk food in the motel, Adam thinks as he chews slowly on a slice. He's going to have a Pavlovian response to pepperoni after this. He's going to order a Meat Lover's one day and start opening up to the server about his relationship with his mother.

"Alright. I've waited long enough, I think," Rao says, mouth full.

Adam blinks at him. "For what?"

"A thank you. I saved your life, Adam."

He's talking about Prophet. Drawing it out of him. Did he?

"Did you?"

"Yes, you prick."

But he can't tell. He can't tell with me. "Today, with Rhodes," Adam says, "you weren't there. It came out of my skin without you around—"

Rao holds up a hand to stop him speaking, looks away, mouth moving silently. He's doing a run. "Well. I obviously know fuck all about what's going on with you. But I can draw it out of people. Other people."

"That . . . changes a few things."

Rao exhales, puffing up his cheeks. "No shit. I think I can cure people," he says, then grins. "I can cure people."

"How?"

"Fuck knows."

"Rao."

"No, really. Adam, I don't know how to run that. I don't know what I can check. I have no idea about the mechanics of this shit, and I don't know why I can draw it out," he says quickly. "It feels right, though. When I did it for you, it felt—" He stops. Shakes his head.

"I have a fucker of a headache, Adam."

"I know, Rao. Do we tell Rhodes about this?"

"We'll have to. I have to," Rao says. He rubs his face. "I'm seeing her first thing tomorrow to go through my scans. I'll do it then."

*

Veronica's office delights Rao. It seems more like a prop-filled stage than a space a human uses for work. When she invites him to join her behind her desk, he takes a seat and looks up at her monitor. It's showing a photograph of a village in the Cotswolds. Honey-coloured stone houses, lush meadows, a ribbon of road climbing a hill. *Bibury*, he thinks. Back when he was a student, he'd visited it with his parents on holiday, staying near Cirencester in a country house hotel. Amiable political talk with his father over breakfast on the terrace, ragged peacocks dragging their tails across dew. Rao necking mimosas under a sky luminous with mist and the promise of a hot summer's day. His mother wrinkling her nose at the state of the peacocks here, she and Rao sharing one of those moments of laughter that punctuate all his memories like gold.

"How are you feeling?" Veronica enquires.

"Fine," he answers. *I miss my mother*, he thinks.

"No symptoms?"

He shakes his head. Trying to explain his episodic hallucinatory experiences would be tedious. Besides, they're private. "Let's look at my brain, Veronica," he says.

She taps at the keyboard and Bibury is replaced with his scan results. The image shifts and roils as she moves through sections of his skull. *Thunderclouds*, he thinks. The way they roil and rise on a summer's afternoon. She raises a pencil, taps the screen with its point. The minute click of graphite on glass as she moves it from place to place. "Frontal, limbic, paralimbic, midbrain regions," she says. "Increased activity in these conforms to previous research in the neurobiology of nostalgia. But your reward centres—hippocampus, substantia nigra, the ventral tegmental area, and ventral striatum—are all in an intense state of arousal."

Rao waggles his eyebrows.

"Not that kind," she says. "Many pointers for further investigation, Rao. For now, let's just say Prophet affects your brain differently than it does other people's."

Maybe, he thinks, *my brain is just different from other people's*. She's dropped the "Mr," he notes. Pity. He'd rather liked the formality.

"Perhaps now might be a good time for us to discuss the passivity you raised, in relation to events in the test room," she murmurs.

"Absolutely we should," he says. "That whole thing in the test room, that was down to me."

"You induced Rubenstein to dose himself?"

He freezes momentarily. "Not . . . not that bit. What happened afterwards. I physically drew the substance out of him. It came out of his skin, right out of the palms of his hands where I was touching them, and it went into mine. Like osmosis."

She looks hungry again. Leans forward. "Not like osmosis. Not at all like osmosis."

"I'm not a bloody biologist, Veronica. Capillary action, osmosis, whatever you want to call it. It came out of Adam, went into me."

"Did it affect you?"

He makes a moue. "A little bit. Got dizzy for a while."

This is by far the greatest understatement of his life, he thinks. He should get an award.

"Are you and Lieutenant Colonel Rubenstein romantically attached?"

He laughs, surprised. But of course she'd ask that. "No."

"You're close?"

"He doesn't really do 'close,' Veronica."

That gets a different smile. She's got a host of them lined up for every occasion, and they're all almost right. "I wonder if we might replicate this phenomenon," she says.

"You want me to take it out of someone else? Very happy to try."

Flores looks worse. Greyer, the smile on his face stranger, his cheeks appreciably more sunken, his skin angrier where the cassette tape is pressed against his jaw. Rao walks closer, sees now that the patch of white hair at his temple runs downwards across the centre of an eyebrow, how his bitten fingernails have grown during his trance. The mark on his face is faded but still visible. "How did he get that bruise?" he enquires lightly. Adam's looking at it too.

"Oh, an accident," Veronica says. It's a lie. "You're sure you want to attempt to extract Prophet from this particular subject?"

"It's Flores or no one."

"And you believe you can cure him?"

"I'm going to try."

"I'll call a porter. We'll take him down to the test suite and set up. It'll take about twenty—"

"We're doing this here. Here and now or not at all."

Veronica isn't happy about that. "Rao—" she begins. He shakes his head firmly, then looks down at Flores, feeling a little self-conscious. Is this a performance? Maybe. He's not worried about his ability to get Prophet out of him. He can do that. It's a fact. But he's less sure how Flores will respond to the process. It's complicated. Too many variables—physiological, psychological. Far too much resting on this.

What's resting on this?

Hunter, he thinks. He's not quite sure when it became important that he stayed in her good books, but life's full of surprises.

"Rao?" Adam's voice, just behind him. He sounds concerned.

"I think he'll be fine, Adam. Really."

Adam frowns.

Rao looks back down at Flores, considers him carefully. It isn't going to matter where he touches him. It just needs to be bare skin. But his arms or wrists don't seem quite enough of a show, and his neck and face don't seem right somehow. "Veronica, be a dear and expose his chest area for me?"

She walks forward, pulls at the cotton bow behind Flores's neck, tugs the blue cotton gown to expose a stretch of skin. Seeing it, Rao holds his own thumbs to steady his hands. They're shaking. A memory, out of nowhere. The morning six days after his seventh birthday when he'd seen what looked like a fat, furry grub clinging to a wall by an oleander bush at the back of his uncle's house. Stubby wings, tiny feet like grappling hooks on pale grains of sandstone. He'd come back to look again a few minutes later and was entranced: the stubby wings had turned to swept-back planes patterned with geometric greens and purples and pinks. It wasn't a grub after all. More like a jewel, alive, and so beautiful it made it kind of hard to breathe to look at. He found out by doing the questions that it was a moth. He wanted to touch it and knew he should not, but most of all he wanted to show his mother, so he went to find her. When he brought her back the moth wasn't just pinned like a brooch on the wall anymore. It was vibrating, wings shivering with a buzzing noise like electricity lines in a storm. His mother saw that he was nervous of it, and she told him that the shivering meant the moth was readying itself for flight, getting itself warmed up before it could leave, and that was true. Scales in his mouth, soft dust. History. Scintillating dots, just for a moment, in front of his eyes. He blinks, steps forward, and lays both hands on Flores's upper chest, fingers spread wide.

A sharp intake of breath. He's surprised that Flores is warm, that's all. Despite the steady rise and fall of his chest, that wasn't a thing he'd expected.

A few seconds tick past and the sensation begins, that hot-cold confusion across his palms and fingers. *Fuck*, he thinks numbly. He knows this feeling, and he's spent a lot of time doing his very, very best to make it go away. *Too late, Sunil*, he thinks. *But you're saving Flores.* And then the thinking stops. Prophet has seeped into his skin and all the thinking is just a dot, a dot smaller than the size of the dot over a letter *i* drifting in the open ocean and the ocean might be water, he thinks it could be, but it doesn't have depths, or tides, or waves, and it's not blue, or even the black of deep water, it's not got edges, either, it's not water, it's definitely not water, and he feels a twist of panic that picks him up and wrenches at him so hard he knows, for one screaming, yawning gulf of a second, that his brain is gone, that this is *madness*—

And then it's done.

He's back, for whatever given value of back this is, he knows he is, and he's looking at his hands. They feel a little unfamiliar, but they're his. And the skin beneath them is Flores. And the sound he's hearing is coughing, and that's Flores too. And the eyes that are looking back at him from Flores's face, between the coughs that wrack his ribcage, are the tiredest he's ever seen. They're trying to focus on his face. He drops his gaze, doesn't want Flores to meet his eyes. Because he feels ashamed of what he's done. Flores didn't ask for this. Flores didn't ask. And Rao swallows, turns his hands, stares at his palms. Nothing. They look normal. But it's in him.

"Rao?"

Rao stands. He feels a thousand years old. And then, a moment later he doesn't. Quite chipper, actually. "Adam," he exclaims, beaming. The expression on Adam's face is perhaps the most complicated he's ever seen it. He has no idea what it means. Obviously.

He bursts out laughing.

"You ok?" Adam asks.

"Yeah, I'm fine. And not the way you use that word, Adam. I'm honestly superb. Hunter's going to be psyched. Look at this Lazarus shit!"

There's a clatter. It's the tape Flores was holding; it's fallen to the floor. Flores is ignoring it, is trying to sit up, Veronica by his side. No, he's not trying to sit up, Rao realises. He's trying to get away from her.

"Veronica, think you should give him a moment, you know? And about twenty feet? Ta."

Rao turns back to Flores and this time looks him right in the eye. "Back with us?"

Flores blinks. Tries to speak.

Adam speaks first. "What do you remember," he says.

Orders, Rao thinks. Adam's good at giving them. Flores's haggard eyes track up to Adam's and stay there. When Adam asks again if he remembers anything at all, Flores nods. The horror in his eyes as he does is naked, unbearable. Worse than anything Rao saw in Kabul. Rao reaches down to take one of his hands, squeezes it gently. Keeps hold of it until Flores's expression slips back to hazy bewilderment. Then Flores rouses himself, tugs at Rao's hand, looks up at him again. Opens his mouth and manages something like a whisper. None of the words are audible, but Rao knows. He knows what gratitude is.

CHAPTER 45

Rhodes tells Rao three times to leave Flores to their nursing team. He ignores her. Now she's clenching her fists. Looks close to attempting physical persuasion. Adam permits himself a brief, therapeutic rehearsal of exactly how he'd take her down, then casts it from his mind. "Rao," he says softly, keeping his eyes on Rhodes. "Let them take over." He gets a weary look but Rao complies.

As Rao sits heavily on the examination couch in the treatment room Rhodes led him to, Adam decides he looks okay. Irritated, more than anything, as Rhodes takes hold of a wrist and examines his hand, telling him she observed filaments of Prophet extruding from Flores's skin into his own. She's speaking animatedly of possible mechanisms for this transferral when a nurse puts his head through the door and requests her attendance.

As soon as she leaves, Adam steps forward.

"I think you need some fresh air."

"What?"

"If you're up to it, we should take a walk," he says. "Outside."

"You think they'll let me out, after this?"

After what Rao just did in there, Rhodes would give him anything he asked for. She'd gift wrap it. Adam keeps that observation to himself.

"Yes," he says.

*

Adam brought him out here, Rao assumes, because he's got something to say he doesn't want anyone else to hear. But he's not speaking, shows no sign of wanting to speak, and it's been more than five minutes, and he's walking fast, and Rao's already bored with the scenery, the marked-up construction plots and rows of half-built townhouses, and he's tired after healing Flores—

"Ok," he says. "What is it?"

Adam slows and turns. His voice is deep and full of concern. "You're sure about all this, Rao?"

"Stop fussing. I'm fine."

He nods, once, after the briefest pause. "You could fix Miller."

"I can, yes."

Another nod. They pace another forty yards in silence. Eventually, Rao stops, exasperated.

"Adam. Why are we out here?"

"You tested if Miller knew about the project."

"Yeah. She didn't."

"What about Richard Clemson?"

"Who's he?"

"Civilian. Defense. Miller's higher-up. I've been taking his orders on this."

"Ah." Rao raises his eyes to the sky. Silver, matted with high cloud. He mutters quietly to himself. "*Shit.* Yeah. He's in on this project. Part of it. Miller didn't know. We should have worked that out. I should have worked that out."

"This is on me," Adam says.

"Fuck that. And fuck them." Rao scratches his beard. "So what are we now? You and me? Ronin?"

Adam smiles slowly at that. "If you like."

Rao looks at him carefully. "What do you want to do?"

"What do *you* want?"

"Heal more people. Find out what the fuck Prophet is. Work out how to fix this bizarro nightmare."

"Yeah," Adam says, face resigned. The expression is familiar to Rao. He used to love it, used to be a dick to Adam specifically to make it happen. He doesn't enjoy what it looks like anymore. "I know you want to fix things, Rao. But this might be too big to fix. You're one person. And in my experience, one person can't—"

"I'm not one person, Adam. I'm *me.*"

Adam's resignation deepens. Rao grimaces, knowing what he's about to say will come out like the worst kind of sop. "Besides, it's not just me, is it? You're here. And you're important in this, love. All this. Somehow."

"You don't know that." Adam shakes his head. "You can't tell shit about me, Rao."

"I know. But I know this, and I don't know how. You're *important*."

Adam shrugs. "I'm an expert shot."

"No—"

"And I don't mind the sight of blood."

"It'd be beyond fucked if you did, love. But, no, shut up—"

"You heal people, Rao. I shoot people. Ok?"

"You're more than that."

"Only when standing near you."

"Fucking *stop* it, Adam," Rao says. "Just stop. You're important in this. I'm not saying that to make you feel better or *do* anything. It's just how it is, and it's true, and I don't know how I know it's true, but I do know this: if we're going to be ronin or knights-errant or rogue agents or whatever, then the first rule is not to fall out about stupid shit. I've seen a lot of movies, and that's always what fucks things up."

Adam's looking at him, evidently amused. "Movies," he says.

"Shut up."

CHAPTER 46

"*Tell me again.*"

Veronica raises a brow. De Witte so rarely asks her to repeat herself.

He's speaking to her from the plant-filled private office in his sprawling Lake Tahoe home. Head tipped back, he's squinting at her now as if she's causing him pain.

"*Sunil Rao has the ability to extract Prophet from our subjects,*" *she repeats.* "*I watched him do it. Skin-to-skin contact, mechanism as yet unknown. And there's more, Steven. He metabolises Prophet. No matter how much he absorbs, his levels remain minimal.*"

"*Your pet test subject continues to demonstrate his uniqueness,*" *De Witte murmurs.* "*He remains asymptomatic?*"

"*Yes.*"

"*And on board with what we're doing?*"

"*I've told him barely anything. But yes, he seems content.*"

"*Say anything to keep him happy.*"

"*Understood. I'm working on modelling the mechanism for his extraction and potential pathways for metabolization. We'll continue monitoring him in the meantime.*"

De Witte doesn't respond for some time. Eventually he clears his throat.

"*You could,*" *he says,* "*do more than monitor him, Veronica.*"

"*I could. But I suggest we hold off from initiating more rigorous investigations.*"

He screws up his face. "*You weren't so, uh, squeamish in Guantánamo.*"

"*This is a different project. And it's a question of exigency, rather than concern for his well-being,*" *she adds lightly.* "*He's very much the goose that lays the golden eggs, don't you agree?*"

"*Fairy tales, Veronica?*"

"*Quite so, Steven.*"

CHAPTER 47

Lunastus-Dainsleif's Aurora facility is nothing like the offices Adam has worked in. Government offices don't get this kind of money, not even Defense. He knew that Lunastus was next-level, but it's another thing to wander its corridors and experience this kind of corporate luxury for real. He and Rao have spent most of their time on the windowless lower levels. But right now he's walking a brightly lit corridor on the fourth floor on his way to Dr. Rhodes's office. There. A frosted glass door with her name on it. He knocks.

"Come in," she calls.

She's at her desk. The room is sparsely furnished. A dark-green filing cabinet. A vibrant monstera. A metal mechanical pencil and a fountain pen, a monitor and keyboard on her desk. She's holding her phone. It's very late in the day: Adam disrupted her plans, he's guessing, to make or take a private call. He doesn't care.

"I want a visitor's pass," he says.

She lifts an eyebrow, puts down her phone, gestures for him to take a seat. He shakes his head. She doesn't push the matter. Gives him a thin, brief smile, nothing like the wide ones Rao gets; they work on him. "And who might this pass be for?"

"Hunter Wood. USAF master sergeant."

"No," she answers. Simple.

Adam can do simple too. "I wasn't really asking."

"Are you threatening me, Colonel Rubenstein?"

"No," he says slowly, seriously. "I'm stating intention."

She likes that. The smile he gets this time isn't as thin or brief as before. He doesn't enjoy the change. "Who is this individual?"

"She tasked me and Rao with finding Flores," Adam says. He realizes his hands are resting behind his back, like he's delivering a verbal debrief. Muscle memory. Rhodes likes that too. "We found him. Rao . . . did what he did. My goal is to return Flores to someone who can care for him outside of the facility."

"And that someone is Sergeant Wood."

"Correct."

"What's your relationship to her?"

"That's not your business, Dr. Rhodes."

She looks at him in silence for a solid ten seconds. She's trying to make him feel uncomfortable. She watches him and he watches her right back.

"We still have tests to run on Flores," she says eventually.

"Run them on someone else. You have a lot of patients, Dr. Rhodes. Ask Rao to wake another one."

"Ah, but you and I both know that our eyes aren't set on that prize," she says, her smile sharpening.

So, that's what it is. That's fine. Makes sense.

"You have my blood already."

Rhodes nods. "I'd like more."

"What else?"

"A biopsy."

Adam frowns. "Of what?"

Her too-sharp smile slips. "Has anyone ever told you that you're far too clever?"

"No." It's the truth, not that anyone can tell.

"You slip under the radar quite often, don't you?" Rhodes says with a thoughtful frown. No, it's not thoughtful. It's considering. There's the slightest of differences, important intel when dealing with Dr. Rhodes. She thrives on people paying no attention to subtle tells. Adam grudgingly admits that he can only see what she's doing because he does it too. He's just better at it.

"Professional habit," he tells her.

"Perhaps." She studies him for a while, then reaches for her pen and opens a drawer. Produces a stack of pale-yellow Post-its, scribbles a note, sticks it to her monitor out of view. "I'll look into issuing

Sergeant Wood a visitor's pass and we can discuss possible procedures in the future."

If he leaves now, he'll be giving her carte blanche to do whatever she likes to him. It's not express permission, but at this point, he thinks, implied permission might hold more weight between them. He doesn't like any of this, but he needs to get Flores out of here and get Hunter through the doors so she can see some of the shit he's had to see. And if he doesn't make it out of Rhodes's tests, he needs Hunter to have some idea of what happened to him.

And he needs Hunter's eyes on Rao.

He'll have to tell Rao. But that can wait until Flores is out and safe.

"Always a pleasure, Dr. Rhodes."

She hums and picks up her phone.

"I'm sure."

Walking back down the corridor, Adam is about to push open the stairwell door when he stops. Stills himself. Something's off. He withdraws his hand from the steel plate it rests against. Backs himself against the wall and quiets his breath. He follows his combat instincts, looks and listens for movement. No obvious threat. No sound except the low grumble of air traffic into Buckley. He takes a breath, exhales. The light in here has changed. Looking up, he sees that the line of halogen spots that ran along the ceiling on his way here has gone. Instead there are eight lamps of a kind he's seen a hundred times before. Upside-down domes tipped with brass finials. Dusty, yellowing glass swirled like the top of an ice cream. The light inside them is soft, and all the lamps are flickering gently in unison. Around them, the plasterwork is the textured popcorn of the ceiling of his childhood bedroom.

Fuck. Adam could be responsible for these, but he can't know that for sure. He doesn't think he is. They don't make him feel anything, but the clock doesn't either. Not now. All he knows is that ten minutes ago the lights were modern, and now they're straight out of a rental from thirty years ago. He looks at his watch, notes the time. Rao told him about his fears back in England. Told him this operation made him feel like he was walking into a haunted house. But it's not really a haunted house, the way things are going. There's momentum to what's happening. It feels more like a ghost train.

Adam steps forward, pushes the door open. Doesn't look back.

CHAPTER 48

The morning is bright; a stiff breeze blows through it. Curling over the rooflines into Lunastus-Dainsleif's courtyard garden, it pushes so hard at the fountains they shiver, breaking intermittently into a host of ephemeral rainbows. Rao bows his head, cups his hands around his lighter, and tries once again to light a cigarette. Success this time. He takes a lungful of smoke and raises his eyes to the miles of blueness above. *It's good to be out here,* he thinks, exhaling slowly. After days of air-conditioned rooms and fluorescent light, the press of the wind on his face is a benison. Makes this mannered quadrangle of pools, fountains, shrubs, and lawn seem close to something real.

His cigarette burns away too fast. He's about to light another when he sees Veronica walking towards him. What the fuck is she doing out here?

"Veronica, is something on fire?" he calls.

"Not to my knowledge," she says as she nears.

"What's the problem, then?"

"There's no problem at all. I saw you and came to give you the happy news that Flores is doing wonderfully well. He's walking now, with the assistance of a nurse. We're about to move him to a private room."

She tilts her head expectantly. All this was prologue. She's about to start on another round of questions about how he did it. What it felt like. Couldn't even wait until he was back in the bastard building. His spirits sink. He's really not in the mood. He could walk away. Or—no. He gestures to the chair opposite. She sits, rests her hands on the table between them, studies him for a while.

"Happy, Rao?"

"Always. You know me. Life's an unmitigated joy."

"Are you experiencing tiredness?" she asks.

"Perpetually."

The wind catches her hair, fans it over her face. She strokes it back into place.

"Your blood shows negligible amounts of Prophet. There's less in your system now than in the first test we took," she says. "So—"

"Before you talk about more tests, Veronica, we need to discuss Miller. You know Elisabeth Miller. Department of Defense. Got dosed with Prophet at Polheath," he says. She widens her eyes with faux innocence. Wants Rao to drop the subject. No chance. "Why don't you tell me about what happened there," he adds. They lock eyes. Rao waits.

"That subproject," she replies tightly, "was not under my aegis. But a degree of compartmentalisation is inevitable in a programme of this nature."

"Whose aegis was it under?"

"That's not relevant." The wind lifts her hair again. Again, she tucks it behind one ear.

Rao waits out ten seconds of silence as she scans the garden. It's deserted. It always is. Despite the tables and seating, Rao's never seen anyone here except a man in a John Deere baseball cap and overalls lackadaisically sweeping leaves.

"Straat died," she says, "while scouting for volunteer test subjects on an overseas base. There was a theory that subjects far from home would experience a different form of nostalgia, provide novel data."

"But it all went tits up."

She nods. "He broke a vial."

"He broke a vial and died."

"His death was accidental and extraordinarily inconvenient."

"But useful. Without the accident, you wouldn't have me." She blinks at him. "Fucking hell, Veronica, I thought you were supposed to be good at faking it. Couldn't you try a bit harder?"

"Hooray," she says flatly.

"Straat was a twat to carry that vial about in his pocket," Rao says. "Accident waiting to happen."

"Well," Veronica says, "he died because his vial was manufactured over five months ago."

"Manufacturing issue? Dodgy glassware?"

"Far from it. At the time, subjects exposed to Prophet weren't creating EPGOs. Straat's vial was perfectly sound. It was foolish to walk around with it in his pocket, yes. But with that particular formulation, he would have assumed that inadvertent exposure would simply have made him sad or made him feel he'd lost something. Perhaps it might have made him miss wherever he came from. Which was Michigan, I believe?"

Rao remembers the diner glowing in the fog, the dreadful roses.

"You know Prophet changes, Rao," she continues. "And you know it isn't a gradual evolution; it's intermittent, saltatory. But what you don't know, what I'm telling you now, is that these alterations have been global in nature. By which I mean all of the substance, wherever it is, undergoes change at the same time."

"Everywhere?"

"Everywhere. But there's a fascinating exception. These changes don't seem to occur in Prophet if it is already inside a test subject. If it was administered before one of these shifts happened."

Rao thinks about that. "You're saying it all changes at the same time when it's on a shelf, but not once it's found itself at home in a brain. Which means," he adds, slowly, "that there are people walking around full of early stage Prophet who never got glued to teddy bears?"

"There are."

"Can I meet one?"

"Why?"

"So I can get it out of them, do my thing, and see what happens. They're walking about full of Prophet and so am I. Nothing might happen. But it seems interesting, you know? You'll get some data from it. Shouldn't be too expensive to set up, if that's what Lunastus is worried about."

"It's not. Very well, Rao. I'll look into setting up a meeting with one of our early test subjects."

"And get me to Miller. I need to heal her too."

"She's in England."

"I *know*. But if you want me onside, Veronica—"

"That will take some time to arrange, you understand."

"Never doubted it. But glad to hear it. And for that, I'll give you a pet theory of mine. It's a good one. You'll love it."

"What?"

"When I first saw your test room, I was surprised how small you'd made it."

She gets it instantly. "Because you'd seen the diner in Polheath."

"Exactly."

She ducks her head. "When we designed the program, we weren't aware that subjects could generate EPGOs of that size."

"You didn't think someone might make an evacuation helicopter."

"We did not."

"Flawed experimental design, Veronica."

"Noted, Rao."

"But I think I know why." Rao sits back, crosses his arms. "So, I reckon the size of the objects it makes maps to the size of the surroundings the test subject is in. If you're in a room, you'll make something that'll fit inside it. If you're in the open air, you could make something of any size, theoretically. The limit's in your head. It's not about how big Prophet can go. It's about our sensing the space available for it. Put someone in a box, they'll make something tiny. Put them on a mountaintop, who knows. Might make something that'll block a valley."

"What's your evidence for this?"

"Call it a hunch."

It's not a hunch. He knows it's true. He did a run on it late yesterday afternoon over a cup of Assam tea. Worked out that Ed could make a diner because he was dosed in the open air. That the smaller things at Polheath were made by people asleep in their dorms or working in rooms. But why they were scattered around the base rather than appearing in their subjects' arms is still a puzzle. He spent twenty minutes throwing statements at it, but all he got in return was a vague intimation of flowers, somehow. Made no sense at all.

She taps her lower lip, then nods. "We might investigate this theory."

"Will I be coauthor on the scientific paper?" Rao says.

"There won't be a paper, Rao."

"*Quelle surprise.*" The wind's dropped. He lights another cigarette. "So, Veronica, have you got any further with the big question?"

"The big question?"

"Why I don't make objects like other people."

"We haven't come up with an answer on that. But with time, we—" She's distracted by a message notification on her phone. "You can tell Colonel Rubenstein," she says, reading it, "that his request for a visitor's pass has been approved."

"What pass? Pass for who?"

Merriment in her eyes. "Out of the loop, Rao?"

"Apparently, yes. So, in the spirit of not being a cunt, you should tell me what's going on."

"The pass is for a Master Sergeant Wood."

Rao sits back, waves his cigarette. "Oh, her. Yeah. Doesn't surprise me. She hates me, you know. But between you and me I'm kind of obsessed."

Evening sun through the motel windows casts bright, burnished rectangles across the carpet of their room. Rao's in a lazy, contemplative mood; he's been lying on his bed watching them lengthen and slide for a while. The sun's now so low they're climbing the far wall. "Gorgeous light, isn't it?" Rao observes, stretching into a luxuriant yawn as Adam pulls up a chair and sits. "Venetian, almost."

Adam looks at him but takes some time to answer. His face is faintly strained, almost sad, as soft as Rao's ever seen it. Maybe Adam's been to Venice. Maybe he's remembering a time there. Dusk over the basilica of San Giorgio Maggiore. More likely blood on marble floors.

"Venice," he clarifies.

"Yeah. I got that. We still clean in here?"

Rao sighs a yes. "Are we doing this now?"

"You want to wait?"

"No." Rao shifts himself up to sit, rolls his neck, regards the sunset light on the wall. "So, the staff are tight-lipped," he begins, "and I can't test silence. The facility isn't a happy ship, is it?"

Adam shakes his head. "Rhodes told them not to talk to us?"

"Yeah. Three-line whip. So much for us all being one big happy family. I got insinuations of fatalities from a couple of nurses and a strong sense that Veronica can be a vicious bitch, but that's old news. She's been quite happy to tell us all about turning people into microscope slides."

"What have you got on her?"

"She's a twenty-four-carat psycho. Vivisected the family cat when she was ten."

"Seriously?"

"Adam, you're asking for intel. This is the bit where I never lie to you."

"Personal life?"

"None. She's renting in Tallyn's Reach. She's untouchable. I've got nothing on her we could plausibly use, even if this weren't the blackest of deep black projects. She's a murderer, but a super-careful one. Not counting the deaths here, they were all work-related fatalities except one. A guy at Harvard who pissed her off. She put a hit on him, used a cutout."

"How many in all?"

"Five. I still like her, though."

"Good to know that murders don't put you off a person."

"We're best friends, after all."

Adam snorts. "All of mine are state sanctioned. Montgomery?"

"Yeah, he's the pivot, isn't he? Or would have been," Rao says, making a face. "Wouldn't have taken long to get him singing, but we missed the window. Veronica came down on him like a ton of bricks the day we signed on the dotted line. He did mention a visit by someone called Lane, five weeks ago. Seems to have been stressful for all concerned. I got his first name. Zachary. Looked him up. He's on the Lunastus board of directors. Clearly an asshole."

"Is that a testable fact?"

"Don't need to test anything with a name like that."

From the look on Adam's face he disagrees with Rao's assessment. "Montgomery's a potential asset."

"If he grows a pair."

"If he doesn't, do we have biographical leverage?"

"Nah. He's so boring, love. Divorcee. Amicable split. Daughter lives with her mother in Ohio. She's thirteen. No debt, no skeletons in his cupboards. His parents are dead. He doesn't have any siblings. And no form at all. Not even a parking ticket."

"Interests?"

"Christ, Adam, don't make me truth-test his hobbies."

Adam grins. "Home brewing."

"Ugh, fuck, of course."

"Anything else?"

"On Monty?"

"On the project."

Rao sighs. The golden light's dimming fast. Shapes losing resolution. Sun's dipped below the horizon. "I've been having a mare with that. I've turned myself inside out trying to find the right statements to test, but all I've got is that there's a lot more to this project and a lot more to Prophet than we know. That's it."

Adam sits up. "You can't tell?"

Rao winces. "It's weird. It's not like with you. It's a bit like those Magic Eye pictures. Autostereograms. Of dinosaurs or desert islands or something. And sometimes you almost get it, you almost see what's there, but it slips away just as you grasp it." He hates this analogy. It's terrible, but it's all he's got. "That's sort of what it's like trying to truth-test Prophet. I don't know if it's because I've got it inside me or whether Prophet and truth don't . . . coincide. It's a metaphysical headache."

"Sounds frustrating," Adam says.

"It fucking is."

"But interesting. Lack of data's still data. Don't stress it, Rao."

A little later, while Adam is out on an evening run, Rao calls Kitty Caldwell in Cambridge. He's sat on his bed with the phone Adam had given him a few times now and not bothered to dial. She's never been free before. Right now, however, he knows she's in her office and isn't teaching. He picks out the number. The wisteria, the old glass in the Gothic windows, the still fenland air in the college squares. The knowledge that those things are all still out there surprises him as he waits for her to answer: the sensation's like changing into too high a gear by mistake.

"Kitty Caldwell."

"Hello, Dr Caldwell. It's Sunil Rao. I don't know if you remember me."

"You weren't very forgettable, Rao. Kitty, please."

"Thank you. Is this a bad time?"

"No, a good time, actually. Why the call?"

"It's complicated," he says, staring at the carpet. "I think I need some help."

"I'm good with complicated. I'm not sure if I can help."

"The thing is, I'm not sure how much I can tell you. I mean, I am sure. I've signed things that make it very clear I'm not allowed to tell you anything. But—"

"You want to know if I can keep a secret?"

"Yeah. Can you?"

There's a pause so long Rao wonders if the line's dropped. It hasn't.

"Yes."

Ok, he's happy with that. She can.

"So I've managed to find my way into a project working with a substance that causes nostalgia."

A beat. "Causes?"

He loves that she's nitpicking semantics. Loves it.

"Provokes. I wanted to talk to you about why this substance doesn't affect me like it does other people."

"Wouldn't you do better with a neuroscientist?"

"There are too many of those fuckers around here already."

She laughs. "Ok, how does it not affect you?"

"It doesn't make me nostalgic," Rao says. "And I think that might be because I have an unusual kind of memory."

He's been trying to truth-test it. Like so much else with Prophet, he's not been able to get clear answers, and he's starting to believe the Prophet inside him won't let him see what it's doing. It won't let him test that either.

"What kind of unusual?"

"I remember everything."

"Is it sensory memory? Emotional?"

"Everything. All of it."

"You're a savant."

"People usually call me a dickhead, Kitty, but that's a word I've heard, yeah."

She laughs. "So, apart from your demonstrating that you have an art historian's distaste for neuroscience, Rao, why did you want to call me?"

"Because your concept of nostalgia isn't based on pictures of brains. Isn't just chemicals and electrical signals. It's more than that. A cultural phenomenon. A historical one. Psychological."

"And social, don't forget."

"I didn't forget. That's just it. I want to ask you about memory. Not how it lights up the brain but how we use it. You said nostalgia can be a response to a sense of dislocation. And your book says it's an act of creation, right? It brings lost things to life, things from your past, things you remember. And the act of nostalgia forges a link between you now and a past self that's always partly imagined. It's comforting. Gives you a sense of continuity. Makes you feel you're the same person through time."

"That's not exactly what my book says, Rao."

"I know exactly what your book says. I was paraphrasing. But, Kitty, this is the thing. The way my memory works, there's no creation. Like, I don't create anything when I remember things. I don't use my imagination at all. I just retrieve the memory. It doesn't get loaded with meaning, you know? I mean, ok, I can read emotional content *off* memories. Like, I can see how the image of my bedside lamp holds associations of comfort and home. But only in retrospect. While I'm remembering it, it's just a lamp. It's that lamp, exactly. It's not an act of creation. It's pure recall."

"Hm." She sounds dubious. "What do you mean by 'pure'?"

"Pure. When I remember a lamp, it's no different from me looking at a lamp right now. It's just an object."

"That's not true," she says. "You look at a lamp right now and it'll make you feel things about lamps and life that aren't what the lamp's made of. Objects are always more than material things."

He knows she's right. He turns his eyes to the bedside lamp, the warm and reassuring light it casts on the wall, the paperbacks heaped at its base. "You can tell the difference between what's real and what's inside your head, if it's right there in front of you," he says a little testily. "Which is, well, I'm wondering if that's the difference, with me. Why I don't get nostalgic. Why I don't miss things."

"You don't miss things?"

"No. I don't have to, do I? Because they're always right there in my mind, exactly as they were. There's no loss of detail. They're perfect. Nostalgia re-creates things, right? Imperfectly. Fills the gaps in memories with feelings. But my memory doesn't have gaps. And that's why I think this substance doesn't work on me. Does that sound plausible?"

"We don't . . ." She's silent for a while. "What are memories like for you?"

Kitty thinks he's missing the point. But she's not challenging him directly, is talking around him to get him nearer to an answer. She's a good teacher.

"Like being inside a movie of my own life," he says. "Which can be pretty fucking grim. But, you know, there've been some good times."

"What about things you don't remember?"

"Pain," he says quickly. "Sleeping. Being unconscious."

"Do you dream?"

"Yeah. Vividly. But they're basically memories. I don't dream about things that haven't happened." He feels the lie. Sharply. Because he has, lately, hasn't he? He's dreamed of a lot of things.

"That's exceptionally unusual. What about emotional content?"

"In dreams?"

"In memories."

"I remember those. Feel them again when I do. Sometimes I worry I don't have emotions like other people."

"Everyone thinks that," she says. It's a throwaway line. She's quiet for a while. "Rao, I have a question for you. I think it's an important one, and I want you to think about it."

"Fire away."

"Do you miss loved ones who are gone, even though you can remember them precisely?"

He bites his lip.

"Yeah."

"Well."

CHAPTER 49

It doesn't take Hunter long to turn up after Adam lights the proverbial flare. He texted her as soon as he got confirmation her pass had been issued. The next morning he's waiting outside the facility for her to arrive. He smiles as she walks into the parking lot. Jeans, leather jacket, black tee, baseball cap. That familiar easy swagger. It's good to see her. It's always good to see Hunter. She externalizes all the things Adam keeps under his skin. Back when the military was molding them into what it estimated they could be, Hunter's externalizing was annoying. At this stage in their friendship, it's steadying. Everything could be upside down, the sky orange, birds flying backward and singing the "Ershter Vals," and Hunter would be the first to state how fucked up it was instead of doing what he would do. Adam always tries to roll with the punch, no matter where it's coming from. Hunter, on the other hand, calls a punch a punch. Their mindsets and responses are different. Complementary. Rao likes to say that Adam is some kind of operational secret weapon, and maybe he is in some scenarios, but not like Hunter is. Hunter is next-level, and she knows it.

"This is fucked up, Rubenstein," she tells him, and it's better than saying hello.

He follows her squint up to the building like he's seeing it for the first time. "Yeah."

"How much do I get to know about this?"

"I'll tell you what I can when we're inside."

"And then what?"

"Then when they release him, you and Flores can go, if you want." Adam shrugs. If she doesn't want to go in, he's pretty sure that he can ruffle different feathers than the ones he's already fucked with to get

Flores out to the front door. She doesn't look like she wants to go in. She takes out a soft box of American Spirit Yellows, taps one out. Doesn't offer one to Adam. For once, he actually wants a smoke, but he doesn't ask.

"Where are you staying?" he says.

"VQ at Buckley. Right across the street," she says, lighting up. "You looking for any help on this?"

"I don't think so."

"The fuck does that mean?"

"It means . . ." he starts, then sighs. It's hard to put it simply sometimes. Everything would be so much easier if people just did what he said when he said it, but that's not how life works. That's not how friends work. Adam doesn't have a lot of experience in that field, but he has enough. "It just means we're good, for now."

"What happens when you're not good?"

"I've got your number."

"And you don't lose that."

"No plans to lose that."

"Good to hear. But you're pulling me in all the same. I didn't haul my ass all the way over here to sit this out on the sidelines, Rubenstein." Hunter exhales an impressive amount of smoke and abandons the cigarette, grinding the unsmoked half into shreds underfoot. She jerks her head to the front doors of the facility. Wordlessly, they head inside. Hunter shows her ID, gets walked through all the paperwork she has to sign before she gets her pass, and when they're through the double doors that lead into the belly of the beast, she elbows him in the ribs. "You want to tell me why the receptionist just pissed themselves at the sight of you?"

"New receptionist. Long story."

"Is it?"

"No," Adam admits with a grin. "I just don't want to tell it. Besides, Rao makes it sound way more interesting than it was. Ask him."

"Rao, huh?"

"Yep." Adam pops his *p*.

"Lead the way, Rubenstein. God fucking help me, I'm actually looking forward to seeing the bastard."

Standing at the bottom of Flores's bed, watching him sleep, Hunter nudges Adam's foot.

"Run it by me again, Rubenstein."

He does. Goes into as much detail as he can. Tells her everything he knows about Prophet, about the project. What happened when he'd dosed himself. How Rao was the first thing he saw when he'd come out of the nightmare of reliving that day. He tells her about Flores. How Rao drew Prophet out of him just by touching him. Skin to skin. The ragged breath Flores had taken. The look on Rao's face.

"How did you get contaminated?" she asks when he's finished. He'd left that part out on purpose, but it's Hunter. She hears silences.

"I did it myself."

"Why?"

"We needed answers."

"You were getting them."

"I needed," he says, "something else."

"What?"

"Some quiet."

"You could have left the room if Rao was pissing you off."

"He wasn't the problem." Adam shakes his head. "I needed a different kind of quiet."

They're waiting for one of the medical team to talk them through the process of releasing Flores. That's all Adam needs to think about. The next task. The next task is easier than actively ignoring Hunter's sharp sideways gaze.

"Are you over this quest for quiet?" she asks.

He nods, once. It's not that simple, but it can look like it is for now. Hunter doesn't need every detail.

"You better not get out of this the stupid way, Rubenstein."

"Nah. You'd kick my ass," he sighs. "How are your folks?"

She rolls her eyes. "They're good."

"Still got our flight photo glued to the wall?"

"Yeah. Me standing next to you, you looking like a fetus dressed as a tree."

"Happy days at Lackland."

"It's all downhill after BMT."

The door opens. It's a doctor, clipboard in hand. Nervous looking and overworked, like all of Rhodes's staff. His voice is soft. Southern. He takes them through the bureaucratic hurdles that will permit Flores to be released into Hunter's care. Says he's sorry that the process will take some time. Retreats with his clipboard after promising to expedite proceedings. It's all bullshit, Adam guesses. Some way to keep Flores for a little longer or to keep Hunter on-site for as long as they need to get more intel on her—or any number of similar shitty tactics Lunastus could be running in the background. All amounts to the same thing in the end.

"Coffee?" Hunter prompts.

"There's a canteen."

"Rubenstein, you're gonna get soft living like this," Hunter observes. Moroccan lamps on every table. Woven Balochi hangings, a host of curved and gilded mirrors on the walls. In the spotlit darkness a full-size fake palm tree. He follows her gaze up to the star-shaped tracery of beams on the concave ceiling, each one set with scores of tiny, glimmering lights.

"It's supposed," he says dryly, "to represent a bedouin tent."

"The canteen? What's with Colorado and tents? Denver airport, now this. It's crazy." She lifts her cup and shakes her head. The coffee here is so good it's unholy. Adam distrusts it. It tastes like dirty corporate money and hazelnut syrup. Rao lives for it. As soon as they get back to their motel room at night, he starts complaining about having to wait all that time before there's decent coffee again. Adam's thankful they get to leave Lunastus in the evenings. Rhodes offered him and Rao accommodation on-site but they both, separately, refused her offer. The motel had been the right call, considering. Weird how quick it got to feel secure and permanent after that.

"So, it was the day your aunt died," Hunter says, breaking Adam's train of thought.

"It was the moment I should have left to go with my aunt," Adam says. Reconsiders. Clarifies. "So I guess, to me, it was the moment she died." Hunter's never heard the whole story about Sasha before. Adam hadn't told anyone before Rao.

She gets it. Doesn't linger on unnecessary questions.

"And your brain made it plop into existence because of this Prophet junk?"

"Pretty much."

"I thought you said you weren't working for the Office, Rubenstein."

"I'm not," he grins.

"Could've fooled me."

Adam's about to reply when Rao walks in. He pulls the chair next to Adam, sits, looks sidelong at Adam's coffee, then makes a series of complicated facial movements indicating his desire to take it. Sighing, Adam slides the cup in front of him.

"It's black," he warns.

"That's okay. I'm feeling *continental* today," Rao says, pleased with himself. "Cheers. What are we talking about? Alright, Hunter."

"Rao," she responds. "Good to see you."

Rao turns. "She means that, Adam."

"Congratulations, Rao."

"We're waiting for them to get the paperwork to release Flores," Hunter explains.

"Yeah," Rao agrees. "But that's not what you were talking about. That's what you're *doing*. Were you telling Hunter about my miracle-working shit?"

"You mean Raoki," Hunter says. "Like Reiki, but Rao."

"Raoflexology," Adam offers. He gets up to pour himself another coffee. Rao's glare of disgust has vanished by the time he returns. "Office Workers," he says.

"What?"

"That's what we were talking about."

Rao huffs. "Adam, I can't help but suspect that you're getting off on being obtuse right now, and I'd like it to be perfectly fucking crystal clear that I don't appreciate it."

"It's what people call the assholes who work in the Extranatural Incident Office," Hunter explains.

"Oh! Mulder and Scully."

"Yes," Adam nods.

Hunter shakes her head. "No."

"Yes," Adam repeats. "Mulder and Scully."

Rao snickers. "And by people, you mean . . ."

"Us," Hunter says.

"Service," Adam adds.

Rao hums sagely. "This would be interdivisional rivalry, then? Like the Chair Force?"

Adam lifts both eyebrows, says nothing.

"What?"

Hunter clears her throat. "He's touchy about that, Rao."

"Your dad was air force, wasn't he, love?"

Adam shrugs. "Still is, as far as I know."

"Adam?"

"Yes, Rao."

"Do you outrank your father?"

Hunter laughs into her mug, mutters something that sounds like "good coffee." Adam smiles, but it's one with teeth. Real.

"Now that you mention it, I think I might," he says slowly.

Rao beams. "You little shit."

"Mm," Adam says, as he tips his coffee and drinks.

Rhodes appears by their table. Adam's impressed he didn't see her coming; she's a natural at silent interception. She'd probably breeze through Peary. Maybe she already did. He doesn't have the intel. She's wearing thin gold bracelets. Her hair has a slight wave today. He gets why Rao's fascinated.

She smiles benevolently. "Dr. Veronica Rhodes," she says. "And you must be Hunter. You've quite a reputation." Hunter opens her mouth to reply. Rhodes doesn't let her. "Colonel Rubenstein was insistent that you be given a visitor's pass. And before it could be issued, of course, we needed to make ourselves intimately informed of your career."

"If you know so much about me, then I guess it's fair to ask about you."

"You may ask what you like, Sergeant Wood."

"I want to know what you're running here."

"I assume that Colonel Rubenstein will have—"

"I don't care what he told me. I want you to tell me."

Veronica moves to stand behind the only unoccupied chair at their table. She doesn't pull it out. Doesn't sit on it. Just rests her hands on its back as if she might.

"Lunastus-Dainsleif is in the fortunate position to have been given the chance to study, to understand, a novel substance with extraordinary properties. We've already determined that with the right application and control, this substance could be used in the field. We're taking the first steps toward completely costless warfare."

Hunter nods. "That's a hell of a spiel. You're shit out of luck, though. I'm not dumb enough to get lost in empty jargon like that."

Rhodes looks amused. "I'm unsurprised our very own Lieutenant Colonel Rubenstein keeps such stellar, straight-talking company."

"*Your* Colonel Rubenstein?"

"Ours, yes. I believe a decision on that will have already been made. What do you think of our project?"

"I think it sounds impossible."

Veronica hums, angles her head a little to one side. "Well, feel free to drop by my office or come see me in the lab if you're interested in the particularities of our impossible research. My door's always open. It's been a pleasure, Sergeant Wood."

Hunter watches her leave. Two seconds pass. Four. Ten.

"I don't like her vibe, Rubenstein," she says.

"No. Neither do I."

"She's just a psycho," Rao explains helpfully. "That's all you need to know about Veronica."

"So?" Hunter hisses, addressing Adam.

"What?"

"You're being headhunted."

"I don't think that's what she was saying, Hunter."

"Is that right?" She narrows her eyes. "Seemed pretty clear to me. What aren't you telling me?"

Adam takes a sip of coffee. "I can tell you later. It's not important right now."

She raises an accusatory finger. "Don't try to feed me that sack of shit and call it a hamburger."

Rao cuts in. "I'm . . . sorry, what seems to be the problem?"

"Rubenstein's keeping secrets," Hunter says.

"From who?"

"Hunter," Adam cautions.

She ignores him. "My guess is that he's keeping secrets from you, Rao."

"Well," Rao says. "We don't do that any longer. Do we, Adam?"

"No."

Rao folds his arms. "So what the fuck is going on?"

"Fucking—fine," Adam says. "My only angle with Rhodes is testing. I have one card to play, so I'm playing it."

"Does that make sense to you, Rao?"

"Yes, it bloody does," Rao says. "You're auctioning your, what, Adam? Your *samples*? For *what*?"

"Hunter's visitor's pass, to begin with."

Rao's eyebrows rise. "To *begin with*? And what did this pass cost?"

"She's pushing for a biopsy."

Hunter's shaking her head. Rao groans. "Fucking hell, Adam. This was phenomenally stupid of you."

"I know what I'm doing. Both of you can stand down."

"Stand down?" Rao raises his voice. "You're not my fucking CO, Adam, and now is not the time for this Captain Oates bullshit."

"Oates?" Hunter says.

"Scott of the Antarctic," Rao says, turning to her. "You know. Everyone on the expedition was starving. Oates was the guy with scurvy and frostbite who kept telling them to leave him behind, and they wouldn't.

So he hobbled out of the tent into a blizzard on purpose, sacrificed himself to save the rest of the team. Said, 'I am just going outside and I may be some time.'" Rao sits back in his seat, lets the silence hang, then turns his head to look pointedly at Adam. "And they all fucking died anyway."

"Rubenstein's not Oates," Hunter says firmly.

"Hunter, that was a spur-of-the-moment analogy, I wasn't—"

"Shut up. I get the analogy, but Rubenstein's got the best operational brains out there. He's a legend at the DIA. My advice is you put your faith in him and your trust in whatever course of action he determines is the most expedient." She looks at Adam. "Even if he is acting like a four-star idiot."

"Hunter," Adam says.

"Tell me I'm wrong."

Adam doesn't reply, just picks at the corner of his left eye. He knows it's a tell. Tiredness. Stress, maybe. Whatever. It doesn't matter.

"Rao," Hunter says. "Are they paying you for this?"

"Spending time with Adam?"

"Putting yourself inside this fucked-up project."

"They are. Lunastus values me at five hundred dollars a day."

Her eyes widen. "Jesus. Well. If you're not busy watching QVC, you're both buying me dinner later. Somewhere that isn't here. Guy on the base says there's an Indian place, it's—"

"Absolutely not," Rao interrupts.

Adam snorts. "Let's find a Vietnamese."

CHAPTER 50

His Tahoe desk is heaped with papers and meal replacement drinks. His lips are bitten raw. He's steepling his fingers. None of these signs are optimal. Veronica steels herself.

"We have to understand the biomechanics of what he does," De Witte whispers.

"That, Steven," she says, "is my goal also."

"So we can replicate it."

She nods. He shakes his head. "Your methodology has been, um, messy, Veronica. We need him in our Pensacola facility. Get him there and put him in one of your restraint units. Immobilize him. Don't give him analgesics. I don't want him sedated. Administer Prophet to him until we can model his extraction method."

Veronica knows this was inevitable. But it doesn't have to happen yet. There's so much she can learn using Rao as he is right now. While he's still willing to help. Still able to talk.

"He's useful here," she murmurs. "I'm—"

"But I don't want him there," De Witte cuts in, looking right at her down the camera. His eyes are pale, peculiarly clear. Veronica makes some rapid calculations.

"I understand," she replies in tones that sound like she doesn't. Waits to see how he responds.

"I hope issues related to his, uh, rendition aren't a concern. He already attempted suicide and was a liability to his previous employers. Elisabeth Miller is, uh, out of the frame. Except for us, nobody wants him. Not even himself."

"What about Rubenstein?"

"*A cog in the war machine*," De Witte says with almost no trace of his usual diffidence. "*He barely exists as it is. Easily removed. To the wider world, neither of them matter.*"

"*I'm sure you're right,*" she replies. "*And of course Rubenstein's air force colleague could be sent back to Afghanistan.*"

He nods. "*She'll be deployed there anyway. She doesn't have to return. Remember the stakes, Veronica.*"

"*They're not forgotten.*"

De Witte's eyes lift beyond the screen for a moment, focus on the far wall. Then, unexpectedly, he smiles. "*Designing a repository for excess stocks of Prophet has been . . . complicated. But now we can cut that expense from our books.*"

"*You want to use him as a live disposal unit.*"

"*Absolutely,*" he says, his smile broadening. "*Our very own human Yucca Mountain.*"

CHAPTER 51

"Where's Hunter?" Rao enquires over his canteen breakfast. "She's with Flores."

He sighs happily. "I must thank you for introducing me to Hunter, Adam. She's so incredibly emasculating. It's brilliant."

"Is she," Adam says, mouth quirked. Then his face shifts wistful. "Miller has that effect on some people too. You should see her on the range. Her groupings are insane."

Silence follows. Rao hastens to fill it. "Veronica said she'll get me to Miller," he assures Adam. "I'll fix what happened. You know I will. She'll be back on the range shrinking everyone's balls before you know it."

"Yeah," Adam says after a while, like he doesn't believe it. "You done? We should join Hunter."

When they walk in, Hunter's perched cross-legged on the bed and Flores is hunched in an armchair, a cream-coloured robe over his shoulders. His face has regained some colour, but it's still haunted. Pinched.

"Hey, Danny," Hunter says. "This is Rao, the guy who woke you up."

"Thanks," he says. "I owe you."

"You really don't. I'm glad to have helped. How are you?"

"Good. Good," Flores says. His hand trembles as he places his mug on the table by his side. "Rubenstein. Been a while. You still DIA?"

"Yeah. They looking after you?"

"Never had food like in this place."

Rao nods enthusiastically. "Have you had the tagliatelle yet?"

"It's good," Flores says, then his eyes rise slowly to the flat-screen TV on the wall, where CNN plays silently with subtitles. Footage of fighter jets. Helicopters. A sixty-billion-dollar weapons deal with Saudi Arabia.

"Fucking with Iran," Flores observes. "Keeping Saudi onside. They've been working on this one for years."

"Pretty intense for convalescence," Rao says. "Want me to switch it over?"

"No thanks. Old shows give me headaches," Flores replies. "News is ok. Hey, sit down." He nods at the button on the table. "I can get coffee, if you want?"

"No, we're all set," Adam says.

They sit watching CNN for a while.

"Flores," Adam says. "Can you tell us what happened to you?"

Flores's face twists with distaste. "I had a bad reaction to that formula. Put me in a coma. I'm just glad they found a doctor who knew what he was doing." His eyes flick towards Rao.

Rao opens his mouth but Adam speaks first. "And now?"

"Disoriented, like a concussion. It's still hard to sleep, but they're taking care of that. I got the shakes. It's sort of like the flu."

"I got dosed," Adam says. "Didn't work the same on me, but that's how I felt too."

"Rough?"

"Rough. It'll pass."

"Adam's therapeutic regimen involved bed rest and beating the shit out of a couple of goons," Rao explains.

"It helped," Adam deadpans.

Flores huffs a mirthless laugh. "June's been taking care of me. My nurse. I get a bunch of vitamins, have to drink a lot of water. But I'll pass your recommendations on."

"I spoke to her," Hunter says. "Looks like you might be able to get out of here soon."

Flores stiffens. "Will they make me go home?" He swallows. "That sounds crazy, I know. I've got to see my mom. She's not doing well. And I miss my dogs. But . . ."

"You got troubles back in Boulder?"

"No. No." He scrubs his face, embarrassed. "Feels safer here, is all. But I'm good. Really."

He doesn't look it, Rao thinks. He might be better than before, but the man's so far from right it's wrong hearing him speak. Every word is like the jolt of expecting a step on a staircase that isn't there. "Danny," he ventures. "Can you tell me what it was like, when you were out?"

His face contorts. Like Rao'd driven a splinter under a nail.

"Dr Rhodes already asked me," he says, eyes flicking towards the door.

"She's not here today," Rao says. "She's on holiday. Back tomorrow. And she doesn't know we're talking." Hunter gives him an accusatory glare. She might not, but she will. There's a security camera right above the door.

Flores bites his lip. One foot taps an anxious rhythm against the carpet. "There was this time I got sick when I was a kid," he says. "My parents put me on the couch with blankets so I could watch TV." He rubs the sore under his jaw. "*Sesame Street.* I had a fever. Bad aches. I hated every second. The blankets were too hot, but I was too weak to push them off. I couldn't even move my head. It felt like I was trapped, like I was falling through the couch, but, you know, it was comfortable, just not the usual comfortable. Comfortable because I couldn't move, and I figured there wasn't anywhere I'd feel any better than where I was. All the time there was *Sesame Street.* Big Bird. Count von Count. Painting a number five. That fucking typewriter. The pinball." He shudders all over. "Didn't matter whether my eyes were open or closed, it was *Sesame Street* inside my head, like I didn't know whether it was on the TV or inside me, and that episode went on for days. Hey Wood, can I get some water?"

Hunter gets up, fills a jug, pours him a glass. He sips at it.

"So your coma, it was like that?" Hunter says.

"Kind of," he exhales. "But . . ." His voice cracks. "I loved it. I hated how much I loved where I was. Even if it was killing me. Like an overdose." Rao's scratching his scalp, hard. White noise of fingernails against his skull. He forces himself to stop.

"The thing I remember most," Flores says, "was the feeling that I hadn't done it right."

"Done what?" Hunter asks.

He shrugs. "I was stuck in a place. It was where I wanted to be, but it was the worst place in the world, and I knew I hadn't done it right. Like when you fuck up a pass on the football field, and everyone's watching. Like that. The feeling hasn't gone away, you know? I still feel like that. Whatever happened, I didn't do it right."

"Withdrawal is a bastard," Rao observes.

An imitation of a smile spreads on Flores's face. "Looks like it."

At eight minutes past ten that evening Adam is watching motel TV. "What is the Leaning Tower of Pisa," he intones.

Jeopardy! Rao grunts, glancing up from the Jackie Collins novel he'd nicked from the lobby. He's never understood this programme. Answers that are questions. It does his fucking head in.

"What is the United States Postal Service?" Adam enquires of the screen, face as deathly serious as if he were testifying at a congressional hearing. Rao shifts his gaze to the curtains, the photographic print of mountains on the wall, then down to Adam's shoes by the door, a sock tucked neatly into each one. *How the hell does this feel so domestic?* he thinks. Decides, eventually, it's because of their daily commute. Driving to work in the morning, just like normal people. Driving back every evening. No wonder this shitty ground-floor room has come to seem like home.

"That was weird," he announces when the show's ended. Adam's on his way back from the fridge with two cans of Sprite. He hands one to Rao, cracks his own, and sits.

"What, *Jeopardy!*?"

"No, but that's weird too. I meant Flores. How he's scared to go home."

"It happens. Trauma response."

"Yeah, well," Rao muses, setting down his unopened can. "I think it might be more than that. You got dosed. How do you feel about home?"

Adam looks at him, doubt in his eyes.

"It's not a trick question, love."

"Yeah, I know." Adam stares at the TV. A Geico car insurance advert involving, for some reason, a dentist. "Home was Aunt Sasha," he says quietly after a long while, like the fact had just occurred to him. Like it was a revelation, one he's not sure what to do with. He raps sharply on the table with his knuckles, picks up Rao's cigarettes. "Smoke?"

Veronica intercepts him on his way to the restroom the next morning. "Good morning, Rao," she begins. "This afternoon—"

"Can this wait until after I've emptied my bladder?" he sighs. "I don't want to have to grab my crotch to keep it in. This is a public area."

"I'll be right here," she says, picking invisible lint from the shoulder of her lab coat.

"The early iteration Prophet test subject you requested to meet is arriving this afternoon," she informs him on his return. "I think she may surprise you."

"Doubt it. I'm losing the capacity for surprise lately."

"I simply meant she'll look quite ordinary. A civilian. Part of a test cohort drawn from a different demographic than our manifestation program. Come to the lab at two thirty, and I'll take you to her."

Veronica's eyes are shining; she's making no move to leave.

"There's more," Rao says.

"There is indeed. I want to show you something."

"Holiday snaps?" he enquires.

"I've not been on holiday."

"Monty said you were in Vermont."

"I was. There's more in Vermont than B&Bs."

"Apples," he throws out.

"Close," she says with an enigmatic smile. Tells him, as they walk to the lab, that she was following up his theory that the size of an EPGO correlates to the space surrounding a subject at the time of exposure. Tells him she'd conducted an open-air experiment on a single volunteer. When Rao asks who the poor sod was, she describes him as an old friend in the intelligence community. Someone who'd served his country admirably and was suffering from a terminal illness.

"Sorry to hear that, Veronica."

"It is terribly sad," she replies. In an improbable moment of accord, both of them smile.

"So what did you do? Stick him in a field?"

"Yes. He made a barn."

Rao makes a face. "That's not that interesting."

She ushers him through the doors. "Yes it is."

Rao sits, watches her bring up a video file on a workstation. "You left him stuck inside it?"

"No. He wasn't drawn to it."

"Why not?"

"He didn't see it. He was instructed to close his eyes during the infusion."

Rao snorts. "So where is he now? Sedated?"

"No. He's in the morgue at Northeastern Vermont Regional Hospital. It was all a little much for him. He was really rather frail."

"Your body count's getting quite impressive, Veronica."

"A blessing, really, for both him and his family. It could have happened at any time."

Rao shakes his head, looks at the screen.

It's a red Vermont barn in the middle of a grassy field on a cloudy day. Dutch roof, weather-worn wooden shingles, white window frames. Hills rise behind it. The image is so evocative Rao feels his mouth water. A vague tang of maple syrup, American apple cider.

"Pretty," he says. "Childhood memory?"

"The original was on his family farm," she says. "It's still standing about thirty miles west, though it's been converted into a home. This is, I think, exactly as the structure looked in the early 1960s."

"You could have shown me photos. Why video?"

"Because he didn't just make a barn. Keep watching."

The camera moves towards the barn at walking pace. Veronica's hand comes to rest on the door. She pushes it open. It swings inwards. Heaps of straw, feed sacks. Columns of dusty sunlight from the upper windows cast elongated pools of brightness across the wooden floor. The camera pans downwards. Lengths of discarded twine, a scrap of hessian. Detailed memories. The camera swings round and Rao starts in his seat.

"Fuck," he says.

It's a horse. Rao loves horses. He's a halfway decent rider. But seeing this one, Rao never wants to ride again. It's not a horse. It's a horror. It looks exactly like a bay Morgan—tackless, coat dappled with sunlight—but as the camera gets closer its eyes are as dead as the wooden walls behind it, and the twitch of its flanks and the shake of its neck, the repeated swish of the tail: they're on a loop.

"Fuck, it's like the radio," he breathes. "It's horrible."

"If you say so," she says. "It looks just like a horse to me."

"It's not a horse."

"Of course it isn't."

As she walks the camera around the thing that isn't a horse, Rao feels a slow wash of vertigo; bile rises in his throat. She stops, extends a hand, runs it down a flank. Presses into it with her fingers. Her hand disappears from view, the image blurs, slips and turns, and when the camera is righted, her hand is holding a penknife. She cuts, deeply. There's no flinch from the horse, but blood flows, thick, from her incision. She steps back. The looping movements continue. The bleeding continues.

The footage cuts out.

Rao sits with his head low, forearms on his thighs, breathing hard, trying to quell a swell of nausea. "Has Adam seen this?" he says, looking at the floor.

"You asked us to leave him alone."

"But you haven't. Get him down here."

Adam's head draws back a fraction as soon as he sees the horse. His jaw tightens. Then he leans towards the screen, intrigued. As the camera tracks around the horse, he says simply, "Why now?"

"Why did he make an animal?" Veronica asks.

He nods.

Rao shrugs. "He thought it should be in the barn."

"That's not what your colleague is asking, I think." Veronica tilts her head at Adam. "I suspect Prophet has undergone another change."

"Like the leap from nostalgia to making physical objects?"

"Perhaps."

When the video ends, Adam sits back, deep in thought. "Did the blood coagulate?"

"It did not."

"Is the thing still there?"

She doesn't quite answer the question. "We conducted a necropsy on-site."

"Can't be a necropsy," Rao says, "if the horse was never alive."

"You don't think it was alive?" She's amused. "Very well. Not a necropsy. We brought it into a position of left lateral recumbency on the barn floor."

"Veronica," Rao chides.

Her mouth twitches. "We laid it on one side. Cut it open. And no, I don't think the word dissection is accurate either. We . . . disassembled it."

"What did you find?" Adam asks.

"What the test subject thought was inside a horse. There's a skeletal structure, of sorts. A skull. A spine. Some ribs, mostly unattached. The lungs were well-defined but resemble human lungs more than equine ones. Rudimentary digestive system. A sac that might have been a stomach, an unconnected anal canal. Most of the horse was undifferentiated muscle tissue."

Rao nods. "Makes sense."

"Really, Mr Rao? Because the horse was nonsense. Fascinating nonsense. This is what I wanted you to see." She takes them to the other side of the lab and pulls a white plastic container printed with a diamond and the legend UN3373 from under a bench. She bends, unlatches it. Inside is a smaller box. She picks it out, lays it on the bench top. "It's the wrong size and shape, of course," she says.

"The box?"

"What's in it." She dons a pair of surgical gloves, opens the lid.

She draws out a heart.

It's a heart.

It looks like a human heart. Pale, muscular, bulbous, slick with blood, the veins and arteries running into it snipped and gaping. Rao stares. It's the worst thing he's ever seen.

It's beating.

It's still beating.

"The heart under the floorboards," Adam whispers.

"What was that?" Veronica says.

"The *Raven* guy. Rao?"

"Poe. *The Tell-Tale Heart*. Fucking hell."

CHAPTER 52

Rao is habitually late to meetings. But he's so early to this one, Adam's not here. His absence gives Rao a sudden sense of covert responsibility: he sneaks through the lab doors as quietly as he can. The lab's not busy: a few white coats sit in front of monitors and a woman with a high-spec mop is silently cleaning the floor. He overhears Veronica talking at the far side of the room.

"Yes. As we discussed. Everything you suggested. After the PET scan on Monday."

She's nodding, holding a phone to her ear. Looks across, catches Rao's eye. "I have to go, Steven."

"Talking about me, Veronica?" Rao says, grinning.

"Yes. I was."

He nods. She's telling the truth for once. Tucking her phone away she takes off her lab coat, revealing clothes of surprising homeliness: pale-grey cardigan, a floral print blouse. Hand her a pair of horn-rimmed glasses, Rao thinks idly, and Veronica would turn full municipal librarian. Behind him, the doors swing open: as Adam walks in, Veronica sends him her sweetest smile. "Glad to see you, Colonel. Shall we all head to the interview room?"

*

Soft lighting. Armchairs, lamps on side tables, a subtly patterned rug. One-way mirror on the wall. Adam sniffs. The sweet, medicinal air of this overcleaned, underused space is sharp, unpleasant.

"So I'll be setting you both in the observation area adjacent to this space," Rhodes explains.

"I want to meet her," Rao says. "I can't meet her if I'm next door picking my nose, can I?"

Rhodes rolls her eyes but not with frustration. If Adam didn't know any better, he'd think that the psychopath in the room was starting to warm up to Rao. He has that effect on people. Wouldn't be the first time he's worn someone down.

"Rao, with respect. You're not white. You're foreign. You have a beard," she lists. "She won't talk freely if you're the first person she sees."

"Did you get her in to meet me because she's a hooting racist or was that just a happy accident?"

"Happy accident."

"Stellar," Rao sighs, rubbing his eyes. "What's your plan?"

"I'll take her through some questions. I won't be mentioning Prophet, and nor will either of you. We've invited her for a qualitative interview on how she's led her town into an era of community renewal—"

"What does that mean?" Adam asks.

Rhodes wrinkles her nose, smug. "Traditional American family values. Community groups. Rallying behind their president and troops. Patriotism."

"Nationalism," he corrects.

"Same coin." Rhodes shrugs. "They're results. Ms. Crossland and the people following her in her community are success stories as far as Lunastus-Dainsleif is concerned."

Adam looks through the tinted glass of the observation room window to where the woman sits waiting. She looks patient and calm. White, graying blonde, slim build. She's wearing a knitted sweater with small appliqué pansies and ducks on the collar and sleeves and reminds him of every single teacher he had in middle school. Rao passes him the file Rhodes had handed him. He opens it and reads. Dinah Crossland. Forty-two years old but only just. Her birthday just passed. Hometown, Pahrump.

"Well," Rhodes says to Rao as she rejoins them in the observation room. "Ms. Crossland is terribly pleased to be here."

"She's from Nevada," Adam says.

Rhodes nods. "Yes, Pahrump. It's about sixty miles northwest of Las Vegas."

"I'm aware. It's an unincorporated town in Nye County. Largest census designated place in the contiguous US."

"Remarkable," she says.

"Remarkable?"

"It didn't occur to me that you'd have such an extensive knowledge of the place."

"Why not?"

Rhodes shrugs. "You're American. American dedication is a powerful weapon to wield, obviously." She gestures vaguely at the woman in the next room. "But it tends to be focused on immediate things."

"She's calling you self-centered, Adam," Rao supplies.

"Thanks, Rao."

"Just being helpful, love."

Rhodes leaves the room. They turn to the window and watch her take a seat with Ms. Crossland in the interview suite. The transition from the Dr. Rhodes they've been working with for the last few days to the charming and affable Dr. Rhodes who wants to make Ms. Dinah Crossland happy and at ease in the facility is remarkable. She laughs and smiles warmly, leans forward, seems fascinated by Crossland's replies. Right now they're discussing Pahrump's Patriot Reaffirmation Ordinance. Flying American flags, making English the town's official language: how terribly important these things are.

"She's very good," Rao breathes. He's fascinated. Adam is, too, but he has the grace to feel bad about it.

"I don't trust her."

Rao snorts. "We've covered this. I know. That's why you never use her name."

"Her name is Rhodes."

"And you're using it to maintain distance."

Adam hums. It's not like Rao's wrong.

"Is that what you do with me?" Rao asks. "Maintain distance. Only use my last name?"

"You prefer using your last name."

"Started at school. It's the path of least resistance for most people."

"Do you want me to call you by your first name, Sunil?"

Rao shudders. "I hated that," he says. Looks horrified. "Never do that again."

"Do what, Sunil?" Adam smirks. It's too easy. Somewhere, distantly, Adam knows he should be having less fun and paying more attention to what Rhodes is doing. She's talking about family. Community. Ms. Crossland lights up, speaks with her hands. They're working. He's working. He and Rao need to know more about this woman, her reaction to her contamination. Why she's like how she is. But in this second he just doesn't care.

Rao glances at him. "Prick. Come on, Veronica's given us a Look, she wants us in there."

"Dinah," Rhodes says as they enter, "I'd like to introduce you to Lieutenant Colonel Rubenstein and Mr. Rao. They'd like to know more about your success story back home."

Adam knows the kind of woman Ms. Crossland is just by how she sits up a little straighter at the sight of him. Here it comes.

"Thank you for your service," she tells him, standing awkwardly to offer an enthusiastic hand.

"Thank you, ma'am," he replies.

"It's just so welcome to meet a fine young patriot like yourself these days. Caring for Little America as well as"—she glances at Rao distrustfully—"as well as on a global scale."

Adam suspects she doubts Rao can speak English. She sits without offering him her hand.

"I've been lucky to be able to work with a range of remarkable people," he tells her mildly. "Mr. Rao here is top of the list. He'd very much like to talk to you about your work in Pahrump."

She frowns, lowers her voice to a whisper. "Arabs don't care about America in a way that keeps the country safe. Who knows what he might want to know."

"I'm from Islington, for the record," Rao says. He pulls a chair to the table, lets it scrape against the floor before he sits.

"London," Adam clarifies.

"England," Rao completes. He considers her. "Ms. Crossland—"

"Mrs."

He sighs minutely. "Mrs. Crossland," he starts again. "I'm perfectly comfortable with the two of us never getting along. Fine with that, actually. I'm not here to convince you to be decent to me. We just have to get through a few questions and then you'll never have to look at me ever again. Won't that be nice?"

"I don't appreciate what you're implying," Mrs. Crossland says icily.

Rao smiles. "I don't believe I was *implying* anything, Dinah."

Mrs. Crossland looks first to Adam, then to Rhodes, her expression shifting from cold distrust to watery discomfort. Rao sighs again, more heavily, as she pleads with Adam and Rhodes. "I didn't come here to be insulted. I can't believe how he's treating me—"

"I'm—" Rhodes starts, but Rao interrupts her.

"No, Veronica. It's fine. No hard feelings, Mrs. Crossland?" he says, getting to his feet and offering his hand. Adam sees what he's doing. He's presenting Mrs. Dinah Crossland, community racist in a hand-knitted sweater, with a choice. She can dig in her heels, or she can take Rao's hand. Be polite.

Social conditioning wins out. She takes his hand, looking furious about it.

But the fury doesn't last. The moment their hands meet, her face turns slack. At first Adam assumes her expression is revulsion, but then he sees Rao's face matches hers. Both stand there, hands clasped, open-mouthed, still as graves. Rao must be drawing Prophet from her just like before, with Flores, he thinks, though this time it looks different. But of course it's different. Dinah Crossland isn't the usual test subject: she's not immune, and she's walking around like Adam. She's special.

Rhodes moves forward. Before she can intervene, both Crossland and Rao take simultaneous, ragged breaths. Crossland stumbles but recovers and, apart from a thin trickle of blood emerging from her right nostril, seems fine. She blinks at them all. Pulls a tiny, embroidered handkerchief from the pocket of her cardigan, dabs at her nose. Her face pales when she pulls it away and sees the cotton stained red.

"I, um," she says quietly, staring at Rao. Then she closes her eyes tight, like she's making a wish. "I want to go home."

"I'd very much prefer it if you spoke to our medical staff before you leave, Mrs. Crossland," Rhodes tells her.

"No. I don't want a fuss. I want to go home."

"Let her go, Veronica," Rao says, sitting back down. He looks exhausted. Dazed. Adam kneels and checks his pupils. They're dilated, but Rao's lucid. "Let her go home."

"Let's get you comfortable first," Rhodes murmurs. Her voice is soft, but her eyes are bright and both her hands are clenched. Adam thinks on that evidence that Crossland's not heading home anytime soon.

CHAPTER 53

Bringing Adam and Hunter back to the Vietnamese restaurant for dinner was, Rao decides, a stroke of genius. After meeting Crossland, after *that*, everything—the wrinkles on his jeans, the shadow under her chair, the angle between Veronica's upraised hand and the floor, the stitching on Crossland's sleeves, the blood on her handkerchief—had shivered with sudden, terrible significance. He could barely breathe against the intuition that a revelation was at hand. That kind of apophenic bullshit is, Rao knows, pretty far down the road towards getting forcibly sectioned under the Mental Health Act—or its Coloradan equivalent. But now? Now everything's good. Everything feels normal. Deeply, wonderfully normal. And fuck he'd been so *hungry*.

He looks at the ceiling tiles, the paintings of lotus flowers, the leggy houseplants under the soft lanterns by the bar and pops a last forkful of food into his mouth. Then he pushes his empty bowl across the tablecloth, sighing with satisfaction. "That's better," he announces. "The universe is back in balance."

Hunter gives him a curious look. "You talking about dharma?"

He grins. "Not in the proper sense, no. But kind of, a bit. I've just fixed a serious injustice."

"What injustice?"

"Adam ordered this dish last time and it was delicious. Far more delicious than the one I chose. So I had to come back and right that wrong. Avenge it."

"Avenge it? You think he ordered it on purpose to annoy you?"

"Absolutely."

"Rubenstein, why did you order chicken vermicelli noodles last time?"

"To annoy Rao."

"Is he lying, Rao?"

"You tell me, Hunter."

Outside, the night air is temperate and smells of mothballs and flowers. They start their walk back to Lunastus in companionable silence.

"What's that noise up there?" Rao enquires after a while.

"Sounds like a nighthawk," Adam says.

"That's a bird."

"It is."

Rao turns to Hunter. "See? You'd never have heard that if we took the car."

"I've heard nighthawks before," she says. "And I don't mind walking. I already said."

"She told you twice," Adam says. "Hunter does a lot of walking in her day job."

"Air traffic control."

"Air traffic control," Hunter repeats, "with added peril."

Banter. Banter and dinner and the walk in soft darkness and that weird noise above them, a metallic, fizzy chime. The world is full of goodness. Rao's spirits are so lifted that he starts humming "Spice Up Your Life" as he steps along the wide sidewalk before the turn into Lunastus's car park. He's replaying the video of the Spice Girls carousing inside a dimly lit spaceship in his mind when Adam throws an arm out in front of him, stopping him in his tracks.

"Adam, what the fuck—"

"Rao," he says, voice tight.

Rao turns to Hunter. "What's he on about?"

"I don't—" she begins, then stops. Stiffens. "Shit. Over there."

She's pointing forwards, farther down the access road, and what she's pointing at is so blisteringly wrong Rao stifles a laugh. There, about thirty feet away, is a patch of blazing, shocking colour. A bright, sunlit puddle running along the edge of the sidewalk. A puddle the blue of a summer afternoon. And all around it, darkness.

"Ah," he says, rubbing the back of his neck. "Hello."

"That is fucking insane," Hunter breathes. "Wait here. I'm gonna take a look."

"She's intrepid," Rao observes as she strides towards it.

"She's fearless. She's always been like that," Adam says.

She stands over the pool of light, considers it for a while, then jerks her head to beckon them over. Adam's face is grim as he looks down at it. Uplit by the brightness at her feet, Hunter's face is set in an expression of puzzled awe.

"It's water?" she asks.

"Yeah," Rao says. "It's a puddle."

"Prophet," Adam announces.

Rao bends down. "A specific memory, this one. It's reflecting the sky on a sunny day, isn't it? And—" He crouches to change the angle. From here he can see the top of a bright-red waterslide, a reflected line of mop-headed palms. He gets down on his hands and knees, brings his head closer to the sunlit surface. More of the waterslide comes into view, and beside it a pile of artfully arranged boulders with a waterfall and beneath the waterfall, bobbing heads and waving arms. "It's a water park," he breathes.

"How did it get out here?" Adam says.

"Dunno. Maybe Lunastus's ventilation containment system doesn't work with Prophet anymore."

"Can't you tell instantly whether that's true?" Hunter says.

Rao shrugs. "Prophet's tricky shit."

"We're due east of the buildings," Adam observes. "Prevailing wind's westward. Rao's theory tracks."

"Is this thing dangerous?" Hunter asks.

"Only to the person who made it. Could be anyone. Passerby, one of the medical staff driving home, anyone."

"Not me?"

"No. You'd be facedown in it if it was yours. Also . . . what do water parks mean to you?"

She shrugs, staring down at the puddle. "Marco Polo."

"What?"

"The swimming game, Rao," Adam says. "Not the guy."

Hunter tilts her head at Adam. "What're we gonna do about this?"

"Enjoy it," Rao says. "It's ludicrously pretty. I'll tell Veronica about it in the morning. She can send someone to clear it up. I'm sure she'll be delighted to hear about another Lunastus fuckup."

Adam shakes his head. "You should call her now."

"With what phone? Besides, I'm off the clock."

"Use my cell."

"She'll never answer your number, love."

"Rao."

"Fuck. Fine. But you owe me."

CHAPTER 54

He wakes suddenly with a surge of adrenaline, heart thrumming under his ribs, eyes wide. The motel room curtains are drawn. Rao's sitting on the edge of the bed across the room, his back to Adam. He's shaking his head and laughing softly. Adam sits up. There's no visible threat, but the surge of alarm that woke him won't go away. "Morning," he calls, voice rough with sleep. Rao looks over his shoulder. His face is amused and guilty. It looks so much like his expression the last time Adam walked in on him jerking off he assumes that's what's going on here. The laughter is weird, but so is Rao. Adam stopped being surprised by what gets Rao off a long time ago.

"Morning, love," Rao says. He turns, crooks one leg up onto the bed, looks down at the covers. He's not jerking off. But he's still snickering.

"What's funny, Rao?"

"There's a lizard," Rao says.

"What?"

Rao gestures at the throw blanket, and Adam sees it. It skitters fast over the patterned cotton to the far end of the bed, where it halts, raises its head, and freezes. It's too dark in the room to make out what color it is, brown or gray, and it's kind of spiny, with a rounded head and a long, whiplike tail. Adam's familiar with lizards. They were everywhere when he was growing up. But he's never seen this kind before.

"That shouldn't be here," he says. This sparks another bout of giggling from Rao. Fuck. *Is he high?*

"No, it shouldn't."

Adam gets out of bed, walks closer, angles his head to study it. Thin toes. Claws. Lizards aren't easy, but he knows how to catch them. Sniper mindset. All you need to do is tell yourself you're part of the scenery, convince yourself you're something like a rock or a tree. Then you strike with confidence, anticipating full success. He puts himself in the right headspace, waits a few seconds, then grabs at it, pressing the wriggling reptile into the cotton, getting a firm hold before picking it up, its spine nestled against his palm, scales rough and warm against his skin, his fingers closed around its neck. Its mouth is slightly open: a line of fine, tiny teeth and a round eye, pupils wide in the darkness of the room. He drops his hand to his side, walks to the door, pushes it open, then crouches and lets the lizard run from his opened hand into the motel parking lot. It disappears over the asphalt into the shadow under a Chrysler minivan.

"You didn't kill it," Rao says as Adam shuts the door.

"Why would I kill it?"

Rao shrugs. "Because you're you?"

"Thanks, Rao. Did you want me to?"

"No. Thank you for not."

"You're welcome."

Rao's laughing again. "Shall we go in? I know it's early, love, but I'm fucking starving. Even thought about hitting reception for a serving of Cheerios in a cardboard bowl, which I tell you is a way worse gastronomic experience than anything they served me in Pentonville."

Adam looks at him and determines, again, that Rao's appreciably thinner than he had been last week. Clavicles more obvious, cheekbones sharper. Which is disturbing considering how much he's been eating every day in the corporate canteen. Rao's never been shy of food, but last night at dinner, there was desperation in how Rao stuffed vermicelli into his mouth. Twice he told Adam how delicious it was, but he was barely chewing, eating so fast Adam doubted he tasted much at all.

"Rao," he says after a second or two of deliberation. "Are you feeling okay?" It's the kind of temperature testing Rao hates, but Rao doesn't roll his eyes. He smiles.

"Never better, love. Tickety-boo."

"Tickety-boo."

"English idiom."

"Right."

"It means I'm doing fine," Rao clarifies.

"Yeah, I got that." Adam sighs inwardly. Working together before, Adam got used to seeing Rao fucked up. He'd laugh, giggle, hum through his highs. Even through his lows. Balance issues, hyperfocus, nonstop talking, eerie silences: Adam's seen them all. But Rao never seemed to lie about it. If Adam asked, he'd own up. Sometimes just to piss Adam off. Always looking for a reaction.

Now, something's off about him. Adam knows it for a fact. The kind of fact that Rao would call flat, immutable, simply the truth. Something's off, but Adam doesn't think Rao is lying when he says he's doing fine. The need to know what's going on makes Adam's skin itch, but he pushes that need away and out of his head.

"Breakfast, Adam? Surely you could eat. Even the Froot Loops there are above average."

"Yeah, Rao. Let me get dressed."

"Ticktock, love."

Adam looks at him. Watches him replay the last few seconds. Watches him wince.

"I didn't mean it like that."

"It's fine."

"Sorry, Adam."

"Rao. It's . . . tickety-boo."

He doesn't know what he was expecting from Rao, but a triumphant howl was not on the list. Grinning, shirtless, Rao starts rummaging around the room for clothes. The weight loss looks good on Rao. Under the circumstances Adam shouldn't think that, but he does. He makes an internal, passive note to get him a new belt. At the rate Rao's losing weight, his pants won't stay up for much longer. They're dipping dangerously low as it is.

"Today's going to be a good day, love. Mark my words."

"Marked, Rao."

CHAPTER 55

De Witte's in the darkened cabin of one of his Lears: in the gloom behind his shoulders Veronica can see tiger-striped wood, cream leather chairs.

"Steven. It's early. Where are you?"

"Right now I'm, uh, over Lincoln, Nebraska, en route to the event. Is Pensacola ready to receive our subject?"

"Event?"

"You don't know about the event?" De Witte closes his eyes, speaks with them shut. "I told Lane he should call you immediately, inform you of the situation."

"He didn't, Steven. He wouldn't. He sees me as a threat to your and his special relationship."

He opens his eyes. "It won't— I'll make sure it doesn't happen again."

"Tell me about the event."

"Lane got a call from security at E-MAD at, uh, three sixteen yesterday. We've had a mass manifestation of EPGOs around the buildings. He's sending in a plane to get a bird's-eye."

"How many objects?"

"Tens of thousands. Plush toys, pianos, Ford pickups, the usual kind of kind. Some are, uh, quite massive."

"How massive?"

"Boeing 747. Pan Am colours."

She takes a deep breath, holds it, exhales. "Do you have a first pass on causation?"

"Considering the quantity, I assume they were generated by our field site cohort."

"That was five months ago," she says.

"*A hundred and thirty-four days since exposure,*" *he corrects.* "*So perhaps this is another case of saltatory evolution? It would strengthen our entanglement thesis if so.*"

"*What do our theoreticians say?*"

He shakes his head. "*We lost another one. Hung himself. He, uh, left a note. It was like the last one. All about how, you know, nothing makes sense anymore.*"

She ignores that irrelevance. Something's just occurred to her.

"*Did you say the call came at three sixteen, Steven?*"

"*Three sixteen, yes.*"

She smiles then. She knows. It's Rao. Rao and Mrs Crossland. Their handshake, that skin-to-skin contact. Veronica's certain Rao somehow triggered the manifestation. Questions are presenting themselves to her now that she's very eager to answer. And right now, she decides, Steven doesn't need to complicate things.

He's looking to her for elaboration, now. "*Does that time have significance to you, Veronica?*"

"*No, Steven. Not at all.*"

CHAPTER 56

Montgomery clears his throat. This morning he grips a clipboard and his eyes are a little vague. Odds-on, Rao thinks, the vagueness is vodka, and the clipboard's partly a defensive prop. *Right*, both counts.

"Let's take you through this once more. You've agreed to extract Prophet from another test subject."

"Yes, Kent."

"And we've scheduled you for a PET scan tomorrow at eleven, to complement the MRI results so far, dig a little deeper into your metabolic processing."

"Yes. Because Prophet's not enough. You want me radioactive as well."

"Only mildly," Veronica offers.

"We'll be administering a radionuclide called fluorodeoxyglucose," Montgomery continues, stumbling a little midway through the word. "It'll leave your system in a few days. Best to keep away from pregnant women in that time."

"I'll try."

"Rao, which subject will you be working with today?"

"With? On? Or for?" Rao rapid fires. "The man with the orange blanket."

"Can you tell us why?"

"Because I'm horrified. Veronica's had his girlfriend sedated for what, a week?"

"Eight days," she says. "Her vital signs are strong."

"Fuck me, that can't be good for her. What'll you do with them both when he wakes?"

She frowns. "They signed the forms. There's no legal avenues for—"

"Lunastus isn't going to bump them off?"

"Rao," Montgomery rebukes.

"Ok, ok. Let's do this."

Rao's chosen subject is at the back of the ward, orange fleece blanket heaped in a soft pile in his arms, the ribbon stitched along one edge pressed against his lips. Tension lines around his mouth and eyes. He's already looking grey. Four nurses are clustered a few feet away. Monty takes himself off to sit on a chair against the far wall. *Fair enough*, Rao thinks. It's not like there's any point to him being here. Veronica's setting up a video recorder on a tripod by the side of the bed. Rao's tempted to step in and start the process before she's ready, but he likes that his next miracle will be on tape for posterity. He's not too proud of that.

Where's Adam? he thinks, turning his head. Standing right behind him, like Adam always is. Maybe he expects blanket man to attack Rao when he wakes. *Maybe*, Rao thinks, *he will*.

"We're ready," Veronica says. "Do you need me to—"

"No. Just make sure you get my best side," Rao says, stepping closer. Reaching out, he cradles the man's face in both hands. A wash of emotion at the sensation. Most of it unidentifiable. A lot of sadness that feels like memory. And the prickling in his palms takes longer this time, but then it catches and holds and Prophet slips through. He's waiting for the terror, but the terror doesn't come. The same intuition of measureless no-water oceans, now lit with dimmest, glimmering stars, almost familiar, and he's falling and rising inside it like breathing, as if—

Done. Like switching on a light, he's back in the room and watching the man's fingers spasm, clutch at the blanket, his eyes open wide. They're blue and bloodshot and absolutely baffled.

"Hi," Rao says.

"Doctor?"

The nurses rush towards him. Rao is pushed aside.

"Very impressive, Rao," Veronica breathes. She's standing too close. Adam's on his other side. "How are you feeling?"

He doesn't answer. Walks to the next bed. In it, a small, short-haired woman has her arms around what Rao had initially thought was a giant pumpkin, albeit one with a spout, red plastic windows, and angry blue eyebrows. Adam had informed him it was the Big Yellow Teapot, and Rao had given him shit for being overly literal. "No, Rao," he'd said. "That's its name."

"Designation."

"Name."

He smiles at the memory, pushes the woman's hospital bracelet a little farther up her arm, and grips her wrists.

This time the no-water ocean is almost a welcoming place, though it's not a place at all, and the way Prophet slips into him reminds him of something he can't quite grasp. The woman wakes with a start. The teapot rolls from her chest, hits the floor with a crack. Parts of it open, and things spill across the floor. Toys, Rao assumes, but he's already moving to the next bed, aware that the woman he's just healed is having a fit. The nurses surround her now, and peripherally he can see her kicking feet. It's not like he can help her out of it, they'll have it under control, there's more—

He studies the occupant of the next bed. Man, early forties, dark hair, gripping a G.I. Joe.

"Rao." Adam, at the foot of the bed, looking warily at him. "Do you know what you're doing?"

"First fucking time in my life, love," he says with feeling, holding Adam's eye as he presses his hands to the man's chest. Keeps looking at Adam as Prophet floods in. But his attention's torn away when he suddenly works out what this sensation reminds him of. A cold day in January in Jaipur, drinking chai from Sahu's on Chaura Rasta Road. Sweet. Hot. Fragrant. *Known.*

He moves on.

They don't all wake the same. Some don't open their eyes, their breathing turning fitful, their fingers twitching as their objects fall from their hands and arms. Others wake gasping. One with a scream. Every time Rao pulls Prophet from their bodies he feels himself sink and rise and by the eighth he's feeling so at home in the not-ocean around him it's more effort leaving it than slipping in. *Chai*, he thinks, as the last sleeper wakes. *Chai on a cold day.*

He heals everyone.

Veronica, staring at him. Hands folded together, pressed to her lips like she's praying. Like she doesn't know what to say.

"Alright, Veronica?"

"We should run some tests."

"Right. Right. But first I require a cup of tea."

*

Adam looks up to see Montgomery walking into the side room off the main ward. He really shouldn't look forward to Rao verbally punching that man as much as he does.

"Oh, *piss off*," Rao growls, setting down his mug. It's weird. Under these fluorescent lights, Monty looks like a corpse; Rao looks glowing with health. "I just healed all your casualties. Whatever the fuck you're bringing to my door, you can piss off with it, okay? Toddle back off to Veronica and tell her to bite the back of my balls. Better yet, tell her to bite yours. It'll shock everyone. You could really take charge for once, Monty. Sorry. *Kent*."

Montgomery opens his mouth, closes it. Adam should feel sorry for him.

"Rao," he says. "I want to take a break."

"Oh! Lunch?"

Obviously. "If you want."

"I could murder a burger."

As they walk the corridors, Rao's savage mood recedes, and he starts reciting lines from his improvised ode to the Lunastus canteen. Adam's heard it on repeat since the first day, but the rhymes are getting worse, the tone more and more evangelical. There's something to be said about Rao's love of luxury and how well he's been doing at ignoring it. Apart from falling off the wagon that night with Hunter, he hasn't indulged in any kind of vice with Adam around—except the canteen.

"It's obscene," Rao says, breaking off from his recital. "I don't know how many Michelin-starred chefs they've kidnapped and got chained up in that kitchen, but eating here feels like I'm doing something highly illegal without actually going down that road."

"I was just thinking the same thing."

Rao laughs. "Go fuck yourself, love. Only I'm allowed to talk about my tendencies so lightly."

"Is that true?"

"No." Rao's smiling. "I suppose you're allowed, all things considered."

Adam shakes his head, quietly embarrassed at how much that means to him. "Very gracious, Rao," he says. He means it. Rao will never know.

Rao's smile slips. "Adam, are you cold?"

"What?"

"I feel cold," he says. He looks up, slow and unnatural. Like a wire connected to his chin is tugging his head into the right position. *Puppet*, Adam thinks. "Marionette," the word Rao would use.

"What is it?" he asks. The question has just left his mouth when he sees something trickle down from Rao's nostrils as he looks up. Blood. It's almost black.

Adam catches him as he crumples. Both of them slide to the floor. Rao's a deadweight in his arms. He's still looking up. His eyes are open, but he's not seeing a damn thing.

"What just happened?" Adam whispers into the air. There's no response from Rao. He doesn't expect one. He doesn't have to sound an alarm, either; there are cameras everywhere. Less than a minute after they hit the floor, there's a team of Rhodes's medical staff right there with a gurney. Adam doesn't fight them, and Rao doesn't react when they move him. He's taking shallow but regular breaths. His eyes are still open, unblinking. As they wheel him down the halls toward an examination room, one of the white coats drops saline onto his corneas. Adam keeps up, hand on the side of the gurney.

They get Rao settled on a bed and are hooking him to monitors when Rhodes arrives. "What happened?" she asks him. Sharp.

"Unknown," he says. "We were walking and then he wasn't."

She reaches over to close Rao's eyes. The action is sickeningly tender, and it takes everything Adam has to keep from telling her to get fucked. She's been delighting in poking and prodding Rao to get answers about what's been happening with him, and Adam's said nothing about it. Not directly. But this act of apparent kindness nearly sends him over the edge. Rhodes doesn't notice him bristling.

"He suffered from epistaxis before losing consciousness."

"You can say nosebleed, Dr. Rhodes."

She glances at Adam. "Why? You understood what I meant. You really are—"

"My ego can handle it if you focus on Rao, Dr. Rhodes, and not on how surprised you still are to learn that I can grasp the concept of synonyms."

"We'll keep him overnight," she says, leaning back enough to give the impression that she's allowing Rao space to breathe.

"No tests," he says. Acquiesces. Negotiates. It's always a negotiation with Rhodes.

"Colonel Rubenstein—"

"Rhodes, don't push me on this," he warns her. "When he wakes up, get his consent as you need it. But right now I'm telling you that the only thing you're going to do is keep him well enough to regain consciousness. Am I understood?"

Rhodes purses her lips. He hasn't used the command tone on her, until now. He doesn't do that anymore. He's not around enough soldiers these days to warrant it. But it has its uses.

"Yes, Colonel. I believe I understand your stance on the matter."

"Glad we're eye-to-eye on this, Dr. Rhodes."

"Adam?"

Rao's voice scratches Adam out of a light nap. Low medical lighting and quiet monitor beeps lulled him into a doze a few hours ago, sometime after Rhodes's people left. One of them even tried to convince him to leave. He rubs his eyes and sits up. Reaches for the glass and jug of water on the bedside table. "Rao," he says.

"What happened?"

"Good question." Adam pours and hands him a glass, watching closely for tremors or signs of weakness. Nothing. Rao looks solid. Confused but solid. "How do you feel?"

"Starving."

"We never ate. You collapsed on the way to lunch."

"What time is it now?"

Adam checks his watch. "Two a.m."

"Fuck," Rao says with feeling. He sits up, scratches his beard. Grimaces at the IV line in his arm. Sighs at his feet poking out of the bottom of the bed. "What does Veronica say?"

"The last thing Dr. Rhodes said to me was 'Tell me when he's awake.' She wants to run more tests."

"She didn't already?"

"No."

"That's not like her."

"She's not happy about it. She's had to reschedule the PET scan."

Rao snorts, settles back down. Looks up at the ceiling. Rhodes's team cleaned the blood from his nose when they brought him in and hooked him up, but Adam can still see it dripping over his lips. He blinks the memory away and tries to refocus.

"Are you defending my honor again, love?"

"Someone has to."

That makes Rao laugh. It echoes flatly. "Do you think they could get me something to eat if we tell them I'm awake?"

Adam looks at Rao seriously. The dim white light makes him look gray, but he seems okay. Maybe a little embarrassed. Distant. He doesn't look at Adam directly. Whenever he smiles or laughs, a little more tension leaves his shoulders. He could be lying about not knowing what happened. Worse, he could be telling the truth.

"Do you think you could find out what happened before they come in here?" he asks. "Do a run?"

Rao groans. "I really don't want to."

"But you could?"

"I could do a fuck ton of things, Adam. I could rip this line out and use it as a skipping rope but I'm not going to do that, am I?"

"Do the run anyway."

Rao groans again, leveling a look of pure malice in Adam's direction, but Adam doesn't care. They need to know what happened. *He* needs to know. He watches Rao give in and mutter to himself.

"Anything?" he prompts eventually.

"Alright, Adam, fuck off," Rao says, rubbing his eyes. Seconds drag past. That kitchen clock's heavy tick is somehow still in Adam's head, and he can almost hear it as he waits. He'd prefer it if Rao were looking at him, but he keeps his hand right there, blocking out the medical lighting and Adam's gaze. "It was an overdose. Run of the mill. Don't fucking talk to me."

CHAPTER 57

Hunter walks into Rao's recovery room with the specific energy of someone on a highly unwelcome mission. She tosses something onto his bed. He watches it arc and fall onto the blanket between his knees. An energy bar. Chocolate chip and peanut butter. Cartoon wrapper of a bear holding a grenade.

"Thank you? Is that beer you're carrying for me too?"

"No, it isn't." She sits at his bedside.

"Why not?"

"Because I'm not an idiot." She crosses one ankle over a knee. "How are you doing? Rubenstein said you passed out."

"Yeah, he's seen that before, nothing unusual. How am I doing? I hate these pyjamas they've given me. I know that's petty, but I am petty, and they're ghastly. Apart from that, I'm just bored. Did he make you come visit me?"

"Who?"

He snickers. "Want to sneak out for a smoke?"

She shrugs. "Sure."

"Pass me that robe on the door?"

They find a door that opens onto a flat roof at the far end of a corridor and duck out into a mild Coloradan morning. The radomes of the airbase across the road sit like unpopped soap bubbles, the sky above dotted with fist-shaped clouds. Rao lights two cigarettes, passes one to Hunter, and they look out across miles of nicotine-coloured grass to the horizon.

"Rao, how the fuck did you end up in this life?" Hunter says.

"Surprised Adam's not told you."

"He probably has," she confesses. "But I hear a lot of stories and I only remember the interesting ones."

"Hunter . . ."

She laughs. "He didn't tell me. *Jesus*, Rao. You're so *easy*."

Rao's quiet for a moment before realising he's going to tell her. Wants to tell her.

"After university," he begins, "I went a bit off the rails. Spent a few years fucking around. Spent too much of my time in the company of posh white wankers with villas and pools and good dealers. Punched out a few. Stole a car from one once."

"Highlight of your criminal career?"

"It was at the time," he says crisply. "Anyway, the last couple of years were in Berlin, and it got full-on ragged. I kind of lost the plot. I wasn't . . ." He shakes his head. He's not going to give her all the grisly details. "Then I got an ultimatum from my father. After a family birthday I try never to think about. *Sort yourself out or the money will stop*."

Hunter blinks at him.

"Don't look like that."

"I'm not." She shakes her head. "I just don't know why you needed his money at all. You've never played poker?"

"Wouldn't be fair."

"That doesn't make sense." She frowns. Rao opens his mouth in protest; she raises a hand to stop him. "Whatever. So you got a job."

"Yeah. At Sotheby's, the auction house. Only got through the door because my mother's a specialist at Christie's. She's a very persuasive woman and she knows everyone. *Everyone*. My job was researching whether artworks were genuine."

Hunter raises an eyebrow, taps ash.

"Yeah, I know. That bit was easy for me, of course, but I still had to get physical evidence to prove it one way or the other, and that was a pain in the arse. So, I'm in my office on a foggy Tuesday afternoon in January, it's nearly dark outside, and there's a call. Someone in reception's asking for me by name. I thought it would be someone I knew from college, you know, or someone who knew someone I knew. But it wasn't."

"Let me guess," she says. "A guy with a painting he wanted you to look at?"

"It wasn't a painting. It was a beautiful red chalk by Sebastiano del Piombo. Totally real, by the way. We talked about it for a while, he got into my space, commented favourably on my cologne. I thought he'd be up for some fun. Said he worked at the British Museum, and two nights later he took me on what I assumed was a date to the Egyptian galleries." He pauses significantly. "After closing time."

"I don't know what that look means, Rao."

"Museums at night, well. You know."

"They give you a hard-on?" she guesses.

"They're *romantic*."

She laughs. "That's the worst lie I've ever heard come out of your mouth."

"Fuck off, but yeah, ok. I was thinking, why would this guy take me to a place full of funerary objects unless he had a pretty specific kink?"

She looks at him enquiringly.

"I've a very open mind," Rao says, very seriously.

She snorts. "Yeah, I know. So, what? He gave you a speech, showed you some wrapped-up mummy, got you to say it was fake, then invited you to a meeting with some people?"

"Yeah," Rao says, faintly crestfallen. Because that was exactly what had happened.

Morten Edwards had wide hazel eyes, a sweep of dark-blond hair, a pocket square that was all affectation, and a deep Welsh voice that wasn't.

"Uh, Morten," Rao had said, both of them staring down into the museum case. "Would you care to tell me what is happening here? I thought you were making a pass."

"Actually I am. In a sense. Indulge us."

"Us?"

"A government department."

"Which government department?"

"It's not Heritage and Sport," Edwards said, amused.

He's a spy, Rao thought and instantaneously *knew*. A punch of excitement under his ribcage. He'd looked back at the mummified cat. "This isn't what it says it is. But it's not a fake. More like a very ancient fraud. Depends. In this case, I don't think it matters, really. Do you?"

"I don't think it does, no. But considering what you can do, some people I know would like to have a bit of a talk with you," he murmured after a while.

"You're MI5," Rao said.

"Not them, no."

Hunter cocks her head, looks at him curiously. "So they didn't know about your lying thing?"

Rao grins. "I'm a fuckwit. I told them. Not all of it," he adds. "Only that I can tell when people aren't speaking the truth."

"When?"

"First meeting."

"You *are* a fuckwit."

He sighs. Sold himself out to the kind of authority he's spent a lifetime kicking against is what he did. That's all he's done. "I really thought I'd be helpful, you know? Save people. Make a difference."

He expects her to laugh. She doesn't. She takes a swig of her beer. "That's why we do it," she says. "I'm not as cynical as Rubenstein. No one is." Her voice is warm but serious.

"You two go back a long way, I hear?"

"Yeah, we went through basic together. This quiet Jewish kid and the asshole mixed kid showing everyone how it's done."

"What was he like back then?"

Her face grows fond. "Next-level. Like he is now." She takes another swig, reconsiders. "No, he's different these days."

"Older and wiser?"

"He's older," she says, looking right at him.

Rao's wondering if he's brave enough to ask for elaboration when the door behind them swings wide. Veronica peers out from the frame, mouth in a tight line.

"Rao. You shouldn't be out here. And you *really* shouldn't be smoking."

"Fuck off, Veronica," Rao says cheerfully.

"We need to discuss your latest blood work."

"Not now. I'm convalescing."

"If you're sufficiently well to smoke barefoot on a rooftop, you're well enough to discuss medical results."

It's phenomenally difficult to argue with that. "Bad news?"

"Inexplicable news."

"Fuck, you do know how to reel me in," he grumbles. "Hunter, where's Adam?"

She shrugs. "I'm not his keeper."

"You don't know where he is?"

"He said he was going for lunch. I don't know where and I didn't ask."

Rao bends to stub out his cigarette, flicks it into a gutter. "Ten to one he'll be eating a burger in the canteen. He hates how good they are. Or maybe . . . Veronica, you don't happen to know what today's specials are?"

"I don't," Veronica says. "But this won't take long. You're welcome to join him in the canteen when we're done."

She stands by the armchair, hands on her hips. Watches Rao get back into bed, prop himself up against the headboard. "Right, Doctor," he says, pulling his robe closer around him. "Give me the inexplicable news. I can take it."

"Your results are bizarre. Yesterday you extracted Prophet from fifteen people."

"I know I did. How are they all?"

"Good," she says. "Apart from one."

He clutches at the bed linen. He hadn't thought to check. "The woman who had the fit. The one with the teapot."

"Yes."

He's going to throw up. He is. He isn't. He might.

"What did I do? Was it broken heart syndrome?"

"You didn't *do* anything except extract Prophet from her," Veronica says tightly. "She suffered a generalised tonic-clonic seizure followed by a stroke. The neurobiology of withdrawal from Prophet will be a wonderfully fertile area for further research."

He stares at the wall miserably, thinking of the hollow crack when her teapot hit the floor. He'd been too eager to do *more*, hadn't looked back. He'd not looked at her. Hadn't even seen her face.

"What was her name?"

"Simmonds. Lab tech."

"First name?"

"Nancy."

"I was trying to help," he says dully. "Why does this always happen. It always happens."

"Rao, this has never happened before, anywhere."

He pulls his knees to his chest, hugs them. The cotton feels greasy. He's suddenly very aware of his shins. Sharp. How frail they are. How everything is.

"But that isn't the reason I wanted to talk to you. Two other things were."

He gestures at her to go on.

"Like you, Colonel Rubenstein has an anomalous response to Prophet. Both with his initial dose and then the follow-up." She purses her lips. "You know about the second dose."

"I do."

She tucks an invisible hair behind an ear. "He requested it. There was full consent."

"What have you done to him now?"

"Nothing. But his case raised the possibility that Prophet . . . refuses, shall we say, to incorporate itself into subjects who've previously been exposed, even if you've extracted all of it from their systems."

He blinks at her. She's expecting him to follow her chain of reasoning, but he's still caught up in the horror that he's killed another person. His body count is getting impressive. He—

"So I gave another dose to one of your miracles, half an hour ago."

He sits up. "For *fuck's sake*," he hisses. "Can't you just leave them alone?"

"You don't want to know what happened?"

He closes his eyes.

"Murray. Jackson Murray. Navy SEAL. Back problems invalided him out. I don't know if you remember him. His EPGO was a G.I. Joe."

He nods, eyes still closed.

"If it helps, Rao, he was barely conscious at the time. It's unlikely he felt the needle at all. But Prophet was very eager to renew its acquaintance. He created another G.I. Joe, held it in exactly the same position as before, and promptly returned to a trance state. His vitals are fine, by the way. So you might drop by the ward when you're feeling better if you're in the mood."

He doesn't engage with that.

"What was the other thing?"

"There's still no trace of Prophet in your system."

He raises his head, stares at her. That doesn't feel right. He feels full of it. Every cell in his body brimming with it. And yet—

"What did you do with it?" she asks.

"You think I'm hiding it?"

Something like a smile. "At this point, Rao, I wouldn't be surprised."

"I have no idea. I took it out of everyone. I don't know where it's gone. Maybe it vanishes into the ether. Gets absorbed. I don't care. I killed someone."

"You didn't kill them. Prophet did."

Rao has a moment of wild confusion. Indeterminacy is everywhere, he knows, but the causal structure of her statement is a fucking bewilderment. Everything true and not true and somehow *in movement*. He rubs his nape. Veronica's talking on her phone.

"Could you tell me what today's specials are? Vichyssoise, pan-fried walleye with artichoke aioli, buffalo tenderloin with prairie butter. Thank you." She cuts the call, smiles, looks expectantly at Rao.

CHAPTER 58

Adam paces around their motel room in silence. He's thinking. Rao isn't about to fuck with that before the time is right. Usually he would—and delight in doing so—but he knows he's up shit creek. He knew things would go pear-shaped if he kept on with this, but somehow thought it would go differently. Which was idiotic. He's an idiot.

The cards. *Shit.*

He'd been desperate to get out of that godawful recovery room and back to the motel but as soon as he'd walked through the door, he didn't want to be there at all. Sick of television, tired of radio, fully over the dog-eared novels the hotel lobby had supplied, he'd simply wanted something to *do*. He'd dropped the deck on the table in front of Adam, asked him to teach him how to do false cuts. Adam had nodded, glanced down, and his face had pulled taut. Shoulders too.

Puzzled, Rao looked at the deck.

The cards from the Tashkent suite. Exactly the same Russian crosshatched backs patterned red and blue, the same card stock, well-thumbed corners. He knows they'd smell the same if he lifted them to his nose and sniffed. Turpentine and bleach.

Adam had looked at them for a long while, then raised his eyes to Rao's, face way beyond demanding an explanation, and Rao, heart thumping, had known he was fucked. No way to bullshit his way out of this one.

And now Adam is pacing around the motel room, and Rao, resigned, is lying on his bed, staring up at the ceiling, waiting for what he knows he's going to get.

"What have you created?" Adam says eventually, stilling himself. "Apart from the cards, Rao. What have you made?"

"You want a list?"

"Honestly, yes. But I know you won't provide that. I'll settle for what you can remember creating and when and why."

"What do you mean, why?"

Adam exhales once, sharply. "Humour me."

"Fine." Rao sits up, positioning himself a little more solidly in the room—though it would be easier to talk to the ceiling than watch Adam's face while he speaks. "I made cigarettes. Smoked them. You had one—"

"Jesus."

"Perfectly safe. Still have three left, if you want to take a look," he offers, gesturing to the jacket hanging on the door. "They're in the front pocket. Then matches. A lighter. A chocolate bar, once, but I didn't finish eating that."

"It wasn't right?"

"No, it was perfect." Rao shakes his head. "I just misjudged how much I wanted to eat chocolate. You know how I get, sometimes, with sweets."

"Stay on target, please," Adam sighs.

"The cards."

"I know about the cards, Rao. I'm looking at them. Anything else?"

There is. There's one more thing. Two more things. They're difficult to talk about because they were the first and because that was when Rao knew he was beyond help. He knows only the worst will come of this, no matter how thrilling it is. Maybe because of how thrilling it is.

"Rao," Adam prompts.

Rao nods. "Yeah. Ok. There were lizards."

Adam freezes. Rao watches his eyes grow wide, darting around the room as he stacks this information high, clicks it into place. "The lizard in our room," he says quietly. He moves closer to Rao. Rao wishes he wouldn't. Drops into a squat so that they're eye-to-eye. "The lizard on the bed."

"Yes."

"And you laughed at it and told me to look." Yes. Rao remembers. Giddy with the sudden creation, the victory of it, the controlled chaos of it. A living thing that had never existed before, skittering on the sheets. "I put it outside."

Rao nods.

"When we were leaving, you took your time in the parking lot. I thought you were tying your laces, but—" He stops, looks at Rao closely. Stills himself to search for whatever truth he's looking for, shakes himself out of it again. The process is fascinating to watch this close. "There were lizards in the parking lot."

"There were two," Rao says. Adam lifts an eyebrow. "What? I couldn't leave the first one out there alone. Contrary to popular belief, I'm not a complete prick."

Adam's lips twitch. It's practically a smile. "I thought you were high."

Ouch. "I suppose that's reasonable enough."

"But, instead, you were creating life."

That surprises a laugh out of Rao. "Bloody hell, Adam. You make it sound so dramatic. 'Creating life,' as though it's as large as that."

"Isn't it?"

"It doesn't feel that large," Rao admits, then shakes his head at the lie. "No. It's large, just not in the way you're imagining."

"Explain it to me."

Rao frowns. "I'm not entirely sure that I can."

"Try."

That's not so easy. Rao knows how it feels, and he knows what it reminds him of. It's like heroin, but without the slowness. It doesn't put distance between him and the world, but it has the same ever-falling stillness. He's not disconnected. He doesn't get that yellow-air-in-a-library feeling, as though everything's old and dry and smells of sweet chemicals. Creating new things makes Rao feel fresh. Cold, a shock to the system. An ice bath. Breathing in morning air in the snow. Bright, sharp, as inviting as any other kind of high.

But there's no way he can say these things to Adam. The hardest thing Adam's ever done in his life is grain alcohol. He tries a different tactic, sticks as close to the truth as he can.

"It's sharp," he starts, and sees Adam focus up. "Like cutting into fabric or digging out a bullet from a wound. Only, instead of fighting to find the bullet within, the wound wants to give it up. When I do this, Adam—it's—it's as though I'm speaking a knife into the world. I make a cut. The wound gives."

Adam sighs, gets to his feet. "I thought that we had cleared up the misconception that I'm a violent psychopath, Rao." He sounds tired. He hadn't before. "You don't have to put it in terms that you think I would understand."

Rao shakes his head. "No, that's not—" He stops, seeing the scepticism on Adam's face. Lifts his hands in peace. "Fine. I might have started with that intention."

"You don't need to—"

Rao interrupts. "But what I said feels exactly right. And, rather more importantly, it's *true*."

Adam is silent again. Steps to the other end of the bed, sits. Rao feels the mattress take his weight. *A concession*, Rao thinks, though Adam's face is unreadable as ever.

"Watch," Rao says. Can hear the urgency in his voice. *Show, don't tell.*

He holds his hand open between them and inhales. Conjures in his mind the full apprehension of what it will be and then exhales, doing the thing he has no words for: opens the world to let it out. He feels the pull, just to his left, and his eyes drag towards a few square inches of bedcover. Adam's attention is drawn to the spot too; he leans towards it, intent. The air around it contracts inwardly, quivers. Like heat haze, but it's not something that can be seen. Sensed. Like an accelerating implosion, air rushing in to fill a vacuum, and—

Rao blinks—and there.

A thick glass ashtray on the coverlet, the cotton beneath it deformed under its weight. He surfs the sensation, but there's the familiar disappointment in its wake. Everything he's made so far has only ever appeared when his eyes have been closed, while he's blinked, has manifested in that fleeting moment of blindness. He's never seen it happen.

He looks over to Adam, hopefully.

"Do it again," Adam says. "I blinked."

"Adam . . ."

"Just . . . I don't know. Another ashtray. Do it again."

"Alright, but—"

"Go ahead."

He prays Adam will see it this time. He needs to know.

No dice: Adam blinks at precisely the same moment, and a second ashtray is laid on the bed.

"I don't think we're ever going to see it happen," Rao says. "Like the static on the cameras at Polheath. It won't let us see it."

"Or we're not letting ourselves see it," Adam says. "Try again."

A crowd of glass ashtrays are strewn across the carpet and piled upon the bed. One rests on the windowsill, another on a ceiling fan blade. Rao's just worked out how to make things appear exactly where he wants them; it requires a form of expectant focus that's somehow orthogonal to the process of creation, and he's thrilled with himself for getting the knack, for having managed to put one right there on the fan. He walks over, reaches to pick it from its perch, drops it next to the others on the bed; it clinks as it hits one of its siblings.

"Housekeeping's going to be a bit freaked out," he snickers, sitting back on the bed.

Adam doesn't respond. His face is no longer lit with fascination. It's turned exceedingly grave. He's picked up the nearest ashtray and is turning it in his hand, watching the light refract through it. "They're all exactly the same. Why make these?"

"I need a smoke, probably."

"No. I mean, is this an ashtray from your childhood?"

Rao shrugs. "Could be. It'll be one I've seen, somewhere, sometime, yeah." He shuts his eyes for a few seconds. "Hotel bar in Istanbul. Long vac, second year at college. Overdid the absinthe."

Adam fits the ashtray in his palm, hoists it a few times to assess its weight. Seeing it, Rao thinks of the Egyptian goddess of truth. Maat. How one of her feathers was weighed against a human heart after its owner's death. The finality of that weighing, the decision it entailed: whether the afterlife would be a fitting place for each individual human soul. He watches Adam weigh the ashtray in his hand and feels the vacancy at his core, the tiny hole that's the foreknowledge of death, and he knows it's speaking to the Prophet inside him. He doesn't know what it's saying, but he knows that Prophet is speaking back. He shivers. *This stuff*, he thinks, *it does this*. Makes him get religious. Hey ho. He's had worse.

"That lizard," Adam says thoughtfully, "wasn't like the horse. It was perfect."

Rao beams. "Yeah. It was. They were. Still are."

Adam puts the ashtray back on the bed, rocks it with a finger. "My guess is, if I'd opened it up, I wouldn't have been able to know it was a telltale."

"Are we calling them telltales now?"

"Rhodes started to use the term for the EPGOs that move. You don't like it?"

"No, it's a good name," Rao admits grudgingly, because it fucking is. For a while he contemplates the way the hotel lights refract through the piles of moulded glass, then clears his throat and assumes his best tutorial voice. "So," he says, "do you know why the lizard was perfect?"

"Because you know the truth about things."

Rao's surprised. "Yeah. Exactly."

"So when you make a telltale—"

"It isn't a telltale at all. I don't make EPGOs. I don't make telltales. What I make is properly, truly alive." He waits for that to sink in. Adam's face shows no sign it has. "You know I'm the only person in the world who can do this?" he adds.

"You made life, Rao," Adam says, low and urgent. "We're not supposed to do that."

Rao smirks. "Nah, people do it all the time. You got made, so did I."

Adam sees his bullshit for what it is, ignores it. "I don't know why I remember this," he goes on slowly, "but there's a word. It's in the first sentence of Genesis. It's *bara*. It means to create things out of nothing. Only God is supposed to create like that, Rao. It's"—he furrows his brow—"it's a serious thing. It's too serious for us to mess with."

Rao rolls his eyes. "So here's another word for you, love. *Lila*. Sanskrit. Means play. Magical creativity. Hindu gods play like that, which is how the world got made. Serious play, but play all the same." He pouts. "Also, monotheism's a drag. No offence."

Adam nods thoughtfully. He took that well, Rao thinks, surprised, before realising the response wasn't acceptance but the patient indulgence Rao's always got from Adam when he's high.

"Ok," Adam says. Glances across the room to the kitchenette. "I'm thirsty. I'm going to get some water, and then—"

"Are you fucking serious? What kind of water do you want? Come on, put your hand out flat in front of you, palm up. I'll make you a glass of water."

Adam doesn't look happy about it. But he proffers his left hand. And a few seconds later Rao watches it dip slightly as it takes the weight of a glass pulled from the air.

Adam focuses on the glass. He swallows. His hand is shaking: the surface of the water shivers. The briefest tremble crosses his features.

"It's not poison. You can drink it."

"Rao," Adam whispers. "This glass."

"Yeah, I dunno why it turned out like that. Just wanted to make you a glass of water." He leans closer. It's plastic, not glass. It's a plastic glass. It's printed with Walt Disney's signature in red at the top, and below it is a cartoon image of Cinderella in a gilded chair. Flat golden hair, an orange-and-white pinafore. She's lifting her foot to her kneeling prince. Behind her, a castle. Mice at her feet. Stars, everywhere.

"I've seen this before. One just like this. When I was a kid."

"Huh," Rao says. "Huh."

CHAPTER 59

istant sirens outside. Rao isn't ready to open his eyes, so he truth-tests his way to the time. It's 8:12 a.m., Sunday the twenty-fourth of October. What happened on this date? He pulls a sheaf of facts from memory. Rosa Parks died. The United Nations was founded. Antonie van Leeuwenhoek's birthday. Ronnie and Reggie Kray's birthday. Release date of *The Manchurian Candidate*. The first one, not the remake. He loves that movie.

He can't smell coffee. He cracks an eye. Adam's bed is made and his running shoes are gone. So selfish. He could have made a pot before he left. Rao hauls himself out of bed, knocks the Disney glass at his feet over as he does. *Fuck.* He'd put the glass on the floor because it'd felt wrong to keep it in Adam's sight. He'd piled the ashtrays on the carpet, too, over on the other side of his bed. Is he ashamed of the things he's made? No, it's not shame. Something else. He's not sure what, but he's not been in the mood to figure it out.

By the time Rao's dressed and made coffee, Adam's returned. He vanishes into the shower, reappears in his usual government white shirt and dark tie and trousers, pours himself a mug from the pot, and stands by the window drinking it.

"See anything exciting on your run, love?"

"No."

"See anything exciting out there now?"

"No."

"That's good, I suppose. We're going in today, yes?"

"It's Sunday."

"Absolutely it is, but I want to go in."

"Ok, Rao."

On Sunday, the Lunastus facility has the hush of a business district hotel at three in the morning. There'll be a skeleton nursing team on the ward, but the upper floors are deserted. Pacing along the main corridor with Adam, Rao starts trying doors. They're all locked except two: one opens into a small meeting room and the other a walk-in cupboard full of office supplies.

"Aha. Want to nick some pens?" he asks.

Adam shakes his head. His expression is tight.

"What is it?"

"You're looking for something."

An observation, not a question. And he's right. Rao *is* looking for something. He just doesn't know what it is. Feels like the first, low ache of wanting to use. Like he's put something down somewhere and forgotten what it is, knowing the only way to remember is to find it. "Veronica's not in today," he announces, closing the cupboard door. "Monty's here, though." The second assertion doesn't feel entirely true. He mutters a few sentences beneath his breath. "He's in the anteroom to the test chamber, doing something with Prophet. Fuck knows what. Probably telling it all his problems."

Adam doesn't smile. "Something's off, Rao," he says.

Something is. Rao's known that since he walked through the doors. "It's just quiet, love," he throws out. "Sundays are always weird in offices. When I was a kid me and some mates broke into a local solicitor's one weekend for shits and grins. It was spooky as hell. *Mary Celeste* with wonky filing cabinets. We stole some biscuits."

His stupid reminiscence doesn't help at all. They both walk faster now, take the elevator to the lower floor in silence. By the time they reach the first of the double doors to the test chamber anteroom, Rao's prickling with disquiet and Adam's holding his left hand open over his sidearm. There's no real reason for this little folie à deux, Rao tells himself, this contagious paranoia. He discovers that's not true.

In the airlock space they look at each other.

"We're not imagining this, Adam," Rao says.

Adam's lips twitch. "Doesn't matter if we are. Won't make any difference if Prophet's involved."

"Ugh," Rao says. "Why does this feel like the end of *Butch Cassidy and the Sundance Kid*?"

"This isn't a movie, Rao. I'm going through."

He's back in seconds with a terse sitrep. "Montgomery's down. His dose of Prophet made a dog. He's hugging it. Unresponsive. Fridge is open, looks like the syringes have been tampered with. You ok to go in?"

"Of course I fucking am."

*

Adam's no stranger to premonition. He's experienced it a bunch of times. Service members talk about it a lot in active combat zones. Could be a sudden conviction of an impending attack, a feeling that alerts you to a hidden IED. "Spidey sense" is the term everyone uses. The Defense Department prefers "precognition involving advanced perceptual competencies." Adam knows it's nothing supernatural. It's experience. Pattern recognition. Gestalt analysis. It's unconscious knowledge is all, and that's how he's been trying to think of what keeps happening with Rao.

But Prophet must be involved. Nobody could've absorbed that much Prophet, like Rao, and not have it affect their brain. Nobody can repel Prophet the way Adam does and not have some consequence. He's pretty sure the threat he feels right now has nothing to do with anything he's seen and everything to do with what Rao is picking up.

That Disney glass last night fucked him up. But it makes sense, somehow, that that's something Rao can do. Pull memories out of Adam and make them real. It's probably his fault. He's not as guarded as he should be. He's getting too attached again, because lately it's been feeling like it felt when they worked together in Central Asia, easy as breathing. He's just obsessing. He shouldn't. But he's trying not to worry about what he's doing and whether it fucks him up. It's paying off. They're getting answers—and new questions—every single day.

Rao pushes by him, muttering that he hates it when Adam goes vacant like this, and makes his way to the fridge where Prophet is kept. Montgomery is curled on the floor in front of it, fingers flared against the fur of what looks like a rust-black-white beagle pressed to his chest, both figures illuminated by the cold light pouring from the open refrigerator door.

"Fuck's sake, Monty," Rao mutters, kneeling beside him. Montgomery's head is bowed, face obscured, forehead pressed to the dog. When Rao goes to place his palm to the bare skin of his exposed nape, the dog Montgomery is holding growls, squirms against his body to try to get to Rao. He snatches his hand back in surprise. Adam kneels, one knee on Montgomery's leg as an anchor, and holds down the dog, now snapping at Rao. It's partially inside Montgomery's chest, he realizes. Only three of its legs are visible, and under that enfolding arm he can make out flashes of teeth and a single eye. The way Montgomery has rounded his back to wrap around the animal inside him reminds Adam of how people curl their own bodies to protect an injury.

He feels an overwhelming need to get away from the beagle, from Montgomery, from this manifestation. As far away as possible from what they have both become. He presses down on the dog's neck, on Montgomery's shoulder. "Do it, Rao," he says. Silently, Rao nods. Reaches again for that exposed skin. The beagle kicks and growls into Montgomery's chest, fighting Adam's hold on them both, but Rao does what he needs to do.

Adam doesn't think he'll ever get used to seeing Rao do this. Heal people. Cure them of Prophet. It's not just that the act should be impossible. It's how Rao looks when he does it. Never the same. Sometimes his jaw goes slack, eyes open, seeing nothing in front of him. Pupils blown and far away. No way for Adam to know what he's feeling or seeing or doing, and he doesn't know how to start asking about it. Sometimes Rao's eyes are closed like he's concentrating. Brows drawn and serious. Only moving to take deep breaths, letting the inhalations move his body. This time, he's bowed over Montgomery with his eyes half closed, lashes fluttering too quickly. Adam watches and, like every other time before, he sees beads of Prophet press themselves out of Montgomery's skin before disappearing into Rao's.

As Rao takes his hand from Montgomery's neck, the arm Montgomery had wrapped around the body of the dog drops onto the tiled floor. His other arm keeps a tight grip, fingers splayed deep across fur.

"This is fucked," Rao says. He sounds far away. Voice thick like he's just woken up or as though he's emotionally overcome. "Monty? Can you let go of the dog?"

Montgomery doesn't respond verbally, just moves his mouth against the top of the dog's head. Adam frowns. Everyone that Rao's cured so far has dropped or moved away from their EPGO as soon as they were able. That's obviously impossible here.

"He can't, Rao," Adam tells him, looking at the hand on the beagle. Montgomery isn't just running his fingers through the fur. There's rust-colored fur growing through his skin. His fingernails. Rao still hasn't seen that the dog's inside Montgomery's chest. Still hasn't seen the fur through the skin. Doesn't seem to comprehend the truth of what this is. Wildly, Adam considers if he can get Rao out of the room before he does—but it's already too late. Rao's attempting to turn Montgomery onto his back, and he's seeing all of it—and more. The wild white of the dog's visible eye as it growls, whines, squirms in Montgomery's chest. The fur growing up from his neck, into his mouth, onto his tongue, as Montgomery tries to speak. "Get," he whispers haltingly. "Call—"

"I'm calling Rhodes," Adam declares, standing up. He needs to get Rao out and he needs her to take charge of this clusterfuck. Montgomery looks terrified, eyes wide, fighting for breath that isn't there. He starts coughing. Then choking.

"Adam," Rao pleads, holding Montgomery down as he convulses. Adam's already on the phone.

"Rhodes," he says as soon as she picks up. "We're in your test room lab. There's been an incident. Contamination. Dr. Montgomery is down." *He's not going to make it*, Adam thinks, looking at him as he twitches out. Lungs aren't meant to have beagles in them. He doesn't say that out loud. "Get down here."

*

Rao's seen a lot of shit. But nothing holds a candle to watching Monty's corpse jerk with the struggles of a beagle trapped half inside him. It's never getting away from him. It's trapped, and it looks terrified. He can't know if this dog is conscious or just acting as if it is. The answer is clouded by Prophet. But it can see. It can definitely see.

It's quietened itself now. Looks defeated. Its head is laid flat against Monty's cooling chest. Occasionally it licks its lips. Monty's mouth has fallen open. There's a thin trail of blood and saliva from its corner. His tongue is frosted with fur. They're waiting for Veronica to arrive. Rao's here on the floor, tightly hugging his knees, and Adam's in front of the fridge, face stark in the light streaming from its open door. *He'll be used to shit like this*, Rao thinks. Not the dog bit. Mortally wounded people he knows dying in front of him because Adam's unable to help. Maybe he does help. Maybe he puts them out of their misery, which is a crime— mercy killings are a crime—but maybe he should have asked Adam to shoot Monty. Shoot him, then the dog. Then turn the gun on Rao.

Adam turns from the fridge, puzzled. "A lot of these syringes are empty, but the seals are intact."

"Doesn't surprise me," Rao says dully. "I've lost the capacity for surprise."

"I think you should take a look."

"I don't think I can get up right now, Adam. I just murdered Monty."

"That wasn't you. Wasn't murder. Prophet killed him."

"He was alive until I took it out."

Adam picks out one of the vacuum-sealed vessels. Walks it over, holds it in front of Rao's eyes. It's perfectly intact, but there's no gleaming liquid inside. Over the surface of the glass, a tracery of frost-like lines. Delicate chasing. Rao thinks of tarakasi. Filigree silver wire. He rubs one ear, hard. Can't stop himself from touching the glass with the outstretched fingertips of his other hand. The lines fade as they sink into his skin. Just the faintest tremor inside him, now. A ticking needle on a seismograph.

"So we're working while we wait for Veronica, are we?" he grates out, when the glass is clear.

"I'm just trying to understand what happened here."

Rao hugs his knees more tightly. "Feel fucking free."

"When did he get exposed?"

Adam doesn't always get sarcasm. Rao sighs and mutters to himself. "Saturday evening," he concludes. "Yesterday. About ten o'clock."

"I think he opened the fridge when Prophet had already escaped the glassware inside. Breathed it in," Adam says.

Rao screws up his face. "He couldn't have breathed in all of it. There wasn't that much inside him, by the feel of it."

There's a faint *clink* as Adam replaces the vessel on its shelf. He walks back and drops into a crouch by Rao's side. He sits silent for a while, looking at the floor. "Rao," he begins. "You said when Prophet changes, it changes everywhere, at the same time."

"Yeah."

"I just thought of something."

"And you're going to enlighten me."

Adam nods. "If I took off my tie and draped it over that chair, the two ends would be in different places, right? If I poured water on the middle of the tie, it'd soak down through the material at the same rate. So both ends would get wet at the same time. Or they would if the tie was all the same width."

"What the fuck are you talking about?"

"It's just a way of visualizing it, Rao. I think all of Prophet's connected, like the tie. Somewhere else. We just see the ends."

Adam's face is expectant. Eager. Rao hasn't a fucking clue. He's absolutely . . . no. *Wait.* "What, you mean connected in another dimension?"

"Maybe."

Here and somewhere else.

"It's just a theory," Adam says. "Is it one you can test?"

He might be able to. He tries. Shakes his head.

"Because it's about Prophet?"

"Or because I'm full of it," he says glumly.

"About that, Rao. If Prophet is connected in another dimension, it could be how the vessels got to be empty in the fridge. Maybe it can move easily between places. And that . . ."

He looks at Rao hesitantly. Cautiously.

"What?"

"That could be why you're still walking, Rao," he says urgently. "This could be why you're ok."

"I'm not ok, you fuckwit," Rao hisses. "In case you'd forgotten, Monty's dead. I killed him. He's lying on the floor right there, and there's a dog inside his chest that's probably never going to die."

At that, Adam's face turns blank and he rises quickly to his feet, eyes fixed upon the door.

"She's here."

Veronica strides into the room in sneakers and velvet loungewear, face pale and free of lipstick, hair drawn back, a black rucksack hanging from one hand. Wordlessly, she kneels to examine Montgomery, propping the bag by her side. Hesitantly, she lowers two fingers to the dog's broad skull. It doesn't growl, just wrinkles its forehead, twitching its eye towards her. She takes her hand away, reaches into the bag, and pulls out the penknife she'd used to cut the horse. Rao winces.

"Can't the postmortem wait?" he protests.

"This isn't a postmortem," she says, running the blade through the plaid of Montgomery's shirt and tugging the fabric away. She runs a finger over the fur that spreads outwards over his chest from the dog's pelt. "Seamless," she whispers, before placing a hand on the beagle's neck, curling her fingers around it. "And a dog without a pulse. How did he die?"

"I did it," Rao says.

"Asphyxiation," Adam says. "As soon as Prophet was pulled out of him."

"Yes," she says. "That would happen." She sits back on her heels, pulls her BlackBerry from the front pocket of the bag, taps the keypad. She's calling someone on her team. Asking them to come in. Deal with the situation. After cutting the call, she gets up to inspect the inside of the fridge. "We'll manage this," she says. "No reason to cancel the test we've scheduled for you, Rao. Colonel Rubenstein, I'd be grateful if you could take him back to your hotel and call me if there's any deterioration in his health. I'll see him tomorrow at one."

PART III

CHAPTER 60

The red LEDs on the motel clock radio swim into focus: 10:36. *Ugh*, Rao grunts. *Why is it light?*

It's morning, he realises, swearing at the clock. Yesterday he'd climbed into bed as soon as they got back, pulled the covers over his head, and curled himself into a foetal position. Two seconds of that was all he could bear; felt far too akin to Monty's fatal canine hug. He'd turned onto his stomach, buried his face in the pillow. Then, like he has too many times before, he took a breath, exhaled, and let his misery and failure in. Let himself sink through it like miles of scalding water, letting it burn. Letting it burn, knowing he'd survive. Because that's the joke, isn't it. It's always other people who die.

For a few hours, that burning descent was all there was. Adam hadn't tried to make him feel better. Rao appreciated that. But he'd brought him water. Asked if he wanted food. Rao'd shaken his head against the pillow. Didn't want it, didn't deserve it.

He'd expected insomnia, a long white night coruscating with memories of Monty's last terrible moments. But he'd passed out and slept for hours. And now he can remember only brief flashes of what happened. Monty's fingernails, stiff with fur. A curved white canine below the dog's raised lip as it growled. The corner of Monty's mouth as he begged for rescue and air. And none of these memories feel like they should. They're clear but distant. Buried. Deep behind glass. Perhaps Prophet's doing this, he thinks. Protecting him from PTSD. He can't tell if that's true. Couldn't care less if it is. Or isn't. His eyes ache. Ghostly patterns branch behind his vision. And most of all he's thirsty. Dust parched. Arid. Death Valley in June. When he remembers he's nil by mouth until the PET scan at one he groans out loud. It's ridiculous Veronica's not cancelled it. Obscene.

He pushes himself up on his elbows. Doesn't feel dizzy. No nausea. He's ok. He's doing ok. And there's a toppling wash of gratitude when he sees Adam at the door of their room, signing for a delivery like a normal person.

"You've got mail," he announces.

"Give it here," Rao croaks.

His name is spelled correctly on the plastic sleeve. He tears it open. Inside is a heavy-stock cream-coloured envelope. Inside that, a letter on Lunastus-Dainsleif stationery. The familiar logo of a stylised warplane silhouetted above the concentric bands of a Wi-Fi signal. He's always been impressed by that logo. Perfectly trite, perfectly blunt.

He squints at the type. His eyes aren't behaving. He wants to ask Adam to read it to him. He doesn't.

"Fuck me," he says, faintly shocked. "They want me on staff."

"They?"

"Lunastus."

"Congratulations," Adam deadpans. A beat of silence. Then, cautiously, he adds, "What do they want you to do?"

"After this project's complete, assist with their corporate negotiations. Fuck that."

"It's a salary, Rao."

"It's a fucking massive salary. Fuck that too." Rao shakes his head. "Stuck in offices and boardrooms all day? In Sunnyvale? I'll fucking perish."

"Sure, but it's not prison."

"Fuck off with your logic, Adam."

"You hate it when I'm right."

"I loathe it." He lets out a long, theatrical sigh. "I should warn you, I'm in a very, very bad mood this morning, Adam."

"I'll survive."

Rao's just dressed when there's another knock on their door. This one is soft, almost shy. Adam moves to the window, narrows his eyes through the sheet of polyester voile.

"The goons are back. Not the same ones as before. They're carrying but they look polite," he murmurs. A twitch of his eyebrows, amused. "They just saw me and put their hands up."

"Did they? You've given us a reputation, love."

Rao pads to the door, puts his mouth to the plywood, and shouts, "Can I help you?"

"We're here for a scheduled pickup on behalf of Lunastus-Dainsleif LLC. We don't want any trouble." The voice is gruff, apologetic.

"Not on my schedule. Where are we going?"

"The airport, sir."

The helicopter is waiting for them at Centennial, rotors turning. It's a Bell 427, Rao observes. He has no interest in aviation but a few years ago he'd flicked through a Bell brochure in a GCHQ meeting room and learned all the models for a laugh.

Inside the cabin, Adam angles his head to locate the sun, checks his watch. Even before the pilot opens the throttle, he's folded his arms, leaned back in his seat, and closed both eyes. Rao envies his composure, knows the mood he's in won't permit him even the semblance of sleep. He watches the ground tilt away, golf courses and streets slipping past, turning to patterned foothills, forests, sluggish valleys.

After forty minutes, the ride gets rougher, the light sharper, brighter, hollowing out the cabin. They're over proper mountains now, snowfields, each fitful negative G plucking at the hollowness in Rao's stomach. When the Bell starts to throttle back, Adam opens his eyes, looks at his watch again, mouths: *Aspen.*

They land on a helipad near the top of a snowy ridge. The doors open into freezing air and their escorts gesture at them to leave. Ducking out onto the pavement, Rao laughs out loud, giddy with the whole Bond-movie knife-edge nonsense of all this on top of last night's horrors. But when the Bell rises through clouds of blade-lifted powder, climbs higher and straight-lines it northeast, its passage fills the valley with a collapsing, proliferating mess of echoes that remind Rao so insistently of the last few seconds before the impossible clock, he looks at Adam worriedly.

Adam's watching the helicopter rise. He doesn't look remotely concerned. In fact, he looks— *Shit.* Snow light does very good things to Adam's face. After the Bell disappears over a jagged row of peaks, he turns to Rao, jaw set tight, snow on his lashes, dusting his hair. Jerks his head towards the chalet above them, windows blank and blue with sky.

The door is unlocked. Rao follows Adam inside, boots dropping hexagons of compacted snow on the mat and across several feet of well-waxed pine. He blinks, eyes slowly adapting, and as the darkness recedes, he sees a space fitted out in full Alpine Cowboy style. A perfect log fire crackles brightly in the grate. The air is rich with cedar and cinnamon.

"Over here!"

The man on the pale-grey couch is wearing a dark-grey Pendleton cardigan and is slitting open the seal on a Cabela's sporting goods catalogue with a deer's-foot pommel knife. But somehow he's also giving the impression he's sitting back with his arms spread along the back of the seat. That's how easy he is here, in one of the many transposable spaces that wealth and power call home. Rao has seen men like him in any number of places like this, but right now it occurs to him that he's never wanted to punch one quite as much. The man's impossibly handsome. Cut glass jaw, a sweep of silvering blond hair over deep-blue eyes. Looks like a Ralph Lauren model. Paul Newman's lovechild if he'd fucked JFK.

"Hey," the man says. "Thanks for coming. I appreciate it."

"That's nice. Who the fuck are you?" Rao says.

"Lane. Just Lane. Hungry?"

Green salad and dauphinoise potatoes. Ribeye steak, very rare. They're served by a silent woman in a black cotton apron with a tight, dark ponytail and a white gold solitaire on her ring finger; she's avoiding everyone's eyes with more, Rao suspects, than purely professional courtesy. After she's finished at the table, Lane calls her over and murmurs something in her ear. She nods unhappily and returns to the kitchen.

Lane drags a bowl towards him, spoons a pile of what look like green peppercorns onto the slick of watery blood on his plate. "I grow these," he says to Rao, picking one up between finger and thumb and crunching it. "Back on the ranch. Bird chilis. You must be a spicy food aficionado. Want some?"

"No, thank you."

Afterwards there's French press coffee with single cream. Chocolate cake. Adam ignores the slice set before him. Rao shovels his down; he's not sure he's ever needed sugar more. Lane watches him eat approvingly. "Ever had cake this good?" he enquires, holding up a forkful. "We call it Death by Chocolate."

"You know, as a matter of fact, I have," Rao grates out. The cake's fucking awful and watching Lane's theatrics as he prepares himself to say whatever the fuck it is he wants to tell them is becoming an agony. Finally, Lane pulls a smear of frosting from his plate with a finger, sucks it clean, then smiles. "So, we have a time-critical situation, and a little bird told me he's a human polygraph, so I'm going to lay it all on the table for you. Literally. Ana?"

Lane pads off once the table's cleared and returns from behind a door with a bulky roll of paper. "PHOTINT," he says almost lubriciously. He flattens it out. Anchors its opposing corners with *A Celebration of Aspen Through the Ages* and a book of alpine cookery.

Rao's stomach is a knot of refusal seeing the familiar colours of it from his seat. Dry hillsides, cloud shadow; an aerial photograph of an arid landscape. He's seen broken men held over tables because of images like these. He doesn't want to give Lane the satisfaction of watching him examine it more closely, but Adam has no such qualms. He stands, bends low over the table, instantly consumed with interest. "Ten centimetre," he says. "161?"

Lane nods, his smile genuine and bright. "Friends in very high places."

Rao assumes 161's a spy satellite. *Yes.* "Where's this of?" he asks.

"Nevada. Area 25."

Adam nods. "Yeah, Jackass Flats. But what's this?" He drops a finger to the paper, taps it.

"That is the situation," Lane says.

Fine, Rao thinks, pushing back his chair.

In the centre of the sheet, milk-coloured shapes that look like the roofs of an industrial facility. Adam's index finger is laid on a darker area encircling them. Tightly packed against the buildings, the darkness lessens the farther from the site it extends, so that the pattern resembles material thrown up by an impact crater. Only the buildings appear undamaged and there is no crater. Rao leans closer. Not rocks. More like a junkyard in the desert. Where the debris is thickest it's incomprehensible, but farther out there are angles that resemble tilted roof ridges, patches of green, a fairground carousel, a stretch of golden sand bisected by what could be a marquee, and on the other side of the building, near Adam's finger, the nose of . . .

"Is that a 747?"

Adam nods. "Pan Am."

"Shit," Rao says. "Yeah, this is a situation."

"EPGOs," Lane says. "You're familiar."

"We are," Adam confirms.

"This is our main facility for the EOS PROPHET program. All this appeared around the site four days ago."

"All at once?"

"All at once."

Rao blinks. "When exactly?"

"Just after three p.m."

Rao's head itches at that. Four days ago, he was—what was he doing at just past three? Scratching his beard, he thinks back. "Fuck," he says, with a sharp inhale. So that was it. The avalanche in his head when he'd taken Dinah Crossland's hand. He'd known instantly something had happened. Something insensibly vast. A shock wave, a slamming door. Somehow, that contact had triggered the deposition of thousands of objects around ground zero. He thinks of Michelangelo's *Creation of Adam* and hates that the fresco came so quickly to mind. A spark across empty air. It's horribly self-absorbed to give himself such a pivotal role, but the problem is it's true. He's a fucking freak. *Sunil the special case.* He feels a corrosive burst of self-loathing, remembering Crossland's ashen face. The blood trickling from her nose as Veronica ushered her out of the room.

"I said, does alcohol mess with your powers, Sunil?"

Adam's giving him a warning look. It's just funny enough to pull him out of his bout of caustic introspection. "No."

Lane nods, satisfied. Produces a bottle of Johnnie Walker Blue Label, to Rao's secret amusement. Rao sets the glass down by his right elbow, surprised how little he wants what's in it. Lane takes a slow mouthful, savours it. "I let you into our Aurora facility, of course. You wouldn't have gotten in otherwise. I already knew how special you were, Sunil. Figured our project could use your ability to detect fakes. But the whole polygraph thing? Finding that out took some serious favours."

"I expect it did."

"It's ok. I was owed a bunch."

"I'm sure," Rao says. He's got Lane's measure now. He's a very particular species of charming bastard, one with an ability Rao has encountered in a few people over the years. Get too close, talk to him too long, and you'll start to feel he's on your side, no matter what bollocks he feeds you. In Rao's experience, this ability to instil entirely unwarranted confidence is the mark of a monster, but that doesn't make it any less effective, and despite his instant dislike of the man, he's having to work surprisingly hard against it. "How are Heather and Bill?"

Lane's smile turns a little frozen. "I'm sorry—?"

"Your friends, I assume? Came with us on a flight from Mildenhall. Got joined by some other friends in a broken-down van."

"Sunil, no offense was meant. We just wanted to know where you were. Keep an eye on you. Protect you," Lane says earnestly. "I thought you'd be potential assets to our project. And I was right. Speaking of which, Montgomery was very worried about what you boys did to yourselves that first day in Aurora. He's a nervous kind of guy, and things like that eat at him, you know? He thought what happened was a test. It wasn't, of course. You know that. It was what scientists call serendipity. It was highly serendipitous." Lane stumbles a little over the word the second time. He's only recently learned it, Rao determines, batting back an unwanted flash of sympathy. Lane hasn't been told about Montgomery.

"I've seen what you can do, Sunil. I watched the footage. It's truly wonderful. Extraordinary. And that's the reason I made the executive decision to pick you up and bring you here." He nods at the satellite photograph. "Let's leave this on the table. We'll get back to it in a sec. I'd like you to meet someone." He pushes back his chair. It grates on the wooden floor; with the noise, Adam rises to his feet. Watching him do so, a soft rush of apprehension climbs Rao's spine. Only lately has he learned the subtle differences between Adam's everyday demeanour and his ready-to-break-necks one. This is breaking necks, for sure. His brows are minutely raised, eyes a little darker, jaw a little tighter, and he's suffused with a sudden sense of ease, like he's just worked out the answer to a complicated question. He puts himself between Rao and Lane as the latter leads them through the lounge to the back of the lodge. Lane knocks on a pine door. A few seconds pass. He gives them both an apologetic glance and opens it.

CHAPTER 61

A large, pine-walled bedroom in near darkness. A rustic king-size bed with geometric-printed linens. An unlit elk antler chandelier. A steer skull mounted by the window, a crack of snowy daylight between the drawn curtains that catches at Rao's eyes like a blade—and a blond man on his knees on a Navajo rug between the bed and the wall. He's surrounded by sheets of paper and is scribing something on one, bent low so Rao can't see his face, just his arms and hands. Blue sweatshirt, sleeves rolled to the elbow. A Garmin watch hanging loose from a wrist that's all bone. His skin—

"Josh?" Lane ventures.

The hush is stifling. There's the deep croaking call of a raven outside and the soft scratch of pencil on paper. "The son of a family friend," Lane informs them sotto voce. "He's a weapons system officer with the 22nd Fighter Wing at Polheath. You can guess what we think happened. He . . . he isn't talking or eating. He isn't doing well." He gestures sadly at the untouched plate of steak on the desk by the window.

An en suite door opens on the far side of the room, and a person in a nurse's tabard and trousers enters. "This is Jo Seul-ki," Lane tells them. "She's taking care of Josh."

"Hi," Rao says. "I'm Rao. This is Adam. Lane told you about our visit?"

She nods. "He did, yes."

"That's good. He didn't tell us," Rao says, stepping farther into the room, soles catching on and lifting the sheets littering the floor, moving until he gets a better view of Josh's face. He's hollow cheeked, fixated on the page he's working on, staring through it to something far, far beneath. The skin of his face, neck, and arms is covered with a palimpsest of grids, some drawn in ink, others not: the darker, thinner, criss-crossing lines are beaded with dried blood.

"He did that to himself, didn't he," Rao observes.

Lane lowers his voice. "Unfortunately, yes. He stopped when we gave him paper."

Rao looks at the papers around him. Some of them are covered in letters, each one surrounded by a box. Some are carefully drawn grids. There are stars and badges and—

"Scrabble," Adam says.

"Scrabble," Rao repeats, rubbing the back of his neck and turning to Lane.

"He was on his morning run when the incident with the fire occurred at Polheath," Lane explains. "But he was fine. Never saw the EPGO we assume he made. He lost his appetite, got headaches, and was apparently a little subdued, but nothing else. He was due some leave and came back stateside to visit his girlfriend in Pismo. They were surfing when this happened. Real lucky he wasn't in the water at the time. He just sat down on the sand and started drawing in it with his fingers for hours. His girlfriend called his parents and they took him in. All the doctors thought it was some kind of psychotic break. We know better, of course. Josh's folks know I know the right people, and they asked me if I could help."

"Have you tried getting him a Scrabble set?" Adam asks. Rao is almost certain it's a joke. No. He's 50 percent certain it wasn't.

"His parents gave him one. He was excited until he picked it up, but then he lost interest and went back to this."

"It wasn't the right one," Adam says, rubbing at his mouth. He looks disgusted, like he had in Polheath after sawing through the Scrabble box that might, Rao realises, have been Josh's EPGO. No. His was the other box, the one with wooden tiles.

"When did this sudden decline happen?" Rao asks.

"A few days ago."

"How many days?"

Lane frowns. "Five?"

Adam looks at Rao.

"Just past three in the afternoon?" Rao says. He's not surprised to find it's true.

"Could be," Lane admits, then his face brightens. "You think there's a connection?"

"Yes, I do. You want me to cure him, I suppose?"

"His family and the United States Air Force would be indebted, Sunil. I'd like you to try."

"I don't try," Rao snaps, then mutters, "There is no try."

He crouches close to Josh, looks at him closely. It seems straight-forward. There's no object. No Scrabble set protruding from his chest. But the emptiness that pours from the man is like chill air through an open window. And after killing Nancy the teapot lady and watching Montgomery breathe his last, after seeing the vacancy in those eyes, he's not optimistic Josh will be back in his fighter jet after this. He turns his head to Adam a little uncertainly. And Adam steps forward. Good. Adam'll be his backstop, should Josh wake in a mood of rabid revenge.

"Mr Rao?" It's Seul-ki. "Do you need assistance?"

"Not for this bit," Rao tells her. "Maybe afterwards. Thank you. Could you give us a bit of space?" He takes a breath, raises a hand, and rests it on Josh's left shoulder. Nothing. He flicks his eyes up to Adam's face.

"Ok?"

"Tickety-boo." Rao smiles, shifting his hand to the back of Josh's neck. He's not warm, he's not cold, he's not anything. There might have been a flinch. Yes. Just the merest twitch of muscles, and then Prophet ticks against his skin and he brings it in. Tides rise and ebb in that dust-wet space between and through all things. There's the familiar host of lights drifting too close, at ineffable distance, but there's more this time, a sense that Prophet's impatient, that it's leaving something deformed irreparably under its weight, and then Rao's back, waiting for the tiredness to pass, wondering not for the first time how long this healing process takes. Because he's not there when it happens, is he. Not quite.

"He's awake!" Lane exclaims. "Look, he's back with us!"

Adam's looking. Rao's looking. Seul-ki's looking. And so is Josh. He's dropped his pencil, has lifted the hand that wielded it, is staring at his fingers. Something like a sob passes through his body, and with that, Seul-ki's there, swift and certain, guiding him up into a sitting position on the rug. Josh is looking around now, as if he's taking in his surroundings, but Rao's not sure he can see them at all. There's not much change in his eyes. Still looking through, not at.

"Josh?" Lane says. "It's Zachary. We met a few years ago in Ketchum, at your folks' place."

Josh doesn't raise his eyes to Lane. "Why," he says. His voice is flat, emptiness still pouring from him.

"It was Christmas and New Year's. How are you feeling?"

"Kay," Josh says.

"Wonderful, Sunil," Lane exclaims as Rao gets up from the floor. "Is all the—"

"There's no Prophet in him anymore."

"And it doesn't . . . affect you?"

"Not dead yet."

"Amazing. Just amazing."

Josh shuffles himself up to hug his own knees, lays his tilted head against them, closing his eyes. His mouth is moving. Rao's close enough to hear him. "Kay," he's whispering. "Five points."

Lane clears his throat. "So I understand it takes time for a patient to fully recover after . . . what you do. We'll leave him in the capable hands of our nurse and you have all our gratitude." He extends a hand for Rao to shake.

"I wouldn't," Adam says.

"No. No, of course. Ha. Head back to the table, I'll join you in a short while. I need a word with Seul-ki, ok?"

"Josh is completely fucked," Rao breathes, after they leave the room.

"Yeah."

"You saw that?"

"I did. Don't know how Lane didn't."

"Wishful thinking?"

"Could be."

Rao shakes his head. "I fucking knew it was going to go tits up."

"How?"

Rao exhales heavily. "Dunno. Everything about him. Soon as I saw him."

"You got the Prophet out," Adam says. "That's all that Lane needed for his little demo."

"That was a demo?"

Adam gives him a sidelong look. "That was a demo. I doubt Lane gives a shit about Josh. Depends."

"On what?"

"On how important Josh's family is. And why we're here."

Lane returns a minute later, ushers them both back to the table, cracks his knuckles. "So," he says. "Let's get to the point."

"Josh wasn't the point?" Rao asks.

"Josh was a miracle," Lane says. "And very much to the point. The reason I brought you here," he continues, tapping the photograph, "is because we have a situation on top of a situation. Our facility has gone dark."

Adam raises his eyes from the tabletop. "Same time the EPGOs manifested?"

"No. After that."

"How long after?"

"A day after. Three days ago."

"Hostiles?"

Lane grimaces. "Yeah. We got a phone call before the lines went down. One of our engineers talking about people trying to get in. It sounded highly kinetic."

"How many personnel on-site?"

"Forty-eight."

"One person, one object. So where did all these come from?" Adam asks, like he's lost interest in the matter of hostiles.

Lane doesn't respond.

"Lane?" Rao prompts. "Do you know why there's so many objects around the site?"

"We're not clear on that," Lane says.

"Why don't we move on to things you are clear on," Rao snaps. "How about telling us exactly why we're here?"

"We need a sitrep."

"Oh, the situation's fucked," Rao announces. Adam grins at that, and Rao's just enjoying how marvellous it looks on his face when it happens. He feels the hit of absolute certainty he'll be going to this place. It begins with one of the full-body shivers like stuttering, igniting sodium, but then it hits him fully; for a few seconds it's almost overwhelming. When it recedes, the undertow continues to pull at him, hard. It's smooth and rich and cold and deep and horrifyingly beautiful. He knows instantly it won't leave him. He pulls his eyes back into focus with difficulty, past afterimages of the encircling EPGOs, the pale glow on the wings of the 747.

When he regains the room, Adam is regarding him with concern. "I'm fine," he mutters. Adam looks unconvinced.

"Everything good?" Lane asks.

"Perfect. Go on."

"You sure? You just did your . . . thing with Josh. I thought a drink would help. But if you need—"

"I'm fine," Rao says, pinching the bridge of his nose.

"Good. Good. You're both immune, and we want you in there," Lane says briskly. "I've put together a small team. Very experienced. Dr Rhodes will accompany you." He looks out of the window. "We're not sure what you'll find inside."

"A lot of corpses clutching Rubik's Cubes."

Lane looks unhappy. "Let's hope not, Sunil. We need an extraction."

"Who?"

The most curious thing, then: Lane's face flushes, his eyes grow wet. His throat moves a few times. Eventually he speaks. "Steven De Witte," he says.

"Lunastus's CEO? Your billionaire? The bonkers recluse? Oh!" Rao breathes. "It's his baby, isn't it, this whole bloody project."

Lane looks defensive, folds his arms.

"Tell us," Adam instructs. "Hiding things from Rao won't work."

The struggle behind Lane's eyes flares a little brighter, then recedes. He holds up a hand in surrender. "Ok, boys. It's just, this stuff is very, very secret. Force of habit, you know? So, when site security told me these EPGOs had appeared, I called Steven."

Lane takes a breath, then: a vague flash of hurt. "He, uh, decided to take a look himself. Flew to Desert Rock early the next morning and drove in. We have him entering the facility at eleven twenty, and everything went dark just after one."

Rao shivers. Just after one. He remembers it. The sudden cold in the corridor, the sense of being stretched and pulled into threads so fine he covered everywhere, and the ice at his core so searing, so sharp, he couldn't move—and then nothing at all. Nothing until he'd woken, starving, in the small hours, with Adam by his side.

Adam's looking at him. Rao twists his mouth and nods. *Exactly, Adam. That's when it happened.*

"Of course, there may be other casualties," Lane is saying. "But De Witte is our priority. He's a brilliant mind. An important mind. We need him."

Rao raises an eyebrow. "We do, do we? Who's we?"

"America."

Rao laughs out loud. Lane is stung. "You wouldn't understand," he says. "Your partner does." He turns to Adam. "Lieutenant Colonel, you believe in America."

"Yes, sir," he says, face blank, an assent halfway between a rebuke and a snapped salute.

Lane is satisfied with this. "So you're on board?"

Adam purses his lips. "We should talk terms."

"Sure. Remuneration."

"Assurances."

"Assurances, yes, of course . . ."

"And logistics. Helo insertion?"

"Ground transport and hike in. Air's off-limits. We had an unfortunate incident."

"Adam, does he mean a plane crash?" Rao cuts in.

Lane nods sadly. "There's airborne contamination at the site. Has a pretty high ceiling."

"What did you lose?" Adam asks.

"Good men," Lane says.

There's silence for a while.

"What *aircraft* did you lose?"

"A Dash 7."

"ARL-M?"

"Yeah."

"Who's your team?"

"Six men, plus you, Sunil, and Dr Rhodes. Good guy in command. Very experienced. Captain Marcus Roberts. Ex-Delta."

"Where's your forward base?"

"Mercury."

"The secret nuclear town in the desert?" Rao interrupts. "Shit. That's brilliant. I've always wanted to go there."

Adam frowns at him. "There's not much to it these days."

"Have you been there, love?"

"Know people who have."

"Are there aliens?"

"Yes, Rao."

Rao beams at Lane's perplexed expression. Adam's taken control of the room, and Rao's having a good time watching it happen. He sees Adam's expression turn pensive, then, his eyes turn to the window. Rao follows his gaze. The light has changed out there. Bruised clouds are massed above the peaks, the shadows shifted violet from blue. Rao has a sudden apprehension of the weight of all that snow, a ghostly taste of ice in his mouth that turns to granite and quartz, salt ticking quickly on his tongue. He looks back at Adam. *He's sad*, he thinks, suddenly. *Adam is sad.*

"We're going to need more details," Adam announces. "But right now I'm taking Rao outside to confer. More coffee when we get back would be appreciated, Mr Lane. We may be some time."

It's started to snow. Outside the cabin, Rao pulls a full packet of Lucky Strikes and a silver Zippo from his jacket pocket. He frowns at the packet, then extracts two cigarettes, passes one to Adam.

"We're doing this," Rao says.

"I know."

"It'll probably end badly."

"I know that too."

Rao watches Adam drag on his cigarette and exhale, eyes closed.

"Do you believe in America?"

"Rao . . ."

"Seriously."

"I've served for a long time," Adam says, frowning. "It's complicated."

"But?"

Adam looks at Rao then. His expression is so unguarded, so openly transparent Rao's almost frightened for him. "How can anyone believe in America," he says after a while, "and keep their eyes open at the same time?"

"Fucking hell, Adam. Who are you?"

"You know who I am, Rao," he says, taking another drag and watching the smoke rise through falling snow. "I'm nobody."

"We've got a nineteen-thirty charter from Centennial to Desert Rock," Adam informs him on the flight back, voice raised against the helicopter's whine. "The team's arriving tonight. Optimally, you'd stay in Mercury and we bring De Witte to you, but Lane wants you to go in, in case we have casualties." Rao nods. He'd spent the rest of their time in Aspen lying on Lane's obscenely comfy sofa, staring at the flames of the log fire, thinking about the hollowed-out airman in the bedroom while struggling with a bout of indigestion. He looks at Adam's face, striped by sun and flickering shadow, and nods again. He's not sure how to treat this version of Colonel Rubenstein. Maybe this is how Adam always gets before action-man sorties. Rao can't know. But being near him—it's like standing at the base of the Hoover Dam, staring up at the concrete wall, millions of tonnes of water banked up behind it. Only it's not water behind Adam; it's something like grief.

"Who's on this plane?" he asks.

"You, me, Rhodes. Maybe Hunter."

"She can't go in. She's not immune."

"We need a good RTO outside."

"Big favour to ask."

"She'll do it."

"For you?"

Adam shakes his head. "No. Hunter always talks about missions like she's out there saving the world. That's how she'll see this."

He's very serious. And as Rao looks at his unsmiling face, it happens again. It's happened a few times, and it's happening more and more frequently. It doesn't go on for long—maybe a second, a second and a half—and Rao feels it like the aftermath of a punch. It's as if Adam's drawn on tracing paper and beneath it is another Adam drawn on a different sheet, and beneath that another, and beneath them a thousand more, all of them moving differently, all visible at once. Rao's been calling it double vision, but he knows it has nothing to do with his eyes at all.

Another lurch in his stomach. This one has nothing to do with Adam. The ride's far rockier than their trip out here. He looks down. Thick pine forest beneath them, verdigris glazed with ultramarine blue. Scumbled with lead white from all the snow in the air. It's cold in here. Getting colder. He thinks of Hunter and smiles. "You want her there, love. I get it. It's really ok to say so. What's Mercury like?"

"Ghost town. But they still do science at the NNSS. Our nuclear arsenal's getting geriatric, so they run experiments to make sure they still work. Conventional explosives testing. Mostly it's a training site. Special ops, counterterrorism, homeland security. How to handle dirty bombs."

"How do you handle a dirty bomb, Adam?"

"You try not to, Rao."

"Fuck's sake."

"There's supposed to be a pretty good steak house."

"That's cheering. How far away is this Prophet place?"

"Forty minutes north-northeast. It's an old building. Went derelict. Lunastus refitted it." He gives Rao a significant look. "Lane was really into telling me about the renovation."

"Christ, not another one of those boardrooms."

"Doubt it. There'll be blueprints in Mercury and an architect's model for the sand table."

"Sand table?"

"Before we go in, we'll need to familiarise ourselves with what's in the building, what's around it."

"A million Mr. Potato Heads."

Adam shakes his head firmly. "There aren't that many objects. Thirty, forty thousand."

"You're being very literal, love."

"I need to be."

CHAPTER 62

Thirty-six years since Rao took his first breath in the world. Four months and six days since he tried to take his last breath and failed. Every breath since. He could find out how many, if he wanted. He won't. He doesn't. Twenty-two days since the diner. Thirteen days since Adam's impossible clock. Since the first time he met Prophet and Prophet met him. One hour and five minutes since they took off from Centennial in a Gulfstream jet. Twelve minutes since he stared out of the window into the darkness and saw, on the horizon, flashes of light that might have been lightning, might have been behind his eyes. Eleven minutes and fifty seconds since he decided it didn't matter either way.

When he was five, Rao ran away from his mother's side when they were shopping in Selfridges on a rainy Thursday afternoon and hopped onto an escalator to the next floor. He'd long been obsessed with moving staircases. Mostly because he was frightened of them. He'd get more and more frightened the nearer to their ends he travelled. He'd turn to his parents and extend his arms, waiting for them to lift him off the ground, rescue him from being trapped and dragged under by the meshing teeth of the inexorable steps.

That long-ago day he'd known the moment he started to rise that he didn't want to be on the escalator. Knew he'd done something incredibly stupid. Gripped with terror, he'd tried to walk back down to her, but the steps were high, and he couldn't get down them fast enough. Kept being carried upwards. Tears blurring his sight, he'd watched her turn and see him. Run towards the escalator. But he knew she wouldn't get to him in time, and he'd be eaten at the end.

He wasn't. Somehow, he jumped over the last step, stood there paralysed with shock after he landed, was swept into his mother's arms a few seconds later.

Being on that escalator is exactly what this flight feels like.

No one's rescuing him from this. He's supposed to be the rescuer here, and life has taught him that's not a role that ends well for him. Not ever. He wants his mother. Her absence is terrible. Tears well up, slip down his cheeks. He brushes them away. Looks at his fingertips. They gleam with Prophet in the gloom. Only for a second before it slips back under his skin. *I'm full of it*, he thinks, self-pity shifting to darkest amusement. *Veronica is wrong, and if I survive this, I can go as a Terminator to Halloween. Scare everyone shitless at parties.*

Parties. He doubts there'll be any more of those. It doesn't matter. The flight is an escalator. They're all on it. He looks over to where Hunter and Adam sit, the walnut table between them glowing in a pool of soft white light from the curved ceiling above. Hunter has her back to Rao. She's eating an apple and nodding. Adam's frowning at her, speaking quickly. Animatedly. Rao can't hear what he's saying over the high note of the engines. His tie's vanished, the top two buttons of his shirt open. It's been like that ever since the doors shut on the plane. Makes him look half naked. Rao has no idea what it means.

Behind him, Veronica emerges from the cabin, walks down the aisle smoothing the wrinkles on her skirt, informs them they're starting their descent. The engine note has changed, and he's already feeling the lift in his chest as it falls fast through air. He buckles his seat belt and knows without knowing that he's not here to save the Lunastus billionaire.

An unsmiling guard with acne, a clipboard, and a sidearm boards the plane as soon as the steps are unfolded. He checks their IDs, issues them security passes, leaves without a word. Rao halts on the topmost step to breathe in a deep lungful of avgas and desert night and looks down to see two trucks waiting on the tarmac, hazard lights flashing. A man in a plaid shirt and a dark gilet is leaning against the bonnet of the nearest. It's Lane. "Sunil! Adam!" he shouts, waving. "Over here!"

As they draw near, Lane gives Veronica a nod. "Dr Rhodes."

"Zachary."

"Joining us for dinner? We've got a table at the steak house."

"Not tonight, thank you."

"Your loss. Food's good." He beams at Hunter. "Master Sergeant Wood? A real pleasure. Thank you for your service. Come eat with us."

"Thanks. I already ate, Mr Lane. Can I head to the dorm?"

"Sure, sure. The driver will take you." He gestures at the second truck. "Roberts is arriving with the rest of the team at midnight. Meeting at eight a.m. in the George Washington Room, classroom block. Cafeteria serves breakfast from six."

"Understood." She climbs into the truck, leans out of the window, jerks her chin at Adam and Rao. "Behave yourselves, girls."

They watch the taillights recede. Lane rubs his hands. "Let's put your cases in the back and get you dinner."

When their driver opens the rear passenger door, Adam climbs in. Rao hesitates. Looks up. The stars are bright here. Sharp. The sky feels too close. Like it could drop. Inside, the vehicle smells of expensive detailing and traces of Creed Tabarome.

After they pull away, Lane turns in his seat and starts on a history of the Nevada National Security Site. Rao ignores him and keeps his eyes on the desert road. Specks of quartz glitter on its surface; above it hangs an auratic haze of dust. After a couple of minutes, he sees the body of a small animal on the road ahead. Pale fur in the lights. Getting closer, he sees it's been crushed. Has left a trail of blood. One leg still twitches.

Their driver swerves to avoid it; the jerk draws Lane's attention back to the road.

"Roadkill. Ran under us on the way here," the driver says.

Fuck, Rao thinks. He shifts himself up against Adam's side. Leans in, whispers into his ear. "You saw that?"

"The jackrabbit?"

"Wasn't a rabbit. Come on, Adam."

Adam takes a deep breath. "You're saying it was a telltale. Out here," he says. "You sure?"

"*Adam*. It was a teddy bear."

"It bled," he exhales.

Rao nods. He doesn't know if Adam's looking at him now; something makes him not want to. He keeps his eyes ahead. Watches drifts of gravel in the headlights as they turn at intersections, rusting trailers and radiation warning signs, runs of glittering chain-link fencing, and suddenly they're in Mercury. Amber bulbs glow dimly on buildings; they pass piles of rubble under pools of light cast by sparse, heron-necked streetlights. The town is eerie as fuck, and the steak house, when they arrive, is just as unsettling. Sitting inside it feels like being trapped in an EPGO. A plastic letter board with today's offerings outside the door, red-checked tablecloths, a tired-looking server, and Lane beaming like he's entertaining at Le Gavroche.

Soon Lane's pouring zinfandel and shaking his head. "Dr Rhodes? No mistake, she's a very, very clever girl. Summa cum laude at Oxford. Before EOS PROPHET, she led Lunastus-Dainsleif's groundbreaking research into pharmacological deradicalisation."

Rao's eyes widen. "Drug-induced brainwashing?"

"Deradicalisation," Lane replies firmly. "She's a great asset to this project. But just between us, she doesn't have the connections. She can't get in the right rooms over here."

"Veronica doesn't go quail hunting with the boys?" Rao says.

"I don't think she does," Lane replies.

"But you have."

"Many times."

"And you get in the right rooms."

"I like people." Lane shrugs.

You're rich, Rao thinks.

"People like De Witte," Adam says.

Lane lays down his cutlery, leans in, crosses his arms over the tablecloth. "It's an honour to know that man. Intellects like his come along once a century. Edison. Einstein. Even when he's not speaking, you can feel him thinking. The energy, you know? His mind . . ." Lane shakes his head. "It's not like ours."

"Ours," Rao says.

Adam gives him a playful, sidelong look. It's great. Rao grins. "Steak again, Lane? It's getting to be a little tradition with us, I see."

Lane picks up his cutlery, starts sawing at his T-bone. "We're in America, Sunil. You know, I was in a place in Montana once, and one of the guys I was with ordered chicken. *Chicken.* Caused a ruckus. You can't beat American beef."

"You serve Japanese beef in the Aurora canteen," Adam points out.

"And it's excellent. Excellent. But wagyu is like foie gras. Cloying, you can't eat it all the time. Not like this." He chews with relish. "You know Steven has a ranch? Two hundred and sixty thousand acres in Wyoming. He's turning it back to prairie. Bison, the whole thing. It's incredible. Incredible."

"Seems a billionaire of many interests," Rao drawls.

"That's what makes him so extraordinary. He's the greatest visionary of our time. But everything we do, he's hands-on. Big data, analytics, defense, infosec, aerospace, energy, life sciences. His range—"

"Yeah, I can see why you want him rescued," Rao cuts in. "Lunastus would go tits up without him."

"America would. We've had this conversation, Sunil. It's not just Lunastus-Dainsleif that's relying on you tomorrow."

"America needs me. I know. So what's the plan?"

Lane chews, takes another sip from his glass. "Mission analysis in the morning, Sunil. Are you sure you don't want wine?"

*

After dinner they're escorted to a low, dimly illuminated, tan-walled dorm block with desert grass and gravel right up to its doors. Adam stands by the vehicle as Rao is ushered into a room. He's been allocated the one next door. Walking in, he sees his kit bag placed at the foot of a varnished wooden bed frame. Green woolen blankets, a single pillow, a wardrobe, a desk with an Anglepoise lamp and a single chair. Sixty-watt bulb in a metal shade suspended from the ceiling. Would have been luxury in its heyday. He peers at the faded, framed photograph of an A-bomb test on one wall. A rising cloudcap the color of rust, the shock wave bleaching the desert white beneath. A carefully inked caption: BUSTER CHARLIE, 14KT, 30 OCTOBER 1951.

He's unlacing his boots when there's a hammering at the door. "Adam?"

"It's open," he calls.

Another knock. "Adam?" He gets up. Outside, Rao's bouncing on the balls of his feet under the light, holding out a pack of cigarettes. "Want a smoke?"

"What is it?"

Rao blinks at the cigarettes, turns them in his hand. "Look, I don't know if I should be left alone right now. What if something happens?"

"What kind of something?"

"I don't know," Rao says hotly. "Aliens. Animate teddy bears with full sets of internal organs. This is a fucking spooky place. What if I lose the plot? Fall off an emotional cliff? This is— Stop looking so unconcerned Adam. I'm freaking out. Not everyone got raised on a military base, this isn't—"

"What do you need?"

Silence.

More silence.

"Can I bring my mattress in here?"

"Yeah," Adam says lightly. "Can I have that cigarette?"

They stand outside and smoke. Rao burns through one cigarette, lights another from its tail. Halfway through the second, his attention is caught by a brown moth the size and shape of an arrowhead clinging to the wall under the light. He leans in, inspects it closely.

"What's with the moth?" Adam says. "Is it real?"

"Yes, Adam. It is. I was just remembering this time when I was small when I found a moth. An oleander hawk moth. It had just come out of its cocoon. It was beautiful. I showed it to my mother."

"You're thinking about your mom," Adam murmurs.

"Yeah."

"You should call her."

"Are you calling yours?"

"Hunter's going to take care of it," Adam says.

Rao obviously doesn't get what that means. He grimaces. "I'm not calling my mum. It's complicated, love. I can't talk to her without it being a whole thing with my dad, and that's not a good situation." He abandons the moth, turns, and leans against the wall. Sighs a lungful of smoke, watches it cloud the night air. "He's never really approved of my life choices," he says, staring into the darkness, studying it keenly.

"Your life choices," Adam repeats after a while.

"Those. He warned me once. Said if I kept sleeping with men, I'd end up ruining my life. Get addicted to drugs, go to prison."

"Huh."

"Exactly," Rao breathes. "Exactly. It's not like I can tell him it was the fucking CIA."

"I'm sorry."

"Fuck off, this isn't— That doesn't matter. You know it doesn't. And I'm not looking for sympathy. Not now I know you've Don't Ask Don't Telled your whole fucking career. I'm just explaining, right? My mother is . . ." He swallows. "She's a wonderful woman, Adam. She's the most beautiful soul. I adore her. And she's got this thing, right? It's impossible to lie to her."

Adam blinks back surprise. "You mean, she's like you?"

"She's my mother."

"No, I mean, she has an ability like yours."

"It's just impossible to lie to her, you know? She doesn't know anything about Kabul. Doesn't know I was there, what I did, the heroin, me trying to top myself, getting arrested, none of it. And I don't want her to know. She'll be disappointed and he'll be right. It's better neither of them finds out."

Adam bends and stubs out his cigarette. "I'll get the mattress."

"Why have I never heard about your mother, Adam?"

"You don't want to know about my mom, Rao."

"I do."

"You need to have another sob story about a high-functioning alcoholic in your head?" Adam shrugs. He doesn't want to talk about this. "She did her best. Her best was too much for her. I don't know what else to say."

"Ah. Is she still alive?"

"Too well-preserved to die of anything natural."

"Fucking hell, Adam."

"I told you that you didn't want to know. I'll get the mattress."

"Give me a sec. I'll come with you."

Back in the dorm, Adam drops the mattress, shoves it against the wall. Looks up to see Rao clutching his bundle of sheets, blankets, and pillow, staring wide-eyed at the framed photograph of the mushroom cloud.

"Cozy, huh?" Adam says.

"Fuck. Least it's honest about what this place is for."

"Yeah, it is," Adam agrees, his chest tight. "You have the bed. I'll take the floor."

CHAPTER 63

I t's three minutes past six. Rao's been lying awake since a quarter to three, and he can't bear the press of darkness, the shape of it, any longer. It's clinging to his throat. Makes him want to cough. Shout. He throws back the blankets. Attempts to dress silently and fails. Adam's already up before Rao comprehends he's awake.

"Walk before breakfast?" Adam enquires, shrugging on a jacket.

"Yeah," Rao croaks gratefully.

The eastern sky is paling over the jagged horizon, but the just-past-full moon is bright in the west. They follow the perimeter fence. A line of Joshua trees, black against the sky. Some anonymous gardener has placed white rocks in careful circles around their trunks. Rao frowns at the absurdity of their effort in a town built for annihilation. Listens for Adam's footfalls next to his own. How does he walk so quietly? He's wearing boots. Rao's in sneakers and he can barely hear him.

"Adam," he begins. "Listen. You know they only need me in there. You don't need to do this."

"You go in, so do I."

"I'm going."

Adam nods, like it's settled.

He doesn't get it.

"I'm going, love, because it's inevitable."

Adam's lips twitch in the gloom. "Thought I was supposed to be the fatalistic one."

"It's not fatalism. It's a fact. I know I'm going to be there because it's true."

Adam doesn't stop walking, but he slows. Looks out over the desert. When he speaks, his voice is hesitant. Like someone walking out onto ice, unsure if it'll support their weight. "You can't read truth in the future, Rao. You've told me that a bunch of times."

"Well," Rao answers. "It's got a bit complicated lately."

"How?"

Rao looks down at the thin scar that runs under the silver kadas on his right wrist. An anchor, a biographical truth, a word, of a kind. He looks at it in the half light and it doesn't seem to belong to him at all. He rubs at it with a finger. "I don't know if I could even do a truth run right now. Full disclosure, the whole world's getting harder to read. Like the light's fading and I can't see what's there. But also, other things, things I really shouldn't be able to assign truth values to, I can now." He makes a face. "I think so, anyway." He takes a deep breath, lets it out very slowly, speaks when it's almost gone. "Adam, I don't think I'm very well."

"I thought—"

"Yeah, me too."

"You tell Rhodes about it?"

He shakes his head. Of course he's fucking not. The only person who's ever going to hear about this is standing next to him.

"What are your symptoms?"

"Double vision. Sometimes."

"Sometimes. Now?"

"No. Look, Adam, have you not wondered why, despite being newly possessed of an ability to make whatever I want, I've not made myself a bunch of drugs and alcohol?"

"You're clean."

"No, I'm not. I've never been less clean."

"But you're not high."

"No. But . . ." He searches for the words. "It feels like Prophet has filled all the spaces where that shit used to go. Feels like those spaces were made for it. And it's getting a little insistent."

"You want more of it."

Rao strokes his beard thoughtfully. "Not like that," he says. "It's more like I can't escape what it wants. The facility. It wants me there. Which makes it inescapable. Like it's a gravity well."

"A gravity well."

"That's a—"

"I know what a gravity well is."

"Shit, of course you do," Rao says. "Your telescope. You were a nerdy astronomy kid, weren't you? Adorable."

It's dark enough now that Adam's face is mostly in shadow, but Rao can see enough of that expression to know he's put his foot in it. Though considering their history, considering the shit Adam's had from him over the years, it'd have to be something pretty fucking bad. Something worse than calling him adorable. "What is it?"

The answer's a long time coming.

"I didn't tell you about that."

"About what?"

"The telescope."

"You did."

Adam holds his gaze, shakes his head. And watching his denial, Rao almost—almost feels it. A sensation of glassy rightness that feels like truth but impossibly distant and deeply disconcerting, like trying to pick up a grain of dust between finger and thumb.

Back at their dorm, Adam disappears for a while. Returns in fatigue pants, a towel slung over a shoulder. Rao glances up from his bed. "How're the showers?"

"Wet."

His hair's longer, now. There are tiny curls behind his ears. Rao's eyes widen in surprise.

"Fuck me, Adam," he says. "Your hair's not straight either?"

Adam snorts. "Never was."

"You're wearing dog tags."

"ID tags. I'm not a marine."

Rao recalls Adam getting beer up his nose in Racks 'n' Butts, spluttering because Hunter had just described the USMC as "lil bitches." He gets up, walks to Adam, reaches to pick the tags from his chest. *They're a big deal to him*, Rao thinks, hearing Adam take a breath and let it out shakily. He'd probably be nursing a life-threatening injury if he'd tried this anytime before. Turning the tags in his fingers he squints, moves them a little farther away. The light isn't bright in here, and the stamped-out text is so small.

"You need glasses."

"My eyes are fine."

Adam snorts again, more softly this time. "Right."

Rao holds a tag between his thumb and index finger. "What the fuck is Protestant B, Adam? I thought you were Jewish."

"I am. I served in Saudi and they don't let Jews in the country."

"Oh, it's a code phrase? That's awful. It's also fucking funny. Did you have secret services in windowless cinder block rooms?"

Adam blinks at him. "How do you know about—"

"Hooked up with a guy who'd been to one."

Adam rolls his eyes. Then, unexpectedly, he grins. "There was a rumour the rabbi smuggled in the siddur in a box of DU rounds. I don't believe it."

Rao looks at Adam's lopsided smile, feels the tension of the chain on the back of his neck, thinks of how many times he's hauled people into a kiss just like this. He lowers the tags incredibly carefully back to Adam's chest.

"You don't always wear them."

"Defeats the purpose of being undercover, Rao."

"And you're wearing them now because—"

Adam looks at him. "Because tags serve a purpose. You know what that purpose is."

Rao sniffs. "We've talked about this, love."

"No, we haven't," Adam sighs. He moves away from Rao, continues towelling his hair, and sits. He jerks his head; an invitation for Rao to join him. "We should."

"Alright, then." Rao sits. Adam doesn't say anything. "Are we not?"

"No, we are. I am."

"Could've fooled me."

"Shut up, Rao. Let me get to it." Adam lets the towel rest on his shoulders. His eyebrows draw in tight. Stressed. Adam is wearing actual human expressions now, Rao realises, but only behind closed doors. He's still full Robot Rubenstein whenever they're around Veronica or Lane. Turns dead behind his eyes. Rao'd always assumed that was just how Adam was. Steel down to the bone. Unfeeling. Because that's how he was when Rao met him. That's how he was when Miller pulled Adam out of the deck like a joker. But Adam's expressive now. Expressive like he is around Hunter, even when she's not there. Expressive like that night with the vodka and missed chances. Expressive like half light in motel rooms after mental breakdowns.

Rao's been a dickhead, hasn't he?

Adam takes a breath. A deep one. He's not looking at Rao any longer. Rao's eyes catch on the end of the scar on his collarbone, move up to the angle of his jaw. He thinks of all the times he's taken a chin in his hand to make someone look at him. He wants to make Adam look.

"This mission isn't going to be standard," Adam says in a low voice.

"No shit, Adam."

He sighs again. "Rao. Just listen to what I'm saying? It's not going to be standard. It's not going to be a case of point A, point B, hostiles, objectives. Those are the words we're using, but it's not going to be that simple with Prophet. Is it?"

Rao relaxes his own jaw to stop his teeth grinding. "It's not going to be standard, love," he agrees.

Adam nods. Reaches behind his neck. Pulls the tags over his head. "I told Hunter to contact my parents. She knows how to find them, when it's time to do that."

"Adam—"

He jerks his head again and Rao opens his hand like the command was obvious. Maybe it was. Maybe Rao knows Adam that well now. Maybe, now, Adam is just expressive enough for him to guess.

The tags and chain pool in Rao's palm. Stainless steel. He's so used to watching bright metal sink into his skin of late that it's surprising the tags just sit in his hand. They feel warm.

"You don't have to worry about contacting anyone. I just want you to have these," Adam says.

"Don't be daft."

"I don't know what that means."

"It means— Oh, fuck off, Adam. You're fucking with me right now, aren't you?"

Adam hums tunelessly. "Not all the way."

It's tempting to leave it there. Like they've cleared the air. Like the heavy shit has been talked about, looked at. And that's almost alright. But Rao can't. He can't let Adam go into this full of doom and gloom. It feels too much like violence.

Rao needs him to know that—

Adam is talking before Rao can piece his words together.

"I'm not letting you out of my sight when we go in," he says, and he's looking at Rao now. He's looking, and he's seeing, and Rao knows that there's no coming back from that promise.

CHAPTER 64

Rao halts by the briefing room door, points at the sign above it. "He totally did lie, Adam."

"George Washington? Old news."

"No, but really," Rao says. "Like, fuck your American myths."

"Yes. I know."

"You're not listening."

"He's listening," Hunter says, striding past.

Chairs, striplights, a whiteboard, projection screen, linoleum tiles. Flyblown blinds. Everything in here is tired except the soldiers sitting on schoolroom chairs. Fuck knows where Lane dragged them in from, but they look so healthy Rao's vaguely cross. He's so used to seeing Spec Ops guys in comas he's surprised by how they look when they're not. Loose-limbed, more trail runner than bodybuilder. Minus the fatigues, the one standing at the whiteboard could be a suburban dad, albeit one who shaves with a blowtorch.

"Lieutenant Colonel Adam Rubenstein," Adam says, stepping forward. "This is Master Sergeant Hunter Wood. And this is Mr Sunil Rao. Our primary asset."

"Captain Marcus Roberts," the man by the board replies. The rest of the team introduce themselves. Estrada, Baker, Garcia, Carlton, Stewart.

"We have six minutes, Colonel," Roberts says. "Mr Lane instructed me to play you the last call out of the facility before he arrives. Should we wait for Dr Rhodes?"

"No. Go ahead."

Roberts hits the key of a chunky laptop. A hiss, then a woman's voice, hushed, tight with panic.

"This is Sandra Evans, core team engineer." There's something off with the line. It's sputtering softly, pulses of silence caught up in it, though her words are perfectly clear. "I'm in the RadSafe counting room. Power's off, but it's not dark anywhere, there are—there are lights, but they're not ours. I need to report a containment failure. It's bad, it's really bad." She swallows, and the sound is louder than her voice. When she speaks again, there's a new noise—something mechanical, with movement to it, like a train going over points, but impossibly deep and slow, far too deep for a telephone line. Far too deep to be coming from the speakers on Roberts's laptop. It's like Sinatra in the diner. Right in the middle of Rao's head. He's not sure if anyone else can hear it. He's not going to ask.

"We're under attack," she's whispering. "I don't know if they'll find me here. I don't know if they can see through copper and shielding. They're everywhere. Please send help. We can't—"

The line cuts.

Dully, Rao listens to the team speculate on how the hostiles arrived, considering there'd been no recorded traffic at any height, no breach of the NNSS perimeter. They're discussing a night operation. He has to say something. But he doesn't know the right way to say it. Not to people like these. He looks to Adam. Adam knows what this is. Why doesn't he bloody say something?

In his peripheral vision, Rao sees Hunter fold her arms and give him an expectant look.

Oh. Adam wants Rao to tell them.

Fine.

"We won't need to go in in darkness," he says, a little roughly. He'd try harder to not sound a dick, but everyone here knows he is already, or will do. "It'd be pointless. Doesn't matter what time we do this."

They're all looking at Adam now.

"Listen to him," Adam says. Six pairs of eyes track back to Rao.

"What did they tell you happened in the facility?" he asks.

"Chemical spill," Roberts says. "A substance with psychotropic effects. Hallucinations, fits, comas. Sometimes fatal."

"Some people are immune," Baker adds.

Not for the first time, Rao wonders how many soldiers are psychos. This one looks remarkably fresh-faced. Just out of school. Maybe Rao's getting old. "Even people who are immune," he says, scratching his beard, "are going to see a ton of shit in there. The substance is called Prophet. It does affect the mind. But it doesn't make you hallucinate. It makes things."

"Makes things," Roberts repeats.

"Yeah. Makes objects. Makes buildings. Makes things that move, look alive but aren't. Those hostiles—they're not going to be human at all." It's true.

"I second that," Adam says. "Their official designation is EPGOs. We've been calling them telltales when they're moving like that. And considering what we heard on that call, they pose a clear threat. To incapacitate, chest and head shots will likely be ineffective. Stopping shots will be ankles and knees, or whatever structure keeps them moving."

The door swings open and Veronica enters, wreathed in floral perfume. She's wearing a light, fur-hooded jacket. *That's not coyote*, Rao thinks. *That's wolf.* There's a red flush high on her cheekbones. Looks like she wants to step on something.

"Ah, Veronica," Rao greets her. "We've just told the boys about telltales."

"Good," she says. "Lane's on his way."

He arrives forty seconds later with two henchmen carrying rolls of paper they proceed to pin upon the walls. The photographic intelligence Rao'd seen in Aspen: blueprints, terrain maps, a weather forecast with pressure lines and predicted cloud. Strange that he's not choosing to display all this digitally on full Lunastus tech, Rao muses. God help them all if it's Lane longing for better, simpler times.

As soon as Lane starts speaking, Rao stretches back in his seat. Tunes out his voice. Lets all that he hears slip into memory. He can pull it out later if he needs to. Because what's intriguing him is how obviously Veronica and Lane loathe each other. He's pointedly not looking at her as he gives his little lecture. She's staring right at him with a deathless expression. Rao smirks. He's looking forward to asking Veronica about her views on Lane.

But Rao sits up after Lane walks to a table and tugs a white sheet away from a bulky shape to reveal a detailed model of the facility. It's a far from elegant structure: a pile of steel-toned brutalist boxes like the offspring of an aircraft hangar and a cement works, a water tower held aloft on a lattice of fine wire. This scaled-down version is mesmerising. Echoes of the diner in the dark. *Scale*, he thinks. Rao's always adored miniature things. Loved how entranced humans are by the small. How we like to remake the world, magic it down to fit in our pockets and palms, turning ourselves into giants. He remembers back at Sotheby's he'd got to hold a Nicholas Hilliard portrait the size of a matchbox. It had been the kind of perfect that hurt to look at. A dark-eyed man with a pale face against depthless, midnight blue. Powdered gold, motes in darkness. It was as perfect a truth as any lie can be, which is why art has always been something Rao's drawn to.

Prophet works like that. Busy making lies that are trying to be true. *Except*, he muses, *with me. With me it makes truths.* And there's a reason for that, and he doesn't know what it is, though it feels like he did. Like it's something he's forgotten. It's a strange sensation. He takes a deep breath, lets it out, watches Lane lift away the model's roof and point inside.

"The hot bay," he says. "So called because it was designed to handle radioactive materials. The purpose of this site was to test nuclear engine assemblies. That's how this building got its name: the Engine Mainte-nance Assembly and Disassembly Facility. E-MAD."

E-MAD, Rao thinks. *Fucking hell, what a name.*

Now the screen shows a different image, a black-and-white photo of the hall in its earliest years. Men in white boiler suits, vast metal manipulator arms, barrels, platforms, everything grained and silvered like Apollo mission shots of the surface of the moon. It's phenomenally evocative but clearly irrelevant to the matter at hand. He suspects Lane's history lesson is because he sees himself as a new Oppenheimer, his fucked-up project a worthy heir to the scariest Cold War Big Science.

Rao sneaks a glance at Veronica; she's looking murderous. There's a different photograph of the hall on the screen now: pools of water on its stained concrete floor, rusting gantries, piles of rotting debris.

"This is what it looked like until our renovation," Lane intones. "And this is what it looks like now." Triumphantly, he clicks to the next image. "We kept the original green to match the historic palette."

Rao clocks the blank looks that gets from the soldier boys. Quells the urge to ask Lane if he'll be handing out special battle dress to match his heritage paint.

The renovated hot bay is spotless. Along the righthand wall, the giant manipulator arms are glossy canary yellow, and beneath them are a series of installations that resemble museum cabinets crossed with industrial machinery. Gleaming pipes, rivets, delicate traceries of glass and copper. Refracted light. Slabs of steel. Thick red lines drawn around them on the concrete floor. A whole forest of warning signs.

"Our Prophet containment system," Lane says. "State of the art. Multiple fail-safes in place. If there's been a breach, we can only assume sabotage."

As soon as Rao hears the word "sabotage," he knows it wasn't sabotage at all. He mutters some statements, finds out the containment system failed catastrophically all at once. And not just here: every single container of Prophet, including the syringes in the medical facility, had failed at exactly the same time. He doesn't have to test to know when that had happened. He knows already. He'd felt it. He'd felt it and it'd laid him out. He'd been walking down a corridor with Adam, reciting a poem, giggling at the violence of forcing entrecôte to rhyme with Truman Capote.

Here and somewhere else.

Lane is showing a series of photographs of De Witte. Most include Lane. Lane at the wheel of an ancient army jeep, De Witte hunched beside him in the passenger seat. A snowy day outside the Aspen cabin, Lane holding an axe triumphantly above a pile of firewood, De Witte swaddled in an orange parka, staring at the snow underfoot. De Witte spotlit at a podium, looking extraordinarily ill at ease in a suit and tie. He has an unprepossessing, strained face and the thin blond hair of a superannuated surfer, and the more photos Lane throws up on the screen, the more obvious it becomes that whatever Lane feels for him is far from mutual.

"We don't know his location," Lane says. "It's likely you'll find him in the hot bay or one of the labs. He was last seen wearing dark jeans, a grey shirt. When you've found him, get your medic to check him over. Then"—he gestures at Rao—"Mr Rao'll take over. Sunil, you're our special secret weapon. Tell the unit what you'll be doing."

"Not really a weapon, but yeah, I can extract this substance from people. If he's not too fucked, De Witte should be able to walk out with us. Or you can bring him out on a stretcher."

Lane opens his mouth again, but Rao's far from finished.

"So, I'm just going to address the elephant in the room," he says. "In fact, there might be an elephant in a room in there. Several. Could be Elmer, even. Or the other one. What's the other one, Adam?"

"Horton," Adam says.

"Yeah. That one. Anyway. Going in there'll be like walking into Disneyland on very, very, *very* bad acid. I'd really like to be able to tell you what you'll see isn't real and can't hurt you, but it is real, and it looks like it absolutely fucking can and will."

"We've had no cases of aggressive EPGOs," Lane protests.

"You've heard the recording," Rao says simply. "Veronica, you want to do this bit?"

Veronica nods. "To clarify, yes, this substance manifests things from people's imagination. Yes, these include animate, moving objects. And the evidence now points to these objects turning . . . being hostile."

Rao looks around the George Washington Room. Lane is standing by his giant photograph of De Witte, arms crossed truculently. Veronica seems entranced at the thought of Prophet-generated horrors. Adam looks impassive. Hunter and the soldier boys appear ready for fucking anything.

No. Someone else can talk now. He's done. "I'm going outside for a smoke," he informs everyone.

CHAPTER 65

He stands on the cracked concrete steps of the classroom block, looks out at sun-peeled trailers, piles of concrete with exposed, corroding rebars. Lighting up, dragging smoke gratefully into his lungs, he studies the desert garden across the road. Cacti, gravel, clumps of yellow grass. It looks exactly like everywhere else, only the gravel is a vaguely different shade of brown, and there's a low fence around it.

The door swings open.

"Veronica," he says as she steps through. "You had enough too?"

"There's a lot of military expertise in that room. They're talking."

"What's Lane doing?"

"Getting in the way, I expect."

He grins. "Yeah. Tell me, what is it with Lane and De Witte?"

Her lips twitch. "You noticed."

"I certainly have. It's a very embarrassing crush."

"It's not a crush. It's a father fixation. Lane lost his own early and tragically. Steven fitted his requirement for a new one."

"Steven, is it? I see."

"I can confidently guarantee that you don't."

He screws up his face. "You're right. I'm talking out of my arse." He takes another drag on his cigarette. "So, we're rescuing De Witte because Lane thinks he's his dad?"

"No," she says. "We're rescuing him because he's in possession of a brain."

He grins. "And Lane isn't?"

"Lane's a competent fixer when it comes to weapons deals. Undeclared ones are his particular speciality. He has *very* important friends."

Rao rolls his eyes. She nods. "Inexplicably, they consider him good company. Steven is a little less . . ."

"What?"

"Hail-fellow-well-met."

"Hard to get on with, is he?"

"You'll see."

"I suppose I will." He inspects the coal of his cigarette, taps ash to the concrete beneath his feet. "Veronica?"

"Yes?"

"What's the plan?"

"I'm sure Colonel Rubenstein will tell you when they're done."

"Not the Action Man plan. Your plan. Do me the courtesy, please."

She frowns. "My role on this mission? Medical assistance."

"That's not what I asked. I'm not talking about your immediate plans. I'm talking about the project. Because whatever the fuck it is, it's never been about getting ex-soldiers with broken legs to make themselves expensive guns."

She shakes her head firmly.

"Look," Rao goes on. "I'm fucked. I'm full of this stuff. Hate to break it to you, but your tests are hopeless. I cried Prophet yesterday. It came out of my tear ducts, sunk right back into my skin. I know there's no happy ending for me. Everyone that's going in is expendable except you. So, you're the one I'm asking. I'm not trying to defeat you and save the day. What am I going to do, truth-test you to death? Fuck saving the day and fuck the saving particularly. I'm over it. I'm . . . *over*, Veronica. I knew that a long time ago. I don't give two shits about De Witte. I'm only doing this because I'm a curious arsehole. That's my motivation, and I really want to know before this shit kills me."

He lets out a long breath. Some of that felt true.

"You're not expendable."

"Don't bullshit me. The next samples you're going to want are postmortem."

She looks at him carefully. He waits her out. Eventually she nods at the packet of Lucky Strikes he's holding.

"May I?"

"Didn't know you smoked."

"I don't."

He lights her cigarette. She lets the smoke slip out of her mouth, drags it back in.

"Ok," she says finally. "The EPGOs around the facility weren't made by the people who worked there."

He blinks. It's true.

"Work it out," she says.

"Can you not just tell me?"

"I don't want to tell you. I want to see you work it out."

"Fine. How much shit is piled up around those buildings?"

"Rough estimate, just under forty thousand objects."

"One person, one object."

"Correct."

He looks out at the desert, at clouds massing over the far slopes. Shivers with sudden comprehension. "It's a town," he breathes.

"It's a town. Pahrump."

"How?"

"Drinking water."

"Fucking hell, Veronica. That's wildly, wildly illegal."

She wrinkles her nose. "It's given us interesting and encouraging data."

"Has it. When was this?"

"Just over five months ago."

"So you poisoned a whole town back when Prophet just made people feel nostalgic. And now the good citizens of Pahrump have suddenly made all this? Veronica, get your story straight. You told me that once it's inside people, its effects don't change."

Her brow furrows. "Until now. In fact, I suspect you're responsible. Your handshake with Mrs Crossland was the trigger. You touched her, and Prophet made a connection. When that happened, forty thousand EPGOs were manifested around the facility."

It's true. He should feel guilty. He *is* guilty. He doesn't feel guilty.

"But why here?" he asks. As she shakes her head, he has the flash of an image that tastes of an answer. Something he saw in a magazine.

Photographs of flowers taken with UV-sensitive film. Bright patches and lines on their petals, invisible to the human eye. But not to bees. He thinks of the appliquéd pansies on Dinah Crossland's sleeves. Thinks of Pahrump. Wonders what it looks like. Like Mercury, perhaps, only with fewer radiation warning signs and more American flags. Yeah, far, far more.

"Community renewal?" he says. "That's what this is for. Right. Yes. And Prophet in the water in Pahrump was, what, a dry run?"

Her eyebrows rise. "Well done."

"What kind of community renewal are we talking about, Veronica?" he says slowly.

"Well, Lane's terribly fond of slogans. He says that just like fluoride in water protects a nation's teeth, Prophet in water protects a nation's idea of itself."

"I'm surprised he's a fluoride fan. Lane's a bit precious bodily fluids, isn't he?"

"I don't know what that means."

"How have you not seen *Dr. Strangelove*, Veronica? What does 'protect a nation's idea of itself' mean?"

"Nostos," she says.

"Now you're just *trying* to be oblique. You're like my auntie Manju. She can't explain anything without—"

"Short version, Rao, is that nostalgia is an emotional weapon. And we're very keen to use it."

"We?"

"I'm not supplying names."

"Wasn't asking for them. Just, I never thought of you as a party person, Veronica."

She raises her eyebrows. "Alliances aren't the same as allegiances. People so often confuse the two. Shall we just say we're working with"— her voice shifts into a creditable Texan drawl—"important folks behind the scenes."

"Ah, yes, the no-oversight brigade. 'Nostos,' you said. Home. Your little cabal wants to dose the population to give them all a hard-on for imaginary America, right?"

"That would be one way of putting it."

"What's another way?"

"Saving America."

He snorts at that. "How is suicide by soft toy going to save America?"

"The purpose of our facility here isn't to store Prophet," she says. "It's to engineer it. We've been working on reversing these step changes in its operation. Attenuating its effects."

"Attenuating? You've been poking away at it to make it weaker? Well that's worked out beautifully for you, hasn't it?"

Veronica is unfazed. "We'll get there."

"So you're weaponizing nostalgia to engineer the conditions for a big populist government takeover."

"Oh no, Rao." She looks at him with something like pity. "No. That's not it at all. Governments are redundant entities these days. They have their uses, but they're not where power lies."

"Corporations."

She shakes her head. "People."

"People? Are we talking socialism, Veronica? Because that's a bit of a surprise, to be honest—"

She laughs. "No. Not *The People*. Persons."

"Like De Witte."

"Steven's part of the network, yes."

"Oh there's a network, is there? This isn't some Elders of Zion shit, because if it is—"

"Of course it isn't. This isn't an anti-Semitic fairy tale. It's real."

It is. Fuck.

"So what's your manifesto?"

"A brave new world, Rao."

"Come on, Veronica, you'll have to do better than that."

She rolls her eyes. "I really don't. But just for you, Rao: Think of the financial crash as the first and necessary step of a great, global reorganisation. We're freeing ourselves of the shackles of regulation to usher in a world where finite resources are managed with rare efficiency by those few, extraordinary individuals who possess the vision, courage, and commitment to see things through. And Prophet is our social engineer, the exquisite silver thread that shall shape the world to our will."

This is monologuing, Rao thinks. Vague as fuck, nonsensical, doubtless genocidal. Prophet notwithstanding, it's almost exactly like the one at the denouement of a Robert Ludlum thriller he'd toiled through a few years ago. Two weeks ago he'd have listened to this, laughed in her face, and frantically tried to work out how to save the day. Now? Fuck knows.

"So when you say 'saving America,' it's not America. It's Lunastus."

"Lunastus-Dainsleif *is* America."

Rao shakes his head, lights another cigarette. "This is some dystopian shit, Veronica."

"I'm rather surprised. I assumed you'd be over the romantic notion the world is divided into heroes and villains by now. But if you insist on that fiction, perhaps I should point out we didn't get you addicted to heroin in order to put you where we wanted you to be."

"No, you've done something worse."

She looks him directly in the eye.

"Rao, please tell me truthfully. Would you *want* to be free of Prophet right now? Would you want to be anywhere else?"

He shivers again. His answer is so perfectly true he almost retches speaking it. "No."

CHAPTER 66

Rao stabs another potato tot, chews it stoically. The cafeteria coffee is undrinkable. He doesn't care. That morning he'd made himself two copies of the finest cup he'd ever had in his life: a latte from a café by Brighton station that punished punters for the quality of their coffee by forcing them to sit on hessian-covered boxes with painfully sharp edges. He watches Adam eat a plate of mushy spaghetti and luminous marinara sauce with grudging admiration. Hunter's finished hers.

He jerks his head subtly at the soldier boys at the other tables. "Who are these guys?" he asks.

"Private security contractors," Hunter explains. "Run out of some office near Dulles, like they all are."

"Yeah, mercenaries. But they're not Blackwater or Triple Canopy."

She shakes her head. "Another outfit. Eagle Aspect. Know a couple of them by reputation. Estrada is sound. Roberts is too. Just don't ask him about God."

"That's not a challenge, Rao," Adam says. "We don't need you locking horns right now."

"I don't feel like locking anything, love. To be quite honest, I feel like a nap. What's happening now?"

"War-gaming," Adam answers.

"They're going to play Dungeons and Dragons?" Rao breathes, eyes wide. No response. *Read the room, Sunil.* "Fine. When's the mission? Tonight?"

"Nope. Lane fucked up," Hunter says. "At this rate, Estrada's going to kill him before I do."

"Estrada."

"Alejandro. Weapons sergeant," Adam explains. "Lane didn't want weapons on the plane he sent. Said he'd bring them separately. They haven't arrived. Now Lane's blaming everyone in the lower forty-eight. We won't get what we need before late this evening. H hour's pushed back to tomorrow a.m."

"Ok. Do I need to be in these war-gaming meetings?"

"You do."

Considering the madness that all this is, Rao probably doesn't need to be so covert. Habit of a lifetime. He sneaks a plastic cup into his jacket pocket as they exit the cafeteria, ducks into the empty office next to the George Washington Room, and makes himself a cup of coffee to fill it. Tucking the earthenware mug he'd magicked into existence behind a window blind, he strolls back into the meeting room, sipping as he walks. Fucking *nectar.* He nods at Veronica, perched on a desk with a bottle of Fiji Water. She beams back. It's not a proprietorial smile. It's relieved. Lane's not here. And the meeting—well. Rao's always had a bit of a thing for competence, and it turns out that watching Adam, Hunter, and six Special Forces types work out a plan of operations really does it for him. They'll be dropped off by vehicle upwind of the building, at the edge of the ring of EPGOs. They'll keep a field ambulance and EMT team from one of Lunastus's private hospitals on the far side of the ridge, leaving Hunter and Carlton with his sniper rifle on the nearside. Carlton will keep an eye on the building. So will Hunter, running the radio and relaying updates to Lane.

Taking EPGO obstacles into account, they calculate it'll take eight minutes to reach the building on foot.

The tape of the engineer's last phone call is replayed twice.

There's speculation on the motivation of the hostiles.

"It may not be hostility per se," Veronica offers. "At least, not how we familiarly use the term. Individuals exposed to Prophet are drawn to the objects they make, want to establish physical contact with them. Once that's achieved, they become unresponsive. It's possible that works both ways. Telltales may simply be searching out the people who made them. Wanting, if that word might be used for an entity of this nature, to establish physical contact with their creators."

"Contact with the people who made them by imagining them," Roberts says hesitantly. He's trying hard, Rao notes, to internalise the reality he's facing. Hasn't quite managed it.

"Yeah," Rao goes on. "Targeting them. To grab hold of them. And then—" He makes a face.

"Physical contact puts their targets down," Roberts concludes.

"Exactly."

"Are they targeting the person who made them, or anyone?"

"Insufficient data to answer that," Veronica says and smiles.

"So these telltales, they're like zombies?" Stewart asks.

"Near enough," Adam replies.

"Fast zombies." It's Estrada. He's not spoken much before.

"Likely." Heads nod.

"But unarmed."

"Who knows," Rao says. "Like, if someone in there imagined Clint Eastwood from *The Good, the Bad and the Ugly* . . ."

"That shot through the rope was bullshit," Estrada snaps immediately. "1874 Sharps at that distance?"

"It's not impossible that cinematic license," Veronica observes, "might carry into a real-world environment in this context."

"Well, that's fucked up," Estrada replies.

More nods. Graver this time.

When Estrada takes the team through their weapons list—suppressed MP5s, Beretta M9s, and a fancy sniper rifle for Carlton—Rao ascertains that everyone going in will be armed except him. Which seems remarkably unfair, considering he's supposed to be their *primary asset*.

"Why don't I get a gun?" he whispers to Adam and Hunter during a break in proceedings.

Hunter gives him a *you're fucking joking me* face.

"Because you've got me," Adam explains.

Hunter rolls her eyes and groans. "You've got more than Rubenstein. Rao, you've got a six-man team whose explicit purpose is to protect you so you can do the job we're here for. You won't need 'a gun.'"

"But—"

"Rao, have you ever fired a weapon?" she asks.

"Depends on how you define a—"

"No weapon, Rao," Adam says. "But you'll have combat uniform."

"What?"

"Battle gear," Adam says with a twitch of his lips. "You're not going in in corduroys."

"Fucking hell. That's a lot. They're not going to make me salute a flag?"

"They'll make you brush your hair." Hunter's serious voice.

"Fuck off."

When they cluster around the model to discuss their entry, sweep, and search, Rao hangs back. All he'll have to do is follow their lead, and the entirety of the model—all its rooms and floors, stairs and halls—is already in his head. So when a woman called Linda turns up with a wheeled case and says she's here with his uniform, Rao nips into the office next door with her to try it on.

It's a little maddening that the first pair of trousers she hands him fit better than the ones he's wearing. So does the shirt, the one she calls a blouse. He brushes his hands down the fractal print in little squares of grey and brown and sand. There are pockets everywhere. The boots are great. The flak vest thing is better. The ballistic helmet is . . . yeah. He hates how much he likes it.

She's looking up at him now. Small and blonde and fierce. To her, he's nothing, and he's so grateful for her lack of interest, her ignorance of whatever conjunction of the planets made him so fucking *special*, he comes perilously close to disaster. Desperately wants to walk out with her right back into ordinary life. Have a beer, a plate of tacos. Complain about the weather. She tells him to bend so she can check the helmet and chin guard. The moment passes. He waggles his eyebrows suggestively when she pulls at his waistband. Force of habit. She doesn't see him do it, thankfully. "How did you get my measurements, Linda?" he asks.

She shrugs. "I didn't. Got a case full of these. I just have to make sure one fits."

"This fits."

He thanks her. He's handed his clothes and shoes in a plastic bag. It's like he's died. Like he's dead and he's picking up the clothes he's died in. When he walks back into the room, Adam looks at him. Says nothing.

Hunter grins. "Fuck me, Rao," she says. "You've joined the marines."

"Am I a lil bitch now, Hunter?"

"Absolutely."

CHAPTER 67

They eat in near silence. There's raucous laughter from a table by the door. All men, Rao observes, none with soldierly physiques. A preponderance of glasses. One wears a Stark Industries tee. Nuclear scientists, he supposes. *Yeah*. Nursemaiding America's arsenal, making sure the end of the world will still happen if the wankers in charge want it to.

After dinner, back at the double dorm they've moved themselves into, Rao has a hot shower in an attempt to shift the blankness he's felt since he held his own clothes and shoes in a plastic bag. It helps a little. He pulls on his Union Jack tee, disconcerted by how much it's faded, a pair of grey sleep pants, then wanders back into the dorm, soles scratching on the sand he's already tracked in over the linoleum floor.

Adam's sitting at the desk examining a detailed terrain map. By his elbow, an elderly Anglepoise lamp, a steel mug, and an open box of Milk Duds. As Rao nears, he doesn't raise his eyes from the map, just murmurs, "Eleven hours fifty-two until we go in."

"Thanks, but that wasn't what I was going to ask," Rao says. Adam looks up, face jagged in the lamplight. "Wasn't going to ask you anything, actually, love. Sorry to disappoint. But now we're alone, I wanted to tell you I found out what's going on. Had a little chat with Veronica this morning. I caught her at an unguarded moment."

"Rhodes doesn't have unguarded moments."

Well, no, Rao thinks. *She doesn't.* She just assumes he's going to die. But they don't need to get into that right now. Could be a bit of a conversational derailer. "Let's just say she took me into her confidence," he says a little haughtily. "Anyway. Listen. This whole project, it's mad. It's fucking insane."

"I know, Rao."

"No. Madder than that. Much, much madder."

That gets a very tight smile. "What's the intel, Rao?"

Rao exhales. Walks to their dorm window. Looks out. The street-lights are dim. He can see high, sallow clouds lit by the moon over the desert. Must hardly ever rain here. He misses rain. Heavy rain. Cold London rain. Monsoon rain in Jaipur. Proper September rain, there, the way it feels on the skin, the way colours flood and burn in it. He doesn't think he's going to feel it again.

"Rao?"

"Sorry." He turns, leans against the frame. "They plan to use Prophet on everyone in America. To make everyone imagine a lost, perfect home and then promise they'll give it to them. They're weapon-izing nostalgia to take over the world. Kitty would lose it."

"Who's they?"

"Not the military. It's a bunch of billionaire fucks and ideologues getting their cocks sucked by the military. De Witte is their little emperor. King Fuck. Veronica's his voice on Earth. The whole mani-festation programme was bullshit cover. White noise. They've already done a field test, put Prophet in drinking water. That memory junkyard around the facility, it was all made by civilians."

Adam reaches to smooth the map against the desk, flattening it with one palm, brow ticking down. "At distance?"

"At distance. Prophet keeps everyone guessing, doesn't it? It's a cunt like that."

"Where's the location of the field test?"

"Pahrump."

"Mrs Crossland."

"Mrs Crossland."

A second later, Adam's wry expression vanishes. "Fucking idiots," he whispers.

"Yeah."

"No, Rao. I mean using Pahrump for field tests."

"It's convenient?"

Adam shakes his head. "You know what happened here."

"Here?"

"Nevada test site. One bomb every three weeks for twelve years. They called Vegas Atomic City back then. You could watch the mushroom clouds from your casino hotel. People came from all over to see that. The reason it's fucking stupid, Rao, is that testing stopped in 1963. There'll be folks in Pahrump who remember those tests from their childhood. You know what that means."

"Fuck," Rao breathes.

"Yep."

"Atom bomb EPGOs? It *couldn't*."

"Have you tested that?"

Rao shivers. "Holy shit. Holy fucking shit."

A long silence. Adam's stopped looking at the blueprints. He's staring into space. He's imagining it, isn't he. Out of the darkness that double flash, so bright you could put your hands in front of your eyes to block it out and see every one of your bones through muscle and skin. The silence, until the noise. The stillness, until the shock wave. The slowly climbing, terrible cloud in the desert. The searing heat of it. The dust, the death. Hard rain.

"Adam," he whispers.

"Well, that's the other way it might go," Adam says.

Rao frowns. "What might?"

"End of the world." He picks up his mug.

"Let's not be overly dramatic, love."

Adam's eyes widen perceptibly as he drinks. He sets the mug back down, stares at it. "Rao," he says very softly. "Prophet is the end of the world. You know it is. They can't contain it and it's making more of itself all the time. Nobody can destroy it. They could vaporize it, sure. But then it's just in the air. It's going to keep growing, and it's going to get everywhere."

Rao blinks at him.

"You haven't run this," Adam says curiously. And Rao shakes his head, just once. It had never occurred to him. Which is, he realises, extraordinary. And he realises something else. He knows now what Adam's sadness is. He'd felt it before. Hadn't known what it meant.

"I always thought the end of the world was going to be, you know," he says, after a deal of silence, "properly apocalyptic. Fires. Tidal waves. Floods."

"No, Rao," Adam says, the tiredness, the resignation in his voice as heavy and obvious as his conclusions. "The end of the world is just people glued to toys."

CHAPTER 68

When Rao wakes it's already light. He pulls the awful green blanket tighter around his shoulders, pushes his face into a pillow that smells of bleach. Keeps his eyes closed as long as he can, but he's so awake, and the squirming press of colourless patterns behind his eyelids is making him nauseated. He gets up, shivers, goes to the door of the dorm, and opens it.

The first thing he thinks is *salt*. Innumerable grains of it blowing in the wind across the flat expanse of gravel outside, collecting on the lee sides of rocks and clumps of grass by the door. The sky is nine tenths cloud, livid, nearly purple, the dawn light yellow, and the air is full of falling grains of salt that isn't salt, is it, of course it's not. It's—

"Snow," comes the familiar baritone. Adam's standing close behind him, already dressed.

"Is this normal?"

"No."

"Fucking hell, Prophet's changing the weather now?" Rao says. "Before anything else, I need coffee. No. Take a piss. No. Coffee first. Priorities."

"We don't have a coffee—" Adam begins, then nods. Rao conjures two mugs of Brighton's finest, one after the other, upon the desk. Hands one to Adam, who accepts it gratefully, even closing his eyes in what Rao presumes is simple pleasure after taking the first sip.

"Last cigarette, Adam?" Rao says, returning from the bathroom to stare down the combat uniform on the chair.

"Sure. You make those too?"

"Yeah, and the lighter. I'm entirely self-sustaining now, Adamski."

"You haven't called me that for a while."

"Haven't I?"

Rao pulls on his combat uniform and boots, leaving the vest and helmet on the seat, and they walk outside to smoke and watch the snow. There's so much silence, and for once in his life, Rao doesn't feel the need to fill it.

He hears the low echoing roar of their idling engines before he sees them. Rao's not seen Humvees since Afghanistan. Four of them in desert tan are parked up where the main street is widest. Snow dusts their familiar squat profiles, glows in the headlights on their toothy, bad-tempered grilles. One of them's an ambulance, red cross high on its sides. He remembers those too. From Kabul. *Shit*, he thinks. All that happened there, it's on the other side of this. But which side, he's not sure. Feels it's all still to come somehow. Garcia nods a greeting and opens the rear passenger door. Rao climbs in, swearing under his breath. Adam follows.

As the convoy pulls away, Rao stares at Garcia's gloved hands resting lightly on the wheel, then up at the wiper blades and beyond, where tunnelling flecks of snow speed towards the windscreen. Rao feels a wrench at leaving their dorm behind. It's absurd to feel so attached to a room he'd slept in for a single night. He turns his head to look out the window. An expanse of low grasses and bushes with tiny leaves silvered by snow. Dark feathery lumps that are yucca trees. About a mile out of town, he thinks he sees something running in the mid distance, ghostly suggestions of movement behind the shifting veils of snow, nothing solid. Deer maybe. Or antelopes. Yes. Those. He wonders what they're running from. Running to.

The team's talking over their radios. Their communications aren't the terse NATO alphabetised sitreps he'd expected. So far, it's mostly Estrada getting shit for that one time he vetoed Starbucks in favour of Peet's. Even Adam had weighed in on that crime. Rao listens to their banter in silence as the convoy makes its way northwest. His hands are laid on his thighs, fingers spread, just the way they were on the way to the diner, but the press on his mind is no longer a dim sense of dissimulation. It's a compass orientation. He knows exactly where they're going. Can feel it, like his bones have been magnetised, his blood. The submarine tow of it is so strong that every time the road veers away from the direction of the E-MAD site, he has the distinct sensation of being pulled onto one side. A car on two wheels. Takes uneasy, shallow breaths that turn deep again as soon as they regain a direct heading in.

They leave the ambulance parked on the far side of the last ridge and climb higher. The snow's falling less strongly now. More and more of the desert around them is revealed. *Prophet wants to draw back the curtain*, Rao thinks. *Wants to let me see.*

And he sees. They crest a rise and through the windscreen Rao views the E-MAD buildings for the first time. They're just above Garcia's hands. They're there, outside. They're inside the toughened glass. They're inside his head. *Scale.* He makes a low sound, tears his eyes away, focuses on his hands. The wrinkles on his knuckles, the hangnail on his thumb. He wants his eyes on their destination more than he wants to breathe, but he's kicking against that need as hard as he ever has for anything. It's a fruitless effort. As soon as he gets close, it'll all be over. Whatever "over" is. But he's trying. He's going to hold out for as long as he can.

They descend a few hundred yards, park up. Rao opens his door, watches his left foot hit the ground a few inches from a Mr. Potato Head. He ducks out and looks around, keeping his eyes low. There's a scattering of objects around the vehicles here. One every fifteen feet or so. Nothing larger than a portable television. Strands of cotton candy snagged in the twigs of desert bushes flapping in the cold wind. Blood singing in his ears. The sounds of doors closing, weapons being readied. The laughter has stopped. Voices are low. Roberts is scanning the buildings through binoculars. Veronica stands by his side, hands on her hips. She's dressed like a CNN reporter in a war zone. Tan ballistic helmet, dark trousers and boots, a down jacket exactly the colour of the vehicles that drove them in. Over it a stab vest and a black shemagh. Pale lipstick like a 1960s snow bunny. It glitters when she smiles at Roberts. *Mad as a box of frogs*, Rao thinks. *Madder than fucking ever.* There's another round of check-ins on the radios. All the headsets are working fine.

After the radio check, Hunter nods to an outcrop fifty yards away. Says she's heading up there with Carlton. "Are you going to be ok?" Rao asks her automatically, feeling a flush of hot humiliation as soon as he hears himself.

"I am and will be," she says evenly. "Behind that BFR we got cover, clear lines, and our guy with the M110 tells me he was top of his class at sniper school. And if he fucks up," she whispers, "I can always call in a hellfire from Creech."

"Don't do that," he says, aghast. "It'll just spread the—"

"Rao," she says, face softening. "You're an idiot. Buy me a beer later."

"Ok," he says. She hoists her rifle and pack, and Rao's back aches sympathetically as he imagines the kind of weight she's carrying. Must hike with a pack like that all the time on ops like these, he thinks. She's so ridiculously badass. Fucking hell. He's within a whisker of asking her to marry him when she turns and looks him directly in the eye. He starts a little guiltily.

"Rubenstein comes back alive, Rao," she says. "You hear me? You have to do two things. You open your fucking eyes, and you make sure he comes back alive."

"Uh, Roger," he says.

She nods. "Then I might even buy *you* a beer."

He watches her walk away, heart strangely bruised. Adam steps in front of him, gives him a tight half smile. "Shit gets weird before this kind of thing," he advises. "Try not to take anything on. Always look to what happens after. It'll be fine."

"Is that Rubenstein fine?"

"Mission fine. Eyes forward, Rao."

The wind blows at their backs and prickles with ice. The sky all the way to the horizon is heaped with clouds. Rao stands by the vehicles, takes a lungful of bitter air. He doesn't want to look forward. Doesn't want to look back. Doesn't want to turn his eyes to the buildings he's keeping behind him. Everything out here but Adam feels unreal. And Adam is somehow almost impossible to look at. These are his real clothes Rao sees now, the reason his suits always look wrong. Helmet, tactical vest, backpack, combat pants, boots. But in battle gear he seems so absurdly slight compared to the guys around him, like a kid play-ing dress-up. When Adam drops to one knee to relace his boots, Rao knows that what he's seeing is an old premission superstition, knows that he has done this many times before. He watches Adam tying his laces tight, and his chest hurts.

"Adam—" he says as Adam rises to his feet, looks at him expectantly. But it's no good. He doesn't know what he was trying to say.

"I'm going to keep you alive," Adam says, low and urgent. "It's going to be the last goddamn thing I do."

Rao snorts. "You're a dramatic cunt, Rubenstein. Did I ever tell you that?"

Adam grins, wipes his mouth with the back of one hand. "Yeah, Rao."

CHAPTER 69

When Roberts gives the order to move out, Veronica smiles at the troops like a benevolent schoolteacher at the commencement of a class excursion. Rao's eyes linger on her smile for far longer than it lasts. She catches him looking. Purses her glimmering lips, falls into step next to him.

"How are we feeling, Rao? Excited?"

"Thrilled," he says. He's trudging behind Adam, close enough that he blocks out the sight of the buildings ahead, keeping his eyes on the ground.

"No last-minute nerves?"

"I'm *all* nerves, Veronica."

"Oh, Rao. Don't be so Cowardly Lion."

A tight laugh. "*Wizard of Oz*, is it?"

"Isn't it?"

"Not as far as I'm concerned it isn't."

"You started it, Rao. Don't you remember?" He does. He shakes his head. "You told me Rubenstein was the Tin Man. No heart."

He's sure Adam heard that.

"Fuck off."

She beams. "So who are you? Dorothy?"

"Toto," he grates.

That gets a peal of laughter. She continues to look amused for a while, then she catches sight of what's ahead and her expression shifts to fascination. The objects are strewn more thickly now and approaching on their left is the first of the larger EPGOs. It's a small section of a municipal park, tinted oddly, skewing faded Kodachrome. Thirty feet of lawn, a regimented bed of glowing red geraniums. Something that might be the back of a dog is moving fitfully among the blooms. Behind it is a houseboat, rocking slowly in the sand. He looks down the line. Credit to the soldier boys, they're still marching. Eyes forward.

A melody. Close by. Carried on the wind with the snow. It's a child's tune: plangent, unearthly. Rao instantly knows what's making those tiny, bell-like tones: it's a Fisher-Price clockwork record player, and it's playing "Jack and Jill." The crunch of feet on glittering buttons spilled over gravel, the crack of boots on a plastic Buckaroo: the music floats over and under everything. Impossible to locate, impossible to ignore.

One of the unit stops. His hands are tight fists. "I'm going to find what's making that noise," he mutters. He looks about, hooded eyes frowning under his helmet. Baker.

"No, you are not," Roberts calls to him. "Eyes forward. We have an objective."

"And I'm not going to make it there, sir, if I've lost my damn mind. I'm gonna find that thing, and I'm gonna kill it."

"It's a music box."

"It's in my fucking teeth."

"Charlie Mike," Roberts says tightly. After a moment of tense irresolution, Baker walks on.

Soon the piles of objects are so densely packed they scramble in single file. Rao slips on the icy roof of a purple Toyota Corolla; Adam grips his hand, helps him over. They have to turn sideways to squeeze their way between the walls of a small Spanish Revival house and a section of rusted chain-link fence covered in kudzu vines. And then, suddenly, they're between the trunks of tall trees, pacing across deep leaf litter, and the air is soft and warm and rich with birdsong, and the light that filters down through the greenery above is so golden, feels so impossibly safe, that Rao finds himself near tears. He hears his next footfall crunch on gravel, not leaves, and as they step out one by one back into snow, a hummingbird the colour of a wine bottle in full sun accompanies them for several feet until it halts in the air, turns back towards the warmth.

Adam stops in his tracks.

"What is it?"

"The surveillance plane," Adam whispers.

It was. Now it's something else. The wreckage is forty feet away, twisted, the plane tipped on one side, but even so Rao can see the shining aluminium wings of a smaller aircraft emerging from the sides of the fuselage near the nose.

"He manifested a Mustang," Adam says. He sounds sad.

"Pilots," Rao says. "Decidedly not immune. Romantics."

"I'm going to check it out," Adam says. He raises one hand; the group halts and waits. Rao follows him to the crash. Close up, Rao runs his fingers down the join between the plastic composite of the modern plane and the unpainted metal of the wartime one. It's seamless. Everything smells strongly of kerosene, the snow melted on the fuel-soaked ground. And though there's no sign of a fire, when Rao rubs one thumb against the shining metal, it pulls a layer of thick black ash from the surface. He wipes it away on his sleeve, looks towards the nose. There's blood inside the canopy, bright splashes of it across the complicated bisecting geometry of windows that are an amalgam of both planes. Adam hops up on one of the silver wings, peers in. "Both cut in half," he calls. "Mustang cockpit's a lot smaller than a Dash 7's. I'll check the cabin for the system ops."

He moves further along the wing, crouches to look in one of the smaller windows, then slides to the ground, walks back to Rao.

"Survivors?"

"Negative. It's a mess in there."

Veronica raises her eyebrows expectantly as they approach. Adam shakes his head. She turns and murmurs something to Roberts; they continue towards the building.

The building. It's close now. It's time. He can't hold out any longer against the need to see it. He takes a deep breath, raises his eyes, and the world clicks into a different shape.

All the photographs Rao's seen of it were taken in sunlight, sheet fasciae of corrugated steel burning white in the Nevada sun. But now the building is grey, the clouds above so low that shreds of vapour cling to gantries, shift over the upper floors. It's huge. An irregular mass of boxes like a collection of hangars, brutalist, uncompromisingly industrial, glacially cold. This close, the structure is oppressive. Feels like it's falling on him. He wants inside so badly he can taste it, feel his fingertips itch. He tries to push the need away, but it pushes back so hard he staggers on his feet.

Veronica notices. Catches at his face with one gloved hand, turns it, looks into his eyes. He looks into hers. Grey. Cold. Speculative. They're conducting a professional assessment, and it irritates the fuck out of him. He takes her wrist and pulls her hand away. "I'm fine, Veronica. Don't fuss."

"But you're so very important, Rao. I'm simply protecting our primary asset," she says. She's smiling. She's crackling with something like elation out here. It's unpleasant standing anywhere near. He's about to respond with a few well-chosen words when he sees Adam is looking at him. Their eyes meet. And with a click, a flash of intuition, of relief, Rao knows that Adam understands.

He grasps the depth of longing Rao has for what's inside those buildings. He knows it. Shares it. He's feeling it too. No. Wait.

A clench of pain deep in Rao's chest. A sudden, searing comprehension. He knows, now, what that longing in Adam is.

It's not for the building.

And now holding Adam's gaze is like trying to swim to shore in a riptide. Feels like every safety the world has ever possessed. But Rao's not strong enough. What's pulling him the other way is too powerful. The gravity well's hauling him in. He'd had no idea what Adam felt for him. How could he? Or maybe he'd known but hadn't been sure. He couldn't be sure. It's Adam. Adam's impossible. It's impossible.

It's impossible.

Adam blinks then, like he's been answered. Lifts his chin, speaks. "I got it, Rhodes."

Rao'd forgotten she was there. He feels her pat him softly, proprietorially on one cheek, sees Adam's eyes narrow as she does. Rao steps back. He's a fucking idiot. All this time. Why hadn't he—

And then what's waiting for him in the buildings ahead pulls on him hard, fanned bright like a fire in a high wind. Too bright, too hard, and he's carried towards it.

But Adam, now, is right by his side.

The objects are smaller around here, less densely packed. The last fifty yards are uneven but easy going: board games, comforters, lampshades, plush toys, sections of Scalextric track. They halt on a stretch of close-mown lawn frosted with snow in front of the personnel entrance of the concrete block annex that leads into the cold bay on the western side. Two small cushions are propped delicately against the door.

Rao knows the drill. He's supposed to wait until the soldier boys have, as they delicately described it, "cleared the room." But he makes to follow them when they file inside. Adam extends an arm across his chest, keeps him in place. He balks at it. Feels like a horse in a starting gate.

"Let them, Rao."

When the clear comes through on their headsets, Rao follows Adam inside, Veronica close behind, Baker taking rear guard cover. The space they enter is the size of a sports hall, angled forests of pipework running across green-painted walls furred with patches of white. The scurf looks old, as if minerals in the bricks had leached out over the years, but Rao doubts that's what he's seeing; the ghostly patterns resemble winter branches.

He drags his eyes to the centre of the room, where two of the soldiers are crouched over bodies on the concrete floor.

"We're not the first team in here," Rao says slowly.

"Of course not," Veronica says, close to his ear. "There've been two others."

"Always good to know we're the last-ditch fallback. Adam, did you know we were the children's fucking crusade?" He walks over, peers down at the nearest corpse. It's clutching a small tub seat upholstered in orange velvet. But the velvet isn't confined to the chair. It runs up the extended arm in a curling patch that spills over one shoulder, edges fused into the camo hazmat suit. The body next to it is curled around a dog. This one isn't a beagle like Monty's. A white feathered tail extends from under an arm, swaying gently, but the rest of its fur is patterned like camouflage. There's condensation in the visor. He's glad of it. He doesn't want to see the face.

The third body lies facedown. Things protrude from its back that look like tubes of half-melted glass.

"Alive?" Adam is asking the medics.

"Unlikely. Doesn't matter," Veronica replies. "We're not here for them."

"Hazmats aren't—"

"NBC suits are not effective, no. They wouldn't be."

The light inside the hall shifts intermittently like sunlight slipping in and out of clouds. Rao looks up. There are no skylights, no windows at all. The light has nothing to do with the weather.

"Radio's down," Roberts says shortly.

"Jammed?"

"Random noise."

"I got cocktail party," Garcia says. "Voices. Music."

"Same," Stewart says. Then, more uneasily, "It's . . . a choir?" He tilts his head, then shakes it. "No. I think I'm hearing a Pan Am commercial."

"That's fucked up."

They futz with their sets, quickly determine the radios are useless. After a brief huddle they decide to continue.

"Old school?" Rao enquires. "Hand signals and shit?"

"Yeah," Adam says. "Keep close."

MP5s readied, Roberts and Stewart slip onwards through the door into the old machine shop, refitted, Rao knows, as a conference room. Ten seconds later, Stewart reappears. "Clear. It's dark. NVGs are fucked. Flashlights."

"What—" Rao begins.

"Torches," Adam says, pulling one.

CHAPTER 70

"**W**hy can't we at least have a go at getting the lights on now that the night vision things have decided to die?" Rao complains as they file into the room. Adam's chin strap tugs; he's not used to smiling, however grimly, when fully dressed. "We're running about in here using fucking mag lights."

"They're easy to shut off," Adam says. Smiles again at Rao's dramatic sigh.

"What's that got to do with shit?"

Roberts answers for him. "If we need to go dark, then we can without issue," he says. Stops moving. Turns around to shine his light in Rao's face. "Without too much issue."

"Fuck off," Rao mutters, squinting.

Roberts sniffs at Rao. Turns. Keeps walking.

"Prick," Rao tells Adam, under his breath.

"Mm," Adam replies. Rao's not wrong.

They continue in silence. The sweeping movements of the flashlights pick out screens, potted plants, poster presentations, the Lunastus logo in silver relief on one wall. Everyday corporate scenes, intermittently broken by EPGOs. A bright-blue bicycle, white and red streamers growing out of the handles like plastic ferns, standing in the middle of the room at an angle, like it's leaning against a wall. Adam's light catches on the face of an American Girl doll moving toward them, stopping, hobbling away. Gesturing and making sure that Rao stays close, Adam breaks rank to check it out.

The doll wears pigtails and red glasses and moves like half a human. The left half, to be precise. That half moves like it's breathing, like there are nerves under its skin, as if its glass eye can see. The left leg steps confidently, drags the right side in a limp. The eye that can see looks up at Adam. The doll stops. Backs up.

"That's weird," he says.

Rao peers over his shoulder, shrugs. "Is it? Prophet made it," he says. Bored. Explaining the obvious. Adam doesn't feel right taking his eyes off the doll, but he glances at Rao. "Prophet doesn't want anything to do with you, love," Rao adds.

"Ladies, are we boring you?" Roberts calls.

Rao shares a withering look with Adam. "Found a doll, Roberts. You know how it is."

"I do not."

"That's not true," Rao whispers.

Adam leads them back to the group. "American Girl doll. It was walking around," he reports. Watches Roberts's face tighten in confusion, maybe frustration, as he forces himself to keep up. All mission, no matter how crazy it is. No matter the struggle to maintain psychological pace.

"Hostile?"

"Complicated," Adam says. "Mobile objects seem drawn to the group but will move away from me."

"You alone, Colonel?"

"Seems to be."

Roberts's expression tightens further, making more of his scars apparent, conjuring them on his face the way Rao can think a cigarette into existence. "This team is immune," he says. Sounds out. An assumption. Adam doesn't interrupt, but he can feel Rao bounce on his heels beside him with the urge to say something. Not a great sign. "So we'll continue as planned and face any kinetic objects when and if that happens."

"Yes, sir."

They file into a wide, dark corridor, where the air is sweet like spun sugar. Reminds Adam of summer heat despite the cold. "Bazooka," Baker says. "That pink gum. You remember that? Smells like that shit."

"Less chatter," Roberts calls from the front. He takes a breath, ready to spout another ass-chewing command, but doesn't get a chance. The noise he makes is cutting. Sudden. Pain. Like he stood on something sharp.

A struggle made of light. Roberts's flashlight slashing through the dark, through the silence. Silence, except the rusty creak of what sounds like pipes to the left of the group. The team drop to their knees. Lights up, weapons switched and forward. Adam tugs on Rao's sleeve and then moves, low, up the line to find Roberts. He's not there.

Adam gestures behind him for the team to stay close, leads them on slowly. The creaking gets louder. Closer. Adam isn't just hearing it on their left any longer. It's in the air. Sharp, metallic, mixing with the sugar-sweet smell around them. His light catches movement, something shiny, polished to perfection. He moves toward it. The creaking pipes are louder, and now Adam can make out another sound underneath.

Choking. Gasping.

The light cutting through the corridor from their flashlights is selective, so it takes Adam too long to figure out what he's looking at: Roberts tangled up in the bars and spokes of the bright-blue bicycle, glittering under their lights. It's twisted around him like a snake, a living thing, but as soon as Adam reaches toward the contorted mass of Roberts's limbs and bike spokes, it starts to loosen up. Begins to move away from him.

But he's too late. He can tell from how wildly Roberts's eyes darted around, by how frantic his gasps sounded before they stopped. He's dead by the time he hits the floor, moments after the bike unfolded from around his body and let him go.

"Fucking hell," Rao breathes, eyes wide.

"Asphyxiation isn't the worst way to go," Adam murmurs. He calls back at the team. "Watch your step."

A pause. Lights tracking through the corridor to his voice, to his face.

Lights tracking down to find Roberts's body.

"Yes, sir." Estrada is the first to speak. The rest echo him.

Baker trots up. Follows orders, watching his step. Quick but careful. "Cleanup after mission success?" he asks.

Adam takes a breath. "Not my area. We continue as planned. Protect the asset, proceed to objective. Estrada, take point. Move forward."

———

The team moves glacially, carefully, after the initial loss. Even Rhodes looks a little rattled when Adam checks formation. She's talking to Rao now, walking in front of him. He can hear every word.

"Roberts wasn't in a trance like the others," Rao says.

"Didn't seem to be," Rhodes agrees. "It's unfortunate that we haven't evidence to know whether he was drawn to that particular EPGO."

"He wasn't."

"Rao—"

"One day you'll trust my hunches," Rao sighs. "If you survive this."

"I'm immune."

"Roberts thought he was too."

"Yes, he did," Rhodes says mildly. "But he wasn't."

Rao exhales. A sharp hiss. "I knew it. Bloody hell, Veronica."

"Soldiers die all the time," she replies. Sounds bored. This kind of mindset isn't new to Adam. People think of soldiers that way. Cannon fodder. Human shields. Sentient robots with guns. "No one enlists thinking they're immune to bullets."

"He thought he was immune when he agreed to this mission."

Sure as shit the others think so too. Adam speaks then, low and quiet. "Volume control, Rao," he warns.

"Shit," Rao whispers. "All of them, Veronica?"

"You'll be perfectly safe, Rao. As will Colonel Rubenstein. As will I."

"D'you think? Because that murderous bike wasn't Roberts's EPGO."

"No. That *was* interesting, wasn't it? He was killed, and quickly. One might go so far as to say purposefully."

Two steps in silence. Creaks of metal behind them. Lights twinkling ahead.

"Actively hostile." Adam finally says what he assumes they're all thinking.

"Which means immunity doesn't count for shit anymore, Veronica," Rao adds. "Not when Fisher-Price fuck knows what is out there braying for blood."

Rhodes makes a thoughtful, almost melodic sound. "That EPGO was notable, yes—"

"Not the point I was making," Rao mutters.

"Since it was free roaming. Unattached from a creator. And a generalized object, wouldn't you agree? Most people had a childhood bicycle. Nostalgia manifested through shared cultural experience rather than from an individual's personal memories."

"Like the radio," Rao says, "in your ward."

"Very good catch."

"Piss off, Veronica."

"Think of what that could imply," she goes on. Adam can hear the hunger in her voice. "We already know Prophet changes periodically to suit its purpose. It could be casting a wider net."

Purpose. Rao looks back at Adam, eyes wide. Adam meets his gaze. He heard it all.

Farther down the corridor, slow, flashing lights shine from under a door, pooling on the floor. "Sweep?" Estrada inquires, calling down the line.

Adam looks back. Gives him the nod. "Go."

A quick reshuffle, with only Rao and Rhodes momentarily confused about where to stand. Adam keeps Rao close. He couldn't give a fuck about where Rhodes finds herself.

"Do you hear that?" Rao murmurs to Adam seconds before he does. Notes trilling electronically.

Adam glances at Rao. "What is that?"

Estrada cuts them off. "It's Pac-Man," he says. "Nothing else sounds like that."

Rao pulls at Adam's arm. "Look," he demands and in the same breath, "Estrada—"

It's too late. Estrada's pushing the door open enough to let the light spill out, blue and bright, getting brighter as the music gets louder.

"Rao," Adam says, stepping aside to let Rao move in. To let him lay hands. Do what he does.

"What's his first name again?" Rao asks. Adam doesn't remember but that doesn't matter. Rao knows Estrada's first name. He isn't asking for information but trying to fill the air with noise, cover the distorted beeps calling out to them. "Alejandro, mate—"

"Boards," Estrada interrupts, dropping his weapon to the floor, "is the name people used to have for levels. It's all different now."

Rao follows after and Adam behind him, but they're not quick enough to stop Estrada from moving to the source of the light. It's an arcade cabinet. Pac-Man, like Estrada said. The room smells like pizza grease and worn cotton. Instinctively, Adam looks down at his feet. He expects the carpet underfoot but not how it grows out from under the cabinet like a rash. Dark woven tendrils with haphazardly dotted russet-tinged geometric shapes designed to look amazing under ultraviolet bulbs. His feet, Rao's feet, Estrada's—their boots pull at the fabric, soaked to saturation. Too thick to be water.

Someone already died in here.

Adam is looking around for the corpse when Estrada reaches the buttons in front of him. He sighs bodily in relief. Pixelated ghosts flicker up, looping electronic notes.

"Rao," Adam says as Estrada bows over the glass in front of him. The game plays at an angle, not straight on, and Estrada's changed his stance to compensate. He bends with the cabinet, a silhouette against the flicker. He isn't suddenly unresponsive, like everyone else coming into contact with their EPGOs, but passive. His fingers are moving, one hand resting on buttons and the other driving a small joystick. Precise movements. He looks calm. In the zone. Whenever Adam hears another burst of celebratory noises, Estrada exhales like he's lining up a shot.

Rao doesn't say anything. He steps forward, puts a hand on the back of Estrada's neck, and closes his eyes. Adam expects the usual: Rao's jaw relaxing, his eyelids fluttering. He expects to see Estrada step back from the video game. He doesn't expect Rao's frown. Doesn't expect it when Rao tugs on Estrada's collar to expose more skin, place a second hand next to the first.

Adam opens his mouth to ask, but Rao is already answering. "I'm trying, Adam," he says, voice strained. Takes his hand away. Adam catches the barest hint of silver on one palm before it disappears into him like every other time. Estrada doesn't back away from the cabinet.

He turns his head. Only his head. Mouth open, eyes wild in silent fear and obvious pain. Adam steps forward to help, sees Estrada's fingers are fused to the brightly colored plastic of the buttons. Still pressing. Still playing the game. And when Adam takes that step forward, the sounds and lights judder in time with Estrada's sudden scream of pain. The cabinet's trying to get away from Adam. It can't.

Estrada doesn't stay lucid for long. As soon as Adam backs off an inch, the game continues. Even the fused hand operates like it's meant to, Estrada's eyes back on the screen.

Rao doesn't try to touch him again. Doesn't reach out to him, doesn't attempt to break the spell he's under. Just stares at the game. There's movement behind Adam. Rhodes, coming into the room to pull Rao out. Rao goes quietly. Doesn't fight her at all.

Now the flickering gets sharper, the lights brighter, the noises louder. A cascade of aural fireworks. Adam should follow Rao out of here. He doesn't. It's not about saving anyone's life in this room. They're too late for that. They were too late as soon as they heard the music in the corridor. Adam's too late. Too late to see Estrada take his other hand off the joystick and press it to the screen. Too late to see the glass get smeared with blood. Too late to realize the cabinet's hood is bowing over Estrada as he bends to get closer to the game. Adam can see the yellow wedge of Pac-Man reflected in Estrada's eyes. Knows what's happening only as it happens. Way too late to help anyone, even if he could get close enough to do something.

The hood's curve is unnatural, and the whole cabinet starts to crumple as a result. It creases like a beer can and takes Estrada's whole body with it. There's no struggle. The *wakkawakkawakka* noise of the game is deafening now. It churns in his stomach like a heavy bass through a speaker. It's the only noise he can hear.

No screams. No nothing.

When the cabinet straightens up again, Adam looks down at his boots. Even wetter now. He understands why he didn't see a body before. The screen flashes, numbers strobing in the dark.

3,333,360.

"Adam."

It's Rao. He's at the door, Rhodes's arm slung across his chest. But he's not trying to pull away. He's waving Adam back away from the puddled remains of Estrada. When Adam gets close, he sees the strain on Rao's face. "I wish I'd made a better job of it in Kabul," Rao mutters. "Because if I were dead now, then I wouldn't have had to see that."

"You don't mean that," Adam responds.

"I *nearly* mean it, Adam."

"You don't mean it."

CHAPTER 71

"Colonel, there's— Shit, what happened here?" It's Stewart, fingers tightening around his MP5. Garcia appears behind him, eyes wide under his helmet.

"We lost Estrada," Adam says. "What's the situation?"

"Baker."

"Details."

"Dead."

"How?"

"Something. I saw hands."

"You didn't investigate?"

"With respect, sir, fuck that all the way home. No, I did not."

"I saw it," Garcia says. "Someone's nonna got him."

"Nonna."

"Something like a grandma, sir."

"Whatever it was, it was fucking fast," Stewart adds. "It's gone."

And then there were five, Rao thinks.

Outside in the corridor the light is rising fast. Pearl and pink, coloured like sunrise. Tastes of distance, sea air. Rao stares at the walls as they brighten and wonders if what he's feeling is usual in lulls like these in the midst of mortal horrors. Everything's smooth and flowing fast inside; everything outside is clear, sharp edged, etched impossibly fine. And the most unaccountable thing of all—he feels entirely himself. Which is, he thinks with a shiver of surprise, an experience he's never, ever had before. Not like this. He's taken a shit ton of stuff over the years, but there's no parallel, no analogy. It's like his soul, his body, his mind have snapped into sudden, perfect alignment. He watches Adam and Garcia return from Baker's body. They've left him where he fell or was dragged;

from here he's a dim smudge of pink-washed camouflage against the wall at the far end of the corridor. Adam walks straight past Rao to Veronica.

"Couldn't close his eyes," he tells her tonelessly. "They've been torn out."

Adam isn't helping, Rao thinks. Or maybe, just maybe, he's not helping on purpose.

Then Garcia starts. Jumps. Mutters. Throws his HK to the ground. Tosses it away from him. It lands without a clatter like it's fallen on carpet, not concrete. Nothing seems wrong apart from his action, but he's frozen to the spot, staring down at his weapon.

Adam raises a hand, is at Garcia's side in moments. Cautiously, he looks him up and down. "Report," he says.

Garcia shakes his head. "I don't . . ." he starts.

"The fuck," Stewart calls. "Pick it up."

Garcia shakes his head rapidly. He's breathing hard.

"What's your situation," Adam commands.

Garcia blinks, shuts his eyes. "Don't touch it."

Rao looks at the gun. It's not right. It's not—

"It moved," Garcia says. "Swear to God. It *squirmed*."

Adam looks over to Rao, raises his eyebrows, and Rao walks over, crouches to examine the thing. It looks fine. It's wrong, wrong, wrong. He puts out a hand—

"Rao?" Adam warns.

"Yeah, you should be doing this, not me," Rao says. He runs his fingertips along the barrel, and the gun flinches like the flank of a horse.

"It's not a gun anymore," he says. "Everyone check their weapons."

Veronica already has. Her pistol has turned to glass. She holds it up in the sunrise light, entranced. Slips it back in its holster. She wants to keep it.

"Mine's ok, I think?" Stewart says. He tilts it, racks it, unclips the magazine. But as he clips the mag back in, the weapon crumbles in his hands, falls to pieces like it's made of charcoal. Soft dust sifts through the air. His gloves are black. A strangled shout from Garcia, a thud by Rao's foot, and when Rao looks down, he nearly shouts too. There's a row of tiny eyes in the slide of the Beretta, and they're blinking at him. He rises rapidly to his feet.

Adam's checking his weapons and ammo. The barrel of his HK is vaguely translucent. He shakes his head and lays it down. But it looks like his two body-carried 9 mils and clips are fine.

"You're *not* normal," Rao says, grinning. "Thank fuck."

Adam ignores that. He's looking intently at Garcia and Stewart. They're backing away from the weapons on the floor, and Rao knows without testing the truth of it what's happening.

"This is fucked," Stewart hisses. "We need to execute a tactical withdrawal."

"We're leaving," Garcia blurts.

Adam blinks, turns to Rao. "Rao?"

"What?"

"What do you want to do?"

"Oh," he says lightly. "I'm not going anywhere."

"Rhodes?"

"I want to see this through," she tells him. She doesn't sound sure, but Adam accepts her words and turns back to Garcia and Stewart.

"We have an objective," he says tightly.

"We're refusing orders, right now, sir," Stewart grits out.

A few seconds pass. Adam sighs. "I won't tell a goddamned soul. You're free to leave."

Relieved, they turn and walk away. Rao's watching their retreating backs when there's a squeal of horror. Veronica. She's got her boot on something, is pressing it to the floor. Rao can't make it out. It's green and rounded, looks like fabric, and there are flailing arms and things that could be legs—two—but somehow he's sure there are more. He watches her stamp down, hard, as if she's dealing with a cockroach, sees the thing turn as her boot descends. It's a Kermit, with bloodshot Ping-Pong eyes and a mouth full of darkness, hands reaching up towards her.

She keeps stamping until it breaks. Shatters into pieces like a bowl. She turns and vomits, moves quickly away, stands behind Adam, wiping her mouth. Garcia and Stewart had been watching, had seen it all too, and they're staring at the shards of Muppet, its limbs still writhing, when the telltale attacks.

It's fast. It's fast and earsplittingly loud. It rings like a bell. A repeated bell, a school bell. The air is chokingly thick with chalk and the scent of ketchup and sour milk. Flat shoes. A skirt. It's short but somehow elongated, a bun of mousy hair, a face that radiates infinite kindness despite lacking any features except a mouth. Rao takes in this sight in one vertiginous split second, because it's fast, it's appalling how fast it is, skittering towards them, metallic splinters pouring from it and clicking to the floor, and somehow, though heading straight for Garcia and Stewart, Rao's sure it's moving sideways, away from them.

It's not. The school bell rings, chalk dust trembling in the air. It has arms, spindly yet somehow plump, rings and fingers on the one hand that reaches as the thing slips fast across the floor. One huge hand grabs Stewart from behind, reaches over his helmet, cupping his skull, and Stewart jerks as the fingers sink into his eyes, burying themselves far past the things pretending to be knuckles, and like a shot-putter uncoiling, the other arm flashes out to grip Garcia around his jaw and throat. The fingers sink deep into Garcia's neck, sheets of blood streaming down his front, and Rao's watching the soldier boys kick out their death throes to the sounds of school. There's drumming feet in corridors, now, high, childish laughter, and there's a series of sharp retorts to his left, gunfire, and the thing's face shreds into tatters. *Automatic*, Rao thinks. *He shot automatically.* Because that headshot damage doesn't even slow it, it's coming towards Rao dragging Garcia and Stewart like they're part of it, and it's moving like a seal on a quayside, now, undulating, but Adam's in front of him now, protecting him, Rao knows, that's what he's doing, because Rubenstein makes things better, doesn't he.

Clink of shell casings. Chalk dust. Sulphur. Adam's walking right towards the thing and it's stopped its advance, is backing away from him fast, and it's going to fuck off into the bowels of the building with its dead soldiers, but it might not. It might not get away, because Adam's shooting at its knees now, and every shot connects, and it's slowing, because Adam.

Who is everything. He's focus in the midst of chaos, sanity in action, the steel-true *i* in the dot of the ocean. All the safety the world possesses, right there, and this stupid line is running through Rao's head: *Adam's brilliant at this*. Because he is, isn't he. Every round rips away more of what that thing is, and Adam is nothing like he was when he fought the goons in the motel, nothing like he was when he sparred in that backroom, it's like he's singing, now, like this is an aria and every note is perfect, pitched to shatter glass. Like the whole building resonates with every step, every shot.

Fuck, Rao thinks. *Adam*.

Adam's above it now. He's pulled a knife. The thing's not able to move away from him anymore, though it's trying to. Rao watches him sink the point of the blade into its wrist, just above Stewart's helmet. He does so speculatively, as if he's expecting to meet resistance, seeking the right path to carve through sinew and joints, but there's no resistance. The point slips right through. He pulls out the blade, changes the angle, and with a single stroke slices the limb away, freeing Stewart from the thing that killed him. He props Stewart's body against the wall, moving what's left of his head upright, then turns back and frees Garcia, whose visible skin is slack and paper white and battle dress red ruin.

Now Adam's standing, looking down at the thing on the floor, frowning. It's down but not out, dragging itself incrementally back along the corridor.

"Rao," he calls.

"Yes, love?"

"Can you make something heavy on top of it, stop it moving?"

"Like what?"

"Whatever you like. Use your imagination."

"I don't—ok."

He magics it into existence, then giggles at his creation. For no good reason he'd imagined a transparent Lucite paperweight, one of those touristic souvenirs with ferns and flowers and shells inside, but he's made it of glass and messed with the scale. It's vast. The thing's caught, trapped motionless inside it.

"Nice," Adam says.

"Shit," Rao exclaims.

"What?"

"I could have . . . before, you know? Done this before."

Adam looks at him. "Let's take five, Rao."

They sit for a while, backs against the wall like the corpses a few feet to their right. Rao doesn't look at them. Stares instead at the staples and spent casings littering the floor, the trail of smeared blood with Adam's boot prints tracked through it. And he wonders why in hell he feels fine.

"I should be more freaked out," he says suddenly. "But watching that, it was like . . ."

"Watching a movie."

"Yeah. Exactly. *The Thing*, to be specific. I saw that when I was thirteen and didn't sleep for a fortnight. The head on the table, the spider with the legs."

Adam smiles. "It was like that, yeah."

"But a teacher."

"*Substitute* teacher."

Rao snorts. "Fucking hell, love. Are you always this funny when staring death in the face?"

A sidelong look, amused. Then the faintest narrowing of eyes. "How are you feeling, Rao?"

"Less frightened than I have any right to be. Is this adrenaline? Is this why you always look so resigned? You feel like this all the time?"

"How are *you* feeling, Rao?"

"Why are you asking?"

"Your pupils are blown."

"It's dark in here."

"No, it isn't. But . . . you look steady. You solid?"

"Yeah, I'm good. Where's Rhodes?"

"No idea."

"We should look for her."

"No, we shouldn't."

"Leave no man behind?"

"She's not my concern."

"Adam—"

"Rhodes can look out for herself."

"So what now?"

"We find De Witte."

CHAPTER 72

Deeper in, the corridors are grim. The light feels singed, flutters arrhythmically. For a while the walls and ceilings are brown velvet, the floor beneath their feet buttoned like leather upholstery. For twenty feet, the stench of roses is so overpowering that Rao is forced to hold his breath; even Adam gags. A small plush purple platypus dragging itself towards them on yellow felt flippers gets pinned to the ground by one of Adam's knives and is left there, squeaking in protest.

Then follows a stretch of wood panelling punctuated with the silver of malformed sporting trophies, which turns, a few yards farther on, into a mess of beige computer casings bled into brickwork, scraps of glossy black screens winking with green DOS prompts.

The first door they try opens into a spacious storage area. Bare walls, a stack of containers and shelves. In the middle of the vinyl floor a heap of brightly coloured Tamagotchis squirm against their own chains. The noise inside the room is atrocious, an ear-splitting mess of voices, advertising jingles, laughter, snatches of *Sugar, Sugar*, the NASA Quindar tone, screams from fairground rides. It cuts out as soon as the door is closed.

The next door is faced with a sheet of polished copper.

"RadSafe counting room," Rao announces.

"Yeah. The engineer."

She's lying in the middle of the floor, a small, broken corpse in a white coat, a hazmat mask next to her, her phone still gripped tightly in one hand. Around her, equidistantly spaced, a grid, a perfect array of green plush worms with nightcaps and glowing plastic faces.

"Night-lights," Rao says. "I had one of these. Fuck. *Fuck*," he adds. There are lights beneath the engineer's skin. Inside her arms, her torso, inside her face. The grid of glowworms manifested itself right through her. He stares, swallows back something like an apology. This death is worse, somehow, than Monty's. Worse than any dealt by the horrors back there. It's so quiet. She looks so terribly alone.

The following room is dark and dense with fog. Dripping water. Smells like fall. Banks of flat-screens flicker with static CRT snow. Adam switches on his flashlight. The beam picks out a column of bark half buried in the far wall, and above and around it a tangle of branches with serrated grey leaves and shining fruit.

Rao speaks through the hiss of white noise that sounds like heavy rain.

"Fuck, it's De Witte."

He's on his knees beneath one of the branches, head bowed, hair dishevelled and damp. Both hands are high above his head, clutching an apple he'd reached for, the branch bowed with his weight. His fingers are golden, fused with the apple, spotted with pores and pits, the backs of his hands bulging horribly. Adam crouches, lifts two fingers to De Witte's throat. Rao thinks of Ed dying in the mud. Thinks of the men in cells in Kabul they kept like this, for longer than this.

"Lucky he didn't get full-body contact," Adam's saying. "His hands are gone but his pulse is strong. I'll get out of the way so you can—"

"Adam."

Adam raises his eyes.

"This isn't why I came."

"You don't want to cure him?"

"Nah. Never wanted to in the first place. Man's a cunt. War criminal. Wants to take over the world. But that's not what I mean. Helping him isn't why I'm here." Adam opens his mouth to speak, and Rao raises a hand to hush him. "Don't hold up your fingers and ask me to count them, love. It's the twenty-seventh of November, 2010, and I know who you are, and I know who the president is, and I continue to know what's true and what isn't. With the usual exception. It's just," he points at De Witte, "he is not why I'm here."

"Ok," Adam says, rising to his feet. "What's your personal objective?"

Rao reaches for an answer. He can't find one. He's pinging between the meanings of the terms "immanent" and "imminent" in his head, and he can't get past them to where the knowledge is. "There aren't words for it," he says shortly. "I know how that sounds but trust me. All I know is it was out there. I mean, it's out there." He gestures behind him. "Also, if I fix De Witte now, he's just going to be another thing for you to worry about, because from what I've heard he's a super-high-maintenance asshole, and that's before spending three days hanging from a tree."

Adam's lips twitch. "Ok. We'll come back for him when you've completed your objective. Please inform me when you know what that objective is."

"Don't nag, love. I'll let you know."

Adam smiles at that, glances up at the tree. Frowns. Looks more closely. "Huh," he says. "These apples aren't apples."

"No shit."

"They're gold. I think they're gold."

"Yeah," Rao says. "Hesperides. Doesn't surprise me in the least. You're not thinking of pocketing a few?"

Adam snorts. "Fuck off."

"Yes, let's." Rao loves it when Adam swears like that. "Things to do, places to be."

"Right. You just don't know what they are."

"You're nagging."

"No, just stating the facts, Rao." They're both grinning. The disaster this mission's become, their walking away from De Witte, shock, adrenaline, Prophet in the air: this sudden surge of elation could come from any of those things and all of them. Rao feels peculiarly porous, permeable. Wonders if Adam's caught this mood from him. The elation is a full-on champagne-bubbles birthday morning coming-up high, and it's making whatever Rao needs to do so exquisitely alluring it's hard not to bolt from the room and run to find it.

But he feels it before he hears it.

Feels it in his head, like in the diner.

Ed's gone. Ed's gone, and that stings inside him, and Nancy's gone, and Roberts is gone, and the others, too, and Polheath is done. Though somewhere, he knows, Polheath is still happening.

But it's not Sinatra he's hearing now.

Adam's already looking at the source of the music. His gun is drawn but pointed down. It's a song. A simple song, sung by someone who's not good at singing. At the end of the corridor is an archway deep enough to be a tunnel and emerging from it is a man in his midforties with greying hair. He looks untouched by any telltales. At first, Rao thinks this man walking towards them, smiling and singing, shrugging off his jacket, must be immune.

But that's not true. He knows that isn't true.

And the words of the song he's hearing are—

Rao shakes his head. He understands the words perfectly, knows what the man is singing, but the words he's using aren't English.

No, they are. They're definitely English but they're also every language he's ever spoken, ever heard, ever heard of, all at once. Each word resonates like . . . Rao thinks of how texts have described the inhuman voices of angels as the man walks easily towards him. He's singing to Rao. He's singing *for* Rao. Singing about how the weather in the neighbourhood is perfect. Asking if Rao would be his . . . if Rao could be his. The words sound like a seduction, but not the usual kind. Rao's being sung to like he's a child.

The man tilts his head. He shrugs off his jacket, lets it fall to the ground. Rao watches it drop and crumple onto the concrete, and when he looks back up, the singing man is holding a cardigan so red it hurts Rao's eyes. Technicolor.

Rao glances at Adam. He's frozen in horror. Which is impossible. Adam doesn't get horrified. Bare minutes ago, they watched a man get eaten by a training bike. *That* was horrifying. Adam's mouth is moving, silently mouthing the words to the song like he knows it by heart.

"Adam," Rao says.

Adam lowers his weapon as the singing man approaches. Silvered hair, brushed to one side. Salt and pepper eyebrows. He's the most charming person Rao has ever seen. But it isn't charm. Rao isn't charmed. The man's smile is warm in a way that speaks of absolute safety. Seeing it, Rao can relax. Like he's just walked through the door after a cold day, like his mum is in the kitchen cooking dinner and his dad is watching the telly too loudly. Safe, familiar, welcome. Warm. All in a smile.

The man is still singing. He sings of the day, how beautiful it is, how it belongs to them, how it's theirs to make the most of. He zips up his cardigan gleefully. When Adam shakes out a breath, it takes everything Rao has to look away from this serenade to check on him. Now the horror is gone from Adam's face. He looks—

Adam looks—

He looks like he does when he's sleeping. He looks like he does moments after he laughs. Glimpses of what happiness might look like on Adam's face.

The song continues. The man is still asking Rao to be his, now they are together again.

Adam's expression shifts. Rao feels it too. A pull to this man. A desperate longing for the welcoming safety his presence offers. *Prophet*, Rao thinks. Knows. No threat but Prophet.

Now the man halts. He's standing in front of Rao, eyes twinkling. That red cardigan is grafted to his skin at his neck. He's not human. But he's not a telltale. This man is different. And he's not perfect. Stupidly, wildly, Rao knows he could have done a better job. He could have made this man *perfectly*.

The smile on the man's face is softer now, as he croons another plea for Rao to be his neighbour. He offers his hand. Adam inhales sharply. All the air is gone from Rao's lungs.

The man speaks, then. A normal voice. Friendly. American. Warm, welcome, familiar. Safe.

He's glad, he tells Rao, they're together again.

Rao takes his hand.

There's Prophet in this man, and it is drawn into Rao. Bigger and badder this time. Silver behind his vision for a breath, forever, for a second. He stands, dizzy and solid, hears a soft thud.

It takes too long, this time, to blink himself back into the room.

Mercury, he reminds himself.

Adam, he remembers.

Adam's kneeling by the body of the man Prophet made. "Rao," he's saying, far away. Distant. Muffled like tinnitus. Underwater. In the past. Far in the future. *Right now*, he reminds himself. They're both right here, and it's now. "Did you just kill Mister Rogers?"

"Did you know him, love?"

Adam looks up at him, mouth open.

"Adam. He came from there. It's in there. He was *welcoming me*."

The door's green paint has curled back in hexagonal patterns to reveal the steel beneath. Very cautiously, Adam walks up, brushes its surface with the back of one hand.

"It's here," Rao says.

"This is what you want?"

"Yeah. It's where I need to be."

Adam's face contorts briefly. He lifts a hand to the side of his face, heel to ear. The tips of his fingers pale with pressure as he pushes them hard against his helmet. "I'm going in," he says. "Stay here." Sliding the door open, he slips through. But Rao can't wait. The draw of the room beyond is inexorable, and it's agony that Adam's out of his sight. He steps over the threshold into the hot bay.

CHAPTER 73

It's cavernous. Vast. An aircraft hangar. It tastes sacred. A temple. A cathedral. It's crushingly silent but singing with noise too deep to hear, a cacophony so appallingly loud Rao's chest hurts with it. Adam's a silhouette in winter light. His jaw has dropped. His eyes are wide. He's holstered his pistol. Knows there's nothing a firearm could do against this. He doesn't move, doesn't budge an inch even when Rao stands against him, shoulder to shoulder.

"Is all this—" Adam's voice is muffled like he's speaking into falling snow.

"Yes, love."

Every inch of the hall is covered with Prophet. It resembles metallic rime ice, flocked lace. Veins. Branches. The threading map of a ravenous fungus. For a moment, Rao's back in Ranthambore, walking in the groves of the banyan tree through slanting sun. His eyes slip across the buried shapes of Lunastus's storage system along the nearside wall. Prophet's slumped over them in drifts, over the far doors, obscuring the inspection windows, furring the pipework, the mezzanine, blanketing the numerous corpses spread across the floor. Rao blinks back what feels like blindness, hears Adam's voice.

"What did you say?" he asks.

"What's the plan," Adam repeats.

"The plan."

"Yes. Is there a plan?"

That's funny. It's genuinely funny, and Rao can't hold back the laugh it provokes. It feels like the struggle for breath after a storm of tears.

"I think there is a plan, love," he says. "But it isn't mine."

"Rao, we should go."

Rao looks at him, laughter gone.

"I can't."

"You can. Come on."

He's standing oddly, one foot pointed slightly inwards, hands crooked and shaking by his sides.

"I can't," he says again.

It's that point inside him. The tiny point buried deep inside. The cold. It's opened its arms and is beckoning everything in. He feels a desperate flash of refusal that's summarily dismissed, and he breathes in once and breathes out once, and knows exactly what he is. What he's for. *Funny*, he thinks. *I always knew*. An absurd memory of the moustached face of his career counsellor at school, the one who told him that his questionnaire showed he wanted to help people, and maybe he should consider medical school or joining the police, fast track. And Rao had shaken his head then, amused as all hell, and he's shaking his head now, but there's no amusement. He's recoiling from what's happening to him, but he can't stop it. The cold has opened its arms and it is beckoning everything in.

*

Adam has to blink. He blinks, and then he can't open his eyes. But he sees it all anyway. Like the afterimage of staring at the sun, the sight burns bright and close and terrible against his lids. All the Prophet in the hot bay changes state at once. It slips liquid as running glass, soft as frost on a frozen vodka bottle. Runs along the floor, slides from the ceiling, pours down the walls, flows toward Rao like it's being pulled by gravity.

It's falling into him. Adam's eyes jerk open and he can't shut them. He wants to. Both Rao's hands are held out from his sides. Sinuous ropes of Prophet are streaming up to them from the floor. His head is thrown back, mouth wide, and there's no sound but still Adam can hear him scream, and when Prophet reaches his chest and throat, it pours into his mouth and with a sickening curl like a silvered fishtail slipping underwater the last of it disappears inside.

It's all in him.

He's still standing. His head is bowed like he's at prayer, his chest is heaving, and there's no Prophet anywhere. The room is empty, and Rao is—

How can it all be in him? *How?*

Rao raises his head and looks toward Adam. Not at him. His eyes are far away. There's blood around his mouth. It's terrible to see Rao's face so still, so devoid of expression.

"Rao—" Adam begins.

"Everything's going to be fine. Wait there."

"I'm not going anywhere."

Rao shuts his eyes. His face is animated again. "I can't know, can I?" The laugh is low, delighted, conspiratorial, the laugh in the motel with the lizard. But there's something in it screwed right to the limit. "So that's why," he says. "Fuck."

A pause. "Fuck," he says again. Low, astounded. He's not talking to Adam.

"Rao?"

Rao raises a hand. "Hang on, love, just wait. Be with you in a second." His voice is precise, teetering on the edge of laughter. His punch-drunk voice. He grins. It's a brilliant smile. But his open eyes are dully shining metal, and the tears falling from them are beads of mercury, disappearing into his skin as they track down his cheeks.

Is he blind now? He's working through how this will impact his exfil in the rapidly narrowing window in which both of them survive when he sees Rao's eyes clear. They're dark now, and steady, and they're looking right at him, but the sight is almost worse. Adam thinks of the time in basic when an idiot kid jokingly put an unloaded M9 to his own head, everyone laughing. Everyone laughing but Adam because he'd seen something far too true in the kid's eyes.

He shivers. The temperature's plummeting. Sharp on his face. Every breath is fog. He looks down. Frost is crawling across the mess on the floor, furring the toes of his boots, climbing up his laces. It's mesmerizing, but his eyes won't stay where they're put.

They're pulled to the space behind Rao, where the air is crackling, rippling like a sheet on a line in the wind. Patterns are meshing through it. They're painful to look at; they tighten his temples like a migraine.

Then slowly, sickeningly, the space between Rao and the far wall begins to open inward. No. Downward. Adam steps back with a lurch of visceral panic, convinced they're both about to plummet into it. No. It's not down. It's not any direction. What's behind Rao is light. Not any color Adam's seen before. It's not bright, but it's sharp, picking at the back of his eyes like sun off a side-view mirror driving east on a winter afternoon.

The light flutters, dims, and now Adam's looking into an endless corridor thick with smoke. Dark, like burn-pit smoke, the aftermath of a high explosive charge. Inside it are flashes like miniature electrical storms that flicker, shift, and resolve themselves into points of fierce white light. The lights hang there. They're moving too. Slow constellations. Impossible to tell how many. Like the desert sky. Somehow too close, crowding in, and so distant they make his skin crawl.

Adam's useless here. Worse than useless. He's doing nothing.

No. He's doing what Rao asked. He's waiting. That makes it easier.

But the cold is a knife now, grating against bone. It's getting hard to stand. He's so tired. He wants to sleep. It's kind of funny. Never thought it'd be hypothermia. Always thought he'd be bleeding out at the end. He sways a little, knows he's seconds away from sinking to the floor and letting it happen. Doesn't seem any good reason not to.

Wait.

Rao asked him to wait.

Rao. He blinks ice away. Rao's standing right there. There's no frost on his skin, no ice in his beard, horror on his face.

"Shit, shit, I'm so sorry, love," he whispers, and Adam feels warmth envelop him, instant and entire, rivulets of water pouring down his scalp as the ice melts, coursing down his cheeks and into his mouth. It tastes, he thinks dimly, of aniseed and rainwater. The warmth brings in its wake a wave of terror. Nothing is moving except the lights behind Rao, but everything is falling toward him and everything's falling away from him, because Rao's the center of all this, and Adam doesn't know what this is. He drags in a breath, starts counting the lights behind Rao's head to keep himself sane, when everything flips. What was darkness is now the soft orange of Los Angeles sunset smog, and the pale points of light have turned into a host of black shapes, tiny flat polygons, jerking slightly, hitching and fluttering as if they're . . .

"They're kites," Adam says—suddenly, stupidly sure.

Rao nods. "They can be anything."

The kites freeze in place. Fall from what isn't the sky. They fall like shot birds, dead projectiles, onto . . . Adam can't make out what they are: things resolving from a chaos of mess and light. Containers. They're things to hold the kites, the stars, in rows. Racks of wooden trays with pale satin linings. So many. An infinity of trays. The ones right by Rao's hands are ordinary sized. The ones in the far distance are little more than dust. But they're all here. All on the same plane. It's like— Adam remembers standing between two mirrors when he was small, putting his hand up to press his fingers against the glass of the mirror he was holding, staring through it at the mirror on the wall, at his bedroom, at the posters, the folded shirts on his desk, the models of aircraft on the windowsill—and past that room into another room behind it, and another behind it, rooms receding into infinity. But flat. All in the same place.

He's standing between two mirrors. That's all.

That's what he's telling himself, though he knows it's not true, as he watches Rao reach out for the trays and start sorting through them. He's looking for something as casually as if he were searching for the right pair of sunglasses on the rack of an airport Hudson's, and he's searching with such speed and assurance Adam feels his fingers twitch, unbidden, with the memory of shuffling cards. Sees Rao halt, stop, pull at a tray. The tray is small, no bigger than a .22 round, but Rao makes it bigger, or it makes itself bigger, or Prophet does, and Rao smiles then and picks something from it. Drops it on his left palm. It's dark, and small, and round, the size of an olive. Adam's throat closes, looking at it. It's *terrifying*.

"Do you want it?" Rao says.

Adam can't speak of it. He tries. His throat won't let him.

Rao blinks, looks perplexed. "How long was that?"

"Was what?"

"Since I said something."

"About two seconds, Rao."

Wonderment. "Was it?" His voice is far shakier now. "I'm in a lot of places at once, Adam. I can't stay long." He proffers his palm again. "Do you want it?"

"Rao, I don't know what it is."

"No. Sorry. Of course you don't." He licks his lips. Swallows. "Well. I guess you could call it a second chance." He picks the thing off his palm. Holds it between his fingers. There's a star in it, Adam sees. No, not in it. It's sliding around, just below the surface.

"Asterism," Rao says. "I used to love these stones. This isn't a black sapphire, though, love, it's just what it's making one look like here. Has to be familiar things for me, for this, know what I mean?"

"Yeah," Adam lies. "So what is it?"

"It's the world where you went with your aunt."

He doesn't know the right thing to say. "Do you want me to wear this?" he tries.

"No. I want you to live it."

A low grinding noise, tectonic plates shifting against one another: Adam can feel it in his chest. Dust blows against him; it's not ice now. It's ash. He's not sure what's under his feet and he doesn't want to look.

"Rao," he says slowly. "I don't understand what you mean."

"It. You know," Rao explains, "it's not just here. Now."

"You mean Prophet?"

"Yeah. That. We brought it here, let it in, sort of. But it's not just here. You were right about that. Runs through all . . ." Rao screws his eyes tight, makes the face he does when he's searching for words when he's high. "Times. Places. Ties? Dimensions." He grimaces. He doesn't like the words he's using. "Universes. But it can't make new things. It needs us to do that." He beams. "Needs me, actually, love. Specifically."

Adam hates this. Rao is talking like he's working on finding the best ramen place in town while Prophet slides across his eyes like ink on water and his mouth is sometimes so full of it his words are unclear. When he chuckles, it sounds like his mouth is full of blood. "Vahana. I'm a vahana. I really am." He shakes his head. His voice clears suddenly. "Now changed then," he says seriously. "No, made then. Fuck. Words. Bear with me, please. Please, Adam. It's important. This is the thing. I've always been here. Right here, because the thing is, it can't create on its own. It needs a mind to do that. And there are a lot of places, universes, that don't have complicated things in them, and it likes things complicated. Complicated is life, yeah? That's what it does. Takes life to places where there's none. So . . ." Rao falls silent. No. He doesn't fall silent. He stops moving.

Everything does. Blurs, stops dead. The sensation is so exactly like looking through a defocused scope Adam wants to reach up and fix it. But he can't move. Wants to scream. Can't. Time has pressed him into glass. Then, with a low, soft crack like the slowed-down noise of ice dropped into warm scotch, everything is back in movement. More ash against his face, blown against his skin, raw citrus in his mouth.

"So I can make anything now. Make a whole world. Remake this one," Rao says, as if he hadn't stopped at all. "So this"—he holds up the sapphire—"this, and all the others, what they are, are alternate worlds. Very close to this one. Like in sci-fi."

"You don't read sci-fi, Rao."

Desperate. He's desperate for everything to be—

"It's why I can't tell. Why I've never been able to tell. Why—" His voice dies away like the words he's using have turned into something else. Adam hates how obviously he's struggling to talk. The pain of witnessing it is clean, deep, unspeakable. Then Rao relaxes, speaks quickly, mouth clear of metal, his voice soft and serious. "With you. As long as I've known you, I've been trying to read you." He frowns. "The way Prophet works, I've always known you. And I've seen all of you, all the Adam Rubensteins in all the universes closest to this one, all the choices they made, all the things they came to be, all the branching ramifications of every decision they made, everything they did and said, everything that happened to them." He pauses. "And all their truths obscure yours. Like . . . you say you grew up in Vegas? I heard that and it never felt true to me because so many of you didn't grow up there. Some didn't grow up at all. Some died later. Some . . . Let's not talk about those," he says hurriedly, face lit like it's night. His eyes are glittering. Everything else is in shadow. "You're an uncountable number of people, Adam. I can't tell what's true about any of you."

Somehow Adam summons a smile. "Figures," he says.

"What?"

"I get it."

"Do you?"

"I promise, Rao. It's not a lie."

Rao looks at the glittering black sphere. "I'm not lying either, love. This thing I'm offering. The world where you went with your aunt. Where she lived. I can show it to you."

Darkness. Instantly, Adam knows it to be persuasion. But it's not the gun-to-the-temple kind. It's like when they're on a tight schedule and Rao's nagging him to stop for lunch. Or when Rao's refusing to get out of bed, pulling the covers over his head, repeatedly insisting he's still asleep and Adam should fuck off. Rao persuasion. Soft. Soft and so familiar he almost smiles.

And there's something else.

It's staggeringly unfamiliar. No. It's not. He's felt it for a long time. He knows what it is. This is more than a place he sleeps in. And he knows, too, that it's only dark because his eyes are shut. But he doesn't need to open them, because he knows where he is. He's home. He's lying in bed, a cool breeze on the skin of his face and his chest and arms from the open window, dust and creosote bushes and desert air just before dawn. He's on leave and he isn't going anywhere soon, and there's the smell of coffee, and there's a dog curled over his feet and he can hear whistling from the kitchen, and Sasha is in Sacramento, she's visiting next weekend, and Rao is—

Rao's not there.

He sits up, opens his eyes, stares at a pair of drapes he knows he chose in a store in Summerlin and has never seen before.

Rao's not *anywhere*.

And that's enough to pull him back to the hall of horrors. The wrench is terrible. He can feel the presence of those other universes now. So close. Like someone looking over your shoulder, reading what you're reading. Exactly that same discomfort, pushed way past the limits of what he can bear. It's insanity, and it's here. He doesn't know how much longer he can stand. But Rao looks so proud of himself. So delighted to help. So expectant of good.

"That wasn't real. That was Prophet," Adam whispers.

"It wasn't *not* Prophet. It was just me showing you what's on offer. I can make that real. Right now. Sasha's alive, you're happy. You're *happy*, love. Go on."

"No, let's get out of here."

An expression chases itself across Rao's face. Bafflement or pain. Both.

"Adam," he says in his most serious voice, and it's terrible how much he manages to put into his name. He holds up the black olive again, the star slipping downward as it moves.

"I don't want it."

"Why not?"

Adam can't answer that if Rao doesn't already know. And there's no time now. He finds the butt of his sidearm, presses at it with his palm. Hands would slip right through.

"Rao, we need to get you out of here," he croaks.

Rao nods sadly, closes his palm, and the thing is gone. All of it disappears. All the trays, all the worlds, the jewels, the stars, the kites, all those possibilities slip inside themselves, pushing out a burst of searing heat that hits Adam's face like sun on an open burn. All that's left is the rippling no-color light. It's brighter now, and so is Rao, like the light is under his skin, illuminating him from within, and then it dims, stopping down incrementally, until Rao looks like himself again, just like he's standing in a bar or in their room in Aurora, though he's so much thinner, so much more fragile, so unsteady on his feet.

"We need to get you out of here," Adam repeats.

Rao looks at the floor. "I can't do what you just said," he says slowly. "I'm really sorry, love."

He raises his face again, holding Adam's eyes. There's mute appeal in his own and behind it—

Adam steps closer. The air around Rao is unreal. The thought cuts through all others, striking Adam so sharply it's almost amusing. *Unreal*, he thinks. Without reality. Like distant heat refraction, cold and close all around him. Thinking about air is a defense mechanism, he knows, because it's hard to think about Rao now. Even harder to look at him. Easier to look at anything else.

But his attention is pulled, like it always is when Rao bids it. Two days ago, Rao would have lazily said Adam's name, made a quiet noise in his throat to get his attention. Maybe he would have announced something ridiculous. That he stole Hunter's underwear and was wearing a pair right now. Anything to attract Adam's attention. As though that had ever been hard to get. But things are different now. Things have always been different.

Rao lifts his right arm. Touches Adam's chin. That's all. *Focus up*, Adam hears himself say in his head, but he stays silent. Rao sucks in a ragged breath. Torn air. What is Adam supposed to say, hearing sounds like that in unreal air?

Struggling to breathe, Rao still manages a half smile. Almost a smirk. Adam's hands hurt with how much he hates that Rao's still smiling right now. A rivulet of Prophet snakes down from Rao's hairline, slips into the corner of his left eye. He shudders. Coughs. Tries to suck in another breath.

"Rao," Adam whispers, because he has to say something over the sound of the deafening nothing around them, over white noise like he's waiting for someone on the other end of the dead comms channel. Over the sound of Rao's lungs stopping and starting. Wildly, he puts a hand on Rao's chest as though he might be able to help. He can feel it, now. The work behind the gasps.

The fingers on his chin shift. Now both hands cradle his face. Rao's movements are as jerky as his breathing, and it should be harder to be in the moment than it is. More difficult to want to cover up the sounds with words Adam doesn't have. But Rao holds Adam's face with unmistakable intent, and his near smirk turns into the kind of full-fledged smugness that's as familiar as home.

Adam tightens his hand into a fist, gripping Rao's vest to pull him down, because there's no way that he's going to end up doing all the work if they're going to kiss. *Asshole*, Adam thinks, utterly devoid of malice. He looks into Rao's eyes, his face, and he sees the smugness smooth into something gentler and far more honest. The longing in the space between them is so fierce Adam is drawn across it like he's swimming up for air, and for a second it turns exquisitely sharp, a glacial blade drawn right through his soul. His breath catches, just as Rao's evens out. The air shifts again, grows heavy and warm. The light flickers, softens, turns candle dim. Sunset light. But Rao doesn't move. Their lips don't meet. The kiss doesn't connect. It's confusing at first. Frustrating, after all this time. Then Rao sways, loses his balance. Drops his hands from Adam's face to catch himself.

He doesn't catch himself.

Adam manages to pull Rao to him before he collapses, but as soon as he feels that certain kind of weight against his own it's obvious he'll never have to worry about Rao getting hurt again. He sinks to the ground, taking Rao with him. The air around them is normal again. He knows that Prophet has gone. The lighting is bland institutional white. Debris everywhere. By their feet the tattered remnants of what once might have been a Teddy Ruxpin bear, a Howdy Doody cookie jar, a bottle promising *No More Tears!* And Adam sits in the silence, in the normal air, cradling Rao's deadweight, feeling the warmth within him, wanting to keep it there. He pulls Rao's head close to his chest, buries his face in his hair. And then what's left of Rao slips like hourglass sand through his hold, falling inward, flowing into points of tunneling absence that for a second are like spines against Adam's eyes. He feels a burst of heat against his face again, and Rao is gone. Rao is dead and Rao is gone and his arms are cradling empty air.

And Adam *wails.*

Time passes. Time passes, and there are footsteps. He raises his eyes, blinks them into focus. Across the mess on the floor of the hot bay a man with a pale, ash-streaked face is walking unsteadily toward him. For a fleeting moment, Adam thinks he's holding a pistol; his hands are linked, held out from his waist, and metal gleams there. When the figure speaks, his voice is weak and hoarse.

"You brought him? The Indian?"

Adam watches him approach. Now the man is looking down at him. His face is impatient. Expectant. Expecting what he's sure he deserves. Expecting he'll get it.

"Where is he?" De Witte demands. "I need him."

Adam pulls his M9, shoots De Witte twice in the chest.

The echoes of the retorts die in the hall. Adam watches him topple. It's done. He's done.

Hunter's voice in his ear, clear and unhurried.

—*Delta 5, Delta 1, over.*

He touches Transmit, speaks automatically. Sounds like a recording of himself.

—*Go ahead Delta 1.*

—*Delta 5 sitrep, over.*

—*Situation's fucked. Over.*

—*Delta 5, do you have a medevac request?*

—*Won't be necessary. Over.*

—*I got your negative on medevac, over.*

—*I'm Oscar Mike. See you in ten, over.*

—*Roger, out.*

When he steps out of the doors into the open air, the light hits him like a scald. The skies have cleared, and the sun has turned the desert gold. Everything is way too close and far too far away, like he's looking through the wrong end of a telescope. Keeping his eyes fixed on the horizon he picks his way through the rubble, the trash of hearts. It occurs to him that his face is wet. When he drags his fingertips down one cheek and pulls them away, they're painted with blood. He doesn't flinch when a jackrabbit gets up at his feet and jinks away between the objects piled around it, the pads of its feet kicking up Monopoly bills and snow. Just wonders, dully, if he'll ever regain the capacity for surprise.

Adam's used to exhaustion. He's lived inside it for months at a time. Everyone who's served has. It's nothing special. He's familiar with the feeling: ash in your blood, grit in your veins, the world turned tissue thin. He's tired, but this isn't exhaustion. He feels old, like his bones are dust, but at the same time so new and terrible it's like he's been skinned. Flayed and rolled in salt. Every step farther from where Rao died is an effort. Wading upstream through a winter flood. He has no sense of time now. The walk takes as long as the walk takes, and then it's done.

One of the hummers has gone. *Rhodes*, he assumes. He stops by the vehicles, feels himself sway, refuses to put out a hand to steady himself. Widens his stance as he watches Hunter make her way toward him.

"I got it, Rubenstein," she says, when she's close. Her face is grim. "Rhodes dropped a panicked exit, explained the situation. Just about."

"Just about."

"Took a vehicle. Said she was heading back to base. Don't know if I believe her."

"Bugged out."

"That was the look in her eyes."

"Don't care."

He hears the falling screech of a hawk above them. He angles his head to the sky, sees it wheeling against the blue. Gets lost in watching it for a while before he drags his eyes back down. Hunter's looking at him.

He looks right back at her and speaks. "He didn't make it."

Silence. "Shit, Adam."

"I need to go. We're leaving."

PART IV

I t's a cutout against the sky. The sky is black. The cutout is blue.
    No.
    No. It's the other way around. The sky is blue, the cutout is black, and it has wings with feathers that look like spread fingers at their tips.
    The bird is very familiar. He's never seen it before.
    The sky it's flying through is familiar too. He knows that blue. It's high and soft and tending to lilac and—he's never seen it before. *Fuck. He's never seen the sky.*
    He's on the ground, there's dust under him and the air smells of woodsmoke and the bird is a kite and there's something in his mouth that tastes of blood and regret. *What have I done this time?*
    And he looks down and realises he's naked, and
    Fuck.

PART V

CHAPTER 74

I t's a cold morning in Mayfair and Adam is walking through Grosvenor Square. Gray skies. Bare trees and muddy grass. Gilded eagle on the American embassy roof, wings spread. He looks up at the building. *Home away from home*, he thinks, feeling nothing.

She's sitting in a soft armchair in a small, richly carpeted room on the third floor, wearing an emerald sweater, jeans, and a silver necklace. Looking solid, despite it all.

"Ma'am."

He sees the concern on her face before she smiles. "Rubenstein. Good to see you."

He takes the other armchair. She pours him coffee from the pot on the side table and asks him about the funeral. He tells her Rao would have liked it. They sit in silence for a while. Then she explains how she'd been woken by the sound of the Smith & Wesson dropping to the floor. How the nurse had put on gloves before he'd picked the revolver up and bagged it in plastic. How he'd stood there, staring at her in silence, until Miller had said eventually that she was hungry. Would appreciate some food.

"They fed me a slice of cold pork pie," Miller says wryly. "It was memorable."

"Where were you held?"

"Suburban house near Banbury. Oxfordshire." He nods. There's an NSA comms hub at Croughton.

She puts her cup down on the table. "Shall we make a start on the debrief? Informal, as requested."

He gives her an abbreviated account, but still it takes some time to relate. She accepts it all with equanimity, as he expected she would.

When he tells her Rao was overwhelmed by Prophet, her jaw tightens. She doesn't ask for details. And when she asks about De Witte, he tells her what he'd told Lane. "He was contaminated. Prophet had changed him. He was a threat."

"I understand that," she says slowly. "But the thing I don't . . . After Rao died, it was gone from *everywhere*?"

"Everywhere. There's no trace of it anymore. I guess it came, then went."

"Like a comet, huh?" There's something like awe on her face. Then she looks down, polishes her watch face with one thumb. "Clemson. My boss. I had no idea. And these people, this network, it's all still in place."

"It is what it is."

That gets him a sad smile and a long silence.

"I'm getting out," she says.

"*Out?*"

She nods. "Not corporate," she clarifies. "My brother manages a dude ranch outside Bozeman. I'll be there for a while. Teaching the worst of the bicoastal elite how to ride and shoot and fish."

"Trout?"

"Rainbow, brown, cutthroat."

"Very spiritual," he replies, smiling, and with that the pain he carries focuses. A stiletto pushing in his chest. Momentarily, he's lost. She sees him fight his way back. He hates that she does.

"Adam," she says softly.

He stares. She's never used his first name.

"You did all you could."

He's thought about that. He's thought about that a lot. Maybe it's true.

"Rao was an irreplaceable asset," he says.

"From what you've told me, he saved the world. I think that makes him more than an asset. I think that makes him a hero." She tilts her head. "You too."

He snorts. "Ma'am."

"Elisabeth," she says.

"Elisabeth."

"Not Betsy, for the love of God."

He smiles. A real one. "I've never seen a dude ranch."

"It's a pretty place. Anytime. You're back in DC now?"

He shakes his head. "I'm in Vegas for a while for cleanup."

"The things piled up around the site?"

"No. They're being moved with backhoes. I'm on disposal of animate objects."

"They escaped from the facility?"

"Some were never in it," he says. "After that's done," he adds, "I'll be moving. I got a lateral transfer."

"Where?"

"Culver City."

Her brows rise. She looks happy for him. Mostly she looks entertained.

"The EIO," she says.

"Yeah," he says. "The assholes wanted me."

CHAPTER 75

He could have put it in an envelope, sent it in the mail. He was back in England for the funeral, anyway. He still could've mailed it. He didn't.

He hesitates before the door, then raps it sharply.

"Dr. Caldwell," he says when it opens, hearing the catch in his voice. It's only a few weeks since he last stood here. Uncountable years have passed. She looks him up and down. "Thought I'd be seeing you again," she says. "Did you solve your case?"

"Yes, ma'am. Thank you for your book." He holds it out. She takes it, regards it. Raises an eyebrow. It's ruined. Rao spilled coffee on it twice and the cover's torn almost in two. "It's not in good condition," he adds.

"No. War wounds, huh?"

He smiles despite himself.

"How's Rao?"

He keeps his eyes on the book, shakes his head.

"Oh," she says. "Oh. I'm sorry."

"It happens."

That gets him a searching look that turns and tightens the corners of her mouth. "I'm very sorry," she adds more softly. "The kettle just boiled. Cup of tea?"

The tea's citrusy. An unnerving hit of childhood; lemon trees and Sunny D. It's scaldingly hot. He cradles the mug in his hands, willing the burn deeper. He can't remember how to do this. He never knew how in the first place.

"Admissions interviews start tomorrow," she says. "It's good you turned up today. Wouldn't have been free tomorrow. Thank you for the book. Was it helpful?"

Adam has no idea.

"Yes, ma'am."

"Kitty, please. And you are?"

"Adam."

She regards him seriously. So seriously he takes another sip of tea— he's surprised how much he likes it—then steels himself to hold her eye.

"So, Adam, I'm not sure if this is permitted. But do you want to tell me about it?"

"About what?"

"What happened."

Adam swallows. He knows he shouldn't want to tell her, but he does. He wants to tell her all of it. Caldwell's like Rao. Someone who inspires unwarranted confidences. He wonders, briefly, if she'd be useful. Speculates on how she'd fit an operational role. Speculates on whether she already has one. It's possible.

But hearing those thoughts—it's like listening to a ghost. He looks past her into her office. The stone windowsills, the lead frames in the glass, the wooden bookcases, the scores of nostalgic objects arranged across shelves and tables that make him feel a little sick inside. He wonders how he can tell her the truth: that without Rao, this whole calm world would have ended up gone.

When he speaks, his words surprise him.

"I miss him," he says.

"I can see that," she says.

"It got unprofessional."

CHAPTER 76

It doesn't require concealment: he's bait. He stands in the open and waits and they come to him. Not all the way. Thirty yards, they'll slow. Hesitate. He'll take the shot before that.

They leave signs everywhere. Three days ago he'd found a thin trail in the sand that wasn't a snake. A V-shaped impression that turned abruptly every few feet, zigzagging for just under thirty yards. He followed it to an animate Rubik's Cube tucked under a creosote bush, rotating itself clockwise, counterclockwise, and back again. That one he almost wanted to keep. Rao'd have loved it.

That got tossed in a bag, like all the smaller ones.

The bags get tossed in the containers in the back of the truck.

It's getting dark and he's been out since dawn. He wants a smoke. He'll have one after he's done here.

He scans the desert ahead. He saw his target in the far distance, has hiked toward it for a while. Couldn't identify it on first sight. Probably got made by someone without a clear imagination. Some of them are like that. Some are small, like the California Raisins figurine he'd trodden into the sand. Some are too big to load into the truck. These he tags and leaves for specialist retrieval. But apart from the truck-sized Very Hungry Caterpillar, which required far heavier ordnance than he was carrying, most are human-sized, like this one. Or smaller. There've been a few dogs. Dealing with those was harder than the others. Something to think about, when thinking is something he'll permit himself at all.

There.

He stands on the plateau, purpled slopes and peaks of Yucca Mountain ahead, and watches it approach. Snorts humorlessly when he sees what it is. An approximation of ALF. Dead eyes. Shambling gait. He waits until it gets closer. Exhales, takes the shot. There's a puff of white. This one is cotton wadding inside. A lot of them are. Which is a plus: ones made of ersatz flesh are heavier, filling the disposal bags with blood. But also a minus: cutting them up blunts his blade.

It takes four minutes to break it down. Twenty more minutes to walk back to the CUCV, drive it to the kill site, bag and load up. He lights a cigarette, leans against the tailgate, and looks down at today's work. There's a low, clicking *woooow* from the bag holding the first retrieval of the day. He'd heard that one before he saw it, a laughing Furby calling *bring, bring, bring* behind a pile of rocks.

A beaded Huichol jaguar. A pillowcase caught on a yucca spike he knew was a target because it was flapping on the wrong heading for the wind. And an orange cat that had walked unsteadily toward him through the desert vegetation, butting greetings at thin air. It had been out here long enough that there were more cactus spines than fur.

When he's done with the cigarette, he'll drive to the NNSS waste disposal site. There'll be the usual exchange with the guy on the gate, the only person he's spoken to for weeks. He'll ask if he's had happy hunting, and Adam will say yeah. Watch him tick them off on a clip-board, then wave to a subordinate to unload the truck and take the bags away. Sealed in shipping containers, they'll join the low-level nuclear waste and classified material in the NNSS landfill, interred under twenty-five feet of sand.

Then the drive back to Vegas. It's better than staying on-site. They've given him an apartment on East Desert Inn Road. He'd smiled grimly when he first pulled in; the place is a faded memory of 1962. Pink-washed brick, wrought iron security screens on the windows and doors, sagging palms in the central courtyard, a long-drained swim-ming pool. He doesn't even see it now. He'll shower. Watch TV. Find something to eat. Might, if the fates are feeling kind, even sleep.

It's Friday. Long past sundown, he sits on the couch, takes out his lighter. It's a shitty plastic one from the 7-Eleven a block away. Yellow. He holds it for a long time, flicking a flame into existence and watch-ing it die over and over again. Darkness. Light. He already knows he won't sleep tonight.

CHAPTER 77

Adam stands by the window at the back of the apartment. Lets everything outside fall through glass into his eyes. A 737 into McCarran at two thousand feet. Palms and pines. The Wynn. The Encore. Utility poles and power lines.

It's Christmas Eve. There's a low thrum of heavy traffic and "Grandma Got Run Over by a Reindeer" playing faintly through the walls for the fifteenth time today. Strings of colored lights along the breeze-block wall of the parking lot below, where a silver Toyota Corolla is driving slowly across the cracked asphalt. He watches it turn, narrowly missing a pole holding up the sunshade roof, then disappear under the awnings. At that angle, it'll be taking up two spaces. He waits for it to back up and try again. It doesn't.

Nine seconds later he stops breathing. Looks again. Walks back through the apartment. The light is dim; the drapes are drawn. Drags a chair across the floor, drops it in the right place. Walks to the door, unlocks it, unchains it, pulls it an inch ajar. He's breathing again, but the air feels taut, full of dust. His throat hurts as he walks back to the chair, draws his pistol, and sits.

After two minutes there's the sound of whistling outside, getting closer: "Driving Home for Christmas." Hearing it brings a punch of nausea. He wills it away.

Five seconds, four.

Three, two, and the door is pushed gently.

"Adam?"

*

He's holding a gun. He's holding a gun and it's pointed right at him. He looks over the front sights and takes Adam in. His shirt collar's undone and his sleeves rolled up. He's unshaven, there's hair curling over the top of his ears, and he's far, far too thin.

"Adam . . ." The name hangs in the air. "You look like shit."

He waits for a reply. Suspects, when it isn't forthcoming, that it might not have been the right thing to say. He tries again.

"It's me."

"You're dead."

"Ah," he says, beaming. "No. It's complicated. Listen, are you going to make me a cup of tea? The drive was dreadful, and I nearly died. This truck driver pulled right out into my lane." He frowns. "No. That's not true, is it. I pulled into his. Fuck." He looks across the apartment. It's dark in here and not what he expected. There are instant ramen cups on the table, pizza boxes and empties on the floor. A small brass menorah by a heap of clothes on a cabinet top, shoes kicked everywhere. "Is that the kitchen over there? I'll put the kettle on."

"Don't move."

"You want me to put my hands up, love?"

Adam doesn't answer, but Rao raises them anyway. "Look, I'm going to explain, but this might take a while. Do I really have to keep my— Ok, fine. Right. First thing, and this is the most important thing: I'm me. I'm really me. *Really*. I remember everything that happened, all of it. I remember you giving Estrada shit for Peet's, and I remember that fucking Pac-Man that killed him, and I remember the singing man, Mister Rogers, and I remember all the rest, the . . . bigger stuff. I was there, with you, and then I wasn't. I was flat on my arse in a field in Rajasthan. Which was a bit of a surprise. As was me being naked." He makes a moue. "Ok, no, that was less surprising. That's happened before. Different circumstances, obviously. So anyway. I was in Nevada with you, and I knew I wasn't going to last much longer, and then I was in a field— You know, I can't help thinking that Prophet was a bit fucking racist putting me just outside Brahmpuri, considering I grew up in North London, but anyway. I lay there for a bit and looked at the sky and tried to work out what happened and—"

"You died."

"Adam, stop saying that. I understand this is a bit of shock, and to be honest it's quite hard trying to explain all this with a bloody gun pointed at me, but I assure you I am really me, and I know I said it's complicated, but it's not *that* complicated if you just let me explain. I got made again, right? Prophet did it. But perfectly. Down to the atom. Every memory, every part of my too-much personality, everything I've ever thought, everything I've felt, all of it. It's all here and it's all me." He makes a face. "The clothes are new, though."

There's a long silence. He speaks carefully into it. "Actually, I wasn't entirely naked. Adam, I'm going to move my arms now. I'd really appreciate it if you didn't shoot me."

He reaches into his shirt, pulls the chain over his neck and head, drops the tags into one hand, sees Adam's eyes widen a little at the sight of them, and he doesn't think he's being stupid when he tosses them across the few feet to where he sits, but afterwards there's a flash of adrenaline when he realises just how close he might have come to dying again.

Adam catches them without taking his eyes off Rao. Closes one hand over them in the air.

*

He holds his tags in one hand. Pistol in the other. Everything in him is screaming not to look away from the obvious threat standing right in front of him, talking perfectly, ceaselessly, in Rao's voice. Clicking Rao's fingers. A perfect mimic of Rao's panicked glances around the room. Everything in him is screaming not to look away. There's a threat.

There's always a threat. So what if this one is Rao-shaped? That's probably okay. If he's going to go, if he's going to lose his mind or have the last remnant of Prophet come along to finally kill him, then he's happier with Rao doing it than someone else, like Bob Ross.

He holsters the Beretta. Looks at the tags in his hand. They're his—or something like his. He'd never be able to tell without Rao around. They look perfect.

"I'm going to sit down now, Adam," it says. "I'm really very pleased you didn't shoot me. Keep that up, please."

Adam keeps his eyes on the tags as it pulls one of his armchairs, scraping loudly across the floor, to sit near him. To the left, opposite. Near the door. It's still open.

He knows that it's a bad idea to put the tags in his pocket because as soon as he does, he can't stop looking at him. It. Him. This Rao that insists he is definitely Rao.

The new Rao's eyebrows tick into a tiny frown. "Fuckload of ash rubbed into this chair, love," he mutters, flicking the fabric on the arm. He's right, the bastard. Adam knocked over an ashtray two days ago and barely bothered to clean up. "Does that mean you're indulging?"

"I don't think you get to comment on any of my habits."

"Don't I?"

Adam can't stop looking at him. Feels dangerous to blink. But he has to cover his face for a second. "You can't just come back from the dead and expect me to—"

"To what, love? Because you opened the door."

"Of course I did."

"Waiting for me. Did you see me coming?"

"Yes."

"And you haven't shot me."

"Yet."

"I understand if you're still mulling it over," Rao says, evidently amused to hell. Adam could kill him. He looks up through his fingers. Could he kill Rao, after everything? Could he have killed him before, if they'd asked? No. Adam's lines in the sand begin and end with Rao. "But, regardless, I'm still here. You're talking to me."

"I'm going insane."

"I'm flesh and blood."

"You're dead and buried."

Rao scratches his chin, looks intrigued. "Buried?"

Adam doesn't know what to say to that, so he defaults to the truth. "Your family burned something symbolic, but I didn't ask. I brought a picture—"

"Did you meet my mum?" Rao interrupts.

Adam frowns. Can't believe he missed the way Rao didn't care, had never cared about Adam getting to finish his thoughts. "Yes, Rao. I met your mother."

"That's agony," Rao says, kicking his feet. Such a childish action. Adam's chest hurts. "I was supposed to be there to smooth that whole thing over."

Adam remembers how Rao's mother had ushered him to sit with the rest of the family. How she'd taken his hand. He rubs fitfully at his wrist. "I think we managed," he mutters. Gets up. Goes to the kitchen. Finds one last beer in the fridge, pulls it out. "I'll split it with you?" he says, walking back in.

"You're day drinking too?"

"If you don't want to split it, you can just say."

*

Grief looks different on different people. Rao's seen it all: the heavy drinking, the hyperproductivity, the empty eyes, the fake smiles, the constant and unstoppable tears, the stoic silence. Kabul had shown him a lot of grief. He'd never expected to see it on Adam. Or, if he'd tried to picture it, he'd never have come up with this day-drinking, scruffy-faced, overtired, nervous-looking version of the man he once knew.

He's suddenly very close to losing it. All this time he thought he could just tell him. Just like that. Tell Adam what he'd worked out, lying in the dust.

Tell him there'd been a miracle.

That across those few closing inches between their lips had leapt a spark of creation. That all of Prophet had felt Adam's longing and known what he wanted and wanted to give it to him. Through Rao himself, it had given it. A goodbye gift, pulled into existence out of nothing.

Out of everything.

I'm made of love, he'd wanted to say. And Adam was going to look at him cynically, and Rao would tell him this wasn't Hallmark Channel shit. It was *true*.

"Are you out here alone?" Rao asks instead, hoping to hear that Hunter's been keeping an eye on him.

No such luck.

"Are you seriously asking about my love life right now?"

"I wasn't, no, but, well, since the subject's come up . . ."

Adam blinks at him. The familiar maybe-angry, maybe-disappointed blink. The slowest blink in the world. "That figures."

"What figures?"

"That this is what it looks like when I finally snap."

Rao frowns. "No, sorry. You'll have to run that past me again, Adam. You think you've lost it because I'm checking if you're single?"

"Hunter always figured I'd go postal."

"So did I, to be honest," Rao mutters. Adam thinks he's a hallucination, and who can blame him? If Rao hadn't been the one who came back from what certainly *felt* like death, he'd be questioning his sanity too.

"And I'm such a dick to myself," Adam continues. He's grimly amused now, leaning forward in his chair, beer hanging lazily from his hand, brazenly taking in Rao's features. His eyes dart around Rao's face like he'll never get another chance to see it. "I'm so inherently damaged I can't even imagine you being anything other than what you were."

"Bloody hell, Adam, that's a bit hurtful," Rao admits.

Adam snorts, waves a dismissive hand. "Shut up. You always knew exactly when to ask me about how lonely I was. We talked about this."

"Did we?"

"In that hotel, after I saw the clock."

"After you made the clock, love." Rao needs to make the distinction.

"After I made the clock and before you became a god," Adam corrects, amends, smiles sadly. Rao can't bear that smile.

"Less of a god, truthfully," Rao mutters, dropping his gaze to the carpet. Anything to get away from that defeated smile. "More like a vahana. They're the beings that carry gods, Adam. Vishnu's is a bird, Garuda. Shiva's is Nandi, the bull. Lakshmi's is an owl. They're . . . vehicles. They take gods from place to place. They help them extend their powers."

"You think Prophet's a god?"

"Why not?" He sees the expression on Adam's face and tries again. "Ok. I was more like a divine aqueduct."

"Rao."

"What?"

"A divine aqueduct?"

"Could you ever have imagined such nonsense?" Rao asks hopefully. "Surely that proves you're in possession of your reason."

Adam shrugs. "Or it's well and truly gone."

This is the worst conversation Rao's ever been part of, which is saying quite a lot. His chest hurts. His breath is gone. This talk feels like a death all by itself. "Does that mean you considered me a god at one point?"

Adam is silent for long enough that Rao has to lift his gaze from the floor to see what's going on. Sees Adam watching him, occasionally taking careful sips of beer. After far too long thinking, after two false starts when Adam takes a breath only to have the words die in his mouth—its own agony to watch—he speaks again.

"That depends on your definition, I guess."

"What was your definition, love?" Rao asks. Does he want Adam to have considered him a god? No. But he still can't help asking questions. Questions that produce answers that are never true, never false. Just Adam.

"Well," Adam says simply. Takes another one of those careful sips. He's never been much of a drinker. But judging by the empties sitting around the apartment, he's been practicing. "That doesn't matter anymore. Everything's different now."

"How so?"

"Asks the dead man."

"Fair point," Rao sighs. This is so much harder than he expected. "Aren't you happy to see me, Adam?"

That slow blink. "You really need to ask?"

"I really do."

"Rao . . ." Adam sighs, laughs, shakes his head. Looks at Rao. That sad smile again, back to strangle the air out of Rao's lungs. "I'd give *anything* to have you back for real. Whenever I go back there—"

"You *what*?"

Adam frowns at the interruption. "I still work. There's still a mess at the NNSS to deal with. I'm still one of the two people from that team that made it out alive. I'm all they have."

The work is all he has.

"You don't have to go back alone again," Rao decides, as though he has the authority. "I'm right here."

Adam laughs again, a strangled noise. Rao thinks this might be too much but he has to understand. He has to believe what's happening here. "Prove it, Rao."

If Rao didn't know better . . .

If Adam were another person . . .

But he is, now, isn't he? They both are. Rao, quite literally so.

That other Rao is gone. He's with Prophet, inside Prophet forever, always, stretched through uncountable dimensions, innumerable universes, helping it bring life to places where there is none.

But Rao is here. Adam remade him. They both, *together*, remade him. "What do you want me to do, love?" he asks, leaning forward. Adam doesn't back away but inhales quietly, sharply. Unflappable, even when flapped.

"I want you to stop calling me that," Adam says. Whispers. He closes his eyes and they're back at that hotel again, after Adam made his clock. Rao knows now what pain looks like on Adam. Or, more accurately, he recognises it. He's always seen it. It's always been right there.

"Do you?"

"No. Yes. No," Adam decides. His next sip of beer isn't quite as careful as the ones before. "I guess it would be weird if you stopped. You always used it against me before."

"What? I never did that."

"Yes, you did." Adam smiles grimly. "And it always worked."

"I was never manipulating you," Rao begins, then falters. Adam's levelling a stare at him that could strip paint. "*Fine*, dickhead, I attempted to manipulate you once or twice, but not like that. I just started calling you that to get up your arse!"

Adam blinks at him. "Rao—"

"It's a *saying*, for fuck's sake." Rao rubs his face. "I started calling you that to annoy you. You were so uptight and straight—"

"One out of two isn't bad," Adam mutters.

"Shut up. How was I supposed to know *anything* about you, Adam? Let alone your sexuality." Rao leans forward enough to snatch the half-drunk beer out of Adam's hand. He doesn't fight. They're splitting it after all. "I can't even know if you're telling the truth about what you had for breakfast—"

"Eggs."

"So the *idea* of figuring you out well enough to use a fucking term of endearment to manipulate you is insane, Adam. It's laughable. It's *mental* is what it is."

"You've never needed to do a run on me to understand what's going on and we both know it," Adam says evenly.

"We both know that, do we?" Rao says. He's supposed to be having a joyous reunion. *You are fucked, Sunil. This is all fucked, and you are the one who fucked it.*

"No one says the things you've said to me without knowing how I felt," Adam says, then takes a breath. "How I feel."

They look at each other in silence. It's too much but, perversely, Rao finds himself loving it as much as it makes him want to squirm. The electricity of it. The near disaster of it, the near triumph. The victory, not insignificant, in getting Adam to actually *say the fucking words.*

"Adam," Rao says. "Have you considered for a moment that maybe I'm just a wanker?"

"Regularly."

"Cheers."

Adam raises his eyebrows in a shrug. "You asked."

"I did," Rao sighs. Fucking Adam and his flat, unreadable, could-be facts. Fucking Adam and his spinning wheel. Adam. "But I think I'm right. Yeah? I think maybe I was just a wanker for a very long time."

No response for a breath too long. "That's a point toward you being real," Adam says eventually.

"Why's that, love?"

Rao sees it happen, this time. He's watching for it. The lightning flash of misery at the endearment. He's done real damage there, hasn't he? And he had no idea.

"As much as I hate myself, I think I would have at least fantasised you apologising properly," Adam says. "Not that I don't appreciate that one."

"Funny way of showing it," Rao huffs before finishing off Adam's now-warm beer. He regrets doing so instantly. It's rank. Flat, body temperature, slightly backwashed. "This wasn't how it was supposed to go, you know."

Adam exhales. "Enlighten me."

"You were supposed to choose happiness," Rao tells him. It's so simple. Couldn't have been simpler. "You were supposed to have a whole new go at it. Why didn't you take it? I know a thing or two about going back for what's never good for you, by the way. I don't have to tell you this, I'm sure, but maybe you're just addicted to misery."

Just like the beer. Instant regret. He shouldn't have said that.

But Adam isn't mad. He isn't anything. That blank face, beyond pain, beyond sadness, beyond grief or anger. Nothing. Smooth features. He rocks himself to standing and grabs the keys from the coffee table. "Come on, Rao."

"What? Where are we going?"

"Beer run."

*

They make it to the car, but that's about as far as Adam can manage. He should have guessed. Should have been ready for it. He wasn't. As soon as the doors close, Rao's cologne fills the car. Terre d'Hermès. Expensive and rich and cloying and somehow unique on him. Adam's seen the bottle in airports. Once, in a fit of weakness that he doesn't like to think about, he bought one. It didn't smell the same. It needed Rao. Even when he was at his best, that smell was sometimes too much for him. He's not at his best right now.

He swears under his breath, drums his fingers on the steering wheel, and ignores the interrogative look he's getting from Rao. Rao, the dead man.

"It's nothing," he lies. Waits a second to see if he gets control over himself. Another second. Another. No. His skin still aches, and he still feels like everything will end if he reaches out and touches Rao's arm. It's all he can think about. Just to reach out and—

"Could you breathe just a little?" Rao asks him carefully.

Adam shakes his head. The cologne will stay in his throat and nose for days, he knows. Linger like a wound. But he doesn't want to open the door. He can't roll down the window. He can't leave. What if this is the last time he gets to have this? His hands throb with the effort to keep from reaching out. He takes a breath.

"Thank you, love," Rao says quietly.

Adam winces. The old litany: *He doesn't mean it, he doesn't know, it's not his fault, it's all your fault, it's just a word, it's just a word you've never understood, it's nothing, it's never meant anything, you've never meant anything.* He's out of practice. He's usually so much better at handling this, at being around Rao. How was he supposed to know that he'd have to stay vigilant even after Rao died?

"It's not fair," Adam says out loud. Doesn't mean to.

"What isn't fair?"

"I'm in the middle of getting over you," he answers. He didn't expect to speak that truth. He sounds petulant to his own ears. Fuck knows what Rao heard when he said it. Nothing, probably. No truth. No lies. Nothing. That's all Adam feels like to Rao. "I'm not even doing it that well, you know? I'm fucking up daily. And you turn up at my door, and you're—"

He looks at Rao. Turns in his seat and *looks.* Sunil Rao, bane of Adam's career, world saver, royal pain in the ass, and genuinely the love of Adam's life. Healthier than he's ever looked since Adam's known him. Breathing and alive. Filling his car with his stupid cologne.

"Complicated?" Rao offers with a smile Adam knows is meant to be charming. It just looks nervous. Adam could kill him.

"You . . . Do you understand why I didn't take you up on that crazy offer?" Adam asks. The facility in Nevada, snow in the sand, lights all around them, nearly freezing to death as Rao showed him jewels. He's not imaginative enough to have made any of that up, and that's the only thought that keeps him sane most nights. It must have happened, because Adam's dull. Too dull for it not to have happened.

"I'm sorry that I said—" Rao starts, but Adam has no time for his apologies.

"Do you understand why I didn't take you up on the offer, Rao?" Adam hardens his voice in an attempt to get Rao back on task. It works. Maybe, even when out of practice, he still knows what he's doing.

"Loss makes us who we are," Rao intones. He's thought about it, and he doesn't like the answer he reached. "If you'd lived a life without the loss you had, you wouldn't be you. I understand, love, I just wish that I could—"

"I chose you," Adam interrupts him again. Rao looks at him, silent. Adam goes on. He has to now. Adam chose Rao, and Rao was supposed to survive. "I was always going to choose you. You know that. You've known that. Haven't you?"

"I know how you feel about me, yes," Rao whispers, like it's still a secret. Adam was ready for him to lie about it, but hearing him admit the truth feels a lot . . . worse, and better, than the cologne. He knows hearing Rao say it will stick to him, in one way or another, for the rest of his life. "Can I ask you a question?"

"You're going to."

"I'm going to, yes." Rao smiles, a brief quirk of lips. "Why don't you ever want to hear how I feel about you?"

That should be obvious. "I know you think that I'm devoid of emotions—"

"Adam—"

"But I genuinely think I wouldn't handle hearing the truth out loud very well," he finishes.

"The truth," Rao repeats.

"Your favorite topic."

Another brief quirk. "Yes. On that subject, in fact, I'm not sure if I've ever mentioned it, but you are aware of how I can't tell with you?"

Adam closes his eyes. *Here we go.* He's going to get some beautiful and devastating poetry about how Adam is a black hole in Rao's universe. "Yes, I'm aware."

"This extends to statements about you," Rao goes on. But Adam knows this. When Rao asked anyone anything about Adam, about his life or professional details, no truth would stick, no matter how hard Rao concentrated. He'd grill people, back when they first worked together. Adam remembers some assuming that Rao was trying to find dirt on him, that he was working an internal audit of some kind. "So I could say anything at all about you and wouldn't be able to run it."

"I knew that, Rao."

"Funniest thing is," Rao continues like he didn't hear Adam. His voice sounds almost nostalgic. "Since I woke up in that field, I've been able to take a run at two statements. I've been able to run them successfully."

The bastard pauses for effect. Adam could kill him, alright.

"I still hear you, from that time, in my head." Rao's voice dips. Not lower in register, but softer. Serious. "Hear you telling me you hated me. And I can taste it, Adam. It was a lie. You don't hate me."

"I don't hate you, Rao. I've never hated you."

Rao nods. After a while, he frowns. "Are you going to ask about the other statement?"

"Are you going to tell me if I don't ask?"

Rao looks away. Turns and looks out the window. The day is nice. Not too hot, but the sun is shining all the same. A real blue sky, no haze. Gentle breeze. Even in the parking lot, it's a nice day. Adam hadn't seen it before Rao looked away.

"Can we go back inside? I don't want more beer."

"Neither do I," Adam lies. "Let's go back in."

*

He follows Adam when they leave the car. He's not been around Adam again for more than an hour, and things between them have already shifted at least three times. Everything feels familiar. But the changes in Adam are killing Rao. New lines and bags under his eyes. The way his hands shake sometimes. Rao leans against the wall by the door while Adam jingles his keys, a quick search for the one to the apartment, and studies his hands. They're funny. Weapons. But right now, the way those weapons are fumbling with a bunch of keys puts Rao in mind of a teenager on a first date. Nerves making it difficult to get fine motor functions to work.

Oh.

He looks at Adam just as he gives up, sighing. "Rao, could you just—back off? For like a full second. Let me fucking think."

Rao speaks quickly. Takes his chance. "And if I don't?"

Adam stills. Nerves, if they were nerves, gone. Licks his lips in thought.

Rao stares at him, floored by his sudden understanding of who Adam is. How he acts. What he feels.

"If you don't back off, then I won't be able to think," Adam says clearly. It sounds like he's saying something else. Rao can almost hear the words he doesn't say. He fights a shiver. He's taller than Adam by several inches, but it doesn't feel like it. Slowly, like he's reaching to take a gun from a madman, Rao takes the keys from Adam's hands. As soon as they're free of that distraction, as though they were the very last barrier between them that Adam could deploy, one hand grips Rao's wrist.

It hurts, for an instant, like a static shock. Skin-to-skin electricity. It hurts, and then it's gone. A pinch, a spark, and then the circuit is closed. Adam sucks in a breath. That's enough. Doesn't say a damn thing and Rao still feels he can almost hear the words in the air.

**

Since the day Rao died, he's had dreams. Longing fantasies. Nightmares. Torture. All about a kiss that never landed. He's replayed the moment over and over. Thinks that if there were any Prophet left in the world, and if he pulled the same act he did back in Rhodes's lab, he'd manifest the room where Rao died.

Regret. It's an old friend of Adam's. And he knows, standing on the balcony outside of an apartment he didn't choose for himself, his fingers wrapped around Rao's wrist in a desperate attempt to keep him exactly where he is, that he won't be able to live with himself if he racks up another wasted chance in his life.

Not this time.

He pulls, telling himself that he'll feel sorry about not being gentle later, pulls until Rao bends, bows, close enough for Adam to close the distance between them. He thought that he had imagined it, a weird current through his fingers and arm when he took Rao's wrist, but then their lips meet—

**

—it's an SSTV transmission. Tones searching for an image. His brain misfiring, then chasing after the feeling. Known, that desperate hunger, but never for another human being. Not like this. Because this is love, isn't it. The *thought* of it. The pure fucking *rush* of the absurdity of that fact as it turns, solid and true, in Rao's head. He's off-balance, but he's not complaining in the slightest. For all he's got wrong about Adam, he was right about him taking charge. It's perfect. All Rao wants is to open the kiss, so he does. Adam lets him, and it's another uncontrollable rush until—

**

—he bites down on Rao's bottom lip. He's not thinking. Can't think. Just searching for the next sensation. The only thing Adam knows for sure is that he wants to know what it feels like to have Rao gasp into his mouth.

It feels like the balcony is too public. Rao is still happy to bend for the kiss, but he arches, the gasp nearing something more—

**

—which is when Adam takes his keys back and pulls out of the kiss.

"Excuse the fuck out of me?" Rao demands a touch breathlessly. "You can't stop there, love, I was just—"

"Shut up, Rao," Adam says, as solid as Rao's heard him since he turned up at his door. "Get inside. Nobody's stopping anything."

"That's a promise, yeah?"

"You're still talking."

Rao laughs and lets Adam push him into the apartment. Once the door is closed, Adam steps into Rao's space. Doesn't push. Doesn't shove. It's sudden. One step and he's sharing Rao's breath. Arresting. His eyes look up at him, knife sharp. Rao shivers. Then Adam's face softens. "Are you sure about this, Rao?" he asks quietly.

Rao's eyebrows rise. "I'm genuinely offended by this temperature check, love."

"I'm asking because—" Adam pauses. Thinks about his words. "I'm not a gentle person. That might not be what you want."

Rao can't hold in the bark of laughter that provokes. "Fuck's sake," he manages eventually. "Do you even know me?"

Adam's brow furrows. His eyes search Rao's face. Then he nods, slowly, infinitely seriously.

"I think so, yes. Yeah. I think I do."

Glossary

AFO Authorised Firearms Officer: Trained UK police officer operationally permitted to carry a firearm.

AFSOC US Air Force Special Operations Command.

ARL-M Airborne Reconnaissance Low - Multifunction: A reconnaissance and surveillance system carried on a modified De Havilland Canada DHC-7 aircraft.

ATC Air Traffic Controller.

BDU Battle Dress Uniform.

BFR Big Fucking Rock (military slang).

BMT Basic Military Training (a.k.a. boot camp).

C4 (a.k.a. Composition C-4): Malleable plastic explosive.

C-17 (a.k.a. Globemaster III): Large US Air Force transport aircraft.

CC Combat Controller.

Charlie Mike Continue Mission (radio jargon).

CIA Central Intelligence Agency (USA).

CONUS Continental United States.

Creech Creech Air Force Base, Nevada: Base for unmanned aerial vehicles/remotely piloted aircraft operations.

CRT Cathode Ray Tube.

CUCV Commercial Utility Cargo Vehicle (USA): Old-style military truck.

DARPA Defense Advanced Research Projects Agency: US Department of Defense agency for research and development into emerging technology for military use.

Dash 7 De Havilland Canada DHC-7 four-engine turboprop aircraft.

DCU Desert Camouflage Uniform.

Delta 1st Special Forces Operational Detachment-Delta (a.k.a. Delta Force): Special Operations force of the US Army.

DFAC Dining facility on US Air Force bases.

DIA Defense Intelligence Agency: Intelligence agency of the US Department of Defense.

DU rounds Depleted uranium munitions used for armor penetration.

EIO Extranatural Incident Office (fictional): Clandestine US government agency investigating unexplained phenomena.

EPGO (fictional) EOS PROPHET Generated Object.

F-15 US Air Force multirole strike fighter.

Fingerspitzengefühl German term meaning "fingertip feeling," connoting instinctive flair and intuition.

FOD walk Foreign Object Debris walk: Routine examination of flight line to remove objects that might damage aircraft on takeoff or landing.

Fort Meade Fort George G. Meade: US Army installation in Maryland, home to the National Security Agency, US Cyber Command, and over a hundred other agencies focusing on cyber operations, intelligence, and information gathering.

FVEY Five Eyes: Intelligence alliance among Australia, Canada, New Zealand, the United Kingdom, and the United States.

GCHQ Government Communications Headquarters: UK signals intelligence organization headquartered in Cheltenham.

H hour (a.k.a. zero hour): Time at which a scheduled tactical operation is set to launch. US military.

HK Heckler & Koch: German small arms manufacturer. *See also* MP5.

HVT High Value Target.

Langley Town in Fairfax County, Virginia; location of the George Bush Center for Intelligence, CIA headquarters.

M9 Beretta 92FS semiautomatic pistol: US military service weapon since 1985.

Medevac Medical evacuation.

MI5 (a.k.a. the Security Service): UK domestic counterintelligence and security agency.

MI6 (a.k.a. the Secret Intelligence Service or SIS): UK foreign intelligence agency.

Mil-spec Military specification.

MoD UK Ministry of Defence.

Moskvich 2140 Car manufactured by Soviet carmaker AZLK between 1976 and 1988.

MP5 Heckler & Koch machine pistol.

Nellis Nellis Air Force Base, Nevada.

NNSS Nevada National Security Site.

NTK Need to Know.

NVG Night Vision Goggles.

Oscar Mike On the move (radio jargon).

OSI Office of Special Investigations, US Air Force.

Peary Camp Peary: Military reservation in Virginia including the CIA training facility known as "the Farm."

Pentonville Category B Prison in Islington, UK.

PET scan Positron emission topography scan: 3D imaging method using radioactive tracers to investigate metabolic and biochemical functions of tissues and organs.

PHOTINT Photographic Intelligence.

PX Post Exchange: Retail store on US military installations.

Quindar Tones The beeping tones heard on NASA Apollo radio transmissions.

Red Zone Unsafe areas in Iraq after the 2003 invasion.

RTO Radio Telephone Operator.

SAP Special Access Program. US Department of Defense program established for special classes of highly classified information that imposes access requirements exceeding those for regular classified information.

SAS Special Air Service: Special Forces unit of the British Army.

SNCO Senior Non-Commissioned Officer.

SSTV Slow Scan TV: Method of sending and receiving static images via radio.

T1 line Historically fast digital data connection.

Telltale (fictional): Animate, moving EPGO.

UAZ Russian utility vehicle manufacturer.

UN3373 International packaging code for Biological Samples B (human or animal tissues, blood, excreta, etc.).

USMC United States Marine Corps.

VQ Visitors Quarters.

Zhen Xian Bao An ingeniously folded paper container from China, most typically used to store needlework items in Miao, Dong, and Yao traditions.

Acknowledgments

Deep thanks to Bill Clegg for his encouragement, critical brilliance, expertise and wisdom, Simon Toop for his genre-saviness and infectious enthusiasm, and everyone else at the Clegg Agency in New York. Huge gratitude to Elisabeth Schmitz, who took this book under her wing, and to Morgan Entrekin, Deb Seager, John Mark Boling, Judy Hottenson, Lilly Sandberg and all at Grove Atlantic. It's a privilege to be published by them. Thank you, Paula Cooper-Hughes and Alicia Burns, for your expert eyes.

And it's a privilege to be published by Jonathan Cape in the UK. Michal Shavit, thank you from the bottom of our hearts for your support and enthusiasm. Special thanks also to Alex Russell, Alison Davies, Suzanne Dean, and everyone on the Cape team.

This book grew from the inspiration, support and assistance of many people, many of whom read and commented on early drafts. Helen would like to thank Tom Adès, Ray Barry, Nick Blackburn, Casey Cep, Sarah Dollard, Paraic O'Donnell, Emma Gilby, James Macdonald, Debbie Patterson, Cornelius Prior, Kathryn Schultz, Anindita Sempere, Andrew Sempere, Grant Shaffer, Murray Shanahan, Denis Villeneuve and Lydia Wilson. Sin would like to thank Peter Breen, Francine Blaché-Breen, Áilbhe Hines, Eben Bernard, Adam McGhee, Ruth McCartney, Moira Purvis, Brodie Smith, Bebhinn Hare, Lauren Mehl and Frank Hicks for all the cheerleading and willingness to listen to the highs and lows. Special thanks to Rachel Purvis, who would have loved being on this journey with us.

Special thanks from both of us to Christina McLeish, Toby Mayhew, Phil Klay, Dan Franklin, Bharat Tandon, Sarah Phelps and Abigail Elek Schor. And a special thanks also to the fic writers of AO3 and the internet.